"Are you worried?" Chance asked.

"About Beatrice? Yes."

"About everything," he responded.

Stella turned away, not wanting to look into his beautiful eyes. She knew what she'd see there. The same compassion and understanding she saw when he was questioning clients or reassuring a victim. He had a way of making people open up to him.

She didn't like opening up to anyone. She didn't like feeling vulnerable. She *hated* being on the receiving end of pity.

"You need to trust me to handle things the way they need to be handled," Chance said. "You're not the only one who's worried. I don't want to see anything happen to you or your grandmother, and I can't do my job effectively with one hand tied behind my back."

"I'm not tying anything. I'm setting boundaries."

"Boundaries that are going to get you killed."

Aside from her faith and her family, there's not much **Shirlee McCoy** enjoys more than a good book! When she's not hanging out with the people she loves most, she can be found plotting her next Love Inspired Suspense story or trekking through the wilderness, training with a local search-and-rescue team. Shirlee loves to hear from readers. If you have time, drop her a line at shirleermccoy@hotmail.com.

An eternal optimist, **Hope White** was born and raised in the Midwest. She and her college sweetheart have been married for thirty years and are blessed with two wonderful sons, two feisty cats and a bossy border collie. When not dreaming up inspirational tales, Hope enjoys hiking, sipping tea with friends and going to the movies. She loves to hear from readers, who can contact her at hopewhiteauthor@gmail.com.

The Christmas Target

New York Times Bestselling Author

Shirlee McCoy

&

Hidden in Shadows

Hope White

LOVE INSPIRED
INSPIRATIONAL ROMANCE

LOVE INSPIRED®
INSPIRATIONAL ROMANCE

Recycling programs for this product may not exist in your area.

ISBN-13: 978-1-335-42496-9

The Christmas Target and Hidden in Shadows

Copyright © 2021 by Harlequin Books S.A.

The Christmas Target
First published in 2016. This edition published in 2021.
Copyright © 2016 by Shirlee McCoy

Hidden in Shadows
First published in 2010. This edition published in 2021.
Copyright © 2010 by Pat White

This edition published by arrangement with Harlequin Books S.A.

For questions and comments about the quality of this book, please contact us at CustomerService@Harlequin.com.

Love Inspired
22 Adelaide St. West, 40th Floor
Toronto, Ontario M5H 4E3, Canada
www.Harlequin.com

Printed in U.S.A.

CONTENTS

THE CHRISTMAS TARGET

Shirlee McCoy

To Marge Garrison. My favorite breakfast buddy.
I sure miss you!

In your unfailing love you will lead the people
you have redeemed. In your strength
you will guide them to your holy dwelling.
—*Exodus* 15:13

Chapter One

Stella Silverstone woke like she often did—bathed in sweat, heart beating frantically, her body screaming for her to run or fight.

She did neither.

She wasn't on a hostage rescue mission in the middle of Vietnam. She wasn't in Egypt, walking through the slums, searching for a missing child. She was just outside of Boonsboro, Maryland, caring for her grandmother because her grandfather was gone.

He'd been eighty-three when he'd taken his last breath. Stella couldn't say that his life had ended too soon, but she would have happily traded a few years of hers to have him back. Henry Radcliff had been a keeper. That's what Stella's grandmother had said at the funeral. She was right. Henry had been a great guy. A wonderful husband, a loving father, a protective and caring grandfather.

Now he was gone, and Stella had to take his place in Beatrice's rambling old Victorian, helping her grandmother do everyday chores that suddenly seemed to be too much for her—laundry, cooking, dry mopping the hardwood floor, paying bills and sending thank-you cards. A year ago, Beatrice could have handled all of that and more. Now she seemed confused, frustrated and a little scared.

That scared Stella.

Which was probably why she'd woken in a panic.

That and the fact that Christmas was only three weeks away.

Her least favorite day of the year.

She shivered, glancing at the glowing numbers on the bedside alarm clock. Nearly 5:00 a.m. Her boss, Chance Miller, and a few members of HEART would be converging on the house in a couple of hours. The hostage extraction and rescue team had bimonthly meetings at headquarters. Meeting outside of that secure environment went against protocol. The team coming to Boonsboro should have been out of the question. Stella had tried to argue with the plan. She could have easily found someone to watch Beatrice for the day while she made the three-hour trip to DC.

Chance had insisted that they do things his way. He knew what he wanted, and he always went after it. When Stella had protested, he'd told her that he wasn't interested in her opinion. Then he'd said goodbye and hung up. If he'd been anyone else, Stella would have seen that as rude, but Chance was never rude. He was almost never wrong, and Stella had been just tired and distraught enough to let things go his way without a fight.

He hadn't gloated, hadn't pointed out that he'd finally won one of their many arguments. He'd just emailed notes for the meeting, told her that he'd update her on a few potential clients and asked if there was anything she needed him to bring when he came.

She'd wanted to be angry with him for insisting on doing things his way. Mostly because she'd spent the past year trying really hard to convince herself she and Chance were past tense. Their brief relationship had burned out faster than a candle in a rainstorm, and she didn't want to relight it.

At least, that's what she kept telling herself.

For a while, that had been really easy to believe. The two had been butting heads for nearly as long as they'd known each other, but there was something very real beneath the constant bickering, some indefinable thing that always made her want to jump to Chance's defense, make certain he was okay, watch his back. She knew he felt the same about her. He proved it every time he did something like this—planning a meeting around her schedule and her life.

Truth? Chance wanted to bring the meeting to Boonsboro because he was worried about her. He'd never say it. He didn't have to. Stella knew it.

Just like she knew that she wanted him there, because she needed someone she could lean on. For just a minute.

She was tired.

Beyond tired.

Her grandfather's death from a sudden heart attack had been shocking, but finding out that her grandmother had been diagnosed with Alzheimer's had pulled the rug out from under every plan Stella had ever made.

Three years. That's how long her grandparents had known about the diagnosis. Three years that they'd kept it secret because they hadn't wanted Stella to give up the job she loved. That's what Beatrice's best friend, Maggie, had said. Stella had wanted to know about the medicine she'd found in the bathroom cabinets, the post-it note reminders plastered all over the house, the forgetfulness and confusion that Beatrice seemed to be suffering from.

Of course, the nurse in Stella had already known what all those things meant. She just hadn't wanted to believe it. Maggie and Beatrice had been friends since elementary school, and Stella had known that her grandmother's friend would have the answers she needed.

She just hadn't expected those answers to hurt so much.

And they did.

It hurt to know that Nana was losing her memories. It hurt to know that the vibrant, cheerful woman who'd raised Stella was going to become a shell of the person she'd once been.

It also hurt to hear that her grandparents had thought she loved and valued her job more than she loved and valued them. But then, why wouldn't they think that? She'd spent so much time away that she hadn't seen the signs and symptoms of Alzheimer's until her grandfather was gone.

It was a regret she'd live with for the rest of her life. If she'd spoken to them on the phone more than once a week, asked the right questions, delved a little deeper into their lives, maybe she would have realized the truth long before Granddad's death. Then she could have told Henry that she'd give up her work at HEART for Beatrice.

So far, it hadn't come to that.

She *had* given up her apartment in DC, moved back

to the huge old Victorian that Beatrice had inherited from her parents decades ago. Stella had even tried to resign from HEART. Working as a member of one of the most well-respected hostage rescue teams in the world took time and energy that she needed to devote to her grandmother.

Chance had refused to accept her resignation. She'd been working for the company since he and his brother Jackson founded it, and he had told her that the team couldn't run without her. That was an exaggeration. They both knew it, but Stella loved her work. She didn't want to give it up. She wasn't even sure who she would be without it. She'd built her entire life around HEART.

Now she was trying to rebuild it around her grandmother.

Chance had made it very clear that he'd support her in any way he could. He'd assigned her paperwork and research, report writing and about six other things that were menial compared to the high-risk jobs she'd been taking before Granddad's death.

Just until you and your grandmother get back on your feet, and you will, Stella. It's just going to take some time.

She could still hear his voice, see the compassion in his dark blue eyes. He'd come to the funeral. Of course he had. Chance always did the right thing. Always.

Stella wasn't sure why that made her feel resentful. Maybe because she often found herself doing the wrong thing. Or maybe because he'd done so many right things the few times they'd dated, and she'd still managed to chase him away.

She stood, her toes curling as her feet hit cold wood. No sense lying in bed fretting about things she couldn't change. She'd be better off making a pot of coffee and finishing up the last of the three hundred thank-you notes she'd been writing out since Granddad's funeral. Keep busy. It had been her motto for as long as she could remember. Especially this time of year.

Wind rattled the old wooden panes and whistled beneath the eaves, the sounds nearly covering another more subtle one. Floorboards creaking? A door opening?

Beatrice?

Had she woken already?

Stella stepped into the dark hall, not bothering with the light. She'd walked through the drafty house thousands of times during the years she'd lived there. She'd memorized the wide hallway, the landing, the stairs and the banister. She knew how many doors were on each side of the hallway and which ones creaked when they opened.

Beatrice slept in the room at the far end of the hall, and Stella went there, knocking on the thick wood door. When Beatrice didn't answer, she turned the old crystal knob and stepped into the room.

"Nana?" she whispered into the darkness, shivering as cold air seeped through her flannel pajamas.

Cold air?

She flicked on the light, her heart stopping when she saw the empty bed, the billowing curtains.

She yanked back gauzy white fabric, nearly sagging with relief when she saw the window screen still in place, the mesh flecked with fat snowflakes.

"Nana!" Stella called, throwing open the closet door. Just in case. Her grandmother had gotten lost walking through the house recently. One day she hadn't been able to find the kitchen. Another day, she'd stood in the hallway, confused about which room she slept in.

"Nana!" Stella yelled it this time, the name echoing through the house as she ran out of the room. She could hear the panic in her voice, could feel it thrumming through her blood. She never panicked. Ever. But she felt frantic, terrified.

"Beatrice!" She yanked open the linen closet, the door to the spare room, the bathroom door.

She thought she heard a faint response. Maybe from the kitchen at the back of the house.

She barreled down the stairs and into the large foyer.

The front door was closed, the bolt locked. Just the way she'd left it. She could feel cold air wafting through the hallway, though, and she spun on her heel, sprinting into the kitchen.

The back door yawned open, the porch beyond it covered with a thin layer of snow. She thought she could see footprints pressed into the vivid white, and she shoved her feet into old galoshes, ran outside.

There! Just like she'd thought. Footprints tracking across the porch and down into the yard. She should have called for help. The practical part of her—the part that was trained as a trauma nurse, who knew protocol and statistics and the necessity of using the brain instead of the heart during stressful times—understood that. The other part, the part that only cared about finding Beatrice as quickly as possible, was calculating just how far an eighty-one-year-old with Alzheimer's could go in the time it took to make a phone call and get the police involved.

Pretty far.

Especially when going just a couple of hundred yards would mean entering thousands of acres of forest.

"Nana!" Stella screamed, sure that she saw a shadow moving at the back edge of the yard. The woods began there—deep and thick, butting up against the state forest, crisscrossed with tributaries of the Patuxent. An easy place to get lost and hurt. Especially if a person was elderly and frail, and probably not dressed for the weather.

Stella ran toward the trees, hoping the shadow she'd seen had been her grandmother. *Praying*, because that's what Beatrice would have wanted her to do. It's what Henry would have expected her to do. Granddad had been a retired preacher. After watching his son take over the pulpit, he'd planned to spend time going on mission trips, traveling with his wife, enjoying the fruit of a life well lived. He'd ended up raising Stella instead.

He'd never complained about that.

He'd never accused God of unfairness, never said he'd been given a rough shake.

He'd believed that everything happened for a reason, and that good could be found in the most trying circumstance if a person took the time to look for it. He'd been an eternal optimist, because he'd believed that God's will trumped all else.

Stella was a pessimist. Mostly because she believed the same thing.

She reached the edge of the yard and found footprints in the snow there, nearly covered by a fresh dusting of white. She should have grabbed her cell phone on the way out. She should have grabbed a coat. A flashlight. Warmer clothes.

Rookie mistakes, but she was committed now. She

couldn't let Beatrice get any farther ahead. She plunged into the thick foliage, branches catching on her hair and tugging at her skin. She thought she heard a car engine, was sure she heard voices coming from the front yard.

No one should be anywhere near the house. They were too far from town for random strangers to show up and none of Beatrice's friends would be out at this time of morning.

Stella would have checked things out, but she had one goal—finding her grandmother.

"Nana!" she shouted.

To her left, branches snapped, and she turned, certain Beatrice would be there.

"What are you doing out—"

Someone lunged from the darkness. Not an eighty-one-year-old; this person moved fast, flying toward Stella, swinging something at her head.

She had a second to react, one heartbeat to duck. The blow glanced off her temple, sent her reeling. She fell into a tree, slid to the ground, but all she could think about was Beatrice. Out in the woods. Near the creek.

She scrambled up, blocked another blow. Dizzy from the first, disoriented, fighting because she'd been trained to do it. Blood in her eyes, sliding down her cheeks, blinding her in the swirling snow. *Nana, Nana, Nana*, chanting through her head.

She landed one blow, then another. She felt something behind her—some*one*. No time to duck, just searing pain, and she was falling into darkness.

Something was wrong. Chance Miller felt it the way he felt the frigid air and the falling snow. He rounded the side of the huge old house, Simon Welsh at his side,

Boone Anderson still at the front door, ringing the bell. For the tenth time.

There was no way Stella had slept through the noise.

She didn't sleep. Not much. When she did, she slept lightly, every noise waking her. He'd learned that during long flights across the Pacific Ocean and long journeys in foreign countries. She also didn't like being surprised. Ever.

And his early morning visit?

It was a surprise.

Stella was expecting him later in the day, but he'd been worried about the coming snowstorm. If it hit the way the meteorologists were predicting, driving later in the morning might have been a problem. He'd decided to leave DC before the snow began to fall. If he got stuck in Boonsboro, no problem. But he'd been worried enough about Stella that he didn't want to postpone seeing her.

She'd been too quiet lately, and quiet wasn't her style. Usually she was loud and decisive, more than willing to explain exactly how she thought things should go.

As a matter of fact, he'd expected her to yank open the door as soon as the bell rang and ream him out for arriving before he was scheduled.

She hadn't, and he figured that could only mean one thing.

Trouble.

It whispered on the cold wind, splashing down in the heavy flakes that fell on his cheeks and neck. Light streamed out from a door that yawned open, the yellowy glow splashing across the back porch. He could see the interior of the house, the bright kitchen, the white cupboards and old wood floor.

He didn't bother walking inside.

No way had Stella left the door open. Not intentionally. Not unless there'd been an emergency that had sent her running from the house.

He eyed the snow-coated ground, crouching to study what looked like boot prints. Not large, and he'd guess a woman had been wearing them. There was another print a few inches away, a different type of shoe. Something without tread and nearly covered by a fresh layer of snow.

"What'd you find?" Simon asked.

"Footprints. Two sets. Heading toward the woods."

"Stella's?"

"I think so, and maybe her grandmother's."

"Looks like she might have left this way," Simon said, moving up the porch stairs and peering inside. "You want me to check things out, or do you want to split up and search the yard and woods?"

The newest member of the team, Simon had worked for SWAT in Houston before joining HEART. He had keen instincts and the kind of work ethic Chance appreciated. He also had the same driving need to reunite families that everyone on the team possessed.

He didn't know Stella, though.

Not well, and he couldn't know just how serious this situation was becoming. Stella didn't leave doors open. She didn't take chances. She played by the rules, and she expected other people to do the same. Something had sent her running, and he was pretty sure he knew what it was.

Who it was.

Her grandmother.

"If Stella were inside, she'd be out on the porch giving us a piece of her mind. She's left for some reason, and I'm worried that reason might be her grandmother."

"She's prone to wandering?"

"She has Alzheimer's, so it's a good possibility." Chance took a penlight from his pocket, flashing it into the yard. Snow fell in sheets now, layering the ground in a thick blanket of white. Soon it would cover whatever tracks the women had left. Once that happened, finding them would be nearly impossible.

Please, God, help us find them before then, he prayed silently as he moved across the yard, his light bouncing over white snow and sprigs of winter-dry grass.

A few yards out, it glanced off what looked like another footprint. Chance moved toward it, studying the ground more carefully, finding another footprint and another one.

"This way," he said, not bothering to see if Simon was following. He would be. They knew how to run a mission. No reason to go over all the variables, discuss a plan. With the temperature below freezing, there was no time to waste.

Frantic people made errors in judgment. Like leaving a house in a snowstorm without letting anyone know they were going. Not that Chance would ever use the word *frantic* to describe Stella. She was one of the most clearheaded people he knew.

If she'd panicked, there had to be a good reason. Her grandmother wandering around in the snow fit the bill. He'd met Beatrice twice. She'd seemed sweet, kind and very fragile.

If she was out in the cold, she'd need medical attention. If the snow continued to fall and her footprints were covered, he and his team would need help searching the woods that surrounded the property.

So, maybe, Stella wasn't the only one who'd panicked.

Maybe he'd been panicking, too. Acting on emotion rather than clear thinking. Not a good way to proceed.

"Change in plans," he said, stopping short and motioning for Simon to do the same. "Call 911. Let's get the local authorities in on this."

"You want me to call it in as a missing person?"

"Yes. I'm going to see how far I can follow the tracks. Get Boone and follow after you've made the call." He jogged across the yard.

The boot prints were faint but obvious. Stella had left the house recently. He wasn't sure about Beatrice. He'd only seen one print that he thought was hers, and it had been left earlier. He hoped not too much earlier. He and Stella had their differences, but he only ever wanted the best for her. The best thing for her right now would be for her grandmother to be okay.

She'd be devastated if something happened to Beatrice, and Chance would be devastated for her. Stella was special. She had depth and character and just enough stubborn determination to keep Chance on his toes. Of all the women he'd dated, she was the only one he hadn't wanted to walk away from.

He'd done it because it was what *she* had wanted.

Or, at least, what she'd said she'd wanted.

There were plenty of days when he regretted letting her go. He never mentioned it, and she never asked, but he'd have rekindled their relationship if she'd given any indication that she wanted to.

Pride goeth before the fall.

How many times had his father said that?

Too many to count, but Chance was still too proud to crawl back to a woman who'd sent him away. That was the truth. Ugly as it was. So, they were stuck in a pattern of butting heads and arguing and caring about each other a little more than coworkers probably should.

A little more?

A lot more.

"Stella!" he called, pushing through thick foliage. Someone had been there ahead of him. Branches were broken, the pine boughs cleared of snow. The thick tree canopy prevented snow from reaching the ground, but he could see depressions in the needles that covered the forest floor.

He followed them, stepping through a thicket and walking onto what looked like a deer trail. Narrow, but clear of brambles and bushes, it would be the path of least resistance for anything or anyone wandering through the woods.

"Stella!" he called again. "Beatrice!" he added. He could imagine the elderly woman wandering through here, finding the open path and heading in whatever direction she thought would lead her home.

A soft whistle echoed through the darkness.

Boone and Simon, moving into the trees behind him. He didn't slow down. They'd find their own way.

Cold wind bit through his heavy coat, and he wondered if Stella had dressed for the weather. If she'd left in a panic, would she have bothered?

He jogged along the path, the dark morning beginning to lighten around him. The sun would rise soon, warming the chilled air. But soon might be too late, and he felt the pressure of that, the knowledge of it, thrumming through his blood.

Somewhere ahead, water burbled across rocks and earth.

A deep creek or river?

He thought he heard movement and ducked under a pine bough, nearly sliding down an embankment that led to the creek he'd been hearing.

He stopped at the edge of the precipice, flashing his light down to the dark water below. A shallow tributary littered with large rocks and fallen branches, it looked easy enough to cross once a person got down to it.

He aimed the beam of light toward the bank, searching for footprints or some other sign that Beatrice or Stella had been there.

Just at the edge of the water, a pink shoe sat abandoned on a rock.

Not Stella's. She never wore pink.

"Beatrice!" he called. He needed to phone Simon and give him the coordinates. They could begin their search from there, spread out along the banks of the creek and work a grid pattern until they found the missing women.

"Beatrice!" he yelled again.

Someone dove from the trees, slamming into him with enough force to send them both flying. He twisted, his arms locked around his assailant as he fell over the edge of the precipice and tumbled to the creek below.

Chapter Two

Stella had to take her attacker down. She knew that, and it was all she knew. Everything else—the darkness, the cold, the blood—they were secondary to the need to survive and to find Beatrice.

She'd been a fool, though.

She should have waited longer. Instead, she'd rushed out when she'd heard the man calling Beatrice's name. Now she was trapped in a vice-like grip, tumbling down, unable to stop the momentum.

Unable to free herself.

She fought the arms clamped around her waist. Blood was still seeping from the cut on her temple and a deeper wound on the back of her head. Sick, dizzy, confused—she knew the symptoms of a concussion, and she knew the damage could be even worse than that. Brain bleed. Fractured skull. She'd been hit hard enough to be knocked unconscious. She needed medical help, but she needed to protect Beatrice more.

She slammed her palm into her attacker's jaw, water seeping through her flannel pajamas. The creek? Had she come that far?

Had her grandmother?

Fear shot through her, adrenaline giving strength to her muscles. She slammed her fist into a rock-hard stomach.

"Enough!" a man growled, his forearm pressing against her throat, his body holding her in place.

"Not hardly!" she gasped, bucking against his hold.

Suddenly he was gone, air filling her lungs, icy water lapping at her shoulders and legs as she gasped for breath.

She thought maybe she'd imagined him, that the head injury was causing hallucinations, or that she was hypothermic and delirious. Then a hand cupped her jaw, and she was looking into Chance Miller's face.

He looked as shocked as she felt.

"You're in DC," she said, surprised at how slurred the words sounded, how difficult they were to get out.

"No," he said, his arm slipping under her back as he lifted her out of the water. "I'm here."

She thought she heard a tremor in his voice, but that wasn't like Chance. He always held it together, always had himself under control.

"Always perfect," she murmured.

"What?" he asked, and she realized they were moving, that somehow he was carrying her up the bank and away from the creek. Snow still fell. She could feel it melting on the crown of her head, sliding into the cut on her temple. None of it hurt. Not really. She just felt numb and scared. Not for herself. For her grandmother.

She had to concentrate, to stay focused on the mission. That was the only way to achieve success. She'd learned that, or maybe she'd always known it, but it had kept her alive in more than one tough situation.

"Put me down." She shoved at Chance's chest. "I have to find my grandmother."

"Boone and Simon will find her. You need medical help."

"What I need," she said, forcing every word to be clear and precise, "is to find my grandmother. Until I do that, I'm not accepting help from anyone."

"We've already called the local authorities. They should be here soon. They can conduct the search while an ambulance transports you to the hospital."

"I'll just transport myself back. So how about we make this easy and do things my way for a change?"

"We do things your way plenty. This time, we're not." He meant it. She could hear it in his voice. She could feel it in the firmness of his grip as he carried her through the snowy woods.

And he was right.

She knew he was right.

She needed medical attention.

She needed help.

But she couldn't go to the hospital. Not while Beatrice was still lost in the woods.

"Chance, I can't leave without her. I can't." Her voice broke—that's how scared she was, how worried. Her grandmother was out in the cold, and someone was out there with her. Someone who'd attacked Stella.

More than one person?

She thought so, thought she'd been hit from behind, but she couldn't quite grasp the memory.

Chance muttered something, then set her on her feet, his hands on her elbows as she found her balance. It took longer than she wanted, the world spinning and whirling, the falling snow making her dizzy. Her stomach heaved, and she swallowed hard. No way was she going to puke. If she did, it would be over. Chance would carry her back to the house and send her off in an ambulance.

Focus on the mission.

"Something is going on," she said, afraid if she didn't get the words out, she'd forget them. "Someone is out here."

"*We're* out here," he said, turning on a penlight and flashing it across the creek bed. Something pink sat near a rock a few yards away.

"Not just us. Someone attacked me."

He stilled, the light holding steady on that pink thing, his gaze suddenly on Stella. "Who?"

"I don't know. He came out of nowhere. One person. Maybe two."

"Did you see his face?"

"No."

"Did he speak? Say anything to you?"

"No."

"How long ago was that?" He strode to the object, lifted it.

Her grandmother's slipper.

Stella had bought them for Beatrice three Christmases ago, knowing her grandmother would love the faux fur and sparkly bows. Funny that she could remember that, but she had no idea how long she'd been out in the snow.

"That's my grandmother's," she said, that thickness back in her throat again.

"Stella," he said, the calmness in his voice the exact opposite of the panic she felt, "how long have you been out here?"

"I don't know. Maybe fifteen minutes."

"Were you unconscious at any point?" His gaze drifted from her eyes to the bleeding cut on her head.

"Yes."

"So it could have been longer than fifteen minutes?"

"Yes. Now how about we stop talking about it and start looking?"

"Okay," he said. Just that, but she felt better hearing it.

Because of all the people she knew, Chance was the one she trusted most to get things done.

His light illuminated the shadowy bank at the far side of the creek. The sun hadn't risen yet, but the forest was tinged with grayish light. No sign of Beatrice that Stella could see, but, then, her eyes didn't seem to be working well, everything shifting in and out of focus.

In the distance, sirens wailed.

Help coming too late?

Please, God. Not too late.

The prayer was there. Just on the edge of her thoughts, and she tried to follow it with more words, more pleas, but her mind was spinning, her thoughts scattering. Her stomach heaved, and she was on her knees retching into dusty snow and pine needles.

"It's okay." Chance crouched beside her, his cool palm on the back of her neck, his coat dropping around her shoulders. She felt him tense, knew he'd realized that she had another head wound. Double the potential for severe injury, and he'd be calculating the risk to her versus the risk of leaving the creek while Beatrice was still wandering around in the snow.

If they went back to the house, Beatrice would probably die before anyone found her.

The temperature was below freezing, the snow falling faster and heavier. And Beatrice's slipper had been in the creek. Which meant she'd been in the creek, too.

"I want you to wait here," Chance said quietly. "I've already texted our coordinates to Boone and Simon. They'll be here soon. One of them will wait with you until the medics get here."

Not a question.

Not a suggestion.

He really thought that she was going to wait at the edge of the creek while Beatrice wandered through the snowy forest.

She struggled to her feet, following him as he stepped across the burbling water. He didn't tell her to go back. He didn't waste time or energy arguing with her. It was one of the things she'd always liked about Chance—he didn't spend time fighting battles when he had wars to win.

"There's a print there." His light settled on an impression in the muddy bank. "Let's see how many more we can find."

He started walking parallel to the creek, and she followed, her heart beating hollowly in her ears, her legs weak, her body still numb.

Voices carried through the woods, men and women calling out to one another. A search party forming, but Stella could only think about taking one step after another, following the tracks that Chance's light kept finding. Bare feet pressed into the muddy earth. Bare feet in below-freezing temperatures.

Stella was shivering uncontrollably, and she had Chance's coat. Beatrice probably had nothing but her cotton nightgown and the gauzy robe she put on each morning when she got out of bed.

She tasted salt on her lips and realized hot tears were mixing with icy snow. She never cried around other people. Ever. She was crying now, because she'd already lost her grandfather, and she wasn't sure she could bear losing her grandmother, too.

She swiped the tears away, tried to clear the fog from her mind at the same time. She had to think. She had to imagine being in Beatrice's shoes, walking outside, making her way to the creek. Had someone been with her? Maybe the person who'd attacked Stella?

Or had she gone off by herself? Maybe reliving some long-ago day? A trip to the creek with Henry, a picnic in the moonlight? Had some memory sent her wandering? Had she—

"There!" Chance shouted, the word sending adrenaline coursing through Stella again.

He sprinted forward, and she followed, tripping over roots and rocks, trying desperately to see what he was seeing.

There! At the edge of the creek! White against the dark ground and glistening water. Gauzy fabric, a thin pale leg peeking out from it.

"Nana!" Stella sprinted forward, grabbing her grandmother's hand as Chance lifted her lifeless body from the water.

They'd always been a good team.

Always.

Worst-case scenario, best-case, didn't matter. Chance and Stella knew how to move in sync. He wasn't sure that was going to save Beatrice. Stella's grandmother was as limp as a rag doll, her skin icy cold. No respiration. Pulse—thready and weak.

"She's not breathing," he said, laying Beatrice on flat ground and checking her airway.

"Nana?" Stella said, giving her grandmother's shoulder a gentle shake. "Can you hear me?"

Beatrice remained silent, her face bone-white.

"Let Boone know where we are so the medics can find us more quickly. She needs help now. Not ten minutes from now." Stella wrapped Beatrice in his coat and began CPR. No chest compressions. Just rescue breaths that made Beatrice's chest rise and fall.

He made the call quickly, his gaze on the trees that edged close to the creek. The morning had gone silent, nothing moving in the shadowy pre-dawn light. It wasn't a safe stillness. It wasn't a good silence. Something was off—the air subtly charged, the shadows seeming to shift and undulate. He pulled his Glock from the holster, stepping away from Stella and her grandmother. Behind him, voices drifted through the trees—the medics moving toward the creek as he moved away from it.

Stella didn't ask him where he was going or what he was doing. She was either so focused on her grandmother she hadn't noticed or she sensed what he did—someone watching.

The woods had lightened imperceptibly, black trees now brown-gray, white snow flecked with green pine needles and fallen leaves.

He used his penlight anyway, training it into the heart of the forest, flicking it across thick tree trunks and winter-brown bushes. He didn't want to go too far. Even with help close at hand, he was worried about leaving Stella and her grandmother. Both were in bad shape. Stella, at her best, could take down almost any well-trained fighter. But she wasn't at her best. Not even close.

He reached the top of a shallow embankment, the snow thicker there, the trees sparser. His light bounced across a fallen log, illuminating a hint of bright pink that peeked out from behind it.

The other slipper. He didn't move closer. He'd spent years in Afghanistan and Iraq, working as part of one of the top ranger teams in the army. He didn't talk about those days, but he'd lived them. They'd been the best preparation in the world for the kind of work he did with HEART.

Always cautious.

Always meticulous.

Always weighing risk versus benefit.

Until there was nothing to do but act, and then he'd do whatever was necessary to get out alive with his comrades.

The slipper?

It looked like one of the dozens of booby traps he'd seen just sitting out in the open, waiting for someone to pick it up. He flashed the light to the left and right of it, searching for wires or leads. Nothing. Not that he'd really expected there to be anything. Booby traps didn't happen all that often in the good old USA, but he was paranoid, and he believed what Stella had said. *Someone's out here.*

Her words had explained the gash on her temple, the blood that stained the collar of her pajama top and matted her dark red hair. She needed the medics almost as badly as her grandmother did. Maybe just as badly. He'd seen people die of head injuries like hers. He knew how dangerous they could be. If she'd been a different

kind of person, he'd have carried her back to her grandmother's house and made sure she was in an ambulance
heading for the hospital, but Stella knew her own mind,
she made her own decisions. He'd have done the same
if he were in her position—insist on being part of the
search. So, he'd let her call the shots.

But he wasn't going to let her get hurt again.

Someone's out here.

Yeah. She was definitely right about that.

He crouched near the slipper, his light trained on the
ground beyond it. He studied the layer of pine needles
and dead leaves, found what he thought were depressions in the surface. He followed the trail with his light,
surprised to see what looked like a path through the
trees. Not a deer trail this time. It looked man-made,
the ground clear of shrubs and undergrowth.

Stella's attacker had gone that way. He was certain of
that. He was also certain that whoever it was wouldn't
be returning. Not now. Too many people crisscrossing
the woods, too many lights flashing above the creek.
Only a fool would risk capture by sticking around.

He saved the coordinates of the trail and holstered
his Glock. He'd pass the information on to the team, let
them figure out where the path led. Once he made sure
Stella and Beatrice were safe, he'd return. By that time,
local law enforcement would have already scoured the
area, but he'd take a look anyway. It was what he did.
Double-check. Look where others might not. Sometimes, a second or third or fourth pair of eyes would
uncover something that no one else had.

If the police came up empty, Chance was going to
make sure he didn't. Right now, he had a lot more questions than answers, and he didn't like it. Had this been

a random act? An opportunistic crime? Or had it been planned?

Stella had worked a lot of missions. She'd made a lot of friends, and she'd made a few enemies. It was possible one of them had followed her to Boonsboro.

He frowned, turning back toward the creek.

She'd have been an easier target in DC. She lived alone there, in an apartment on the top floor of an old brownstone. He'd been to her place twice, and he'd lectured her both times. Not enough security. The doors were flimsy. The locks were a joke.

She'd told him to mind his own business, but that was Stella. She liked to do things her way. When it really mattered, though, she knew how to follow protocol and work as part of a team.

He moved toward the creek, retracing his steps, following the sound of voices and the flashes of lights through the forest. He thought he heard Stella, her voice about as familiar as his own. They'd known each other for a long time. Long enough to know each other well.

And to care about each other deeply.

He'd seen her crying while they searched for Beatrice. He wasn't going to mention it. Not to her. Not to anyone on the team. Stella was indestructible and unflappable. At least, that's what she wanted everyone to think.

The air changed, and he knew he wasn't alone, that someone was just out of sight, hidden by the heavy boughs of a giant conifer. He didn't pull his firearm. Anyone who wanted to take a shot at him would have already done it. A shadow separated itself from the trees, the gray edge of dawn highlighting red hair and a tall, narrow frame.

Despite his height, Boone Anderson moved quietly, his footfalls silent on the pine needles. "Find anything?" he asked.

"One of Beatrice's slippers and a path through the woods."

"We going to follow it?"

"You and Simon can. Let the local PD know what you're doing and where you're heading."

"You'll be at the hospital?"

"Someone has to be."

"Stella can usually take care of herself."

"She's in bad shape. I don't think she'll be doing much of anything for a while."

"How bad?" Boone cut to the chase. No extra questions. No speculating. He was a straight shooter. He did his job and he did it well, but his heart was with his family—his wife, his new baby, the daughter he'd lost years ago and had recently been reunited with.

"Probably a lot worse than she's going to admit. A pretty deep gash to the temple and one on the back of her head."

"And she probably thinks she's going to be up running a marathon tomorrow."

True. That was Stella. To a T.

"Where's Simon?"

"Sent him down to the creek to see what the ruckus was about. Looked like the medics were carrying a gurney in. I'm assuming they've got to carry someone out. The grandmother?"

"We found her in the creek. She wasn't breathing."

"Pulse?"

"Yeah."

"Then she's alive, and we're going to pray she stays

that way." Boone pulled out his cell phone, texted something, then slid it back in his pocket. "I told Simon you
were on your way. You go do what you need to do for
Stella and her grandmother. We'll keep you in the loop,
and we'll play nice with the local PD."

"You'd better. I don't think you'll like prison food."

Boone snorted, pulling something out of his pocket
and holding it up for Chance to see.

A bag of homemade cookies.

Typical of Boone. The guy never stopped eating.

Any other time, Chance might have smiled.

Right at that moment, all he could do was think about
the tears that had been sliding down Stella's cheeks.
He'd never seen her cry. Not on the worst missions.
Not when she'd been exhausted or tired or injured. Not
when things had seemed hopeless or the person they'd
been looking for had been found too late.

Not even at her grandfather's funeral.

Never.

Not once.

Because Stella didn't cry.

Except that she did, and he'd seen it, and he didn't
think he'd ever forget that.

Boone opened the bag and took out a cookie. Unflappable. Just like always. He'd done what he'd been
asked to do, and he'd keep doing it, but first, he'd eat.

"I always come prepared. Tonight, it's a dozen homemade chocolate chip cookies," he said. "I'll share, but
only because my wife told me I have to."

"You can tell her that you tried, but I'm not in the
mood for cookies."

"Worrying won't change anything. You know that,

right?" Boone bit into the cookie, his gaze as direct as his comment.

"That won't stop me from doing it. Keep your nose clean, Boone. I'm heading out." Chance jogged back to the creek, every nerve in his body on high alert. He hadn't expected trouble. He'd found it.

Now he was going to deal with it.

A dozen people were standing near the creek—police, park rangers, paramedics. Simon stood next to Stella, his hand on her shoulder, not holding her up but pretty close to it.

He met Chance's eyes, mouthed, *She's done.*

"I am not," Stella bit out, her body shaking beneath a blanket someone had tossed over her shoulders. "Done."

"That's a matter of opinion," Simon countered as paramedics lifted Beatrice onto a backboard. She'd been swaddled in blankets and had an IV in her hand, but she was breathing, an oxygen mask covering her mouth and nose. That was an improvement, and it gave Chance hope that she might recover.

"My opinion is the only one that matters," Stella muttered, but she didn't seem interested in the argument. She was watching as the medics strapped Beatrice to the board and lifted her.

"Careful," she warned, as if the team needed to be reminded.

They ignored her.

Which was surprising since she had blood dripping down the side of her face and more of it seeping from beneath her hair. She was also pale as paper, her skin completely leached of color. Chance would have thought every available medic would be hovering around, cleaning her wounds and getting her ready to be transported.

She must have refused treatment, insisted that the attention be given to her grandmother.

Now her grandmother was on the move, and Stella looked like she planned to follow.

"I don't think so," he said, grabbing her arm.

"You don't think what?" she asked, trying to pull away.

He didn't have to put much effort into keeping that from happening. Which concerned him. A lot. "That you're going to walk back to the house."

"I don't think you have a choice in the matter."

"Sure I do. Just like I had a choice when I didn't drag your butt back to the house. I let you decide then. This time, I decide."

"This is not the time to go macho on me, Chance," she growled. "I'm in no mood."

"And I'm in no mood scrape you off the forest floor. So, how about we stop arguing and get this done? Your grandmother needs to get to the hospital, and you're slowing things down."

She pressed her lips together, and didn't say another word as an EMT urged her to sit down, then cleaned both wounds.

"This one looks okay," the EMT said, pressing gauze to Stella's temple, "but you're probably going to need stitches to close the other one."

"I've had worse," Stella muttered, brushing the young woman's hands away and holding the gauze in place herself. "Has the ambulance left with my grandmother?"

"Yes," the EMT admitted. "She's in a very critical state and needed to be transported immediately. We've called another one for you."

"There's no need for another ambulance. I'll drive myself. My grandmother might be confused, and I really need to be there with her."

If she hadn't been dead serious, Chance would have laughed.

"Ma'am," the EMT said before Chance could, "you're in no condition to drive."

Stella must have agreed, because she eyed Chance with a look he'd seen many times before. It was the one that said she needed him, but she didn't want to. The one that said she couldn't do it alone, but wished she could.

He understood the look and the feelings behind it.

"I'll give you a ride," he offered before she could decide whether or not to ask, and she smiled. A real smile that softened her face and made her look sweet and young and vulnerable. It surprised him, because she hadn't directed a smile like that at him since they'd broken up. He'd forgotten how powerful it was; forgotten how it made his pulse race and his heart pound.

"Thanks. I really appreciate it."

"You know I'd do anything for you, Stella," he said, and meant it.

Her smile faded, and she was just staring into his eyes, looking wounded and tired and a little too fragile for Chance's peace of mind.

Finally, she shrugged. "You're the first guy to ever say that to me."

Odd considering that she'd been married for years. Her husband had died serving his country, and she'd mentioned once or twice just how proud she'd been of him.

That was about as much information as she'd given. Even when Chance had asked.

Even when they were dating.

"Then you haven't had the right guys in your life," he responded, keeping his tone light.

She wasn't herself.

That was obvious. He didn't want her to regret their conversation or be embarrassed by it.

He took her arm, helped her to her feet. "Do you have a spare key to the house? Boone and Simon might need to get inside."

"I left the door open."

"There are police everywhere. Someone might have closed it."

"There's probably a key in the flower box outside the kitchen window. If you want to look for it, I can—"

"No."

"You don't even know what I was going to say."

"Whatever it was, the answer is still no. We're getting out of these woods, and I'm driving you straight to the hospital. No stops for anything."

"You're awfully bossy when I'm hurt," she muttered. There was no heat in her words and no real complaint.

"Awfully worried," he corrected, taking her elbow and helping her up the embankment.

"Don't be. I'm fine."

"You always are. Until you aren't, and then I have to ride to the rescue," he replied, baiting her the way he had a hundred times before. He knew how she'd react. Her back would go up, her chin would lift, and she'd march to the house like she hadn't been knocked unconscious and nearly frozen.

It almost worked out that way.

"I've rescued you more times than you've ever rescued me," she said.

Just like he knew she would.

Then she shrugged away from his hold, marching forward with just enough energy to convince him she might actually be okay.

They made it through the trees and out into the yard, white snow swirling through the grayish light. He could see how pale she was, see how much she was trembling. She was cold or in shock or both, and he had about two seconds to realize that baiting her hadn't worked out the way he'd wanted before her steps faltered.

Just a little hitch in her stride, a soft sigh that he barely heard, and she was crumbling to the ground so quickly Chance barely had time to catch her.

Chapter Three

She was in the car again, the beautiful book her grandparents had given her for Christmas in her hands.

"Don't touch it," she snapped at Eva. Her sister was only four, and she liked to ruin things—paintings, drawings, schoolwork. Eva was always scribbling on them.

"Be kind," her mother admonished, turning in her seat and smiling, her beautiful red hair curled, a pretty green Christmas ribbon woven through it.

Matching hairstyles. Stella and Eva had ribbons, too. Even tiny little Bailey had a bow in her fuzzy hair.

That kind of made Stella proud.

She loved her family. Even Eva.

"Okay, you can touch it," she said, and her sister smiled with Daddy's dark brown eyes, and then the world exploded in heat and flames and horrible screams.

She was screaming, too. Screaming and screaming, her throat raw, her head pounding. Someone calling her name over and over again.

Stella woke with a start, bathed in sweat, pain throbbing somewhere so deep inside she wasn't sure where it came from or how to get rid of it.

"Shhhhh," someone said, hands brushing across her cheeks, wiping away the tears that always came with the Christmas dream.

Christmas *nightmare*.

She took a deep, shuddering breath, realized she was hooked to something. An IV?

Was she in the hospital?

Suddenly the fog cleared, and she knew where she was, what had happened.

"Nana!" She shoved aside blankets, tried to get to her feet, but those hands—the warm, rough ones that had wiped her tears—were on her shoulders, holding her still.

"Slow down, Stella."

Chance.

She should have known, should have recognized the hands, the deep voice.

"Where's my grandmother?" she asked.

"In ICU. Stable." He was leaning over her, his dress shirt unbuttoned at the neck, his tie dangling loose, his gaze steady and focused.

He was the most handsome man she'd ever seen, the kindest man she'd ever known. She tried really hard not to think about that when they were working together.

Right now, they weren't working.

For a moment, it was just the two of them, looking into each other's eyes, everything else flying away. If she let herself, she could drift into sleep again, let herself relax knowing that Chance was there. She wouldn't let herself. Her grandmother needed her.

Stable. That's what Chance had said.

It was a good word, but she wanted more. Like *conscious, talking. Fine.*

"I need to see her."

"You're in no shape to go anywhere or see anyone."

"I'm seeing you," she retorted, sitting up a little too quickly. Pain jolted through her skull, and she would have closed her eyes if she hadn't been afraid she'd be in the nightmare again.

"You're funny, Stella. Even when your skull is cracked open," he responded, his hand on her back. He smelled like pine needles and snow, and she realized that his shirt was damp, his hair mussed.

Not perfect Chance anymore.

Except that he was—the way he was supporting her weight, looking into her eyes, teasing her because he probably knew she needed the distraction. All of it was perfect, and that made it really hard to remember all the reasons why she and Chance hadn't worked out.

All the reasons?

She could only really think of one—she'd been a coward, too afraid of being disappointed to risk her heart again.

She shoved the covers off, turned so her feet were dangling over the side of the bed. She was wearing a hospital gown. Of course. Her feet bare, her legs speckled with mud and crisscrossed with scratches. She could have died out in the woods. If Chance hadn't shown up, she probably would have.

If she'd died, what would have happened to Beatrice? She knew the answer. Beatrice would have died, too.

It didn't make sense.

The town she'd grown up in was quiet and cozy. Movie theaters, shopping centers, a bowling alley and an ice-skating rink. The nice-sized hospital she was in had been built in the sixties and had a level one trauma center. People hiked and biked and ran, and they generally died of old age or disease. Not murder.

She frowned.

Was that what all this had been? Attempted murder? It didn't seem possible. Not in Boonsboro. Trouble didn't happen there. At least, not the kind that took people's lives. Not usually. Not often. One of the worst things that had ever happened in town was the accident that had killed Stella's family. It had been the worst tragedy since the old Harman house had gone up in flames at the turn of the nineteenth century. Four children died in the fire. Two adults. The grave plot was still tended by someone in the family, but Stella had never paid much attention to it. She'd had her own family to mourn, her own graves to tend.

She shoved the thought and the memory away, pushed against the mattress and tried to stand. Failed.

"Need some help?" Chance slid his arm around her waist, and she was up on her feet before she realized she was moving.

The room was moving, too, spinning around her, making her sick and woozy. Maybe Chance was right. She wasn't in any shape to go anywhere.

In for a penny. In for a pound.

That's what her grandfather had always said.

She was already standing. She might as well try to walk.

She took a step, realized she was clutching something. Chance's belt, her fingers digging into smooth leather, her shoulder pressing into his side. He was tall and solid, not an ounce of fat on his lean, hard body.

He could hold her weight easily, but she tried to ease back, stand on her own two feet, because it's what she'd always done. Even when she was married. Even when she should have been able to rely on someone else, she'd taken care of herself, handled her own business, stood alone more than she'd stood beside Daniel.

"There is no way you're going to make it. You know that, right?" Chance said.

"Sure I am." She grabbed hold of the IV pole and took a step to prove him wrong. Took another one to prove to herself that she could do it. Her legs wobbled, but she didn't fall. She made it to the door and put her hand on the jamb for support, the hospital gown slipping from one shoulder.

Chance hitched it back into place, and she knew his fingers must be grazing the scars that stretched from her collarbone to her shoulder blade. She didn't feel his touch. The scars were too thick for that, the skin too damaged.

His gaze dropped to the spot where his fingers had been, and she knew he wanted to ask. Not how she'd gotten them. He knew the answer to that. He did background checks on every HEART operative. No, he wouldn't ask how she'd gotten them. He'd ask if they hurt, if there was something he could do to take the pain away, if the memories were as difficult to ignore as the thick webbed flesh.

He'd asked those things before, and he'd told her how beautiful she was. Not despite the scars. Because of them. They made her who she was, and he wanted to know more about how they defined her.

She hadn't answered the questions, because getting close to someone meant being hurt when they left. She'd been hurt enough for one lifetime, and she didn't want to be hurt again. If that made her a coward, so be it.

"How about I get you a wheelchair?" Chance said, his breath tickling the hair near her temple, his hands on her shoulders. Somehow, he was in front of her, blocking the doorway, and she wasn't even sure how it had happened.

She was worse off than she'd thought.

But she still needed to see Beatrice. For both of their sakes.

"Okay," she agreed, because she didn't know how she'd make it to the ICU any other way.

"And how about you sit and wait while I do it? I don't want you to fall while I'm gone." He was moving her backward, his hands still on her shoulders.

She could have stood her ground. But her legs were shaky, and when the back of them hit the bed, she would have fallen if he hadn't been holding her.

"Careful." He helped her sit, his tie brushing her cheek as he reached for the blanket and pulled it around her shoulders. Yellow. That's what color the tie was. With a handprint turkey right in the center of it. Only a guy like Chance could wear a tie like that and still lead the most prestigious hostage rescue team in North America.

"Nice tie," she murmured.

He crouched so they were eye to eye, smiled the easy smile she'd noticed the first day they'd met. The one that spoke of confidence, kindness and strength.

"A gift from my niece for Thanksgiving. I promised I'd wear it to my next meeting."

"And you always keep your promises."

For a moment, he just stared into her eyes. She could see flecks of silver in the dark blue irises. He had the thickest, longest lashes she'd ever seen, and when they'd dated, she'd told him that.

"I try," he finally said. "I'll be back in a minute. Don't leave the room without me. They still haven't found the guy who attacked you, and I don't want to take chances. Boone is outside the ICU, making sure your grandmother is protected. You're my assignment."

"I'm your *what*?" she asked, but he'd already straightened and was heading out the door, pretending that he hadn't heard.

If she'd had the energy, she would have followed him into the hall and told him just how likely it was that she was going to be anyone's assignment. She'd been taking care of herself for years. Daniel had been part of an elite Special Forces unit and had been gone more than he'd been home during their marriage. When he was home, he'd been distant and unapproachable. She'd loved him, but their three-year marriage had been tough. If she was honest with herself, she'd admit that she wasn't sure if it would have survived.

She'd wanted it to, but she and Daniel had both had their demons. They'd only ever fought them alone. That didn't make for a good partnership. She knew that now. Maybe because she'd spent the last few years fighting beside and with Chance.

"Not the time," she muttered. She had more important things to think about. Like the fact that the police hadn't found the man who'd attacked her.

Men?

She still wasn't certain.

If she had her cell phone, she'd call the local sheriff's department for an update, but she'd left it at the house. There was a phone beside the bed and she picked up the receiver, tried to remember the sheriff's number. Her mind was blank, her thoughts muddled. She dropped the phone back into the cradle and grabbed her pajamas from a chair near the window. Someone had folded them neatly. Her galoshes sat beneath the chair, side by side.

Chance?

She could picture him folding the clothes, setting the boots in place. Everything precise and meticulous.

She walked into the bathroom. It took a second to pull the IV from her arm, took a couple of minutes to wrangle herself into the pajamas. Her hands were shaky, her movements sluggish, but she didn't want to be running from the bad guys in a too-big hospital grown.

Running?

She'd be fortunate if she could crawl.

Damp flannel clung to her legs and arms as she splashed cold water onto her face and tried to get her brain to function again. No dice. She was still woozy and off balance. A concussion? Had to be. She lifted the gauze that covered her temple, eyeing the wound in the mirror. The bump was huge and several shades of green and purple. No stitches. Just a long gash that looked like it had been glued shut.

She had a bandage on the back of her head, too. She didn't bother trying to see. She felt sick enough from the effort she'd already put in.

Someone knocked on the bathroom door. One hard, quick rap that made her jump.

"Hold on," she called, grabbing the handle and pulling open the door.

Chance was there.

He didn't look happy.

As a matter of fact, he looked pretty unhappy.

"Why am I not surprised?" he asked, his gaze dropping to her pajamas and then jumping to the IV pole.

"You'd have done the same," she responded.

"True, but that doesn't mean I approve. You have a concussion. You're supposed to be resting."

"I'll rest better after I see my grandmother."

"You won't rest. You'll be out hunting down your attacker unless someone is there to stop you." He took her arm, the gentleness of his touch belying the irritation in his eyes.

"No one would dare try," she responded, jabbing at him like she always did. Usually, he jabbed right back, but this time he just shook his head.

"How about we not test that theory, Stella? Because I have better things to do with my time than babysit someone who won't follow the rules."

"I hope you're not talking about me."

"I told you. You're my assignment. Or rather, keeping you safe is."

"Since when?"

"Since about two nanoseconds after you collapsed on your way to my car. Sit." He gestured to the wheelchair that was near the bathroom door.

"I'm not a dog."

"Trust me. I am very, *very* aware of that."

She was suddenly self-conscious in her wet pajamas. But this was Chance. He'd seen her looking a lot better, and he'd seen her looking a whole lot worse. They'd crossed a river together once, emerging on the other side soaked to the skin and shivering with cold.

Yeah.

This was Chance. There was nothing he didn't know about her and no situation he hadn't seen her in.

She blushed anyway, dropping into the wheelchair so quickly that pain exploded through her head.

Her eyes teared but she didn't close them.

If Chance realized how much pain she was in, he'd insist that she get back into bed. Truth? She didn't think she'd have the energy to fight him. She felt so tired, she thought she could close her eyes and sleep forever.

"Maybe this isn't a good idea," Chance muttered, grabbing the blanket and tossing it over her legs.

"Did you ever think it was?"

"No," he replied, pushing the chair out into the hallway.

There was too much noise there, too many lights—her head spun with all of it. She had to see Beatrice, though, and then she needed to talk to the sheriff. She didn't have time to give in to pain or to lie in bed feeling sorry for herself.

Someone had attacked her.

She had to hold on to that, had to keep it in the front of her mind so that she stayed focused on the goal—find the guy, figure out his agenda.

Maybe he'd been a vagrant, wandering through the woods, startled by a woman suddenly appearing.

Maybe, but it didn't feel right. The entire thing felt too coincidental.

"Have you spoken with the sheriff?" she asked as Chance wheeled her into the elevator. "I know you said that they didn't find the perp, but I'm wondering if they found anything else."

"They traced the guy to an old logging road that runs through the woods behind your property. They've cast tread marks that he probably left behind. Other than that, they've come up empty."

"That's not the news I wanted."

"I know."

"Maybe he was a vagrant." She tossed the theory out, because Chance was as likely to see the strengths and weaknesses in it as she was. More likely. He wasn't concussed, and he wasn't sitting in a wheelchair with bandages on his head.

"Someone just moving through who was squatting out in the woods and panicked when you showed up?"

"It's possible, right?"

"Anything is possible, Stell. That doesn't make it likely. Right now, I don't have enough information to speculate, but if I were going to guess, I'd guess the attack wasn't random." The elevator door opened, and he wheeled her out.

"You've got a reason for that. Care to explain?"

"You said there were two perpetrators."

"Possibly two," she corrected.

"I've never known you to make a mistake. If you say there might have been two, it's because there probably were. If that's the case, a squatter who panicked seems unlikely."

"Squatters don't always live alone."

"It sounds like you want to believe the attack was random."

"Don't you?"

"I want to believe the truth. For right now, I'm keeping an open mind. Sheriff Brighton is still on the scene with half a dozen men. He said he'll stop by the hospital when he's finished. We'll know more then."

"Did they—"

"Stella, this isn't your case. It's not your mission. You are the victim, and you've got to let the local police handle the investigation."

"I plan to, but I'd like to talk to Cooper—"

"You and the sheriff are on a first-name basis?"

"We went to school together. I want to talk to him."

"You'll have plenty of opportunities to do that. After you rest. The doctor said three or four days in bed."

She snorted, then wished she hadn't. Pain shot through her skull and her ears rang.

Up ahead, double wide doors opened into the ICU unit. Several nurses sat at a desk there.

Stella scanned their faces, trying to see if she knew any of them. She volunteered at the hospital once a week. It kept her sane, helped her focus on something besides her own problems and her own sorrow. She probably knew half the nurses who worked there, but her vision was too blurry, everything dancing and swaying as she tried to focus.

"Stella!" one of them cried, rushing around the counter and running toward her.

Not a nurse. A volunteer.

The uniform came into focus. The name tag. The pretty brunette. Karen Woods. A nursing student at the local college and the person who stayed with Beatrice when Stella had to be away from home for more than a few hours.

She should have recognized her immediately.

She probably would have if the world had been standing still.

"Are you okay?" Karen had reached her side and was leaning toward her, the smell of her perfume mixing with antiseptic and floor cleaner and making Stella's head swim. "I was working on the pediatric floor and heard Beatrice had been admitted. What happened?"

"She—"

"Tell you what," Chance interrupted. "How about we hash it all out after Stella sees her grandmother?"

Karen frowned. "Of course. I was just so relieved to see her, I wasn't thinking. I was going to visit Beatrice, but there's a guy outside the door who says she can't have visitors. I told the nurses, but they said you want him there, Stella."

"I do," she responded, the words echoing hollowly in her ears. She felt light-headed and sick, and she wanted to grab Chance's hand, hold on tight so she didn't float away.

"Why? Are you worried that Beatrice wandered off? Do you think she's getting worse? I heard she left the house without a coat or shoes." Karen's words came in quick staccato beats that slammed into Stella's head and made her want to close her eyes.

She liked Karen.

The young woman was smart and helpful, and she'd been wonderful with Beatrice, but right at the moment, Stella wanted to tell her to go away.

She needed to think.

She couldn't do that with someone talking nonstop, asking questions she had no answers for.

"Karen," she began, but Chance's hand settled on her shoulder, his thumb sliding against her neck, and she lost what she was going to say. Felt herself just give it over to him, because he was there, and he could handle it and she was more than willing to let him.

She'd think about what that meant later.

When she wasn't so tired, so scared, so concerned.

"It seems like you've heard a lot of information in a very short amount of time," he said, his tone conversational and light.

* * *

Chance waited for the young woman to respond. Karen Woods. That's what her name tag said. He'd seen her before. Probably at the funeral. He remembered the brown hair and the big smile. If she remembered him, she didn't let on. Just offered a quick shrug.

"The entire hospital is buzzing with the news. Beatrice and her husband helped fund the pediatric wing. They're a big deal here."

Stella looked like she was trying to think of a suitable response, her brow furrowed as if she couldn't quite come up with the words.

Chance figured no response was necessary.

"Big deal or not, Beatrice isn't to have any visitors unless they're approved by the police or by Stella. You know that, right?"

"I'm not stupid."

"It's not about stupidity. It's about knowledge. Were you informed?"

"Yes."

"Then you'll understand that Stella is going to have to say goodbye for now. She wants to see her grandmother, and—"

"I'm not invited?" Karen smiled, but there was something hard in her eyes. "No need to hit me over the head with it."

"I'm not trying to. I just want to make certain we're all clear on the rules."

"Because you're so big on them," Stella murmured, and he smiled.

She was right.

But that was why they got along so well.

"Only when they matter. We'll see you when we come out," he said, pushing the chair past Karen.

He wasn't asking permission, and he didn't wait for a response. He wanted Stella to see her grandmother, and then he wanted her back in the hospital bed.

She was two shades too pale, red hair falling lank against her neck and cheeks. Her hand trembled as she tucked a strand behind her ear, and he wanted to turn the chair around and go straight back to her room.

He knew Stella, though.

She'd find her way back.

With or without him.

Family was everything.

She'd told him that dozens of times when they were on a mission together. She'd proven how much she meant it when she'd tried to give up her job to take care of her grandmother. Chance hadn't been able to let her go. She was too valuable a team member. And the team was its own sort of family.

He pushed her through the hallway of the ICU, Karen following along behind despite the fact that he'd made it really clear that she wasn't going in Beatrice's room. She looked well-meaning enough, but there was a glimmer in her dark eyes that bothered him. A little bit of excitement that shouldn't be there. He'd seen it before—some otherwise harmless person determined to get the juiciest bit of gossip and spread it to the four corners of the earth.

He imagined she had a nice little group of friends that she'd love to give all the details to. She'd be the star, have her five minutes of fame because she'd brushed shoulders with a couple of people who'd almost died.

She wasn't getting any information from him, and

he doubted Stella would share anything. Not if she was thinking clearly.

Several closed doors lined the hall. Boone was in front of one, sitting in a chair, his legs stretched out, the bag of cookies in his hand. He'd eaten half. Chance was surprised he hadn't eaten them all.

"I see you finally made it up here," he said, his gaze on Stella. "You look like death warmed over, Silverstone."

"Thanks."

"It wasn't a compliment. It was a hint that you should go back to bed." His gaze shifted to Karen, and he frowned. "Are you here to try to kick me out again, Karen?" he asked, and the young woman blushed.

"I wasn't trying to kick you out. I just didn't understand why you were sitting here."

"I told you why," he said with typical Boone patience. The guy was almost never bothered by anything or anyone. "Next thing I knew, hospital security was trying to kick me to the curb."

"I know, but—"

"Karen," Stella cut in. "I appreciate you wanting to visit with Beatrice. Tomorrow will probably be a better day."

It was a dismissal, and Karen seemed to get it.

Finally.

She patted Stella's shoulder. "Of course. If you need anything, you know how to reach me. I have classes tomorrow and Friday, but I'm free Saturday and Sunday if you want me to clean the house and do some shopping."

"I'll let you know."

"I can also stay here with Beatrice, if you need me to."

"I think we've got everything under control." The

words were kind and a lot more patient than was typical of Stella.

"Okay. Great. Good. Like I said, you know how to reach me." Karen hurried off, and Stella sighed.

"She means well," she said, and Chance wasn't sure if the words were a reminder to herself or information for him and Boone.

"It didn't feel like it when security was trying to strong-arm me out of here," Boone muttered, pulling a cookie from the bag. "I nearly lost these babies fighting for my right to stay."

"I'm sorry she called security on you, Boone."

"Not your fault." He stood, brushed crumbs from his lap. "If you two are going to be in there for a few minutes, I'm going to run and get coffee. Maybe see how the cafeteria food looks. You want anything?"

"Juice. Orange. And a black coffee," Chance responded. He'd drink the coffee, and hopefully he could convince Stella to drink the juice. She still looked shaky, and that worried him. She also looked thinner than she had the last time he'd seen her. A month ago. Maybe a little longer than that. She'd come to DC to pick up a computer system that she could use for work.

She'd said she was fine, that her grandmother was fine, that things were going well. He'd heard a lot that she hadn't said. Or maybe he'd just assumed that things weren't as easy as she claimed, that life wasn't quite as fine as she was making it out to be, because that's the way Stella was.

She didn't need help.

She didn't want it.

Everything was always okay and fine and good.

When a guy got too close, when he asked too many questions, she backed off and walked away.

He'd watched it happen over and over again.

He'd experienced it firsthand.

She wasn't the kind of woman who wanted more than an easy and light relationship. She didn't want to share her soul. That's what she'd told him on their last date when he'd asked about her family, about the accident that had taken them from her.

I don't go out to dinner with a guy so I can share my soul with him. Sharing a meal is good enough.

He'd told her that he only ever wanted to be with someone who could share every part of herself.

That was it.

A bad ending to a story that should have had a great one. He and Stella had a lot in common. They clicked in a way he'd never clicked with any other woman. He could have made a life with her, but he wasn't going to insist. He wasn't going to beg. He wasn't going to do anything but give her exactly what she'd said she wanted.

"You want anything, Stella?" Boone asked, calling her by her first name. Something he almost never did.

That seemed to shake her out of whatever stupor she'd fallen into.

She frowned, locking the brake on the wheelchair and getting to her feet. "Just to see my grandmother."

"You go do that. I won't be long," Boone continued, meeting Chance's eyes. "I'll call Simon and let him know what's going on here."

"See if he's got anything new from the local police."

"And ask when the sheriff is going to get here. I

want to speak with him." Stella took a wobbly step toward the door.

"Take it easy," Chance said, taking her arm before she could face-plant into the door.

"If I take it any easier, I'll be prone in a bed."

"That's where you should be."

"Not yet." She opened the door and stepped into the quiet room.

A heart monitor beeped a steady rhythm, and the soft hiss of an oxygen machine filled the room. From what Chance could see, Beatrice's vitals were normal. Or close to it. Her oxygen level was low, but the mask over her face should help with that.

Stella leaned over the bed rail and kissed her grandmother's cheek. "Nana?"

When Beatrice didn't respond, Stella lifted her hand, studied the gnarled joints and short nails. "She used to love having her nails done."

"Did she?" Chance pulled a chair over to the bed and nudged Stella into it.

"She thought it made a woman feel feminine. She always wanted me to have mine done, too, but I was never a girly girl, and I hated it. One year, we had matching nails for Christmas. Hers were green with little red Christmas trees. Mine were red with little green Christmas trees. Christmas morning, I realized she'd bought us matching outfits, too. Long red skirts and white blouses with high collars. I think she was going for a Victorian vibe."

"How old were you?"

"Fifteen."

"I guess the Victorian theme didn't go over well with you."

"No." She smiled at the memory. "But I wore the outfit to church anyway. Becky Snyder never did let me live that down. I heard about it every other day for my entire high school career."

"I'm surprised you didn't shut Becky down." That was another thing Chance had watched happen over and over again. Stella knew how to put people in their places and how to keep them there. She also knew how to lift them up when they needed it, offer support when no one else could. It made her fantastic at her job, and it drew people to her. No matter how many times she tried to push them away.

"Why would I? I never cared what anyone else thought. Beatrice was happy. That made me happy."

"I'm sure your grandmother wouldn't have been happy if she'd known you were being teased."

"She knew. We used to laugh about how ridiculous Becky was for bringing up something *so last year.* And about how silly she was to think that someone who'd survived what I had would be bothered by her opinion." She smiled at the memory.

"Your grandmother was a smart lady."

Maybe she'd heard the past tense. Maybe she'd realized just how much of herself she'd just shared.

Whatever the case, her smile faded, her gaze shifting to Beatrice's face. "I hope she weathers this. She's already frail, and her memory isn't good. Sometimes older people don't recover from—"

A siren split the air, the sound shrieking through the silent ICU.

Stella jumped from the chair, swayed.

Chance just managed to grab her waist, holding her upright as her grandmother bolted into a sitting position.

"What's happening?" she cried, her voice muffled by the oxygen mask.

Good question.

Chance wanted an answer as badly as she did.

"I don't know, but I plan to find out. Stay here," he said, looking straight into Stella's eyes.

She didn't argue.

She wouldn't leave her grandmother's side. That was one blessing. For once, he absolutely knew that Stella would stay exactly where he'd left her.

He sprinted from the room, the siren still screaming as he raced down the hall to the nurses' station.

Chapter Four

The siren cut off as abruptly as it had begun.

Stella listened to the sudden silence.

No. Not silence. There were sounds. Subtle noises mixing with the beep and hiss of machines.

She could hear voices. Nurses and doctors talking, their excited chatter drifting in from the hall. They weren't moving patients. That was good news, but it didn't make her feel better. It didn't make her feel confident that things were okay.

She didn't like this.

She didn't like it at all.

"Is there a fire?" Beatrice asked, her voice hoarse, her face pale.

"Probably just a drill," Stella assured her and tried to reassure herself.

No one would be foolish enough to launch an attack in the hospital.

Would they?

"Are you sure? Because where there's sirens, there's bread."

"Where there's smoke, there's fire, Nana, but there's

no smoke. Sometimes hospitals check their equipment. Just to make sure everything is working." Sometimes, but not often. Not with sirens that could scare heart patients into cardiac arrest.

"I hope you're right, dear. After last night…"

"You remember last night?"

"How could I not? People shouldn't throw rocks at glass. It can cause all kinds of problems."

"Rocks at glass?" She was listening with half an ear, most of her attention on the door. She wasn't sure what she expected. Maybe some masked gunman rushing in, ready to take Beatrice out.

Or take her out.

She had a lot more enemies than her grandmother.

As a matter of fact, she'd be surprised if Beatrice had any enemies at all. Stella? She'd earned plenty of them. In her line of work, that went with the territory.

"I had to tell him to leave, but he told me that he had a message from Henry, and I had to come down and get it."

"Who had a message from Henry?" Now she was focused, now she was really listening, and she *still* wasn't sure what she was hearing.

"The man with the rocks. The one who woke me up."

"Nana, there was no man with rocks."

But maybe there was.

Maybe that's what had woken Beatrice and sent her out into the storm.

Beatrice pulled the oxygen mask away from her face, her blue eyes blazing with irritation. "Of course there was, Stella. I may be losing my marbles, but I don't imagine things. Yet." She let the mask drop back, and her eyes closed.

She was either tired of talking or tired of trying to

explain what had happened. Either way, Stella let her be. She had bigger things to worry about and more pressing matters to attend to. She'd figure out the window and the rocks and the man with the message after she figured out why the siren had gone off.

She walked to the door, her legs like noodles, her knees weak. She hated to admit it, but Chance had been right when he'd said she'd be better off in bed. The injuries to her head weren't the worst she'd had, but they sure didn't feel good, and they sure didn't make her steady on her feet.

The room seemed to tilt as she moved, the walls swaying. She needed Chance's steadying hand, and she wasn't sure how she felt about that.

She hadn't ever wanted to need him, but she thought that she always had. From the moment she'd met him, she'd known he was going to be trouble, that he was going to ask for a lot more than she wanted to give. She'd joined his team anyway. She'd dated him.

She'd sent him packing.

And she'd regretted it.

She still regretted it.

She frowned and opened the door, her hand clammy, her skin damp with sweat. She felt sick and she felt scared, and she didn't like either.

The corridor was empty. No nurses running to prep patients for evacuation. No security officers rushing through looking for trouble. Just the soft beep of machinery, the quiet hiss of ventilators. Everything seemed to be functioning normally.

But the alarm had gone off. That meant something wasn't normal.

Rocks at glass.

The words ran through her head as she took a step toward the nurses' station.

Rocks at glass.

She thought about Beatrice's room, the curtains billowing from the open window, the dusting of snow beneath it.

Had there been footprints?

Had she looked?

Her sluggish brain clicked along, the connections harder to make because her mind was functioning at super-slow speed.

Rocks at glass.

Someone had been throwing something at the window and woken Beatrice. That was the easiest explanation for what had happened. A few rocks, a little noise, and Beatrice had woken and gone to the window.

And had been given a message that she couldn't ignore? One that had sent her outside into the snow? Why would anyone do that to a harmless elderly woman?

A nurse stepped through the double doors. Male. Tall. A mask covering his face, his hair a dark shade of brown that didn't look natural. Too monotone. Too dull.

Her brain was still chugging along slowly, but she knew. Even before he moved. Even before she realized he was heading in her direction.

Trouble.

It was written in the lines of his body—tense and rigid.

She didn't question the instinct to move back, to put herself in a position to guard the doorway to Beatrice's room.

His gaze was on the floor, trained away from her with such determination that she knew he felt her gaze. He moved past, and she almost believed that was it, that she'd imagined the shiver of unease, the feeling that he wasn't what he seemed.

Then he was on her, turning so quickly she almost didn't see the movement. A knife flashed in the light, and if she hadn't been so well-trained, if her muscles hadn't been conditioned to react before her brain, he'd have taken her out with one swipe of the blade.

She blocked the attack, shoved him back, tried to rip at the mask on his face. She was seeing double and maybe triple, her head pounding sickeningly, her movements too slow.

The blade came up again, and she slammed her fist into his throat, heard him gag as the knife clattered to the floor. She dove for it, landing with a thud, her fingers grasping the handle. She had it in her hand, and she was up, nearly blinded by the pain in her head, praying that the guy didn't have another weapon.

She expected him to come at her again, to try to wrest the knife from her grip, but he was gone, the corridor empty and quiet.

If she hadn't been holding the knife, she might have believed she'd imagined it all.

The doors he'd entered through were closed. None of the patients' rooms were open. There was a right turn at the end of the corridor, though. He must have run that way.

She wanted to go after him, but she was afraid to leave Beatrice. She was also afraid she wouldn't be quick or strong enough to apprehend him. She felt shaky and off balance, and that wasn't a good way to go into a battle.

She turned back to the room, fumbled with the doorknob, her grip clumsier than before, her heart beating hollowly in her ears. She needed to sit, but first she needed to buzz for a nurse, explain what had happened.

"Stella!" Chance called, and she turned, saw that he'd walked into the corridor and she hadn't even heard him.

His gaze dropped to the knife, jumped back to her face.

"What happened?" He took the knife from her hand, using his shirttail to keep from touching it. Then he cupped her cheek. His palm was warm and calloused, his touch light.

She wanted to lean into the comfort of it.

Lean into him, but she'd made her choice, and what she'd chosen was to go it alone. Live life without the connections that could break a heart and bruise a soul.

"Some guy thought he could go through me and get to Beatrice," she said, and was surprised to hear the shakiness in her voice.

She never got shaky. Ever.

"That explains the fire in the stairwell," he muttered. "A great diversionary tactic. I shouldn't have left you here alone."

"How could you have known?" she asked.

"Easily. I shouldn't ever be surprised at the lengths a criminal will go to get what he wants. Did you get a good look at him?"

"He was wearing scrubs. I thought he was a nurse. He had dark brown hair. Tall. He was wearing a surgical mask, so I didn't see his face."

He didn't ask for more details. He already had his cell phone out, was dialing a number. Probably Cooper's. Or, maybe Boone's.

Seconds later, he tucked the phone away, set the knife on the ground and studied her face.

Carefully.

Thoroughly.

She wasn't sure what he was looking for.

Maybe signs of her weakness. Of her desperate need for support.

"Are you okay?" he finally asked.

"Yes."

"He didn't hurt you?"

"I didn't give him a chance."

He offered a grim smile.

"Typical," he said, and it didn't sound like a compliment.

"What's that supposed to mean?"

"Just that you could have called for help. There are nurses, doctors and security guards all over the place."

"I didn't have a whole lot of time to think about that. I barely had time to react," she said. No heat in her words. She was too tired for that. Too sick.

"Right. Sorry." He glanced at the knife. "He meant business."

"I know. I'm just glad I was able to keep him from getting to my grandmother."

"You're assuming he was going after her."

True.

She was.

Because of the rocks on the glass and the message Beatrice said she'd been given.

She would have told him that, but two security officers ran into the corridor, Boone right behind them. Everyone seemed to be talking at once, the noise tearing through Stella's skull.

She leaned against the wall, closing her eyes and trying to stop the whirling, swirling world.

Warm hands wrapped around her waist, slid along her sides, and she was being lifted, carried somewhere by someone. She'd have opened her eyes to see who, but she felt the edges of a silky tie brush her face, caught a whiff of pine needles and snow and familiar cologne.

"I can walk," she said without opening her eyes.

"And?" he responded, the words rumbling against her cheek.

"I *should* walk."

"We're not going far."

He set her down, and she finally opened her eyes.

He'd brought her back to Beatrice, and she was sitting in the chair by the bed again.

"Law enforcement will be here soon," Chance said, crouching in front of her. He had the bluest eyes she'd ever seen, the longest lashes, and if she hadn't been such a coward, she'd have stuck it out with him. Because he wasn't just handsome. He was smart, driven, kind. All the things any woman could want.

And she had wanted him.

She just hadn't wanted to lose him.

"I want you to rest until they get here. All right?" She could have argued.

She could have insisted that she should be out in the hall, helping him run the show. That's what she usually did, and he was usually happy enough to let her.

But she didn't think she could walk if she wanted to, and she didn't think she'd do anyone any good if she passed out in the hallway.

She nodded, wincing as pain shot through her head again.

"Good." He smiled, tucking a blanket around her, touching her cheek as if they were exactly what they should have been—a couple, tied together by years of seeing and meeting each other's needs.

She wanted to tell him how stupid she'd been, how

foolish. She wanted to tell him how much she longed to go back to that day when she'd let him walk away and make a different choice, a braver one.

But her words seemed to be coming as sluggishly as her thoughts, and before she could even open her mouth, he was gone.

It was for the best.

She knew that.

So, why was she having such a difficult time believing it?

Chance didn't like being played for a fool. He liked it even less when someone he cared about was nearly killed because of it.

He closed the door to Beatrice's room and pulled out his phone, snapping a few pictures of the abandoned knife. He'd wanted to ask Stella if the guy had been wearing gloves, but she'd been so close to passing out, he'd decided to wait. Security was already combing the hospital, trying to find the perpetrator. A tall guy in scrubs with brown hair.

Only the guy had probably already changed back into street clothes and was moving through the hospital unchallenged by security guards. He'd be outside before law enforcement arrived with the K-9 team Chance had asked for.

"Strange-looking knife," Boone commented, crouching beside the weapon.

He was right. The blade looked typical enough, but there were odd symbols and pictures carved into the wooden handle. "Looks like an old bowie knife."

"*Old* being the operative word," Boone murmured. "Weird carvings, but the blade is all business."

"Yeah," Chance responded. "Stella said the guy was trying to get through her to get to Beatrice. I'm wondering why anyone would want to kill a lady who already has Alzheimer's."

"Inheritance? Does she have other family? Maybe someone who's a little too anxious to get that big old house and whatever money she might have?"

"Maybe. We'll check into it."

"But you think this is about Stella, right?" Boone straightened.

"It makes more sense."

"She's got more enemies, but that doesn't mean it makes more sense," Boone argued. "If someone wanted to go after Stella, why do it this way? Why not shoot her while she was walking outside? Set the house on fire? Plant a bo—"

"I'm sure I can think of just as many ways she could die as you can," Chance said dryly.

"All I'm saying is that Stella's grandmother is vulnerable. Without Stella to look out for her, she's an easy target for an accident like what happened tonight."

"You're saying someone wants Stella out of the way so he can get to Beatrice?" It was something Chance hadn't thought of.

"I'm not saying that's a fact. I'm just saying it's a possibility."

Maybe it was.

But accidents could happen with or without Stella dead. According to Stella, Beatrice still had an active social life, going to book club meetings with friends, participating in a women's mission group that met at church every week. She and Stella weren't always together.

"There are a lot of possibilities. I'm going to ask

Trinity to do a little research for me, go back through the reports from some of Stella's more recent missions. Maybe there's a clue there. If she comes up empty, we'll know to focus things closer to home."

"Trinity never comes up empty," Boone said.

True. Chance's younger sister was an expert in computer forensics, was training to be a search and rescue worker, and had been an integral part of HEART for several years.

She excelled at finding people and at coordinating missions from headquarters. She kept track of the team members as they went out on missions, got them help quickly when they needed it. She also filed reports, wrote up bids and generally made things run a lot more smoothly than they would have without her.

Office work.

That's what Trinity called it.

Chance called it necessary and safe. His parents had already lost one daughter, and he was going to make sure they didn't lose another. He'd been six years younger than his older sister. Old enough to remember her leaving for mission work. Old enough to remember his mother and father crying when they'd heard that the village she was working in had been attacked.

She'd been kidnapped, and she'd never been found.

He wasn't going to let that happen to Trinity.

He'd call her, ask her to do some research.

Maybe that would make her happier than she'd been in recent weeks.

"She never comes up empty, and she's never slow. That's going to pay off in this situation," he said, eyeing the knife. He'd already snapped a few pictures. He texted one to his sister. Asked her to find out what it was and if it was rare.

"You should have her look at Stella's personal life, too. Didn't she just break up with someone?"

"How should I know?" But he was pretty certain she hadn't been in a serious relationship with anyone since they'd broken up.

Boone snorted. "You know everything about everyone on the team. Especially Stella."

"What's that supposed to mean?"

"None of us are guaranteed another day. It would be a shame to wait for tomorrow only to find out that tomorrow isn't going to come."

"Since when did you become a philosopher?" he asked, and Boone grinned.

"Since always. It's one of my best characteristics."

"That and your ability to down more food than sixteen truckers?"

"Exactly. So didn't she just break up with someone?" Boone pressed for the answer that he knew Chance had, because he was right. Chance made it his business to know about his operatives' lives.

"If you're talking about the navy guy, they went out twice. I don't think saying no to a third date could be considered breaking up."

"He might be Navy. Stella mentioned him to my wife a few months ago."

"Like I said, they went out twice. I don't think that can be considered a breakup."

"Maybe you don't, but what about the guy she was with?"

Good question.

Stella didn't date often.

He knew that. Just like he knew that if she'd ever planned to be serious about anyone, it would have been him.

No pride in that thought.

Just honesty.

They were made for each other. Two halves of the same whole. As corny as it sounded, he thought it was true. If he'd been another kind of guy, he would have tried to prove it to her.

He wasn't, so he'd let her go.

And here they were—her dating life the subject of a conversation he'd rather not be having. He might keep close tabs on his team, but he tried hard not to stick his nose into their personal business.

"I'll have Trinity check into that relationship. Just to make sure the guy was in DC when all this went down."

He dialed his sister's number, waiting impatiently as the phone rang. He needed to find the guy who'd gone after Stella, and he needed to return to his life, because he could feel himself being pulled back into that nice little fantasy—the one where he and Stella were exactly what each other needed, where both of them were willing to admit it and where happily-ever-after became the ending they both longed for.

A pipe dream, and he'd never been much of a dreamer.

He was a doer, and what he was going to do was make certain Stella and her grandmother were safe. Then he was going back to DC, back to the life that only ever seemed lonely when Stella was around to remind him of what he was missing out on.

Chapter Five

Sheriff Cooper Brighton had been the town bad boy when Stella was growing up—the guy every girl wanted to be with, the boy every father distrusted and the rival every young man wanted to defeat.

Now he was the town sheriff, and he wore the uniform and the badge as easily as he'd worn the bad-boy label.

She watched him as he jotted something into his notepad, waiting impatiently for the next question. He'd asked at least a hundred already. Most of them just repeats of earlier ones. Same question worded in a different way.

At least he hadn't insisted that he conduct the interview somewhere besides Beatrice's room. He'd been agreeable and cooperative, telling Stella that they could talk wherever she felt most comfortable.

She felt most comfortable right beside Beatrice, Chance standing behind her. She didn't have to glance over her shoulder to assure herself that he was still there. She knew he was.

She also knew that Boone was outside the door, sitting in the chair again, firearm holstered beneath his jacket.

Beatrice was safe. For now.

"Is there anything you want to add to what you've told me?" Cooper finally asked, looking up from the pad and meeting her eyes.

There *was* something. It had been scratching at the back of her mind since the sheriff arrived, trying to catch and hold her attention. If she hadn't had the headache to end all headaches, she'd have already mentioned it.

"Beatrice said someone tossed rocks at her window and woke her up. She also said that he told her he had a message from Henry."

"Is that why she went outside this morning?" Cooper asked, and she nodded.

"That's what she said. It's possible she was confused."

"It's also possible that she wasn't," Chance broke in.

"I know. But I don't know why anyone would want to hurt her. What other motivation would someone have for luring her outside during a winter storm?"

"That's a good question." Cooper stood, grabbed his coat from the back of the chair and handed Stella his business card. "That's my direct number. I'm going back to your place. I want to see if there's any evidence that someone was outside Beatrice's window. Which room is she in?"

"It's at the back of the house. The far left window. Pink curtains."

"I bet Henry loved that," Cooper said, a half smile curving his lips. He'd always had a soft spot for her grandparents, because they'd never bought into the town's view of him. When he was a tween and teen, they'd given him odd jobs to do around the property, and they'd paid him well for the work.

"He loved anything that my grandmother loved."

"I know. And who could blame him? Beatrice has the best heart of anyone I've ever known. Remember that old donkey she insisted on rescuing? That thing was as ugly as sin. Swaybacked and old as the hills. She paid me to brush its tail and mane and put little pink ribbons in both." He glanced at Beatrice, smiling at the memory.

"I remember. Granddad was afraid she'd want you to paint its hooves pink, too."

"She asked. I refused. It was a male donkey. I figured it deserved a little dignity."

She laughed, the sound ending on a groan as pain shot through her already aching head.

"You okay?" Chance touched her shoulder, the warmth of his hand seeping through her damp flannel, chasing away some of the chill she hadn't realized she'd been feeling.

"I will be once we figure out what's going on."

"Hopefully that will be soon." Cooper shrugged into his coat. "Beatrice is a good lady. I'm going to do everything I can to make sure she stays safe. Call if you remember anything else. I've got a couple of guys going over the hospital security footage. I'll keep you updated." He walked out into the hall and disappeared from view.

"Here." Chance pressed a cup into her hand. "You need some sugar."

"I need some answers." She sipped the lukewarm orange juice, her stomach twisting. "I also need Tylenol."

"I have that, too." He handed her two tablets. "Cleared by the nurse, so it's safe to take."

"Did any of the nurses see the guy who attacked me?"

"They saw him. He had a badge, and they didn't bother checking his ID. The security guards already found it with the scrubs in a bathroom on the main floor."

"Near the lobby?" She swallowed the pills with the rest of the juice.

"Yes. The sheriff has a K-9 unit moving through. It's possible they'll track him."

"You know it isn't, Chance. He walked out the lobby door and he got in a car. He drove away in a vehicle that was either stolen or unregistered."

"Probably."

"There's no *probably* about it. We've done this thing dozens of times together. We know how it works."

"We know how it *usually* works. Let's leave some room for surprises, okay?" He pulled a chair up next to hers and took her hand, the gesture intimate and gentle, and so surprising she didn't pull away. They'd sat like this before. Years ago. When they'd thought they might be able to make something special out of the thing that was between them—the admiration, the respect, the chemistry that always seemed to steal Stella's breath.

She glanced away, her fingers curving through his, her heart slamming against her ribs.

"I've never liked surprises," she murmured, hoping he couldn't feel the wild throbbing of her pulse.

"Then leave room for possibilities. You seem to think the guy was coming after Beatrice. The team is checking into the theory that you're the target."

It was a possibility. She knew that. Her work put her in contact with lots of people who knew how to hold grudges and get revenge. Most of them were far away, and it would be difficult for them to get visas into the country. Money talked, though, and it could accomplish a lot.

"My last mission was in Egypt," she said as if he hadn't been there with her, as if they hadn't found a child kidnapped by her abusive father and brought her back to the United States. She'd known then just how wrong she'd been to close herself off to Chance. She'd had a dozen opportunities to tell him, a dozen moments when she'd wanted to.

Fear had kept her silent.

Fear of loving him and losing him.

Just like she had her family.

"We're checking the whereabouts of the people involved in that. Is there anyone else we should look into?"

"You know exactly what I've been involved in, where I've gone and who I've angered."

"I do, but we also need to think on a more personal level." He still had her hand, his thumb running across her knuckles. She could have been distracted by that if she let herself be, but she knew he was getting at something, moving toward a subject that he didn't think she'd want to discuss.

Her brain might be moving slowly, but she knew exactly what he was asking. She didn't care. Talking about her personal life—what little she had of it—didn't bother her. "There's no one in my life who'd want to kill me out of jealousy or anger. I don't have an ex-boyfriend stalking me, and I didn't rebuff some guy who might be holding a grudge."

"You've been out on a couple of dates recently."

"I didn't realize you were keeping track," she responded, a little hint of something zinging through her.

Happiness?

Pleasure?

It sure wasn't annoyance.

"The last date I went on was a week before my grandfather died. I haven't seen Noah since then."

"Maybe Noah isn't happy about that?"

"I'm sure he didn't give it a second thought. We're friends. That's all."

"Can I have his contact information? I'd like to verify that with him."

"No," she snapped, and then wished she hadn't. Beatrice stirred, moaning softly in her sleep. She looked tiny, the bed and linens nearly swallowing her up.

"Look," Stella continued more quietly. "Noah was a member of my husband's special ops unit. We've been friends for years. We went out because he'd broken up with his fiancée and was feeling lonely. That's it."

"If that's it, then why don't you want me to contact him?"

"The last thing Noah needs is people butting into his business." He'd been wounded during an operation three years ago, and he hadn't been the same since.

"It's not butting in to check on someone's whereabouts."

"Chance—"

"You can trust me to do things discreetly," he cut her off.

Any other day, she might have argued with him, given him a dozen reasons why she knew Noah hadn't been the guy who'd attacked her.

She stood instead, placing the juice on the table near Beatrice's bed and walking to the window. Snow still fell, drifting to the ground in huge flakes. She wanted to walk outside, let the frigid air clear the cobwebs from her head. More than that, she wanted to hunt down the guy who'd attacked her, make sure he didn't get another opportunity.

If she hadn't felt so weak, she might have left Chance with Beatrice and tracked down the K-9 unit that was searching for the perp, but she was weak, and she'd be stupid to go out looking for trouble.

"It's not a good idea to stand in front of the window, Stella," Chance cautioned, but he didn't pull her away and he didn't close the curtains.

He probably thought he was giving her what she wanted, what she always said she needed—space, distance, platonic friendship.

Except that they could never be friends, because they'd always been meant to be something more.

"I need to keep Beatrice safe," she murmured, trying to refocus her thoughts, keep them where they needed to be. "The guy who attacked me is still out there, and I can't count on him not returning."

Chance heard the worry in Stella's voice, and the weariness. She wasn't asking for help, but they both knew she needed it.

"We'll keep her safe."

We'll keep you *safe, too*, was on the tip of his tongue, but he didn't say it. Stella prided herself on being able to handle just about anything. She didn't like needing help, but she'd take it when necessary. This was one of the few times when it absolutely was.

"I appreciate that, Chance, but Cooper and his department—"

"Aren't going to be able to provide twenty-four-hour protection. HEART can."

"At what cost? Another job? A client who really needs your help not getting it because you're here helping me?"

"We have plenty of man power, Stella, and you know it. If you don't want us here, you'll have to come up with a better reason than that." She wouldn't. Because she knew HEART could do what needed to be done faster and better than just about anyone else.

He was as confident of that as he was that the sun would rise every morning.

She shrugged, her shoulders narrow and thin beneath her pajama top. He caught a glimpse of her scar again—purple against her pale skin. He knew a little about the story—that she'd been in a car accident that had killed her entire family. That she'd escaped with terrible burns.

And terrible nightmares.

She'd never told him that, but he'd heard her talking in her sleep more than once. They'd camped out in dozens of places with the team, and he'd heard her muttering about flames, and then saying a name over and over again.

Her sister's name.

When he let himself, he could imagine Stella as a little girl, trying desperately to save her sister from the fire.

"If you want HEART out, say so," he prodded, and she sighed.

"I would, but I do need the help. Much as I hate to

admit it, my brain isn't functioning at a fast enough pace to keep Beatrice safe."

"It functioned fast enough to stop a knife attack."

"Muscle memory."

"And God?"

"He does always seem to come through for me. Even when I doubt that He will. I should probably learn something from that."

"Like?"

"I don't always have to fight my battles alone." She brushed hair from Beatrice's face, her palm settling on her forehead. "She feels warm."

"She's under a few blankets."

"Warm as in feverish." She pressed the call button for the nurse and removed one of the blankets that covered her grandmother. "I hope it's not pneumonia. She inhaled water, and she was hypothermic. She could—"

"Stop," he said, taking the blanket from her hand and setting it on the chair. They were so close he could see the flecks of violet in her blue eyes, see the gold tips of her red lashes. "Worrying won't change a thing."

"I'm not worrying. I'm speculating."

"That's not going to change anything, either."

"It's going to keep me going," she said, turning to her grandmother again, putting some space between them, because it would have been way too easy to walk into each other's arms.

Chance knew it, and he kept his distance, because there was more to a relationship than heat and passion. There was deep sharing and vulnerability and a dozen other things that Stella didn't want.

"Who says you have to keep going?" he asked, and she shrugged.

"Me. If I don't keep moving, I'm going to fall over. Then where will Beatrice be?"

"In this bed with me watching over her."

She looked like she was going to say something in response, but a nurse bustled in, her scrubs swishing as she moved to the bed.

"Is everything okay?" she asked, and Stella began filling her in, questioning whether or not X-rays had been ordered, asking if there'd been any sign of fluid in the lungs.

Chance could have waited for the answers, but he had other things to do, a few phone calls to make while Stella was focused on her grandmother.

He wanted to give Trinity Noah's name. She might be able to come up with a surname, maybe figure out who the guy was. HEART had plenty of contacts in the military, and it shouldn't take any time at all to track down a buddy of Stella's deceased husband. Daniel Silverstone was a military legend. Smart, quick and deadly, he'd died a hero's death, saving his unit from enemy fire. Stella never talked about him. She never talked about her marriage or what it had felt like to be widowed at such a young age. It was another reason why they'd broken up. Chance had wanted to know, and he hadn't understood her need to keep it from him.

"How are things going in there?" Boone asked as Chance stepped into the hall. He'd taken a seat in the chair again, his legs blocking half the corridor. To the untrained eye, he looked relaxed, but Chance sensed the tension in him. He was ready for more trouble.

They might get it, but it wasn't going to be at the hospital. Not with so many deputies and security guards roaming the hallways.

"Beatrice seems to be holding her own, but Stella's worried."

"I meant with the interview. Was she able to remember anything else?"

"Nothing that is going to help us put a name to her attacker. I do have the name of the last guy she dated."

"Noah Ridgewood?"

"She didn't give me a last name."

"It's Ridgewood. I texted Scout to see if she remembered."

"Thanks. I'm going to have Trinity see what she can dig up on the guy. I'm also going to have her call in another team member. You need to get home to your family."

"I can stay a few days. Scout will understand."

"Maybe, but your kids won't. They need you home when you can be there, and this isn't a paid mission. It's a favor for a friend."

Several HEART members had been married in the past year. Chance tried to give them as much family time as possible. It was important for their marriages, their homes and their work. If he had a wife and kids, they'd be his priority. God first. Then family. Then business.

That was the way his father had raised him.

It was the way he'd planned to be if he'd gotten married.

At this point, he doubted that would happen.

He'd found the woman he wanted to be with. He'd probably end up waiting a lifetime for her to realize she wanted to be with him.

He frowned, glancing at the door and calling himself every kind of fool for falling for Stella again and again and again.

"Kids do grow up fast at this age." Boone said. "And I have lots of lost time to make up for with Jubilee."

"You guys are doing okay, right?" Chance had asked the question so many times he was sure Boone was tired of it, but being reunited with a daughter who'd been missing for five years was challenging. Even in the best of circumstances.

"Better than I anticipated. She's a smart kid, and she's eager to fit in with the family. The counselor seems to think she's doing remarkably well."

"Anything I can do to help?"

"You've already done enough. You helped find her. You helped keep her safe. You gave me two months of leave." Boone shook his head. "I owe you. We both know it."

"A person can never owe family, Boone. We do what we can for one another, and we don't keep score."

"Exactly." Boone stood and stretched. "Keep that in mind when you're dealing with Silverstone."

"What's that supposed to mean?"

"She's been thrown off the horse more than once. It's not surprising she's afraid to get back on it."

"You're talking in riddles, and I'm not in the mood."

"I'll make it plain then. Family is everything. Stella is family. To me, she's like a sister. To you…" He shrugged. "You get to decide, but I'd say she's a lot more, and I'd say you'd be a fool to let her keep avoiding what you both so obviously want."

"And what, exactly, would that be?" he asked, irritated with the conversation and with the fact that Boone could read him and Stella so easily.

"Like I said, that's for you to decide. Just make sure you don't let the past get in the way of whatever the future could be. Family should never keep score of the good things, but we shouldn't keep score of the bad, either." He pulled a bag out of his pocket. Not cookies this time. Chips. "You going to call your sister? Maybe we can get that information before the sun goes down."

"Sure," Chance said, gladly allowing the direction of the conversation to change. Whatever was between him and Stella, it was theirs to deal with. Hopefully, Boone would keep that in mind.

He dialed his sister's number as he walked to the end of the hall, following the same route the K-9 team had tracked earlier. Down a longer hall. Around another corner. Through doors that led into a stairwell.

The guy had run to the lobby, changed his clothes in a bathroom there and escaped completely unnoticed.

The security cameras had to have captured him, though. There were cameras in the stairwell and in the lobby. Chance was anxious to see the footage and to find out whether or not they'd gotten a clear picture of the guy's face.

Because if they had, he'd be that much closer to keeping Stella and her grandmother safe.

He left a message for Trinity as he walked into the hospital lobby. A few police officers were gathered there, a large German shepherd beside one of them. It looked like the K-9 team had followed the trail as far as it could and then returned to the hospital.

Chance wanted to know exactly where the trail had ended, what they had found at the end of it. A parking space? A dirt road? A shed or house of some sort?

There was no time like the present to find out.

He pasted on the easy smile he'd trained himself to use, the one that said he wasn't a threat, that he only wanted a friendly conversation. He'd learned long ago that he could catch more flies with honey than with vinegar, so he kept the vinegar for cleaning up messes and for making reluctant people give him the information he wanted.

The honey, though?

He used it as often as he needed it.

The officers eyed him as he approached, and he was sure they were noticing the bright tie and the starched white shirt, the tailored pants and jacket. He liked people to underestimate him, to assume he was a business man who just happened to run a hostage rescue team.

He introduced himself the same way he always did. Handshake, smile, business card. Once everyone was on the same page, he asked how the search had gone.

Next thing he knew, he was being given the tour, through the hospital lobby and out into the swirling snow. It was amazing that the dog had tracked anything in this, but it still seemed to have the scent. Nose down, it moved unerringly toward the corner of the building, around the side and then into a back lot that stretched into an empty field. They crossed that and moved onto a paved street in the town's main business section. Lots of buildings. Cars. Trucks. They passed a restaurant, a bank, a drug store, then went into the parking lot of a small movie theater.

"This is it," the K-9 officer said. "We have security footage from the theater's external camera. It shows the vehicle and the guy getting into it."

"You've already seen it?"

"Sure have." The officer was young, maybe midtwenties, and he seemed eager to prove himself. "Got the make of the car, but not the license plate, off it. No visual of the perp's face. If you want to take a look, I can check with the sheriff and see if he'll approve it."

"That would be great," Chance replied, eyeing the empty lot. He could see the tire tracks in the snow, nearly covered now but visible. The lot itself was behind the building and hidden from the street.

The perp must have known that.

Did that mean he knew the area? Or that he'd spent a few days staking it out, finding places where he could easily blend in and hide out?

Too many questions and not enough answers. Chance wanted to see that footage. Once he got a make and model for the vehicle, he could send the information to Trinity, see if she could connect it with any of Stella's known associates.

Or any of Beatrice's.

It was still possible that the attacker was after Stella's grandmother. Especially if Beatrice was right about rocks being thrown at the window. Boone had suggested inheritance as a motive, but Chance didn't know of any family aside from Stella who might benefit from the elderly woman's death.

He frowned, pulling out his cell phone as he followed the officer and dog back to the hospital. He texted Simon to ask him to check for evidence under the window. Sure, the sheriff was going to do that, but Simon knew how to assess a crime scene without disturbing it, and Chance needed to know exactly what had happened at the house. Then he texted Trinity and asked her to do some digging into Beatrice's family tree. Maybe someone, somewhere, would gain if Stella lost her grandmother.

He had to find out, and he had to do it quickly.

Whoever this guy was, he had motive, he had means, and he wasn't messing around. Two attempts in a few hours meant he was also desperate.

For what?

That was the question Chance needed to answer.

If he did, he'd have the answer to everything else.

Except what he was going to do once Stella was safe and there was nothing standing between them but her reluctance to be hurt and his decision to let her walk away.

Chapter Six

They wheeled Beatrice out for a chest X-ray at midnight. Stella followed the nurse and orderly through the quiet hallway and into the elevator, her body heavy with fatigue, her mind numb with it. Chance stood a few feet away, grim and silent, his jaw shadowed with the faintest hint of a beard. He met her eyes but didn't speak. She knew he didn't approve of her leaving the room to follow Beatrice. He'd wanted her to stay behind the closed door, Boone guarding her until he returned.

Usually, she didn't care about other people's opinions. She did her thing, followed her gut. Generally with good results.

Right now, though, she wasn't thinking clearly, and that was a terrifying place to be.

Chance, on the other hand, was clearheaded. He'd told her that the best thing she could do was stay in the room. Then he'd let it drop.

Just like always.

That was the way Chance operated.

No fuss or muss. No debates. Just stating facts and

expecting people to get on board with his logic because, most of the time, his logic was flawless.

Of course, this wasn't about logic.

This was about love, and Stella loved her grandmother too much to leave her alone and confused.

And she *was* confused.

She'd spent most of the day and night asking where she was, what had happened, where Henry was.

Even now, she was pulling at the oxygen mask, trying to drag it away so she could speak without her voice being muffled.

Stella reached for her hand, but Chance already had it. "Better leave that mask where it is, Ms. Beatrice," he said. "Your oxygen level is a little low."

"I'm sick?"

"Yes." He set her hand back on the gurney and patted it. "But you'll be better soon."

"You're Chance," Beatrice said as if she were trying to hold on to the name and remind herself of who he was. "Stella's friend."

"That's right."

"You two went out a few times."

"Nana," Stella cut in hurriedly. "Chance and I work together."

"I know that, dear, but you *did* date."

"Now you choose to remember things?" she muttered, and Chance laughed, steering her out of the elevator as the doors opened. They went toward radiology and Stella would have walked in, but the nurse shook her head.

"Sorry. Only patients past this point. We'll bring her out to you when she's done. It shouldn't be long."

They rolled her away, and Stella wasn't sure what

to do with herself. She'd spent most of the day sitting in the seat beside Beatrice or pacing the ICU trying to piece together how they'd gotten there. She'd run everything through in her mind dozens of times, and she still didn't have any answers that made sense.

Things had been fine since her grandfather's funeral. She hadn't sensed any trouble. Aside from Beatrice's health, there'd been nothing to worry about. Just everyday things to take care of. Even that hadn't been difficult. Her great-uncle Larry was a financial planner, and he knew exactly what Beatrice had, what Henry had left her and how long she could support herself without digging into retirement funds.

A long time.

Probably much longer than she'd live.

That had surprised Stella. Henry had been a pastor, and he hadn't made much money. She'd learned to live frugally when her grandparents were raising her. The house was beautiful. The antiques it contained stunning. But they were Beatrice's heritage, an inheritance from a father and grandfather who'd left her much wealthier than Stella would have ever guessed.

Stella's childhood had been nice, but modest. She'd had what she needed. Nothing more. No big parties or expensive clothes. Nothing excessive. She'd worked for her own car, and she'd paid for the gas and insurance on it. She hadn't minded. She'd been too grateful to her grandparents to ever complain that she didn't have the fanciest or most expensive things.

"Worried?" Chance asked, his hand settling between her shoulder blades.

"About Beatrice? Yes."

"About everything," he responded.

She turned to face him and realized just how close they were. Barely a breath between them, his bright tie at eye level, hanging loose. She tugged at the end of it, pulling it from his neck and tucking it into his shirt pocket.

"It's a little late in the day for a tie, don't you think?" she asked, avoiding his comment because she really didn't want to go into all the reasons why she was worried.

"It's a little late in the day for avoiding my questions, don't you think?"

"Probably," she admitted, turning away, not wanting to look into his beautiful eyes. She knew what she'd see there. The same compassion and understanding she saw when he was questioning clients or reassuring a victim. He had a way of making people open up to him.

She didn't like opening up to anyone.

She didn't like feeling vulnerable.

She *hated* being on the receiving end of pity.

She'd felt all of those things in the past few hours, and she needed some time to regroup, get herself together, take a little control back.

"Not talking about it isn't going to make it go away," Chance pointed out as she dropped into one of the chairs.

"Talking about it won't help, either."

"Stop lobbing volleys, Stell. If we're going to find the guy who attacked you, we need to work together."

"We are working together. I told you everything I know."

"Not Noah's contact information."

"Are we back to that?" She sighed, pulled her knees up to her chest and rested her chin on them.

"You need to trust me to handle things the way they need to be handled." He sidestepped the question, got right back to his point.

"Unless I've missed my guess," she muttered, turning her head just enough to meet his dark blue eyes, "you've already obtained Noah's full name, his address, his last known whereabouts. So why bring this up again?"

"You're not the only one who's worried. I don't want to see anything happen to you or your grandmother, and I can't do my job effectively with one hand tied behind my back."

"I'm not tying anything. I'm setting boundaries."

"Boundaries that are going to get you killed." His words were calm, his voice quiet, but the irritation in his eyes was impossible to miss.

"You're angry about nothing, Chance. If I'd thought that Noah—"

"You have a concussion. Do you actually believe you're making a rational assessment of the situation?" He stood, pacing across the room, his hands shoved into the pockets of his suit jacket.

"Probably not," she admitted. "But I know Noah well. We've been friends for years. There's no way—"

"There's always a way, Stella," he said gently, and she had a cold, horrible feeling that he knew something she didn't.

"What did you find out about Noah?"

"His ex-fiancée filed for a restraining order two days ago. She said he's been abusive and violent for the past year."

"I don't believe her. Noah is about the least violent person I know."

"She had proof enough to convince a judge that she needed the order of protection." He stalked back toward her, his legs long and muscular beneath his black dress pants. Most days he looked like an easygoing business-man, but Stella had seen him fight. She'd seen him win against powerful opponents. She knew just how dangerous he could be, and just how smart.

If he was worried about Noah, she should be worried, too.

But... Noah?

They'd been friends for a decade. She'd seen him at his best and at his worst, and she'd never ever seen him lay a hand on anyone.

"I'll talk to him. See what the order of protection is all about." She didn't have her phone with her, but there was one in Beatrice's room.

"He hasn't been at his apartment in a week. And my guess is he won't be answering his cell."

"How do you know?"

"Trinity talked to a few neighbors, called his work. Noah took a ten-day vacation. It started a week ago."

"And?"

"I'm interested to see if he returns home in three days and goes back to work."

"He will," she insisted, but she wasn't really sure. "He's just looking for a change. He told me that. He's tired of climbing the corporate ladder. He's been talking about rejoining the DC police department."

"That will be difficult to do with a restraining order out against him. A restraining order he apparently felt no need to mention to you. Why do you think that is?" he asked, his expression cold and hard.

"I'm not sure, but I'm guessing you're going to give me some ideas."

"Maybe the change he really wanted is you in his life, Stella. Maybe he was looking for a little more than what you were willing to give. Maybe he didn't tell you about the restraining order because he didn't want to scare you off, and when you stopped seeing him, maybe he got a little angry. Maybe he wanted a little revenge."

"That's a lot of maybes, and a lot of speculation about a guy who isn't around to defend himself."

She did not want to believe that Noah had anything to do with the attack.

She *didn't* believe it.

Footsteps sounded in the hall, voices drifting into the waiting area. She thought the nurse and orderly had returned with Beatrice, but Simon strode into the room, his black hair falling across his forehead, his light-colored eyes cutting from her to Chance and back again.

"Law enforcement is finished at the house. I locked up." He handed Stella her purse. "The keys are in there. I tossed your phone in, too, but I don't know if it's charged."

"Thanks."

"How's your grandma?" he asked, a hint of a Southern drawl in his voice.

"We're waiting on X-rays. Was someone out in the hall with you?" She was sure she'd heard voices.

"Yeah." His gaze shifted to Chance. "Don't blow a gasket over this, Miller."

"Over wh…?"

Chance's words trailed off as a pretty young woman walked into the room. Tall, slender, honey-blond hair, freckles. The same dark blue eyes as her brother.

Trinity Miller.

There was absolutely no doubt in Stella's mind that Chance really was going to blow up about it because he'd hired Trinity to work at headquarters. He'd never had any intention of letting her work in the field. He'd told Trinity that. He'd told Stella that. He'd told everyone at HEART that. He'd lost one sister, and he had no intention of losing another.

Stella understood that.

She supported it.

Trinity was young. She was a little naive. She'd spent most of her life being protected and cared for by her very well-meaning family. She had no business walking into the kind of situations HEART went into every day.

Stella had talked to Trinity about it, explaining everything in detail, telling her just how dangerous this line of work was and just how easily she could break her family's heart by being hurt or killed.

Stella had thought Trinity understood, but here she was. In the flesh. And unless Stella was mistaken, she had a gun holster strapped on beneath her coat.

Chance had taught his sister to use firearms.

He'd taught her self-defense.

He'd taught her everything she needed to know to survive, but there was no way in the world he was going to let her walk into this situation.

He didn't know why she'd come.

He didn't know what she thought she was going to add to the investigation beyond the information she'd already dug up for them.

What he did know was that she wasn't going to stay.

Not if he had anything to do with it.

"Go home," he said.

Trinity had the nerve to sashay across the room, kiss his cheek and smile.

"It's good to see you, too, bro."

"Bro?"

"Would you rather me call you 'Killjoy'?"

"I'd rather you were back at headquarters," he retorted, not bothering to keep the edge out of his voice. He had enough to worry about. He didn't want to add his sister to the list.

"You said you needed someone to take Boone's place. Here I am." She opened her arms wide, and he could see her shoulder holster under her thick pink parka.

"You are not taking Boone's place," he said, and she frowned.

"I don't see why not."

"Did you tell Jackson you were coming?" He sidestepped her comment, knowing that she hadn't consulted with their brother. Jackson was the co-founder of HEART, and he was just as protective of Trinity as Chance was.

"I left a note at the office."

"Coward," he muttered, and her smile broadened.

"No. Just smart. I figured by the time he read it, it would be too late for him to sabotage my car or come up with some busy work for me to do."

"That would have been fine by me. In case you haven't gotten the hint, I don't want you here."

"Because you don't think I can handle it. But I can." She brushed past him and wrapped her arms around Stella.

"I'm so glad you're all right," she said, and Chance knew she meant it from the bottom of her heart. He still wasn't going to let her take Boone's place. He'd call Jackson and have him send someone else, but it wouldn't hurt for Trinity to stick around. She'd be good for Stella, and she'd be good for Beatrice. She had that kind of personality—the kind that made people comfortable. He appreciated that about her, but she loved her family and friends with the kind of zealous loyalty that could get her into all kinds of trouble if she let it.

"Thanks, sweetie," Stella said, extracting herself from the hug and smiling at Trinity. "But your brother is probably right. You should go home."

"Give me a break, Stella. You've seen me on the gun range, and you've seen me in training. You know I can handle this. Besides, I have some information that I thought you might be interested in."

"About Noah?" Stella's smile fell away, and she took Trinity's arm, dragging her to the seats and pulling her down into one.

"Actually, no. The last record I have of him is a plane ticket he bought two weeks ago. Baltimore–Washington International to Dallas–Fort Worth."

"Fort Worth? I wonder who he knows there," Stella murmured.

Trinity shrugged. "I have no idea, but I can tell you this. Your uncle has a lot to gain if something happens to your grandmother."

"I don't have an uncle," Stella replied.

"Great-uncle. Your grandmother's brother."

"Uncle Larry?" Stella asked.

Trinity nodded as she pulled a folder out of her oversize bag, thumbed through some papers and pulled one out. "See this?"

She thrust the paper toward Stella and jabbed at

the top of it. "This is your great-grandfather's last will and testament. When he passed, his wife was already dead. He bequeathed his estate to your grandmother and great-uncle, and he had an executor make sure it was divided equally."

"And?" Stella took the paper from Trinity, her brow furrowed as she scanned the document. "As far as I know there was never any conflict between my great-uncle Larry and Beatrice regarding the estate."

"I couldn't find anything to disprove that theory. No legal action. No lawyers. Everything seems to have gone off without a hitch. The thing is, I searched on-line databases and found the name of your grandfather's attorney."

"William Tate. I could have saved you some effort and given the information to you, if you'd asked."

"I was just working off a hunch, and I didn't want to bother you." Maybe not, but Trinity must have thought she should have. Her cheeks were bright pink, her gaze lowered as she pulled another sheet from the folder. "Mr. Tate wouldn't tell me much, but he did say your grandfather was his client. Did you know that your grandmother is not?"

"The subject never came up," Stella said wryly.

"Do you know if your grandmother has a will?"

"Another subject that never came up."

"It needs to." Trinity held out the second sheet. "See this? It's an addendum to your great-grandfather's will. Written about three months before he died. He left the house to your grandmother along with all its contents. She has the legal right to bequeath it to whomever she wants, but if she dies without a will, the house goes to your great-uncle."

Stella took the paper and read it, her brow furrowed. She looked intrigued and a little anxious, as if she was worried that there might be something to Trinity's find.

Chance was intrigued, too.

He'd have asked to see the paper, but Stella passed it to him, handing it over before he could.

"I'll admit that it looks bad," she said as he scanned it. "But there is no way my great-uncle would try to kill Beatrice to get the house. He and my great-aunt love Beatrice and were close to my grandfather."

"Love of money is the root of all evil," Trinity said. "And it can motivate people to do some really horrible things. I ran a credit check on Larry, and he's having some serious trouble paying his bills. He's three months behind on his car. The boat? He's behind on that, too. I called a couple of his buddies at the country club and—"

"Enough." Chance cut her off before she could go any further. He loved his sister, but she wasn't thinking about Stella's feelings. She was thinking about proving herself.

"There's plenty more," she said, her cheeks pink. She obviously knew she'd gone too far, and she glanced at Stella. "I'm sorry, Stell. I should have given you the write-up instead of shouting it to the world."

"It's okay. I know you're just trying to help," Stella said, her face ashen. "Larry is out of town. I don't think he's involved in any of this, but I'll talk to him. See what he has to say."

Trinity frowned. "You know your uncle better than any of us. If you don't think he's involved, you're probably right."

"I think I'm right. I hope I am, but it still bears checking out. I called Larry earlier to let him know that Beatrice was in the hospital. Hopefully, I'll hear from him soon." She stood stiffly, her cheeks gaunt. She hadn't eaten and the last thing Chance had seen her drink was the few sips of orange juice.

"Tell you what," he said, cupping Stella's elbow and leading her back into the corridor. "How about we go back to the house once your grandmother is finished? You can shower, put on some warmer clothes, get something to eat."

"Food," she muttered, "would not be my friend right now."

"Juice, then," he insisted, and she sighed.

"Chance, I can take care of myself. I've always been able to take care of myself."

"That's the problem, isn't it, Stella? You can always take care of yourself, and you're never willing to let anyone step in and help out even when you really need it. You don't want to be vulnerable, but right now, you are. How about you just admit it, and we move on?" The words slipped out, and she frowned.

"You want me to admit it? Fine. I'm vulnerable right now, and you've helped me plenty. We both know it, and I appreciate it, but I can't leave Beatrice. She'll—"

"Be fine, Stella. Boone and Simon know what they're doing, and they're not going to let anything happen to her."

"Your sister knows what she's doing, too. She dug up a lot of information very quickly."

"My sister has a big mouth and doesn't know when to keep it shut."

"I heard that," Trinity called as she stepped into the hall. "Sadly, I can't argue with it. I really am sorry, Stella. I was so excited to have something to share—"

"You don't need to apologize."

"I do, and I have. Twice, because I feel terrible. And now I'm going to agree with my brother for probably the first time ever. You need to go home for a while. You look like death warmed over."

"You were eavesdropping," Stella accused.

"I was, and it didn't make me agree any less."

"I'll make a note of that," Stella murmured, her gaze on the radiology department doors. Maybe she thought if she stared long enough, they'd open.

"Notes don't do squat if we don't learn from them," Trinity responded, and for the first time in a long time, Chance wanted her to just keep on doing what she was doing, because he needed the break, too.

He needed a few minutes away from the hospital and the bright lights and the people. He needed to look into Stella's eyes, make sure that she really was okay before he decided whether or not to let her stay involved in the investigation.

Sure, it was her problem and her trouble, but she was emotionally invested. That could be dangerous for all of them. If he thought she couldn't handle it, if he thought she was going to get herself or someone else hurt, he'd put her under armed protection until the team figured things out. She wouldn't like it, but she'd allow it.

He knew she would. For her grandmother's sake.

Stella was pragmatic. She understood how easily emotion could sway judgment.

She was also hard-core and determined, willing to do anything to achieve a goal.

That came with a price.

It wore a person down, made him want to hide away

for a while, sit in solitude and replenish the stores that had been depleted.

He frowned.

Yeah. He knew that feeling. He'd been there a lot lately.

Maybe Stella knew it, because she touched his wrist, cool fingers against his warm skin.

Nothing else.

No words.

No arguments.

No concern that Trinity was a few steps away, watching them both.

He didn't care, either.

Everyone on the team knew that he and Stella had dated. Everyone on the team thought they belonged together.

In his opinion, everyone on the team was right.

All he had to do was convince Stella of that.

He captured her hand when she would have pulled away, linking their fingers and pressing a kiss to her knuckles. She seemed surprised, but she didn't pull away.

"What was that for?" she asked.

"It's a promise," he responded, "that everything is going to be okay."

And then the double doors swung open and Beatrice was wheeled out.

Chapter Seven

Stella waited in Beatrice's room until the X-ray results were in and her grandmother was sound asleep,
her raspy breath filling the room. Pneumonia. That was
the verdict the doctor had given. He'd put Beatrice on
an antibiotic and upped her oxygen. In a few days, he
hoped to wean her off that and get her out of the ICU.

A few days.

That seemed like a lifetime to Stella. She wanted to
bring Beatrice home now, back to the familiarity of her
bed and her bedroom, fix her favorite tea and feed her
one of the fancy chocolates she loved so much.

Since she couldn't do that, she'd go home, get her
grandmother's robe and her spare slippers, maybe even
one of the pretty nightgowns Beatrice loved so much.
Then she'd grab the brush Beatrice kept on her nightstand, the loose powder that she liked to pat on her
cheeks, the well-worn Bible that sat on the rocking
chair. Beatrice might not be able to use any of those
things, but it would make her feel better to have them
nearby.

That was all Stella cared about.

That and figuring out what was going on and how to stop it.

And then there was Chance. The kiss on her knuckles that she could still feel. Those whispered words—*It's a promise that everything is going to be okay.*

She'd been trying to put both out of her mind, but of course, she couldn't. Because she could never put Chance out of her mind. He was always there. The one guy who could be everything to her if she let him.

She grabbed her purse and tossed her phone into it. The battery was dead, and it was useless. She'd grab the charger when she went home.

"You going somewhere?" Trinity asked, looking up from the book she'd been reading. She'd taken position near the window, the oversize chair she was sitting in squeaking every time she moved. She looked tired and she looked young.

Stella could understand why Chance wanted her to return home.

She could also understand why Trinity had refused.

She'd been begging to take a more active part in HEART rescues, but neither of her brothers would allow it. She probably thought this was the perfect opportunity to prove her mettle. No need to get a visa, no need for pre-planning or travel approval. Just hop in a car and drive to a small town, bring information that might prove valuable, take part in the investigation on the ground rather than in the corner office at HEART headquarters.

If Stella had been in Trinity's shoes, she'd probably have done the same.

"I'm going back to the house. I want to get a few things for my grandmother."

Trinity set the book down and stood. "Does my brother know?"

"He will." He and Boone had gone to look at security footage obtained by the sheriff's department. If she hadn't been worried sick about Beatrice, Stella would have insisted on going with them.

"You know you can't go by yourself, right?"

"Seeing as I don't have a ride, yes."

"Even if you had a ride, it wouldn't be smart."

"I know, Trinity."

"So what are you going to do if Chance is still at the sheriff's office?"

"Find another ride."

"That's not a good idea."

"It wasn't a good idea for you to come here, but you did it anyway."

"I'm not the one who was nearly killed." She returned to the chair, picked up the book. "But you're an adult. You can make your own decisions."

"And you're going to text Chance as soon as I walk out the door."

"Something like that." Trinity smiled. "As a matter of fact, I may as well do it now." She pulled the phone from her pocket. "Or you can call and see if he's finished yet."

"Good idea." She took the phone, dialed Chance's number.

He picked up immediately.

"Trinity, we're not discussing anything unless it's you going home," he growled.

"It's Stella, and home is exactly where I was planning to go. That's why I'm calling. Are you still with Cooper?"

The door opened, and Chance walked in, tucking his phone away. "We just got back."

"And?" she asked, relieved that Chance was there and surprised by the feeling. She'd never needed Daniel. Not ever. Not when they'd met. Not when they'd married. Not when she'd spent long nights alone. She'd been happy when he'd returned, but she'd never been relieved, never felt the weight of responsibility, the burden of it, lifting as he walked through the door.

She'd felt that when Chance walked in. Felt it even more when he crossed the room and stood beside her.

"The perp must have known exactly where the cameras were. He kept his face hidden. No prints on the knife. No ID on the vehicle."

"That's not what I was hoping for."

"Me, neither." His gaze cut to Trinity who was studiously looking at her book. "We both know you're listening to every word. How about you don't pretend otherwise?"

"I was trying to avoid your wrath." She set the book on the window ledge and stood, taking her phone from Stella's hand. "But if you want to go head-to-head in front of Stella, that's fine."

"There's no need. I've already called Jackson. We agree that you should stay."

"Really?" She looked surprised and doubtful.

"As long as you follow instructions and do your part, yes."

"What, exactly, is my part going to be?"

"Sit with Beatrice when Stella can't be here."

"Fine," she agreed.

"That was a little too easy," Chance muttered.

"You give me what I want, I make your life easy. This is a good lesson for both of us," Trinity said solemnly. "Now you two go on and have fun. I'll take care of things here."

"Are you sure—" Stella began, because she was worried about her grandmother, terrified that she'd wake up and be confused and scared.

"I won't leave her side," Trinity promised.

"Okay." Stella touched her grandmother's cheek, remembering all the times Beatrice had done the same for her. Remembering those long, painful days and nights after the accident when the only thing that had kept her from giving up was her grandmother's soft hand against her cheek, her quiet words, her fervent prayers.

"God be with you," she whispered in her grandmother's ear, remembering the words she'd heard so many times, "when I cannot. God give you strength when mine is not enough for both of us. God give you hope when we both feel hopeless, and when I am gone, may He give you love that stretches beyond this world and into the next."

She kissed Beatrice's temple, told herself she wasn't going to cry.

"That was beautiful," Trinity said quietly.

Chance didn't say a thing. Just took her arm and led her out of the room, down the hall, into the elevator. And she was still trying not to cry. Still telling herself that she had nothing to cry about.

The first tear fell as they stepped outside.

The second one fell as she slid into the passenger seat of Chance's SUV.

He still didn't say a word. Just rounded the side of the vehicle and got in, turning on the engine and the heat.

She sniffed back more tears. Annoyed. Irritated. Broken.

Because she was more tired than she'd ever been before. Because her head hurt and her stomach churned and the one man who could always make her feel better was sitting right beside her, and she wouldn't reach for him because she was too much of a chicken.

"I don't cry," she felt the need to say.

"Everyone cries sometimes, Stella. Even me."

"I've never seen it."

"You've never seen me stand at the hospital bed of someone I love, either." He leaned toward her, his lips brushing her temple, her cheek, her lips.

She should have told him to stop, but she wanted more. Of him. Of this.

When he backed away, she wanted to follow, wanted to cling to his solid strength.

"Are you going to ask me what that was for?" he asked, his voice raspy and rough.

"Are you going to tell me?"

"It's a promise, Stella, that I'm not walking away from you. Not again."

He pulled out of the parking lot, the silence thick and filled with a dozen protests she could have made.

Didn't make, because she didn't want him to walk away.

Finally, he broke the silence. "I asked the sheriff about your uncle."

"And?"

"He said that Larry is a good guy who seems to really love his family. Including his sister and you."

"I agree."

"Sometimes people aren't what they seem."

"I agree with that, too."

"Did Larry return your call?"

"Not yet."

"Do you think that's odd?"

"He might have his phone turned off. People do that at night."

"Some people do, but would he?"

"I don't know."

"Do you want me to have some people track him down?"

"If he doesn't call tomorrow, we're not going to have a choice."

"Do you have any idea where he was going?"

"His property in Florida. He heard the storm was coming in, and he and Aunt Patty wanted to avoid it."

"When did he make the plans?"

"The first I heard of it was a week ago. Aunt Patty mentioned it when she came to visit. She was excited. Usually, they don't go until after Christmas."

"That's what she said?"

"Yes."

"And a sudden winter storm changed all that, huh?" He turned into the snow-covered driveway, headlights splashing across tracks left from dozens of other vehicles.

The house jutted up from the landscape, black against the grayish sky, a light on in the attic and one on in the living room. A car was parked close to the porch, the paint gleaming dully in the moonlight. She thought it was familiar, but she couldn't quite place it.

"I wonder whose—" The attic light went off, and the rest of the sentence caught in her throat.

Chance thrust his phone into her hand. "Call the sheriff." He put the vehicle into Park. "And stay put."

Then he was out of the SUV, sprinting toward the house.

Whoever had entered the house was going to exit it. Chance had no doubt about that.

Front door or back?

That was the question.

He sprinted up the porch stairs, tried the knob and wasn't surprised when the door swung open. He stepped inside, listening for the sound of footsteps. The house seemed empty, the silence echoing hollowly as he moved deeper into the foyer.

He glanced in the living room, the bright light there revealing a room that had been torn apart. Books pulled from shelves. Couch cushions tossed on the floor. A lamp had been overturned, the bulb shattered.

He flicked off the light, backing out of the room and leaving it for the police to process.

Right now, he had more important things to deal with.

There were servant stairs that led from the upper levels into the kitchen. If Chance were the one trying to avoid detection, he'd take those and go out the back door. He moved through the hallway, tensing as someone walked into the house behind him.

Stella. He could hear her pant cuffs brushing against the floor, hear the whisper of her breath as she stepped closer.

She didn't ask questions, didn't offer a plan, just kept pace with him as he walked into the kitchen. Like the foyer and hallway, it was empty, a small light above the stove illuminating the darkness. He flicked it off and walked to the servant stairs. The stairwell was pitch-black, the silence eerie.

Someone was there.

He could feel it like he felt the flash of adrenaline that shot through his blood.

He pulled out his Glock, motioning for Stella to move back. Somewhere above, a floorboard creaked. Then another. The perp was retreating, probably heading back toward the front steps.

Chance followed, the sound of creaking boards and running feet carrying through the house.

He reached the front stairs, saw a shadowy figure barreling down them. He didn't announce his presence, didn't give the guy a chance to see him. He lunged, forearm to throat, gun pressed to the underside of the jaw, slamming the guy up against the wall.

"Don't move," he growled, knowing the barrel of the gun was digging into flesh and his forearm was cutting off air. "Understand?" he asked, and the guy didn't nod. He whimpered.

"Do you have him?" Stella called.

"Yeah. Get the lights," he responded.

Seconds later, the foyer lit up, and he was looking into the face of a man who had to be in his seventies. Salt-and-pepper hair, tan skin, blue eyes.

Larry Bentley.

Stella's great-uncle.

Chance had met the guy at Henry's funeral.

He eased his hold and backed off.

"You have any weapons on you, Larry?" he asked, and the older man shook his head, his hand trembling as he smoothed his hair.

"Of course not! I'm not a hoodlum." Larry's gaze darted to Chance's gun and then settled on his face again. "What's the meaning of this? Why are you in my sister's house?" he demanded.

"I was going to ask you the same thing."

"Uncle Larry?" Stella walked into the foyer, her skin nearly translucent with fatigue. "What are you doing here?"

"Picking up a few things for Beatrice. I planned to head to the hospital when I was done."

"At two in the morning?" she asked.

"She's my sister. She's ill. Does it really matter what time it is?"

"What I'd like to know," Chance said, "is why you were in the attic."

"I told you," Larry huffed. "I was looking for some things to bring to Beatrice."

"Is that why you tore the living room apart?"

"What?" Stella brushed past and stalked into the living room. She muttered something under her breath, and then returned, her eyes flashing with anger.

"What were you thinking?" she demanded, and Larry frowned.

"I didn't make that mess. It was already like that when I got here. I thought maybe the police had gone through the room looking for evidence."

"How did you even know that the police were here?" she asked. "I didn't tell you that in the message I left."

"Cooper left a message, too. He said they were conducting a full investigation."

"And to do that they needed to tear apart Nana's house? Come on, Uncle Larry," she said. "You're smarter than that."

"No need to get riled up, Stella. Like you said, it's the wee hours of the morning, and my brain isn't functioning well. I traveled all day to get here, and I drove straight from the airport to the house."

"You could have let me know you were on the way," Stella responded. She didn't look mollified by his explanation.

Chance wasn't, either.

"I would have, but I left my cell phone in Florida. I was in such a hurry after I heard the news, I guess I wasn't thinking straight."

Either that, or he hadn't wanted anyone to be able to track his movements. "What time did you arrive at the house?" Chance asked.

"Twenty minutes ago." He glanced at his watch. "Maybe a little longer."

"It took you a long time to gather things for your sister."

"I was looking for something specific. A wedding photo of our parents. It was in a beautiful Victorian frame. My great-grandmother's wedding brooch was worked into the frame. Do you remember it, Stella?"

"Of course. I saw it every day when I was growing up."

"It was on the fireplace mantel right before Henry passed," Larry said. "I haven't seen it since. I thought maybe Beatrice put it in her room or stored it in the attic."

"Why would she do that?" Stella walked into the living room, and Chance followed, watching as she studied the fireplace mantel. There were a few items there. A blue vase. A photo of Stella when she was ten, her bright red hair hanging nearly to her waist. Another one of Beatrice, Henry and Stella, all of them standing in front of the house, smiling at the camera. Stella was even younger in this one, the scars on her shoulder and upper arm revealed by a yellow tank top.

"Why does she do anything lately?" Larry responded.

"We could talk about that forever," Stella said, her gaze on the bookshelf and the books that had been pulled from it. "I'd rather talk about what happened here. If you didn't make this mess—"

"I didn't."

"Someone else did, then. Not the police. Cooper would never allow his deputies to leave a mess like this."

"Did you check any of the other rooms?" Chance asked, because if someone had been searching the house, it seemed unlikely he would have only torn apart the living room.

"I came in here and I went to the attic. That was it."

And yet, he'd been there twenty minutes.

Seemed like a long time to spend in two rooms.

Chance met Stella's eyes, saw his doubt reflected in her gaze.

Outside, emergency lights flashed as the sheriff's squad car raced up the driveway.

"Here comes the cavalry," Chance said. "Let's see what they have to say."

"I need to get those things for my grandmother," she responded, turning and heading up the stairs.

He wanted to follow, but Larry was hovering on the living room threshold, and Chance had the strange feeling that he was waiting for an opportunity to leave the scene.

Wasn't going to happen.

The guy had some explaining to do, and Chance was going to make sure he did it.

He offered a smile that he knew was anything but friendly, tucked his Glock into its holster and opened the front door. He waited there as the sheriff got out of his vehicle and headed across the snowy yard.

Chapter Eight

For days after she'd been knocked unconscious, Stella was finally beginning to feel more like herself. A mild headache, an ugly bruise and itchy stitches were a small price to pay for surviving what could have been deadly.

She couldn't complain.

Especially with Beatrice improving so much.

After two nights, her condition had been upgraded, and she'd been moved out of the intensive care unit. The private room she'd switched to had plenty of room for a cot, and the nursing staff had been happy to provide one for Stella. That had made it easy to keep an eye on Beatrice *and* rest.

She'd have rested better if Trinity hadn't insisted on bringing a tiny Christmas tree into the room. The potted plant stood about a foot high, its spindly branches barely covered by needles. Trinity had tried to make up for that by wrapping it in gold tinsel and decorating it with miniature ornaments.

For the past two nights, Stella had lain on the cot, staring at that tree, willing herself not to have nightmares. She'd thought of a dozen different ways she could get rid of the thing. Sneak it out in the middle of the night, toss it into the Dumpster behind the hospital, give it to the lady across the hall who never seemed to have any visitors.

Beatrice, of course, loved the tree.

As a matter of fact, she hadn't stopped talking about it.

"It's such a lovely little tree, don't you think, dear?" she asked for the umpteenth time, and, for the umpteenth time, Stella smiled and agreed.

"It is."

"We could hang stockings, too. Wouldn't that be nice?"

"I can—" Trinity began, and Stella shook her head. Sharply.

"We'll do that when you go home. We can get the stockings out of the attic and hang them from the fireplace mantel. Like we used to."

"Let's go, then." Beatrice sat up, the frilly nightgown she'd insisted on changing into hanging from her bony shoulders. She was still attached to an IV, and Stella put a hand on her arm, holding her in place.

"We will. Once the doctor releases you."

"When will that be?"

"Tomorrow. If you're still feeling good."

"Will that be a Sunday? I feel like I missed church this week. Did I?"

"Tomorrow is Tuesday. Yesterday was Sunday. Your friends came to visit you after church, remember?" Beatrice had had a steady stream of visitors since she'd left the ICU.

Chance had kept a list of every one of them.

He'd also made a list of people who'd visited Beatrice

in the weeks after the funeral, because the framed photo hadn't been found. Someone had removed it. Larry had insisted it wasn't him, and Stella wanted to believe him.

Except for the fact that he really was in financial trouble, and the brooch that had been built into the frame was twenty-four-carat gold with a two-carat diamond surrounded by sapphires. Early twentieth-century Tiffany.

Stella had always thought the piece was paste.

She'd been wrong.

If she'd known it was worth nearly ten thousand dollars, she'd have asked her grandparents to lock it in the safe long ago.

Larry and Patty had traveled to Florida. They could have brought the piece with them, sold it to some antiques dealer somewhere and pocketed the money.

They absolutely needed the cash.

Larry had admitted that he and Patty had put their vacation property on the market while they were down there. That had been the real reason for the spur-of-the-moment visit. He'd had to sign the paperwork, get things rolling. He'd told Cooper that he'd made some bad investments and lost a lot of money, but he'd never take anything from his sister.

Stella *really* wanted to believe him.

But who else had access to the piece and knew its value? Stella was certain the frame and photo had been missing since the day she'd returned to town. It hadn't been taken by whoever had torn the living room apart. Which left few options. Or, maybe, many. People liked Beatrice, and she often had visitors.

"I think I might remember them coming," Beatrice

murmured, plucking at the lace on her nightgown. "And Karen. She came by this morning."

"That's right."

"And brought me chocolates. Where did they go?"

"You ate them."

"My goodness. I must have been hungry."

"Or you really like chocolate," Trinity said cheerfully.

"I do like chocolate." Beatrice sighed. "I also like home, and I'd really like to go there. I'm sure you can pull some strings, Stella. You're a nurse. Just tell the doctor you'll take care of me. Or have your grandfather do it. I'm sure Henry is anxious for me to come home."

"Nana," Stella began, but she couldn't get the rest of the words past the lump in her throat.

How many times would she have to tell her grandmother the truth? That the man she'd loved for sixty years was gone? That he wasn't waiting at the house for her return? That he would never tell a silly joke or compliment her cooking ever again? How many times would she have to see the tears fill Beatrice's eyes? How many times would she have to break her heart?

"Beatrice," Trinity said, pulling a chair over beside the bed and taking a seat. "How about I read you more of *Little Women*?"

"My favorite story," Beatrice replied, but she looked as sad as Stella felt.

Sad because she wasn't going home, or sad because she suddenly remembered the truth?

"While you two do that, I'm going to run some errands," Stella said. She couldn't sit in the room for another minute, listening to her grandmother's favorite book, staring at the gaudy little Christmas tree.

"I'd love some chocolate, if you have time to stop at the shop," Beatrice said. "It's been months since I've had any."

Stella just kissed her cheek and promised chocolate, and then she walked out of the room.

Simon was sitting beside the door, scrolling through something on his phone. He looked up as she walked out, but he didn't ask where she was going. He wasn't the kind of guy to get involved in other people's business. Chance had told him to guard Beatrice; that's what he was going to do.

Which meant that Stella didn't have anyone following her around the hospital. Not that she needed anyone to do that. She wasn't foolish enough to think she was safe. There'd been no progress made in identifying the guy who'd attacked her.

Not Noah.

She was sure of that.

Now that her mind was clear again, she realized Noah was taller, broader and stronger than her attacker. If he'd wanted to kill her, he would have succeeded. It wasn't Larry, either. His alibi had panned out, and he'd passed a lie detector test.

Whoever it was, he hadn't tried again.

Chance thought there was too much man power on the ground, and that the guy would bide his time, strike again when he thought he had a shot at succeeding.

Chance...

She'd been trying not to think about him because she didn't want to focus on how nice it was to have him around. She didn't want to remember the kisses, the promises, the sweet words.

She didn't want to think about what he'd meant when he'd said he didn't plan to walk away.

Because she was falling harder than she'd ever fallen before. Harder than she'd ever thought she could. For a man who spent his life going into dangerous situations and getting people out of them.

Christmas carols were playing over the hospital intercom, and that only added to Stella's bad mood.

"Can't we just skip Christmas this year?" she muttered, yanking open the stairwell door.

"I don't think my niece and nephew would approve," Chance said, behind her. "But you could put together a petition and see if you can get anyone to sign it."

Startled, she turned around to face him, her heart beating double-time, her stomach doing a funny little dance. He looked like he always did. Handsome. Together. Confident. But he hadn't shaved in a couple of days, he'd traded his dress shirt and tie for jeans, flannel and a heavy coat, and he looked like he spent most of his time outside rather than in a boardroom.

"Where'd you come from?" she asked, her pulse still racing. She wanted to chalk up her fast heartbeat to his sudden appearance. But she couldn't. It was from looking into his eyes and seeing the man who'd been with her through the good and bad and everything in between.

For years.

For longer than Daniel had been with her, and that was odd to think about. That she and Chance had known each other for nearly double the amount of time she'd been married.

"I was getting coffee and saw you leaving the room as I got off the elevator." He held up a carryout cup. "I guess Simon didn't mention that I'd be right back. But then, I'm assuming you didn't ask."

"I needed some air," she responded. "I wasn't going far."

"You shouldn't be going anywhere on your own."

"Now I won't have to."

He smiled, and her pulse jumped again, her thoughts flying back to that moment in his SUV, those tender kisses.

"So why the sudden need for air?" he asked, taking her arm as they walked into the stairwell.

"*Little Women*, Christmas, Beatrice mentioning Henry again," she answered honestly. "Take your pick."

"I'd say that the last is the worst."

He nudged his coffee into her hand, and she took a sip. They'd done all of this dozens of times before. Walking together, talking, sharing coffee. It felt different this time. Maybe because he was there to protect her, and she knew it. Maybe because they were on her home territory, close to all the things that she longed for deep down where it mattered most—home, family, love.

"You're right. I hate breaking her heart over and over again."

"You're not breaking it," he reminded her as he pushed open the lobby-level door. "Losing Henry is."

"Semantics, Chance. It all boils down to the same thing. I have to keep reminding her of the one thing she'd love to forget."

"Is there another choice? Could you live with yourself if you lied to her? Let her think that Henry was alive? Kept building her expectation that she was going to see him again?"

She'd thought about that a lot the last couple of days.

She'd asked herself whether or not lying would bring Beatrice comfort or if it would just bring more pain. In the end, she'd decided to stick with what she knew—honesty.

It's what Beatrice would have wanted if she hadn't had Alzheimer's, and it was what Henry would have expected from his only grandchild.

"Right now, I don't know what I could live with. I only know what my grandmother would want—honesty."

"Then don't feel bad about giving it to her."

He took off his coat and draped it around her shoulders, pulling her hair out from under the collar. "How about we go get something to eat?"

"I'm not hungry."

"You haven't been hungry in four days."

"Are you counting?"

"Yes."

"You know how head injuries are," she said as he tucked strands of hair behind her ear and eyed the bump on her temple. She knew how it looked—green and purple and yellow but better than it had been yesterday and the day before that.

"How are the stitches?" he asked, moving around her and parting the hair near her nape. She hadn't bothered looking at the stitches. They itched, and she knew they were healing. That had been enough information to go on.

"Fine."

"You're going to have a pretty little scar, Stella."

"It'll be the perfect complement to all the big ugly ones."

"Your scars aren't ugly. Nothing about you could

ever be ugly." He let her hair drop back into place as
he adjusted the coat again. She could feel the warmth
of his hands near her skin.

And she just stood there and let it all happen.

She didn't brush his hand away or tell him to stop
fussing.

She didn't explain that she was perfectly capable of
taking care of herself.

She didn't offer a word of protest when his lips
brushed hers. A sweet, gentle kiss, and she wanted
more because this was Chance and they'd known each
other forever, had been there for each other over and
over again.

If that wasn't love, she didn't know what was.

But the sweetness of love had always come with the
bitterness of loss. She didn't know if she could take
what she wanted and not suffer for it. She didn't know
if she could lose Chance and survive it.

Kissing Stella was the best thing he'd ever done and
probably the biggest mistake he'd made in a long time,
but Chance wasn't about to apologize for it. He knew
what he wanted. He'd known for a long time. After
spending four days thinking about what could have happened if he hadn't shown up at Beatrice's house at just
the right time, he'd decided that he'd be a fool to keep
skirting around the thing that was between them.

"Chance—" Stella began as he stepped back.

"If you're going to say I shouldn't have done that,
forget it."

"I wasn't."

"Then what were you going to say?"

"That…" She shook her head.

"Tell you what, Stella. For once, how about you just be honest with both of us?"

"You want honesty?" She started walking, his coat still around her shoulders. "I'm terrified."

"Of loving me?"

"Of losing you."

"Who says you have to?"

"Life? Experience? I've lost everyone I've ever loved, Chance. Everyone."

"Do you wish you hadn't loved them?" he asked, his heart breaking for her, but his mind clear and sharp and focused. He knew what she needed to hear. Not a bunch of platitudes. The truth, and this was it—love always had risk, and it was always worth it.

"Of course not."

"Then what's to fear?"

"I don't want to be hurt again."

"Neither do I. But when I weigh the risk versus the benefit, I'm all for giving it a try," he responded as they walked past a Christmas tree that had been set up in the lobby. Colored lights twinkled in the branches and brightly wrapped packages were piled beneath it. A few people were hanging ornaments. Others sat on benches and in chairs, talking and laughing as carols continued to be piped through the intercom.

"You're braver than I am."

"And yet, we both face danger every day."

"You know what I mean, Chance," she said quietly, stopping short in front of the doors. "Even if I weren't afraid to risk my heart, the timing isn't right. My grand-mother—"

"Is very happy to know that you've found someone

who cares about you. Do you really think she wants to leave you alone when she's gone?"

Her expression tightened, her lips pressing together.

"I'll take your silence as a no, so how about you stop trying to use Beatrice as an excuse?"

"Fine." She shrugged, walking again, her shoulders stiff and straight, her head high.

He followed her into the sunny day, the crisp, cold air cutting through his flannel shirt. He'd strapped his holster beneath it, his Glock loaded and ready.

He opened the SUV door for her, and he wanted to kiss her again, taste the cold winter air on her lips.

Not the time.

Not when they were both upset.

He closed the door and rounded the vehicle, someone at the edge of the lot catching his eye.

Not a man. A woman. Medium height. Light brown hair. Familiar. But the sun was so bright behind her that he couldn't see her face.

She was watching. He felt that.

He wanted to know why.

He opened the door, leaned in.

"See that woman over there?"

Stella nodded. "I noticed her when you closed the door."

"She's watching us. I'm going to ask why."

"Hold on." She grabbed his hand, her fingers cold, her skin rough from years of climbing, shooting and training. "I think it's Karen," she whispered as if she was afraid the woman would hear.

"She was here earlier," he said. He'd looked through the bag she'd been carrying, and she hadn't been happy about it.

Twenty-two, a nursing student, a hospital volunteer. Active in church. Young and happy and kind. Maybe she thought she was above suspicion.

She was wrong.

He'd done a little digging, found out that she'd moved to town with her father two years ago. No one had actually been able to tell him why.

He figured this was as good a time as any to ask.

"I'm going to talk to her, see why she's still hanging around."

"She does volunteer here," Stella pointed out.

"She has classes. She should be at school."

"You looked at her college schedule?"

"Trinity did."

"I'm not going to ask how she managed that."

"Me, neither, but she printed it out, and I know where Karen should be. I want to know why she's here instead."

"Looks like she's coming this way," Stella responded.

She was right, Karen was walking across the parking lot. Hurrying, really, her narrow frame encased in a long wool coat. She could be carrying a dozen weapons beneath it, and that bothered Chance.

A lot.

"Stay in the car," he said, closing the door and turning to face Karen.

She was smiling.

Of course. He had yet to see her without a wide grin and a cheerful expression.

"Hi, Chance!" she called. "I thought that was you and Stella. I guess I was right."

"I thought you left a couple of hours ago," he responded, and her smile fell away.

"I did, but my afternoon class was canceled, and I figured I'd get a few more volunteer hours in. Is that a problem?"

"Just a curiosity."

She laughed. "I like what I do. Is that so curious?"

"Not at all." Simple. To the point. Let her do the talking and see where she went with it.

"I want to do mission work overseas. There are several orphanages supported by our church, and I'd like to use my nursing degree to help there."

"That's charitable of you," he said.

Apparently, that wasn't the response she wanted. She frowned.

"It's not about charity. I just have a heart for orphans. Everyone thinks I'm too young to know what I really want. My father wants me to find a nice guy, get married, spend my life trying to…"

Her voice trailed off, and her cheeks went bright red.

"Anyway, I just came over to say hi to Stella." She leaned down, waved through the closed window.

Stella waved back but didn't get out of the vehicle.

Either she was tired or she was cold or she was as worried as Chance was that someone would take a potshot across the parking lot.

"I'm coming by tomorrow to clean Beatrice's room and get things ready for her, okay?" Karen yelled through the glass, and Stella gave her a thumbs-up.

"She might be released early in the morning. It's what she wants," Stella responded, her voice muffled by the glass.

"I can't make it until the evening. I have college singles group at church at seven. I can stop by your place at five and paint her nails. I'll bring her a sandwich from the diner. She'll like that."

"Sounds good. If plans change and she isn't released—"

"I'll bring everything to the hospital. See you then." Karen walked away, not giving Chance a backward glance.

He slid behind the steering wheel and started the SUV, watching in the rearview mirror as Karen walked into the hospital. "She's an interesting kid."

"She's a hard worker."

"I know a lot of hard workers who work hard at being criminals."

"You don't really think she had anything to do with the attack, do you?" she responded, reaching forward to adjust the heat. Her hand was white from cold, her knuckles red.

She did her own volunteering.

She hadn't mentioned it, and he hadn't asked, but he knew. She spent one morning a week in the NICU, holding premature babies while Beatrice attended occupational therapy and craft classes for dementia patients. She'd scrubbed her skin raw to keep from spreading germs.

He grabbed her hand, and she went completely still, her eyes wide in her pale face. She had fine lines near the corners of her eyes and a tiny scar near her left ear. He'd been there when she'd been hit by shrapnel. He knew exactly how she'd looked as blood seeped from the wound while she ran for a helicopter, an injured child in her arms.

They'd saved the kid, but he'd lost a couple of years off his life thinking she'd been severely injured.

"You need some lotion," he said, running his thumb across her knuckles.

"I need answers more," she responded. "So how about we go by the house? I want to look around. When we're done, we can stop and get Beatrice more of her favorite chocolates."

"It might be better if you take a nap once you get to the house."

"No way. Now that my head is clearer, I want to walk through the woods, see if there's anything that will spark my memory and help me figure out who was out there with me."

"You said there might have been two people."

"I know."

"Do you still think that?"

"I don't know what I think. I just know that I have to keep searching until I find what I'm looking for."

"There's a lot I could say about that," Chance murmured as he backed out of the parking space.

"Like what?"

"Maybe what you're looking for is right in front of you?"

She shook her head, strands of bright red hair sliding across her cheeks. "You know that's not what I'm talking about."

"Maybe it should be. God gives us each a certain amount of time. If we're not careful, it will run out, and we won't have gone after what we really wanted."

"My grandfather always used to say that." She smiled, leaning her head back against the seat and closing her eyes.

"I wish I'd had a chance to meet him. From what I've heard, he was a great guy."

"Did you know he was a pastor?" she asked, her eyes still closed as she seemed to be drifting in some long-ago place, some sweet memory. Her lips were curved, her face soft.

"Yes."

"He really believed that God would make something wonderful out of what happened to my family, and he never stopped telling me that I lived because God had great work for me to do."

"You didn't believe him?"

"I had a hard time believing that a God who had great plans would take my whole family from me and then expect me to still keep on going toward whatever wonderful thing was in store."

"I'm sorry."

"Yeah. Me, too."

"But your grandfather was right. Your family is gone, but dozens of other families are together because of the work you do and the passion you have for it. I know that's cold comfort—"

"No." She opened her eyes. "It isn't. I'm older now. I can accept that the tragedy I lived through brought me to a place where I could help other people. I just find it hard to believe that I'm ever going to find the kind of peace that my grandparents had. An easy, nice, lovely life with all kinds of ordinary miracles—babies and kittens and Christmases filled with happiness and laughter."

"Those things are all around you, Stella," he said, because he thought that she'd missed them too often, so busy pursuing the next rescue, the next big victory, that she'd forgotten to look for the little ones.

"Maybe." She turned on the radio, frowning as a carol filled air. "More Christmas songs."

"It *is* the most wonderful time of year," he joked, but Stella didn't seem amused. She sighed, smoothing her hair and rubbing the back of her neck.

"For some people. For me, it just brings back a lot of bad memories."

"You could change that. You could make some good ones."

She said something, but he didn't hear the words. He was glancing in the rearview mirror, eyeing the truck that had just sped out from a side road.

Black. Shiny. Looked like a newer model, and it was coming fast.

"What's going on?" Stella asked, twisting in her seat and looking out the back window. "That looks like trouble."

"And *that's* an understatement," he muttered, because they were out in the middle of nowhere, the truck speeding toward them, tinted windows keeping him from seeing how many people were in it. The road stretched straight out in front of them, a steep tree-covered hill to the right, a slush-filled ditch to the left. Too deep to try to drive through. He'd bottom out the SUV.

"There's a driveway about a mile from here," Stella said, her voice tense, her hand gripping the back of the seat as she watched the truck career toward them. "On the left. Very hard to see. Look for a giant spruce and a white mailbox. Turn hard when you see it. There's a small bridge that goes over the ditch."

He stepped on the accelerator, focusing his attention on the road and on keeping a distance between the SUV and the truck.

"He's still coming," Stella murmured, pulling her phone from her pocket and calling for help.

That was great.

Except the truck was closing in, and he could see the barrel of a rifle poking out the window.

"Get down!" he shouted as he caught sight of the spruce and the mailbox. He could see a hint of wood planks. Not much of a bridge, but he yanked the wheel to the left, the SUV skidding sideways and bouncing onto wood, then dirt and grass.

The truck sped past, tires squealing as it tried to brake, glass shattering in the back of the SUV. The guy had taken out the back window.

"Keep going!" Stella yelled. "He's turning around."

Chance didn't need the warning. He was already stepping on the accelerator, speeding toward a distant house and, hopefully, a place to take cover.

Chapter Nine

"Do you know what's on the other side of the house?" Chance asked, his voice razor-sharp. He was calculating risk, formulating a plan, doing everything he'd done hundreds of times before.

Stella was doing the same.

It was what they'd been trained for, and she didn't feel panic as much as she felt adrenaline flooding through her, clearing the last cobwebs from her concussed brain.

"A field. Probably not enough coverage, though," she responded, her gaze on the truck. The driver had skidded to a stop and turned around, searching for the entrance to the driveway. Going too fast. He'd have to slow down if he was going to find it.

"Is there another access road to the property?"

"No." The driver had slowed, was backing up, probably knowing that they were cornered. Maybe not realizing who he was going up against. Not an elderly woman wandering through the snowy woods, and not an unsuspecting caretaker rushing to find her. Two well-trained operatives who weren't going to be taken out easily.

"Anyone in the house? It looks empty, but I don't want to take chances that we're going to put civilians in the crosshairs of a gunfight."

"The place has been abandoned for years." As a teenager, she'd spent time exploring the house with her friends, walking through the dusty rooms and looking at furniture that had been left behind decades ago. Eventually, the town council had opted to board up the windows and doors to keep the teenage crowd from partying there, but Stella hadn't let that stop her. She'd found a way into the cellar and brought friends there to tell scary stories.

"Any way to get inside?" Chance asked, that edge still in his voice.

"Yes. There's a cellar door in the back. I broke the lock years ago. Unless someone has fixed it, we should be able to get in."

"You called 911. Did you let Simon and Boone know we've got trouble?"

"Yes." She'd texted coordinates to both of them. She didn't have time to check for a response. She was too focused on the truck. The driver had finally found the entrance and was bouncing over the planks that led to the driveway.

"He's in," she said.

"And we're out of sight," Chance replied, pulling around the side of the house and throwing the SUV into Park. "Let's go," he commanded, but she was already moving, jumping out and running to the cellar door.

It was covered with debris—snow and grass and dirt.

She found the handle and tugged, trying to pull it open. She could hear the truck's engine, the swish of tires on grass and dirt. A quarter mile. That's how far it was from the road to the house. A few seconds of driving, and the guy would be there.

Chance grabbed the handle, wrapping his hand over hers and yanking hard. The old door finally gave, swinging up and open.

"Get in!" Chance shouted, nearly shoving her into the cellar. She stumbled down rickety steps, tripped over an old box and fell, sliding on hands and knees across the earthen floor.

Chance scrambled down the stairs behind her, letting the door drop back into place and plunging the cellar into darkness.

"You okay?" he asked, finding her hand and hauling her to her feet.

"Yes."

"Can we get into the house from here?"

"There's a door..."

"Shhhhh." He pressed a finger against her lips, and she froze.

She could hear the truck's engine, the tires on the frozen yard. Then silence, thick and heavy and horrible.

She grabbed Chance's sleeve and led him across the root cellar. She knew the way. She'd been here dozens of times, and she hadn't forgotten. The cellar was ripe with the scent of dirt and decay, the air frigid with winter. Years ago, fruit and vegetables were stored there, old wooden shelves jutting from the walls, still hosting cans of peaches and pears and pickles.

She couldn't see them through the darkness, but she knew they were there. Just like she knew there was a door in the far wall that led to the stairs. She ran her hand along the packed earth until she felt wood. There'd once been a doorknob. Now it was just a hole. She stuck her fingers through and dragged the door inward, the wood scraping against the floor and sending up a cloud of dust that she could feel on her face.

She didn't dare cough.

"Duck," she whispered in Chance's ear, and then she moved through the small opening, felt cement under her feet, smelled must and mildew.

Chance was right behind her. She could feel the warmth of his chest against her back, feel his hand on her waist and his breath ruffling her hair.

He pulled the door closed, the quiet whoosh of it mixing with another sound. Wood creaking. The cellar door opening?

Faint gray light shone beneath the door, and Stella knew it was filtering in from outside.

She stepped back, pulling Chance with her.

She expected the door to open, and what she wanted more than anything was her Glock. She'd put it in a lockbox on the top shelf of her closet, afraid that Beatrice might find it and hurt herself.

She hadn't had time to retrieve it.

Now she wished she'd made the time.

Fabric rustled, and she knew Chance had pulled out his firearm. She stayed behind him, out of the line of fire, her gaze trained on the sliver of light that seeped under the door.

They moved in sync, still facing the door, still waiting for it to fly open. One step after another across the basement and to the rickety stairs that led to the main level of the house.

She put her weight on the first step, testing to see if it would hold her, then clambered up the rest, anxiety clawing at her stomach, a warning whispering up her spine.

Something was off.

Really off.

She'd expected their pursuer to rush into the basement, gun drawn, bullets flying. Instead, he was still in the cellar.

Doing what?

That's what she wanted to know.

She reached the basement door, tried the knob.

Locked.

"Let me," Chance whispered, the words tickling the hair near her ear, the sound of them barely carrying over the pulse of blood in her head.

They needed to get out.

She didn't know anything else, but she absolutely knew that.

She eased to the side. Chance squeezed in between her and the wall, his weight bowing the step they were standing on. She took one step down, glancing at the cellar door, that little wedge of light still visible beneath it.

A shadow passed in front of it.

Once. Twice.

She caught a whiff of something sharp and pungent.

Gasoline?

She had about two seconds to realize it before the cellar door went up in flames, fire licking at the wood and devouring it.

Every nightmare she'd ever had was coming true again. The flames. The smell of gasoline. The screams.

She didn't realize they were coming from her until

Chance pulled her against his chest, whispered against her ear. "It's okay. I'm going to get us out of here."

She choked down another scream, her throat raw, her hands trembling as she reached around Chance and started banging on the door.

Panicking.

Terrified because she'd lived this before. A different time. A different place. And she'd lost almost everyone she'd loved.

"Stella." Chance grabbed her arms, held them down at her sides, his grip gentle. "Let me do this, okay? Because I can. I just need you to give me a minute. Trust me."

We don't have a minute, she wanted to shout, but the light from the flames had illuminated the basement, and she could see the cement floor, the rotting stairs. She could see Chance, too, everything about him calm.

He wasn't panicking, and she shouldn't, either.

It was a fire.

Which was probably better than a barrage of bullets shot into the dark.

Below, the flames crackled and hissed, spreading along wooden support beams. It wouldn't be long before the entire place went up.

If they weren't out…

She pushed the thought away, tried to push away the terror, too. Beatrice needed her, and giving in to fear wasn't going to save her.

Please, God, she prayed silently, and she wasn't even sure what she was asking for. Safety? Help? Protection?

All of those things?

Chance jiggled the doorknob, a utility tool in hand. Still no panic in his face.

"Chance," she said, her mouth dry with fear as flames crawled across the ceiling, eating away at the beam that supported the upper floor. "We're running out of time."

They *were* running out of time, the old-fashioned lock trickier to pick than newer ones. Tricky. But not impossible.

Chance twisted the utility tool he always carried, fishing around in the lock for the mechanism that would open it. It caught, the knob finally turning, the door flying open.

He grabbed Stella's hand, dragging her into an empty hall. Pictures hung from the walls, all of them too covered with dust for any details to be visible. Not that he had time to stop and look. Smoke billowed up through warped floorboards, swirling into the air and filling his lungs.

Up ahead, the front door stood dark against the lighter-colored walls. The arsonist could be waiting outside, ready to take a shot when the door opened.

Chance didn't think so, though.

The guy was a coward. He'd shot at them through the truck window, then set fire to the basement door rather than follow them into the darkness and risk being ambushed. He'd taken off by now. Chance could almost guarantee it.

Even if he hadn't, there was no choice but to go out the front door. Heading to the back of the house with the fire blazing in the basement would be a fatal mistake.

"The door is boarded up," Stella said, her voice tight and controlled as if she were afraid of falling apart again. She was moving with him, briskly down the hall.

No more screams. No more panic. She was terrified, though. He'd seen it in her face and he'd felt a gut-deep need to find the guy who'd done that to her—who'd terrorized her, who'd made her scream and panic and nearly climb through Chance to get away.

He *would* find the guy.

He would make him pay.

First, he needed to get Stella out of the house and away from the fire.

He opened the front door, eyeing the heavy plywood that blocked the opening. Bits of sunlight shone through cracks near the center, and he aimed for that, kicking once and then again. The wood splintered and then gave, cold air sweeping in.

Outside, the day was silent, the snow-speckled driveway crisscrossed with tire marks. No sign of the truck, but Chance could see a Jeep speeding toward them. Trinity's. She'd better not be in it. He'd told her to stay at the hospital and stick with Beatrice.

"Is that Trinity?" Stella asked, her teeth chattering, her body trembling.

"Let's find out." He led her down the stairs, hurrying her away from the building. The place was old, the structure compromised, fire eating away at the foundation.

It wouldn't be long before the entire thing came down.

If he hadn't gotten the door unlocked, it wouldn't have mattered. They'd have been overtaken by smoke before the house fell. Black clouds billowed from the back of the house, spiraling into the sky. Fueled by old wood and dry weather, the fire continued to grow.

In the distance, sirens were screaming. Police. Fire

trucks. Rescue units. Chance had no doubt they were all on the way. Too late. At least as far as the house was concerned. And as far as catching the perp.

The Jeep stopped a hundred yards from the house, pulling off to the side of the driveway and leaving room for the emergency vehicles to get past. Simon hopped out of the driver's seat and jogged toward them.

"The perp?" he asked, and Chance shook his head.

"Gone."

"You're sure?"

"About as sure as I can be before I check things out." He led Stella to the Jeep.

"I want you to wait here," he said. "The sheriff won't be long. Fill him in when he arrives. Simon and I will head around to the back of the house. Make sure the guy really is gone."

"I'm not going to sit on my behind while you two go do the manly work," Stella said, some of the color back in her cheeks, all of the fear gone from her eyes. She looked like herself now—tough, confident, strong.

"This isn't about fair division of labor, Stella," he responded, using the same tone of voice he always did when they were working together. "I want you to fill Cooper in, because you're the witness. Simon isn't. Get in the Jeep."

It was an order.

She knew it.

Knowing her, he was sure she'd take her sweet time deciding if she was going to follow it. They'd been down this road before. Half the time, she won. Half the time, he did.

This time he wasn't playing games.

"I mean it, Stella. Somebody wants you dead, and if

he gets his way, Beatrice is going to be on her own, facing down a threat she can't even begin to understand. Get in the Jeep."

Her lips pressed together and her eyes flashed, but she did what he said, sliding into the Jeep and slamming the door. She had her cell phone in hand, and he could see her making a call as he motioned for Simon.

"We're heading to the back of the house. You head left. I'll head right. I think the guy is gone, but play it cautious. And cut a wide swath around the building. The basement is on fire, and the place is going to come down."

Simon gave a quick nod and took off, jogging toward the edge of the yard and then moving in the direction of the back field.

A squad car was racing along the driveway. Chance didn't wait around to see if the sheriff was driving it. He'd given Stella her instructions. Whether she liked them or not, she'd follow them.

He headed around the side of the building, running parallel to a set of tire tracks. The guy had been in a truck and he'd fired a rifle. Chance knew that much.

He needed to know more.

A face would be nice. A name.

Not Noah Ridgewood. Stella's friend had checked out. He was currently staying at a ranch just outside Fort Worth, and he hadn't been happy when HEART member Dallas Morgan had shown up. Or so Dallas had said. He'd been given about two seconds to state his case, and then the door had slammed in his face.

Didn't matter. Dallas had confirmed Noah's whereabouts, and he should be at the hospital in an hour, ready to take over for Boone.

So the perp wasn't Noah, and Chance didn't think
Larry was directly responsible for the violence. He was
lying low, staying at home and keeping quiet about his
troubles. The guy didn't seem capable of hurting anyone. Although it was possible he'd hired someone to
do it. He'd taken funds out of his savings account several times over the past year. The amount had added
up to just over twenty thousand dollars. He'd told the
sheriff that he'd been using it to pay off debts that he'd
accrued, but there'd been no trace of the money. No
cashed checks. No deposits. It had been there and then
it was gone.

Which could mean a lot of things.

Could mean he had some bad habits—gambling,
drugs, women. Could mean he owed the wrong people
money and had paid it back in cash.

It didn't necessarily mean that he'd hired a hit man
to take out his sister and niece.

But it also didn't mean that he hadn't.

The backyard was empty, just like Chance had expected. No truck. No gunman. Just his SUV parked
too close to the house. Too late to move it. The fire
had spread across the back facade and had set several
shrubs ablaze.

He could see the area where the truck had been
parked, the packed snow and crushed grass. Smudges
of gray from the exhaust. A few feet away, an old gas
canister and a lighter lay abandoned, half hidden by
snow. Chance crouched in front of them.

"What did you find?" Simon asked beside him.

"Looks like the accelerant. We'll have to have the
local PD look for prints."

"If the guy set the place ablaze with gasoline and a lighter, he's an idiot."

"I'd say he soaked the door with gasoline, lit a piece of cloth or paper and tossed it. He'd have a pretty good chance of igniting the gas that way, and he'd avoid going up in flames himself."

"Guy is still an idiot. He's not going to get away with this."

"He already did."

"You know what I mean, Chance." Simon straightened. "We're going to find him, and we're going to make him really sorry."

"Law enforcement will hand out the consequences," Chance reminded him. "But you're right. We are going to find him."

"Chance!" Sheriff Brighton strode toward them, his expression grim and hard. "You need to clear out. Fire crews are moving in."

"We've got a gas canister here. A lighter."

"I'll have one of my men collect it. Right now, we want all civilians clear."

Chance wasn't going to argue.

One thing he'd learned early in his career—get on the good side of local law enforcement, play by their rules and you might just get a favor when you needed one.

"Did you see Stella?" he asked, and Cooper nodded.

"I have a deputy questioning her. She gave a description of the vehicle. Dark truck. Newer model. Ford or Chevy."

"That's right."

"I spotted one parked on the side of the road on my way here. Looked like one of the tires was blown."

"You stop to check it out?"

"I was in a hurry to save your hide. So, no. I'm going back there now."

"Mind if I come along? I'll know if it's the right vehicle."

"As long as you keep your distance, keep your hands off the evidence and don't ask questions."

"I can manage that," he responded.

"We'll see," Cooper muttered as he led the way to his squad car.

Chapter Ten

Midnight, and Chance hadn't returned to the hospital.

Stella had been back for hours, clean clothes on, chocolate in hand, every trace of smoke washed from her skin and hair. She'd been back to the house, gotten the things she needed. She'd smiled at Beatrice, listened to her talk about Henry and their wedding and the beautiful life they'd lived together. For a while, it had seemed like she remembered it all. The years they'd spent loving each other, the wonderful home they'd shared, even his death.

Eventually, she'd asked to go home, and then she'd asked why Henry hadn't visited, and the whole cycle of grief began again. She'd cried herself to sleep, and Stella had wanted to cry with her. She hadn't because it would only have upset Beatrice more.

She still wanted to cry.

The fire had been too much.

After everything else—Granddad's death, her return to Boonsboro, the nightmares, the attacks—it seemed like the last straw. For the first time in longer than she could remember, she wanted to throw in the towel and call it quits.

"Everything okay in here?" Boone peeked in the open door, a cup of coffee in one hand and a pretzel in the other.

"Have you heard from Chance?"

"Not yet, but Dallas finally arrived. I'm going to be heading home in a minute. Just thought I'd ask if you needed anything before I go."

"I need to speak with Chance."

"Sorry, I can't help you with that." He smiled and took a bite of the pretzel.

"Boone, do you ever stop eating?" Trinity asked groggily. She'd been sleeping in the chair, head on her knees, doing exactly what her brother had asked. As far as Stella knew, she hadn't left Beatrice's side all day.

"Not if I can help it. Got a couple of these babies from the cafeteria a few hours ago. They're just as good cold as they were warm. You want one?"

"No. Simon brought me a sandwich a couple of hours ago." Trinity yawned and stood. "You said Dallas is here?"

"Should be on the elevator up."

"I guess he found out what he wanted to know."

"What did he want to know?" Stella asked, and Trinity blushed.

"Nothing."

"If it's nothing, why do you look like you just spilled top secret information?"

"I—"

"Tell you what," Boone said. "I'm going to leave you two to figure this all out. I'm heading to the elevator. As soon as Dallas gets off, I'm getting on. Got a wife and some kids who are missing me." He took another bite of his pretzel and walked away.

"Well?" Stella demanded, keeping her voice low enough not to wake Beatrice.

"Well what?"

"What was Dallas doing that I'm not supposed to know about?"

"He went to talk to Noah."

"Wonderful." She snagged her phone from the table near Beatrice's bed. No messages. No angry texts. Whatever had happened, Noah seemed willing to let it drop. "We've been friends for years. I told your brother—"

"What did you tell me?" Chance asked, walking into the room. He looked tired—his eyes shadowed, his hair mussed—and all her irritation slipped away. She wanted to tell him to sit down, ask him if he'd eaten, get him a hot cup of coffee and a warm blanket.

More than anything, she wanted to pull him into her arms and kiss him. She forced the thought from her mind.

"It's not important."

"It was important enough five seconds ago," Trinity muttered.

"Tell you what, sis," Chance said, his gaze on Stella. "How about you take a break? I'm sure Stella wouldn't mind you spending the night at her grandmother's place. The sheriff is running patrols by there every few minutes, you'll be safe enough."

"A real bed?" Trinity perked up, her blue eyes bright with happiness. "Are you serious?"

"You've worked three days without a break. Now that

Dallas is here, you need to get some rest. Come back in the morning, and we'll set you up with Beatrice again."

"Do you mind?" Trinity asked, and Stella shook her head.

"Here's the key." She dug it out of her purse and handed it to Trinity. "Use any of the bedrooms. If you want clean linens—"

"All I want is a bed. And maybe a pillow. I'll see you in the morning." She took off without a backward glance.

"Maybe she's finally cured," Chance said.

"Of what?"

"Her desire to go on missions."

She snorted. "Not hardly. She'll be back in the morning, armed for bear."

He smiled at that, crossing the distance between them in two long strides.

He was right there, in her space, and she didn't move back, just reached up and smoothed his hair, let her hand settle on his shoulder. His coat was cold and damp as if winter had soaked into it, and everything about him was so right and so wonderfully familiar. She wanted so badly to believe that what they had could last. That she could give herself over to love and not be sorry for it.

"You look tired," she said. "And cold."

"I'm both. The truck Cooper spotted? It was the one that chased us down."

Her pulse jumped, hope springing to life. If they'd found the truck, they might have found the perp. "Were you able to find the driver?"

"He was long gone, and the truck was reported stolen yesterday, so we can't trace him through that. We found something, though."

"What?"

"An old Remington 22. A long rifle. Probably from the early twentieth century. Same caliber as the bullet that was found in the SUV."

"That's an odd weapon to choose."

"It certainly isn't a common one. What's interesting is that the knife was old, too. An old bowie knife. Probably close to a hundred years old. At least, that's what the expert Cooper hired said."

"An antiques buff?" she asked, surprised by the information and intrigued by it.

"Sounds like it. Or like someone who has access to antiques. Ring any bells?"

She wished it did, but she shook her head. "None. Is Cooper checking the serial number on the rifle? Maybe—"

"It's too old."

"So we've still got nothing to go on."

"We've got the rifle, we have the knife and we have a lighter the guy dropped. Cooper pulled a print off it. He's running it through the database, trying to get a match."

"Was he able to get any prints from my place?"

"A couple of partials. He said he was going to come by tomorrow to get Beatrice's prints and yours. Anyone else who has spent a lot of time in your house?"

"Just Karen."

"He'll have to get hers, too."

"I'll text her and let her know." She grabbed her phone and typed a quick message. "She's supposed to stop by the house tomorrow evening. Maybe he can just come there."

"You think Beatrice is going to be ready to go home."

"I hope she is." She walked to the bed, touched her grandmother's forehead. She felt warm, her cheeks pink.

Too many blankets? Or a fever?

Concerned, she checked Beatrice's pulse. A little rapid, but steady.

"What's wrong?" Chance asked, and she shook her head.

"I'm probably worrying about nothing."

"You never worry about nothing. What's wrong?"

"She feels warm. Or maybe I'm just cold."

Chance's hand settled on Beatrice's brow, his skin tan against her pallor. "She does feel warm. Why don't you call a nurse? Have her vitals taken. If nothing else it will give you peace of mind."

"Peace of mind," Beatrice murmured, her eyes opening.

Did they look glassy?

Or was that Stella's imagination, too?

"If you take a piece of my mind, I won't have any left. I've already lost too many of my marbles," she continued, and Chance chuckled, his hand dropping away.

"You're as funny as your granddaughter, Ms. Beatrice."

"Call me Nana. All my family does."

"We're not family, but I'll be happy to call you Nana."

"We're not family *yet*," Beatrice said with a sly smile.

"Nana—" Stella began, but Beatrice coughed, the wheezy rasp alarming. "Are you okay?"

She grabbed the pitcher of water, poured some into cup and handed it to Beatrice.

"I'm fine. Just still a little under the weather. Maybe it was the chocolates I ate. They tasted funny."

"You said they were delicious earlier," she reminded her. "Hopefully, your pneumonia isn't getting worse."

"Do I have pneumonia?"

"Yes, but you're on the mend."

"That's good, dear. Now let's talk about the wedding."

"What wedding?"

"Yours. I have my mother's wedding dress packed in a box in the attic. It will look lovely on you."

"Nana," she said gently, "I'm not even engaged."

"Yet," Beatrice said, her gaze shifting to Chance. "Christmas is the perfect time for an engagement. Don't you think?"

"I think that Christmas is the perfect time for just about anything," he responded.

Not quite, Stella wanted to say. With all the bad memories and nightmares so tied to the holiday, she didn't think she'd ever be able to enjoy it. For Beatrice's sake, she'd have to try.

"I knew I liked you, young man," Beatrice murmured, her eyes drifting closed again, her face going slack. Awake and then asleep. That didn't seem right to Stella. Sure, it was late. Sure, Beatrice had had a rough few days, but she'd been her usual spunky and energetic self the past two days.

This seemed like a setback.

She pushed the call button for the nurse, felt Beatrice's forehead again.

"Hovering isn't going to help her get better," Chance said, dropping into a chair. His long legs stretched out in front of him, his shoes speckled with mud. She'd forgotten how tired he'd looked, forgotten how cold he'd been.

She took a blanket from the end of Beatrice's bed and tucked it around his shoulders.

"You were outside for too long," she chided, and he smiled.

"I think we both know that I've spent way more time outside in the cold and survived it."

"I think we both know that I need someone to fuss over. It might as well be you." She moved away, though, because she shouldn't be so close. Shouldn't be tempting herself so much.

"Come here." He snagged her hand, tugging her so close that their knees were touching, and something warm and wonderful welled up in the region of her heart. Something filled with sweetness and beauty. Something she'd never really looked for and hadn't ever expected to find.

She should pull away.

She knew she should.

She should guard her heart, because she was going to get hurt again. She'd never ever wanted this kind of love. The kind that consumed everything, filled every empty spot in her heart.

Even during her marriage, she hadn't looked for it. She'd loved Daniel. She had, but she'd known that she couldn't count on him to be there for her. Not for birthdays or holidays. Not for funerals or weddings. She'd planned every life event knowing that she'd probably be alone because Daniel's work demanded all of his time and energy and commitment, and there hadn't been anything left for her.

And that had been fine.

It was the way she'd wanted it.

It wouldn't be that way with Chance.

She knew it.

And it terrified her.

"I was worried about you earlier," he said. "I've never seen you so scared."

"You've never seen me scared," she corrected, her voice tight from the memory of those flames lapping at the door, the smoke pouring into the basement.

"Was it the fire?" He ignored the comment, his hands settling on her waist.

"Did I ever tell you that I can remember it all? The accident I was in?"

"No."

"It was Christmas day, and we'd just been to my grandparents' house. My sisters and I were all sitting in the backseat of the old car my dad drove, and I was holding the gift my grandparents had given me. A copy of *Little Women*. Only it wasn't an ordinary copy. It was old with beautiful watercolor illustrations inside."

"You don't have to talk about this, Stella," he said, but she did have to because Chance deserved more than the little pieces of herself that she was always giving, he deserved more than the tiny glimpses of her heart that she allowed others to see.

"I think I do. I think you deserve to know. I'm sure you *do* know." She laughed, the sound harsh and painful. "Some of it anyway. You do background checks on all your employees. I know you read the newspaper reports about the accident."

He didn't deny it, just watched her through those deep blue eyes, his hands still on her waist.

"My sister and I were bickering because she wanted

to touch the illustrations in the book. Eva was six years younger than me, and she was always tearing up papers and scribbling on things." She could remember that, just like she could remember Eva's dark brown eyes, her pretty smile, her soft red hair.

She blinked, surprised at the sting of tears in her eyes.

"I don't think my parents even saw the truck that hit us. The guy had been drinking all night, and he was probably going seventy in a thirty-miles-an-hour zone. He lost control and hit us head-on. One minute, my life was normal and happy. The next, flames were everywhere. The window beside me had shattered, and I managed to unbuckle my seat belt. I could see my parents, and... I knew they were dead. My baby sister was gone, too, but Eva was alive. At least, I thought she was, and I couldn't leave without her."

Her voice broke, and Chance was up, wrapping his arms around her, pressing her head to his chest.

"I couldn't save her," she said, the words muffled. "I was trying so hard to get her seat belt unbuckled, and my shoulder was burning, my hair was on fire, and I didn't want to leave her, but some man...some guy dressed like Santa...yanked me through the window, and I didn't have a choice."

Her arms slid around him, her hands clutching his shirt. She wanted to burrow deeper into his arms, disappear into the comfort of his embrace, let all the horrible memories be chased away and replaced by better ones.

"If there is one thing I know, Stella, it's this," he responded. "If it had been possible to save your family, you would have done it. I also know that, while you've spent years focusing on the tragedy, your grandparents focused on the gift they received. They could have lost everyone. Instead, you were pulled from the wreck and returned to them. That's amazing. I'd say they spent every day after that Christmas thanking God for it."

She'd never thought of that.

But maybe she should have.

All these years that she'd wondered why her grandparents still loved Christmas, all the times when she'd wondered how they could stand to put up a tree, sing the old carols, go to church and thank God for His gifts, and she'd never thought that she was one of the gifts they had been most thankful for.

She glanced at the tree that Trinity had brought, thought about how happy Beatrice had been to see it. Not just a symbol of Christmas but of grace and mercy.

"I'm going to have to dig the stockings out of the attic," she said, and Chance smiled.

"I'll help you," he said, his lips brushing her forehead, her cheek, her mouth.

He lingered there, and she was lost, all the memories and nightmares gone, the longing for home and family and love taking their place.

Someone knocked on the door, and Chance broke away, his pulse racing wildly. He wanted to hold on to Stella, to keep her close, but she moved away, her hand shaking as she pressed her palm to Beatrice's forehead as a nurse walked in.

She was worried.

Chance couldn't blame her. Beatrice was pallid, her cheeks gaunt, her body frail. She'd faded since he'd seen her at the funeral, and even then she'd been fragile.

Stella explained the situation to the nurse, her voice

shaking. Maybe from nerves or maybe from the aftermath of the kiss. He didn't ask. Wouldn't ask. There were more important things to think about. More important things to worry about.

For now.

Later, they'd talk about it again.

"She does feel a little warm," the nurse confirmed, taking out a thermometer and running it across Beatrice's forehead. "Ninety-nine point eight. Not too bad. I'm going to make a note of this and call the attending physician."

She pressed a stethoscope to Beatrice's chest, and the older woman shifted in her sleep. "Sounds clear, but I think I hear bronchial wheezing."

"Are you going to check her oxygen levels?" Stella asked.

"I know how to do my job, ma'am." The nurse offered a tight smile as she attached a sensor to Beatrice's finger. "She seems to be sleeping deeply. Is that normal for her?"

"Not usually." Stella touched Beatrice's cheek. "Nana?"

Beatrice moaned but didn't open her eyes.

"Oxygen levels are at 90. So that's good. I'm going to call the doctor, though. We'll see what he says. He may want to order some blood work. Maybe run an X-ray. Hold tight. If anything changes, buzz me."

"I should call my great-uncle and let him know what's going on," Stella murmured as the nurse walked away.

"I'm not sure Larry needs to be informed of anything."

"We don't know what he's involved in, but the lie detector test—"

"Can be cheated."

"He loves Beatrice, Chance," she said, her hair mussed from their kiss, her lips still pink. She was a beautiful woman. He'd always thought that. Over the years, he'd seen just how deep that beauty went. Her attention to her grandmother, her need to make sure she was okay, her desire to believe her uncle—it was all part of that beauty, and Chance wouldn't try to change it.

"Call him. If he comes, we'll keep an eye on things."

"And maybe we'll ask him a few questions," she responded. "He did give that money to someone, and I do think that's the key to all of this." She met his eyes. "When I say *we'll* ask questions, I mean *I'll* ask questions. My great-uncle is older, and—"

"Make the call, Stella." He cut her off because he wasn't going to make any promises. He'd seen Larry a couple times, but the guy had scurried in and out, staying as far away from Chance as possible.

Because of what had happened at Beatrice's house?

Or because he was hiding something and was afraid that Chance would uncover it?

One way or another, Chance was going to discover the truth. Stella and her grandmother had been through a lot, and they deserved a little peace.

He touched the Christmas tree.

Stella had been right. He'd known the bare basics of her story. He'd read the articles. He knew about the drunk driver, the crash, the fire, the broken window, the father of three who'd been playing Santa for his kids when he'd heard the crash.

He knew that Stella's Christmas dress had been on

fire when she'd been yanked from the wreck, that the man who'd saved her had been sure she was going to die because her body was broken, her skin peeling from her arm and shoulder, but he'd run with her into his house, laying her on the wood floor, covering her with a blanket, handing her a little stuffed toy one of his kids had abandoned—all while the car with her family in it burned.

Yeah. He'd read all that.

But he'd never heard the hitch in Stella's voice. He'd never seen the pain in her eyes, the regret and sorrow and heartbreak. He'd never heard her tell the story in her own words, with all the details of the moments before and the moments after.

He'd only heard her cry out in her dreams, and now he knew what the nightmare was, knew exactly what chased her from sleep.

He couldn't change it.

He couldn't make it different than what it was.

He couldn't ease the pain of loss or protect her from losing someone else, but he could be there for her. He could make the way a little easier. He could offer the best of himself and hope that it filled some of the holes in her life, made the empty spots less painful.

If she let him.

For now, he'd do what he knew—his job.

Three times, someone had tried to kill Stella. If she were a different kind of person, she'd be dead. He could assume that the assassin didn't know her background or her training. First, he'd come after her in the woods. Then in the hospital. Both times, he'd used the element of surprise, but he'd been willing to go hand to hand with her. Maybe assuming that a woman would be easy to overpower.

The third time, he'd taken the coward's way—avoiding direct contact.

He was learning from his mistakes, and that could make him even more dangerous.

He was also using some very odd weapons.

Not a handgun or a typical hunting rifle. A Remington 22. Antique. Same for the bowie knife. It had been handcrafted in the 1800s.

Stella had said she didn't know anyone involved in the antiques trade, but she'd been busy since she'd returned to Boonsboro. Caring for Beatrice had become her job. He'd been calling weekly since she'd arrived, and she always had a list of therapies she had to bring Beatrice to, doctor's appointments. Hair. Nails. Little outings to keep Beatrice happy and engaged.

He met her eyes, realized she'd been watching him, her hand still on Beatrice's cheek, her eyes still filled with all the memories she'd shared.

"We're going to figure this out," he said.

"I know."

"And then we're going to find those stockings, and we're going to hang them on the fireplace mantel, and we're going to give your grandmother the best Christmas she's had in years."

"We?"

"Why not?" he responded. "Unless you'd rather go it alone."

"I've been going it alone for a while," she said. "I don't think I know how to do anything else."

"You can learn."

"I can also lose. Again. Don't make me rehash it all,

Chance, just so you can understand why I can't think of Christmas and family and gifts and fun." She swallowed hard, and he knew she was fighting tears.

When she turned away, he let her.

He wouldn't push her.

Wouldn't beg her.

He'd offered what he had.

It would be enough or it wouldn't.

Either way, he was there for her.

"I'm going to talk to Dallas and Simon," he said. "There's something about the choice of weapons that's bothering me. This guy has to have access to antiques."

"You know what I've been thinking about?" she asked, obviously relieved by the switch in topics. "The frame that's missing. Not many people would know how much it was worth. *I* just thought it was a gaudy little bauble, and I lived in that house for years. Whoever took it had to have knowledge enough to know what he was taking."

"So we're back to the antiques angle."

"I'm going to ask my uncle to stop by the house tomorrow. I want him to see if anything else is missing. There are a lot of valuables in the house, and he has probably kept a record of them."

"You think he's the right person to ask?"

"I think that he's the only person who will know if something is missing. Beatrice…" She shook her head. "He's the only one."

"Ask him, then. I'll have Trinity and Simon stay here. We'll supervise Larry's visit to the house. Dallas can help us with that."

"I don't think—"

"Let me do this my way, okay? My heart isn't involved. Not in the way that yours is." It was involved, though. With her. With wanting the best outcome, the best ending.

With wanting to make good on his promise that everything was going to be okay.

She hesitated, her gaze dropping back to Beatrice and then returning to him. "Fine. We'll do it your way, but don't expect my acquiescence to become a habit."

He laughed, opening the door and stepping out into the hall. Dallas and Simon were waiting there, one sitting in the chair, the other leaning against the wall. Both newer to the team. Both as hard-core and well-trained as anyone.

A good team. A ready team.

The guy who was after Stella?

He'd made a big mistake going up against a member of HEART. He probably didn't realize that yet, but he would.

Chance was going to make certain of it.

Chapter Eleven

Beatrice's fever got worse overnight and, by seven in the morning, her cheeks were pink, her eyes glassy. She seemed in good spirits and even managed to eat one of the chocolates, but Stella was concerned. So was Larry. He'd stayed at the hospital through the night, pacing the small room and driving Stella nearly insane with his worry.

She thought Larry was driving Chance insane, too. He'd taken a seat near the door, his long legs stretched out in front of him, his arms crossed over his chest. He'd asked Larry a few questions, but Larry had brushed off the interrogation, his focus on Beatrice.

Either Chance had wanted to keep the peace, or he hadn't believed Larry had anything else to offer. Either way, he'd retreated to the chair an hour ago and had been sitting there silently ever since. She should have been able to ignore him, but that had proved impossible. Even in his silence he was a loud presence in her life.

She'd found her eyes drawn to him again and again. Found herself moving in his direction more than once.

She'd stayed way, because she needed to.

She couldn't do Christmas and family and stockings and gifts, and she didn't want to keep him from having all those things. She cared too much, loved too much to ever be the one to make him miserable.

"You'd think they'd have come to get her for the X-rays already," Larry muttered for what seemed like the fiftieth time. He was sitting next to the bed, his shoulders stooped, his hair uncombed.

"Who is having an X-ray?" Beatrice asked, and Larry patted her hand.

"You are, sis."

"Am I sick?"

"I certainly hope not." He smiled, and Stella saw the gentleness of his expression, the kindness in his eyes. He loved his sister. He'd never hurt her.

Not for money. Not for anything.

"Me, too, because I'm ready to go home." Beatrice looked around and frowned. "Where's the girl?"

"Girl?" Stella asked. "Karen, you mean?"

"Not Karen. She and I don't see eye to eye. It's the other one that I like."

"Since when do you and Karen not get along?" Stella asked, surprised by Beatrice's comment. Karen had been working for Beatrice before Stella arrived—cleaning the house every Monday and Thursday, taking her to the store when Henry couldn't. At least, that's what Larry had told her when he'd recommended that Stella keep Karen on as a part-time home care aide.

"Since the day she walked into my house," Beatrice responded. "Now Henry? He thought she was wonderful, and who was I to argue with your grandfather. The man had the softest heart." She closed her eyes and smiled, caught in some long-ago memory.

"Nana," Stella prodded, "why didn't you tell me you didn't like Karen?"

"Of course she likes Karen. Of course you like her," Larry cut in. "You've told me she's a great housekeeper and a good driver."

"And nosy. I don't like people digging around in my home." Beatrice frowned. "What were we talking about, dear?"

"Karen?" Stella said.

"Right. She's a hard worker, but the other girl reads to me. What's her name? Charlie?"

"Trinity?" Stella offered.

"That's it! Trinity. She's a lovely girl. Where is she?"

"At the house. She'll be back soon."

"Maybe she can bring Henry when she comes. Do I have her number? I'll call her and tell her to bring him."

Larry looked stricken, his eyes watery, his cheeks pale. "Beatrice—"

"Remember that game we used to play when we were kids, Larry?"

"Which game was that?"

"The one with the flashlights. You'd make all those little animals with your hands. You always were the clever one out of the two of us, and I never could figure out why Dad left me the house."

"Because he'd already bought me a place, remember?" he responded gently. "I got married, and he bought me that house in town. It seemed only right that you and Henry have the family home. Besides, you always loved it more than I did."

"If I don't ever get back there—" she began, but Stella couldn't listen to it.

"You're going to get back there, Nana. Soon. You just need to get a little better. That's all."

"You can't know what tomorrow will bring, sweetie. If I don't get back there, it's yours. You know that, right? I want you to fill it with happiness. Just the way your grandfather and I did. Just the way your parents would have when we handed it over to them. You know that was our gift to them that Christmas, right?"

"What are you talking about?"

"We had that wonderful Christmas lunch together, and Henry and I told your mother and father that the house was going to be theirs." She was crying, tears sliding down her cheeks.

Stella wiped them away, tears burning her own eyes and clogging her throat. She wouldn't let them fall, because Beatrice needed her to be strong.

"Nana, you and Henry were the best parents anyone could ask for, and I love you for it, but I'm not going to listen to any more talk about me inheriting the house. We're going to live there together for a long time before that ever happens."

"She's right, sis," Larry cut in, pouring water into a cup and handing it to Beatrice. "You've got many more years ahead of you. A lot of good years. You'll see."

"And Christmas is coming." Beatrice wiped at the last of her tears, offered a watery smile that made Stella's heart hurt even more. "I love Christmas. Are you hosting a party this year, Larry?"

The two began discussing parties and Christmas and family, and Stella tried to listen, to contribute, to act cheerful. Inside, she still wanted to cry. Mostly because seeing her grandmother lying in a hospital bed, her hold on reality tenuous, was as painful as remembering the accident.

"You okay?" Chance asked.

"I will be."

"Trinity is on her way. I texted her." He leaned close, his lips against her ear as he whispered, "I don't think I can take another second of your uncle's pacing or worrying." The confession surprised a laugh out of her, and Larry glanced their way, frowning.

"You're standing a little close to my niece, young man," he snapped. "How about you go out in the hall and wait there?"

"How about we both go out in the hall? I have a few questions I'd like to ask you."

"You already asked me plenty. So has the sheriff. I've answered them all, and I'm not in the mood to answer again."

"Where did you meet Karen?" Chance asked, the question as surprising to Stella as it seemed to be to Larry. His mouth opened. Closed.

"What do you mean, where did I meet her?" he hedged, and every nerve in Stella's body jumped to attention.

Karen.

She'd been knit into the fabric of Beatrice's life before Stella returned to Boonsboro. She had a key to the house. She had full access to every room in it. She cleaned and polished and ran errands. Stella hadn't thought much about that when she'd arrived. She'd been too concerned about Beatrice, too focused on dealing with Henry's death. Karen had just been a side note in the drama that had been unfolding.

Only maybe she wasn't a side note.

That's what Chance was thinking. She could see it in his face—the grim set of his jaw, the hardness in his eyes.

"It's a simple question, Larry. You met her somewhere. I'd like to know where."

"Church," he rushed to say, but the damage was done. He'd already taken too long, and Stella wanted to know why.

"When Trinity gets here, we're going to the house, Uncle Larry," she said, "you can come with us. I want to see if anything besides the picture frame is missing."

"What frame?" Beatrice asked, and Stella wished she'd kept quiet.

"Just one of the ones on the mantel. I was looking for it."

Beatrice seemed satisfied with that answer, but Larry looked...

The only way to describe it was sick.

"I'd rather stay with my sister. She needs someone looking out for her best interests."

"Don't worry," Chance said. "I'll have people here to make sure she's okay."

"I'd rather—"

"You're coming to the house, Larry," Chance said. "If you don't, I'm going to wonder why."

That was it.

Larry pressed his lips together and didn't say another word.

Maybe Larry *had* met Karen at church, but it seemed odd that a man his age would make such a quick connection with a college student. If his wife had been the one to suggest that Beatrice and Henry hire the young woman, Stella might have believed the story. As it was, things didn't make sense.

That bothered her. A lot.

She eyed her uncle. He was a nice-looking man. Still fit and handsome, despite his advanced age. Was it possible he and Karen…

No way.

There was no way the two had been having an affair. Was there?

If they were, that might explain the missing money, the nervousness that Larry exhibited every time his financial situation came up.

It might also explain the attacks.

With Beatrice and Stella out of the way, there'd be nothing to prevent Larry from giving Karen everything she might want. Money, expensive things. Was it possible that's what the young woman wanted? Could she be the one responsible for luring Beatrice outside, for attacking Stella?

No. The person with the knife had been a man. Stella was certain of that.

But…

Karen. Yeah. She might be the piece of the puzzle that had been missing. If Stella could figure out who she was and what she wanted, she just might find the answers she'd been looking for.

After too many hours watching Larry pace the room, worry over his sister and avoid answering questions, Chance was ready to shake the truth out of the guy. Despite his obvious affection for Beatrice and Stella, it was clear he was hiding something. Whatever it was, it was wearing him down. Even Chance could see that.

He wanted to know what it was.

Something that had to do with Karen?

Maybe.

Chance texted Trinity and requested that she run a full background check on the young woman. Sure, she'd looked at Karen's class schedule, confirmed how long she'd been in town, found her address, but she hadn't run her photo through HEART's face-match program. It was possible Karen had changed her identity before moving to Boonsboro. It was possible she wasn't the person she was claiming to be.

Twenty minutes later, Trinity walked into the room, her computer in one hand, a cup of coffee in the other and a huge duffel bag tossed over her shoulder.

"What's the word?" she asked, going straight to Beatrice's bed. "I hear you've got a fever and won't be going home."

"That's what they tell me. A clever girl like you could probably find a way to sneak me out."

"Probably, but I want you healthy, so I did something better." She put the duffel on the bed and unzipped it. "Christmas stuff! I found the stockings in your attic. I also found some really cool old Christmas cards. Let's hang them on the door. We'll make this place festive for as long as you're in it."

"I told them," Beatrice said, beaming. "I told them you were wonderful."

"Did you?" Trinity pulled out a pile of cards. "How about you look through these, Beatrice? Just to make sure there aren't any that are really special to you."

"Call me Nana," Beatrice responded. "All my family does."

"I'd tell you to call me what my family does, but

generally, my siblings call me brat, so we'll just stick with my given name."

Beatrice chuckled, her gnarled fingers thumbing through cards that looked to be decades old. "These are all before my time. My mother just loved to collect things. Perhaps we won't hang them since they're so old."

"I can take them back to the house, if you'd like, Nana," Stella said. "While you and Trinity decorate, I'm going to make a quick trip home."

"Bring me a sandwich when you come back, will you, dear?" Beatrice asked, handing the cards back to Stella and accepting a kiss on her cheek.

"Of course. I'll bring you a fresh nightgown, too."

"And my pink kneesocks. The ones you bought me. They're my favorite." She inhaled deeply, and Chance thought he heard a quiet rattle in her lungs.

"Maybe I should stay," Stella said, and Beatrice gestured her away.

"Of course you shouldn't. I'm perfectly fine, and Trinity and I have Christmas plans to make. I haven't gotten my shopping done. You don't mind helping me with that, do you, dear?" she asked.

"Not at all. We can make a list, and I'll go out later. After Stella returns."

"Come on," Chance said, cupping Stella's elbow. "Standing over the bed worrying isn't going to change anything, so we may as well proceed with the plan."

"You're right," she agreed. "And the sooner we go, the sooner we can return. Come on, Uncle Larry."

"I'd prefer to stay here."

"I don't think you were given that option," Chance said, and Larry blanched.

"Are you threatening me?"

"I don't make threats. I act," Chance responded, walking out into the hall with Stella.

Larry followed. Just like Chance knew he would.

"I don't know what you're thinking," he sputtered, his gaze jumping to Dallas who'd moved into step beside them. "But whatever it is, you're wrong."

"I'm looking for answers. I think you might have them." Chance led the group to the stairwell, motioning for Dallas to move ahead.

"Answers to what? Why Stella was attacked? If you think I have anything to do with that—"

"You want to know what I think, Uncle Larry?" Stella asked quietly, her words barely carrying over the sound of their footfalls.

"You know I do, honey." Larry took her hand. "You're as important to me as any of my own children or grandchildren. You know that, right? I'd never do anything to hurt you."

"That's what I think. That you wouldn't hurt me or Beatrice, but that someone you know might."

"What are you talking about?"

They'd stepped into the lobby, and Dallas jogged outside to get the car.

"Who is Karen?" Stella asked.

"I already told you. We met at church."

"I don't believe you."

"I'm not a liar."

"Are you a cheat?" Stella responded.

"How can you say something like that?" he asked, his cheeks flaming red.

"You're not denying it," Chance pointed out, and the older man shot him a look filled with anger.

He didn't say a word, though. Not as Dallas pulled up in front of the doors. Not as Chance hurried Stella to the SUV. Not as he climbed in beside her.

Dallas took Larry's arm, ushered him around to the front passenger seat.

"Get in," he ordered, and waited impatiently while Larry did so.

Still not a word from Stella's uncle.

"Well?" Stella demanded. "You were going to answer my question, Larry. Weren't you?"

No uncle this time, and Chance was certain Larry noticed.

They pulled away from the hospital entrance and onto the highway, the seconds ticking by, Larry's breathing harsh and a little hitched. He'd gone from bright red to stark white, and Dallas must have noticed. He put a hand on Larry's arm.

"Calm down, Granddad. Nothing is going to be fixed if you drop dead."

"I'm not your granddad," Larry muttered. "And if you think I had an affair with a little girl who is young enough to be my great-granddaughter, you can think again, Stella. Patty is everything to me, and I couldn't bear the thought of hurting her."

"People cheat," Dallas cut in, taking over the questioning, playing the good guy, the sympathetic interrogator. "And Karen? She's an attractive young woman. No one could blame you if—"

"She's a baby!" Larry protested. "What could I possibly have in common with someone like her?"

"You're right," Dallas agreed. "She's way too young. But maybe she saw you with someone else? Maybe she has information that you don't want shared?"

"Are you crazy?" Larry snapped. "She got to town two years ago. What could she possibly know that could hurt me?"

"That's a good question," Stella said. "How about you answer it?"

Chance's phone buzzed, and he saw that Trinity had texted him.

Interesting tidbit. Guess whose father owns an antiques store in town?

He didn't have to ask. He knew.

Everything was clicking into place. All the little clues— the overeager young woman, the antique weapons, the missing antique frame, Beatrice's comment about Karen nosing around in the house.

"What is it?" Stella asked, and he handed her the phone, watching as she read the message.

He knew the moment the truth hit her, saw her eyes narrow, her expression tighten.

"Change of plans," she said, thrusting the phone back. "We're going to town. There's a little antiques shop I'd like to visit."

Larry stiffened, his shoulders suddenly straight, his face even paler. He didn't argue. Didn't try to make them change their mind.

Chance got the address from Trinity, gave it to Dallas, then texted his sister.

Keep Karen out of the room and away from Beatrice. Don't let Beatrice out of your sight. We're going to the antiques shop. Will keep you posted.

He shoved the phone into his pocket and detached the ankle strap he used to carry his extra pistol.

"Just in case," he said, handing it to Stella. She nodded, adjusting the straps so they'd fit her calf, checking the firearm to be sure it was loaded, the safety on. She looked confident, assured, ready.

She also looked heartbroken.

"It's going to be okay," he said.

"You keep telling me that."

"Because I believe it." He squeezed her hand, and her fingers wove through his. They sat just like that as Dallas sped toward town.

Chapter Twelve

Everything was about to change.

Stella felt that to the depth of her soul.

The fact that Larry hadn't said one word, asked one question or protested the change in plans seemed to confirm that.

She wanted to poke at him a little, ask more questions that she knew he wouldn't answer, but he looked terrible—his face ashen, his lips colorless.

She thought he might pass out and, despite the fact that she knew he had something to do with the attacks, despite the fact that she was sure he'd withheld important information, she couldn't stop herself from caring.

"Are you okay, Uncle Larry?" she asked.

When he didn't answer, she leaned over the seat, felt the pulse in his carotid artery. Steady but too fast, his heart beating at an alarming rate.

"You need to calm down, take a couple of deep breaths. Whatever is going on, we'll handle it," she said.

"This is all my fault," he responded so softly she almost didn't hear.

"Whatever *this* is," she responded, "it can be fixed. You just have to tell us what's going on."

"I can't."

"You *won't*," Chance replied, his tone harsh. He'd always put his family first. He'd never have made the choice to keep silent if it would hurt the people he loved.

There was no way he could understand someone like Larry.

Stella couldn't, either, but he was her family, and she wanted to believe there'd been extenuating circumstances, some reason besides money or lust that had driven him to keep secrets that had almost gotten Beatrice and Stella killed.

"I can't," Larry repeated, the words breaking, his hands trembling as he smoothed his hair, tried to pull himself together. "It's a horrible choice. Like trying to decide which child to feed when you only have enough food for one and both are starving, and you know one of them is going to die, and all you can do is hope that you can save the other."

"What are you talking about, old man?" Dallas asked, his hands tight on the steering wheel.

"He said he'd kill Patty. He told me that if I said anything to anyone about who he was, he'd kill her."

"Who?" Chance asked, but Larry was done, his lips pressed together, his jaw tight.

"Better call local law enforcement," Dallas suggested. "We might want backup when we get to the antiques shop."

Stella called Cooper's direct number, gave him as much information as she had as quickly as she could. He promised to meet them at the shop. Old Thymes. That's what it was called. He knew it, had been there on several occasions. He even knew that the owner was Karen's father. Camden Woods was the guy's name. He'd been in town for a couple of years, and Cooper hadn't heard any complaints about him or the business. Maybe that's why he hadn't put the shop and Camden together with the attack.

That's what he'd said to Stella, but she could hear the frustration and irritation in his words. He was frustrated with himself, annoyed that he hadn't made the connection.

By the time he disconnected, they were in town, the familiar buildings and pretty streets belying whatever secret was hiding there. Stella had walked Main Street hundreds of times. As a kid, she'd hung out on the street corners, playing tag with friends and eating ice cream from the local shop.

Despite all the heartache, she'd had a good childhood.

She needed to remember that just as clearly as she remembered the rest.

"Looks like we're here," Dallas said, pulling around the side of the old brick building that housed the shop. "It would be good to know what we're walking into, don't you think?" He shifted so that he was looking straight at Larry.

"I told you, if I talk—"

"Your wife dies. Yeah. We got that part, man," Dallas said. "But you know what? She's probably going to die anyway. Along with other people you love. All because you decided to keep your mouth shut."

Larry blinked, shook his head. "I can't."

"Then the consequences are going to be on your head. Get out. We're going in that shop, and we're going to have a little talk with the guy who owns it," Chance said, none of the usual politeness in his voice.

He was angry.

So was Stella.

She waited until Chance got out of the SUV, then she followed, the weight of the gun strapped to her ankle comfortingly familiar. She'd been trained by the navy, and she'd continue to train in combat and self-defense since she'd left it. She didn't take things for granted, and she wasn't content to rest on her laurels.

She hadn't done her due diligence, though.

As angry as she was with her uncle, she was just as upset with herself. She should have run a background check on Karen, asked for references, talked to some of the people who knew her. Someone somewhere might have known something that would have kept Beatrice safe.

Too late now.

All Stella could do was move forward.

She walked to the front of the shop with Chance, Larry shuffling along behind them. Dallas was there, too, hanging back, flanking them and searching for trouble.

A sign hung from the shop window, the bold letters declaring that the place was closed.

"Odd for a shop in this area of town to be closed during business hours, don't you think?" Chance asked, banging on the door.

"Odder that it looks nearly empty inside." She peered in through the storefront window, eyeing shelves that looked mostly empty. Someone had left a light on in the back room.

As she watched, a shadow moved, blocking the light for a split second.

"There's someone in there," she said.

Chance yanked her away from the window, placing his body between hers and the glass. "Let's not take chances, Stella. A bullet can go through a store window just as easily as it can go through the window of an SUV."

"How many entrances does this building have?" Dallas asked, stepping back and looking at the upper stories. Three of them. All with windows glinting in the sunlight.

"Front and back," Larry said. "And a fire escape in the alley."

"Whoever is in there is going to have to come out," Chance said, moving to the window and peering into the shop. "Light is off, so he or she may be on the way. You want to take the back door, Dallas? Stella and I will watch the fire escape. My guess is that he's going that way."

"Will do," Dallas responded, jogging around the side of the building.

"We should wait for Cooper," Larry suggested, his voice shaking. "Whoever is in there probably isn't the kind of person you should mess with."

Chance laughed, the sound harsh and ugly. "You've got that wrong, Larry. We're not the kind of people *he* should mess with. There's the sheriff's car. I suggest that you stay here and explain things to him."

He took off before Larry could respond.

Stella followed.

As much as she wanted to hear the truth, as much

as she wanted to force it out of her uncle, she wanted to help Chance more.

Despite Chance's suggestion, Larry followed along behind them, his breath hitched with fear as they entered the narrow alley.

"This isn't a good idea," he said nervously, beads of sweat on his brow despite the frigid temperature. "He's not a nice guy."

"Who?" Chance asked. "Or are you content to just let whoever it is get away with terrorizing you and your family?"

Larry closed his eyes, swayed. "Camden Woods," he whispered. "My youngest son."

Chance heard the words. He even understood them. He just wasn't sure how it all fit. Now wasn't the time to figure it out. They needed to get in the shop, see if the person moving around in there was Camden.

Larry's son?

If so, he wasn't a son that anyone in the family had known about. That explained a lot, but it didn't explain everything.

Stella looked stunned, but she didn't question her uncle's assertion.

"Go to the front of the shop," she said. "Tell Cooper everything you know. Being honest is the best thing you can do right now. I'm going up the fire escape. If the guy doesn't want to come out on ground level, he'll head to the roof and try to escape to the next building."

She was probably right. Less than four feet wide, the alley was little more than a space between buildings, the ground littered with debris and dusted with snow. The fire escape was near the back corner, the metal rusted and old. If a person were brave enough to try it, they could make it to the roof and jump to the next roof.

Brave enough or desperate enough.

"I've ruined everything, Stella," Larry said. "I didn't mean to. I just never thought that a mistake I made forty-five years ago would come back to haunt me. I panicked, and I made everything worse. I hope you can forgive me. I hope Patty and Beatrice and my kids can."

He looked…lost. Like a man who'd been walking in one direction for a long time and suddenly realized he'd taken the wrong path and had no idea where he was or how to get back.

Stella must have seen that.

She pulled him into a quick hug, then gave him a gentle shove away. "We'll work it out. Now go talk to Cooper."

Larry looked stricken, but he turned and walked away.

"Let's get this done," Stella said, impatience in her voice as she reached the fire escape. Above it, someone had fashioned a bridge between buildings. From Chance's angle, it looked like several two-by-fours side by side.

"Careful," he cautioned as Stella grabbed hold of the rail and put her foot on the first rung of the fire escape. "That thing doesn't look like it will bear weight."

"It should. There's got to be a code, right? Fire safety inspections? Something that guarantees this thing is functional in case of emergency."

"I wouldn't count on it," he said, yanking at the metal frame. It held firm, but he still didn't trust it.

A soft sound came from somewhere above—wood against wood as a window opened. Third floor. Chance could see someone in the window, climbing over the ledge and onto the metal landing.

Female.

That was his first impression.

Karen. That was his second. Same hair. Same build. Young, moving like she'd done this a dozen times before. She reached back inside, pulled out a large duffel and set it on the landing. Then she levered half her body into the window, dragged what looked like an oversize flowerpot from inside.

She hefted it in both arms, wobbled to the railing.

Looked down.

Chance had about a millisecond to realize what she was going to do. Then the pot was falling, and he was diving toward Stella, tackling her to the ground, twisting so that his body hit the pavement first.

The pot landed a foot away, bits of clay flying into the air, dirt sprinkling Chance's face and arms.

He jumped up, dragging Stella with him.

He brushed the debris from her hair and shoulders. "You okay?"

"Dandy. Now how about we get that little monster? Because I've about had enough of her." She was climbing the first set of fire escape stairs before he could respond.

He followed, the metal vibrating as they raced toward the roof.

Karen had already made it there. Chance could see her, easing out onto the makeshift bridge on her hands and knees, the duffel hanging from her shoulders, bumping against her back as she crawled across the area between the buildings.

Didn't matter.

She wasn't going far.

Dallas was waiting for her, standing on the roof of the other building, just far enough away that Karen probably couldn't see him. Oblivious, she just kept crawling, completely focused on her escape.

Stella reached the roof a second ahead of Chance, and by the time he was up, she'd made it to the bridge. She didn't pull her gun, didn't call out to try to stop Karen. She just watched as the young woman eased across the boards.

"How long do you think it's going to take for her to realize she's been caught?" she asked as he reached her side.

"I'd say about three seconds."

"One," Stella said. "Two."

Karen had reached the other side and was scrambling over the roof ledge. She straightened and looked right at them, smiling triumphantly.

"Sorry about this, Stella. No hard feelings, right?" she called, pushing the boards so that they tumbled down into the alley. "See you around, cousin!"

She turned, saw Dallas and screamed so loudly Chance was certain the foundations of the buildings shook.

She pulled the duffel from her back, tossed it with all her strength. It fell short of Dallas, but she was already running to whatever entrance Dallas had used to gain access to the roof.

Another fire escape?

A door from the building?

"Should I call Cooper and tell him what's going on?" Stella asked.

"Not unless you think Dallas can't handle this."

"He can."

He did. A quick sprint, and Dallas had Karen by the arm, hauling her up against his side.

"Looks like he's got it under control. Let's head back down. Cooper should be there with your uncle, and I'm anxious to hear what he has to say."

"You and me both." She turned away from the drama unfolding on the other roof. Not much of a drama, really. Dallas was nudging Karen toward the opposite side of the building.

She wasn't screaming anymore.

She looked like a kid caught with her hand in the cookie jar, the duffel she'd been trying to escape with now in Dallas's hands. "Wonder what is in the bag?" Chance said more to himself than to Stella.

"I have a feeling some of it came from Beatrice's house."

"Do you think Larry was telling the truth?"

"About Camden being his son?" She shrugged, stepping onto the fire escape and beginning her descent. "Why would he lie?"

"Why wouldn't he have acknowledged Camden two years ago, when he moved to town?"

"Knowing my uncle, he didn't want to hurt Patty. He was probably hoping he could keep the relationship a secret, maybe have some kind of connection with Camden but not one that anyone would be suspicious of."

"Have you ever met the guy?"

"No." She'd reached street level and stood waiting for him, her hair shimmering in the sunlight that shone between the buildings, her cheeks red from exertion or emotion or both.

This couldn't be easy for her, but she was handling

it like she did every mission—with focus and determination.

When he reached her side, she smiled, shaking her head. "You're a mess, Chance."

"Thanks?"

She laughed, brushing dirt from his shoulders, then from his hair, her hands lingering a little longer than was necessary. He knew that. She knew it, and that smile was still in place, her gaze direct and unapologetic. "We have a lot to talk about. One day. When we're not dodging bullets or clay pots."

"What is there to say, Stella? We either go for it or we don't. There's never going to be any in-between for us."

Her smile slipped away, and she nodded. Solemnly. Carefully. As if that one gesture spoke every word that needed to be said. "I don't ever want to be hurt again, Chance. I don't ever want to love and then be left alone. The thought of that terrifies me. But you know what terrifies me more?"

"What?"

"The thought of never having that kind of love. The kind that takes up all the empty places in my heart. The kind that would hurt to lose, but that would leave memories that would make the pain worth it. Come on. Let's go find Cooper and Larry. Let's figure out what Karen had in that bag. Let's get this mess cleaned up because Christmas is coming and I promised Beatrice we'd hang the stockings."

He could have said a dozen things to that. He could have given her all sorts of reassurances. She didn't want that, though. He knew Stella. Just like he knew himself.

"Chance? Stella?" Cooper appeared at the end of the alley, Larry beside him. "Everything okay here?"

"One of my men caught Karen Woods trying to escape through the building next door," Chance responded.

"I've got a man over there now."

"I guess my uncle told you what's going on," Stella said, and Cooper nodded.

"Most of it."

"All of it," Larry corrected.

"We'll see if your story checks out, Larry," Cooper responded, and Larry flinched.

"Why would I lie about something like this?"

"Because you're in deeper than you want to admit?" Cooper suggested. "Because maybe you're having financial difficulties and you want your sister's estate to help you get back on your feet. Maybe you hired Camden to make sure you got it?"

"He's been blackmailing me for two years. That's how I got into the financial trouble I'm in."

"Because he's your long-lost son?" Cooper asked.

"I told you he is! Patty had no idea that I'd had an affair, and I never thought…" His voice trailed off and he shook his head.

He hadn't thought he'd get caught?

He hadn't thought he'd have to pay the consequences of his sin?

Chance didn't ask.

He'd seen it too many times. The sin. The results. The sadness that followed.

"Maybe you should have thought," Stella said quietly, and Larry started to cry. Quiet tears that streamed down his face.

"When Camden's mother told me she was pregnant, she asked for ten thousand dollars cash so she could leave town. I gave it to her, because I didn't know what else to do."

"Maybe confess?" Chance suggested.

"I couldn't hurt my wife like that. I thought I could pay the money, and it would all go away, but then Camden showed up and told me that if I didn't pay, he'd go to Patty."

"So you did?" Cooper asked, and Larry nodded.

"What else could I do?"

A lot, but Chance didn't say it.

He could picture the first meeting, could imagine Larry's shock. He'd been living a lie for forty-five years, and now it was all going to unravel.

"I paid until I was out of money, but he kept wanting more," Larry continued. "I told him that, and he told me he'd take care of it."

"He must have known Beatrice didn't have a will," Stella said. "He must have known about your father's stipulation regarding the house and the property."

"He knows everything. More than me. He's fixated on the family." Larry wiped moisture from his cheeks. "If he could get you out of the way, Stella, it was only a matter of time before—"

"Stop," Cooper ordered. "You have rights, Larry. You're well aware of them."

"I gave up my rights when I betrayed my wife and my family."

"I'd still rather you get a lawyer," Cooper said. "I've got a warrant issued for Camden, and I've petitioned for a search warrant of this property and of Camden and Karen's house. They live about a mile from here."

"Has anyone been over there yet?"

"I sent a deputy. No one's home."

"I don't like the sound of that," Stella muttered, meeting Chance's eyes.

He knew what she was thinking.

Exactly what he thought—they needed to get back to the hospital. He pivoted, headed back toward the SUV.

"You don't think he's at the hospital, do you?" She was following him now, running behind him as he sprinted for the vehicle.

"Where's Dallas?" she asked as they reached it. "We need the keys."

"I'll get—" His phone rang, and he saw that it was Trinity.

"Hello?" he said.

"She's gone!" Trinity cried. "You've got to get back here because she's gone!"

"Beatrice?" he asked, and Stella froze, all the blood draining from her face.

"She went for an X-ray. They said an orderly would bring her back out. I waited outside radiology, but she never came back."

"We'll be there as quickly as we can. Contact hospital security."

"Simon is already with them. I can't believe I let this happen. I should have—"

"We'll be there soon."

He disconnected and sprinted back to the front of the store, adrenaline pouring through him because he knew beyond a shadow of a doubt that Camden had Beatrice.

How long had she been missing?

How far could he have gotten?

Cooper would need to put on an APB on whatever vehicle was registered to Camden. He'd have to—

Stella grabbed his arm, yanked him to a stop.

"He has her, doesn't he?" Her eyes were bright with tears, but she didn't let them fall.

"Yes," he said, hating having to say it. "But it's going to be okay," he promised, and he prayed that he was right. Prayed that she wouldn't be disappointed, heartbroken, hurt. Because Beatrice was all she had left of her little family, and he thought it just might destroy Stella to lose her.

She took a shaky breath, nodded stiffly.

"Okay. Let's go find her." Then she took off, sprinting toward Cooper and the deputy.

Chapter Thirteen

By the time they'd arrived at the hospital, Beatrice had been missing for forty minutes. Not long, but to Stella it seemed like a lifetime. She'd listened while Cooper had questioned the hospital staff; she'd ridden with Chance as they'd headed over to the sheriff's department.

Now she was pacing Cooper's office, waiting while he questioned Karen. Chance and Simon were with him in the interrogation room. They'd left Stella and Trinity together. Stella wasn't sure where Uncle Larry was. All she really cared about was finding Beatrice.

Trinity sat a few feet away, slouched in a chair and crying. "I should have insisted," she said, her eyes red-rimmed from tears. "I should have told them that I had to go with her." She'd said it a dozen times before, and Stella had responded the same way each time.

"It wasn't your fault," Stella assured her, her throat dry with fear. Did Beatrice understand what had happened? Was she afraid? Was she hurt?

The thought left a dull ache in her chest and a twisting pain in her gut. She couldn't just sit around hoping that Beatrice would be found. She had to act.

She walked to the door, yanked it open.

"I'm going to look for her," she said.

"You can't!" Trinity protested.

"Watch me," she replied, stalking down the corridor and pausing outside a closed door.

She could hear voices. Female. Male.

She knocked. Didn't wait for an invitation. Just walked into the room.

They were all there—Chance, Simon, Dallas. Larry. Cooper.

Karen.

For the first time in longer than she could remember, Stella saw red. Her body went cold with rage, her skin crawling with anger.

She walked across the room, ignoring Chance's look of caution.

"You'd better hope that my grandmother is okay," she nearly spat, and Karen frowned.

"My father would never hurt her," she responded blithely, her legs crossed, her fingers tapping impatiently on her thigh. "She's family."

"I'm family, too," Stella responded. "He tried to kill me."

"You're kidding, right? My father barely even knew you existed," Karen scoffed. "I'm sure he was too busy cashing the checks Uncle Larry was writing to bother with you."

"I never wrote him a check," Larry said faintly.

"You gave him cash. Same difference, really." She shrugged. "He's just taking what he's owed. That's all."

"What does he think he's owed?" Chance asked.

"Whatever the rest of the family has." She shrugged again. "It's only fair. At first, he just wanted to get me through college and get his shop going, but once I started working for Beatrice and realized how much money the family has, the plans changed. Things should be split equally in a family like this, and my father deserves his cut."

"Based on what Larry has said, your father got more than his cut," Cooper said. "And he extorted it. Which is a crime and could get him jail time."

"*Extorted?* That's a heavy word, Sheriff." She flipped her hair over her shoulder, studied her nails. "Go ahead, Granddad," she said, "tell him that's not what happened. You were more than willing to help with the shop and with my education."

"It's true. I was happy to help him. At first. Then he kept coming back for more. He thinks I'm a bottomless well that he can keep pulling from."

"You should have told him that you weren't." She frowned. "It's not like he wanted to drive you into bankruptcy."

"Karen, he didn't care if I had nothing. As long as he got what he wanted. He told me that I'd either find a way to pay or he'd take something more valuable than money from me. He threatened to kill my wife." He put his head in his hands, closed his eyes. "I've made a mess of everything."

"No," Chance broke in. "You made mistakes. Camden is making the mess, and Karen is helping him."

"I haven't done anything," she protested.

Chance reached down and opened the duffel that was sitting on the floor beside him, pulling out a beautiful gilt vase that Stella remembered from her childhood. It had a crack down the center now. Probably from being tossed at Dallas.

"Where'd this come from?" he asked, and Karen blushed.

"Beatrice gave it to me."

"Did she give you this, too?" He lifted a gold bracelet decorated with rubies and sapphires.

"I want a lawyer," Karen responded.

"I'll get you one," Cooper said. "Once we book you. Of course, if you want to tell us where your father has taken Beatrice—"

"He didn't take her anywhere! He wouldn't. I keep telling you—"

"Does your father have an old bowie knife in the shop? One with symbols carved into the handle?" Chance asked.

Karen frowned. "Yes. Why?"

"That's what was used the night Stella was attacked at the hospital."

"My father isn't a murderer," she responded, but her brow furrowed, and she bit her lip.

"You're wondering if he is, kid," Dallas broke in. "So I'd say you have your doubts. How about you try some honesty and either prove your doubts or put them to rest?"

"I've already told you everything I know."

"You haven't told us where you were going with this stuff." Chance nudged the bag with his foot.

"If I tell you, will you agree not to press charges?" She was looking straight into Stella's eyes and, for the first time since she'd met her, Stella saw the resemblance to Larry. The shape of the eyes. The color. They were almost identical.

"That depends on what you know and what you've done," she answered honestly, and Karen blushed.

"I did take a few things. Dad asked me to. He said he just wanted a few family heirlooms to remind him of where he'd really come from. Not the rat-infested house his mother raised him in. You guys were like royalty to us, and Dad said Beatrice would never know anything was missing. He told me that we wouldn't sell anything until after she was gone. We'd just keep them and enjoy them. I let him convince me. I bought the whole we're-family-and-we-deserve-it thing. I knew it was wrong, though. And I'm sorry. I was going to bring everything back before we left town. That's why I was in the shop. I was getting the things I'd stored there."

"You were leaving town?" Stella asked, her heart beating wildly, her mind jumping from thought to thought so rapidly she couldn't quite hold on to any of them.

"Dad said we needed to. He said the guys you had with you were snooping around, and he didn't want to cause any trouble for Larry. He and Derrick—"

"Who's Derrick?" Cooper asked.

"Derrick Smith. He and Dad go way back. They were buddies in the army. When they got out, they both got married and lived right next door to each other. When my mom died, Derrick's wife kind of stepped in and mothered me. She left him a couple of years ago, and he and Dad started thinking up schemes to get money and open their own business. That's how all this started."

"Is Derrick living in town?" Cooper asked, and Karen shook her head.

"No. He lives in Florida. Where we came from. He came up here a few weeks ago for a visit. He's renting a little cabin in the mountains. One of those hunting lodges."

"Have you been there?" Stella asked, all her thoughts

suddenly sharply focused. A cabin would be the perfect place for Camden and Derrick to take Beatrice. The perfect place to get what they wanted and discard what they didn't.

And, of course, they wouldn't want Beatrice.

Not once they got what they needed from her.

Bank account information, maybe?

Would she remember that?

What would they do if she didn't?

"I was there once. He doesn't even have hot water or heat. Just a wood stove that he has to keep lit." She wrinkled her nose, brushed a smudge of dirt from her pants. "I was going to meet them there after I returned Beatrice's things."

"Kid," Dallas cut in, his frustration obvious. "You weren't returning anything."

He was right about that. Karen had nearly dropped a flowerpot on Stella's head, and she'd gloated about her victory.

Obviously, she wasn't as innocent as she'd like everyone to think.

But maybe she wasn't as guilty as she looked.

She seemed willing to share some information, and Stella was willing to listen.

"I was, too," Karen protested. "Anyway, we were going to drive from there to Florida. Straight shot. No stops. That's what Dad said. I'd have rather stayed here, but with the shop closed—"

"There's an old hunting lodge twenty minutes west of here," Trinity suddenly said, her gaze on her phone. "Looks like they rent cabins during hunting season."

"That's probably the place," Karen said. "No one is there right now. I can tell you that."

"Your father is," Stella responded, just barely managing to hold in her anger. "Call him. Ask him about Beatrice."

"He doesn't have your grandmother! Besides, if I call him, he'll know something is wrong. He'll hear it in my voice. We're really close, and—"

"Then text him. Ask if Beatrice is okay."

"But—"

"Do it," she demanded. "Because I'm the one who's been most hurt in all of this, and I'm the one who gets to decide whether or not to press charges."

Karen scowled, pulling the phone from her pocket and sending a quick text. Seconds later, her phone buzzed. She glanced at it, her face going white.

"I swear, I didn't know—" she began.

Stella snatched the phone from her hand and read the text.

No worries, hun. The old lady is fine. Go ahead and hang out at the hospital for a while. Don't want anyone getting suspicious, right? Derrick and I have some business to take care of. Meet us at the cabin at midnight. You packed?

"He's got her," she murmured, handing the phone back.

The room was buzzing. People talking and planning.

That was fine.

They could plan all they wanted.

She was leaving.

She walked out without a word, made it all the way to the end of the hall before Chance caught up with her.

He took her arm. Held it. No pressure, just his fingers wrapped around her bicep.

"Running off without a plan is a good way to get killed," he said quietly.

"She's there. I have to find her."

"My statement still stands."

"You know what they're going to do. Get her financial information. Find out where her accounts are, move the money into their accounts. Then they'll kill her."

"You don't know that."

"Of course I do. They tried to kill me three times because they wanted me out of the way so they could do this. You know that's what it was about. She's vulnerable, and they wanted to take advantage of that. Then I showed up with a bunch of people who weren't going to let that happen, so they kidnapped her. They're going to take what they want and—"

"Stella," he said. Just that, and she stopped talking, looked into his eyes.

Waited, because she knew whatever he said, it was going to be important. This was the Chance she knew best. The one in charge. The one who knew how to run a mission and to save a life.

"Here's how it's going to be," he continued. "I'm sending Trinity back to Beatrice's hospital room. She's going to clean it out and meet us at the house. That's where we're headed. Not to the hunting lodge. Not yet."

"Going to the house will be a waste of time." Stella pulled away, walked out into the cold afternoon. Heavy clouds were moving in from the west, drifting over distant mountains, carrying snow or rain or both. Stella could feel the storm in the air, and all she could think about was Beatrice, in her frilly nightgown, sitting in a freezing cabin with two men who wanted her dead.

"Have I ever led you in the wrong direction?" Chance

asked from behind her, and she turned, wanting to rail at him, to yell and scream and demand that he take her straight to Beatrice.

Only he didn't deserve to be treated badly because she was upset. He knew just how scared she was, just how worried she was and just how right *he* was. They needed a plan. Going into a situation like this without one *would* get someone killed.

"What direction do you think we should go?" she asked, forcing a calmness into her voice that she didn't feel.

"We go to your place. We get your car. Give Cooper a chance to get some men together. Then we go to the hunting lodge as a team."

"Chance, what if we're too late?" she asked. "What if they…hurt her before we arrive?"

"It's more likely that they'll keep her alive. At least until they have what they want."

"Okay," she conceded. "We'll do things your way, but I'm going to the hunting lodge as part of the team."

He nodded, motioning for Dallas to get their ride.

She waited impatiently, every beat of her heart reminding her that time was slipping away and, with it, their chances of bringing Beatrice home. She knew how these things worked. She'd recovered hostages in dozens of countries, helped them out of more than a few desperate situations. She'd also failed to bring them out. Not often, but sometimes. Enough that she always worked harder, planned better, prepared more for every mission that she went on.

Time was the enemy.

That was the hard and fast rule of hostage rescue.

The longer the kidnapper had his victim, the less likely it was that the victim would be returned.

She shivered, felt Chance's coat settle around her shoulders. He didn't offer any words of comfort. He didn't tell her that everything would be just fine.

He knew the truth, and as he helped her into Dallas's SUV he whispered in her ear, "God is in control, Stella. Don't forget that."

She nodded, the hard knot of fear still in her stomach.

God was in control.

She knew that.

She just didn't know what He wanted from this.

She didn't know what He'd leave her with when it was over.

Lord, please keep Beatrice safe. And whatever happens, she prayed, *help me make something good out of it.*

It's what her grandfather would have wanted. It's what Beatrice would have wanted.

All *she* wanted was to bring Beatrice home.

After that, she could think about other things. Like the future. Like God's plan. Like Chance, waiting for her to say that she was willing to risk being hurt to love him.

Chance had worked with plenty of local law enforcement officers. He'd been impressed by most of them, irritated by a few and downright uncivil to any who tried to get in the way of a mission.

Cooper fell into the first category.

He was smart, quick and willing to work as a team. That made things easier, but it still didn't make them good.

Chance eyed the map that had been spread out on

Beatrice's kitchen table. Twelve men and women stood around it, taking notes and listening as Cooper outlined the plan.

It was simple enough. They'd park their vehicles at the end of the three-mile gravel road that led to the hunting lodge. Walk in from there. Once they found the cabin, they'd signal the group, and the real fun would begin. They'd take position outside the cabin and wait for Stella to arrive. She'd be driving Karen's car, carrying Karen's cell phone, doing all the things Karen would be doing if she were actually going to meet her father.

Dressed in a winter coat and hood, a scarf over the lower part of her face, Stella would be able to get to the front door without alarming the men.

Once there, she'd knock and walk in like she belonged there, leaving the door wide open for Chance, Dallas and Simon to enter.

Simple.

Easy, even.

Only they had no idea what weapons the two men might have. They had no idea where Beatrice was being kept. Basically, Stella would be walking in blind.

That bothered Chance. A lot.

"We need to rethink the plan," he said, and Cooper frowned.

"Why?"

"Sending Stella in alone is too risky."

"She's not going to be alone. She's going to have nearly a dozen people outside, ready to run to her rescue."

"Not good enough."

"It's plenty good enough," Stella said.

"It won't be if you're dead," he retorted, his blunt words doing absolutely nothing to change Stella's mind.

She grabbed the coat, hat and gloves that one of the deputies had brought from the station. Karen had willingly lent them to the mission. She'd also handed over her cell phone and the keys to her car.

That should have made Chance happy.

It would have, if Stella hadn't been the one going in.

"Why would you think she's going to die?" Dallas asked, leaning against the doorjamb that separated the kitchen from the dining room. "We've been on way more dangerous missions than this one, and we've all come out of them alive."

"This is personal. Emotions are involved. Emotions can get people killed."

"So can standing around discussing things that aren't up for discussion." Stella had strapped on her shoulder holster, and she slid her Glock into place. She still had his ankle holster, and he was pretty certain she had a stun gun hidden in one of the coat pockets. "The sun is going down. By the time we reach the lodge, it will be dark. We've already wasted enough time. Let's head out."

"You cool with that?" Cooper asked, meeting Chance's eyes.

He nodded because Stella was right.

The plan wasn't up for discussion. They'd hashed it out, made decisions and agreed as a team that this was the best way, the *only* way, to get to Beatrice.

No second-guessing.

No backing out.

That had always been his policy. The team knew it. Cooper gave the signal and his deputies walked out.

Dallas and Simon followed.

"You going to stand there all night looking dejected?" Stella asked, pulling on the cap that Karen had lent. Her red hair peeked out from under it, bright against the light blue knit.

"Only if you walk out looking like that."

"What's wrong with the way I look?" She grabbed the duffel that Karen had been carrying. Empty now except for some old books that Stella had tossed in to make it look heavy.

"They get one look at your hair, and it's going to be all over," he murmured, tucking the strands under the knit cap and pulling the hood up over her head. "There. That's better."

"Thanks," she said, and he realized how close they were, how beautiful she looked, standing there in her borrowed snow gear. How big a hole would be left in his life if she were suddenly gone.

"Thank me by staying safe."

"So that we can get through the wretched Christmas season together?" she asked, making light of the situation. She always cracked a joke when they were heading out on a mission, and it always made him smile.

"No, Scrooge," he responded, brushing her lips with his. "You get yourself killed, and all Beatrice's plans for a Christmas engagement will be out the window. She and I will both be devastated."

The words popped out. Unexpected. Right.

He didn't regret them, and she didn't argue with them.

A surprise, because she'd always been the one to back away, deny what they felt.

"Scrooge?" she said. "I guess I've earned my reputation. We'll see if we can fix that when I get back."

He wanted to ask her what she meant, but she was already moving, hefting the duffel onto her shoulder, tossing a scarf around her neck and patting Chance's shoulder like she had a thousand times before. "Let's head out, boss. I've got a grandmother to save."

Outside, snow was beginning to fall, the heavy flakes dancing in the headlights of the three vehicles that sat at the ready.

Stella walked to Karen's small SUV, tossed the bag into the passenger seat and then turned to face him again.

She touched his cheek, her palm warm against his cool skin.

"Just so you know, I'll be careful. I want to come back. For Nana. And for you."

She got into the car, closed the door and turned on the engine.

That was his cue to get moving.

He and his team were leading the caravan.

Twenty miles on snowy roads could take an hour, and they didn't have that much time. Eventually, Woods and Smith would get impatient with Beatrice. They'd get tired of whatever game they were playing. Once they did, anything could happen.

He climbed into Dallas's vehicle, ignoring the worry in the back of his mind. Stella was one of the best operatives he'd ever known. She could handle this, and he had to let her.

"Let's go," he said, and the vehicle jumped forward, bouncing along the long driveway and out onto the snow-dusted road.

Chapter Fourteen

Stella had been in a lot of dangerous situations. She'd faced a lot of enemies who were much deadlier than Camden Woods or his buddy Derrick Smith. Cooper had provided her with photos of both, and she knew that Derrick had been the one who'd come after her at the hospital. Camden was shorter, stockier and more muscular. She thought that he'd been out in the woods with her, but she couldn't be sure.

Both were former army, but they'd been out of the military for over a decade, and Stella didn't think either had done anything to maintain self-defense or fitness training.

Yeah. She'd faced worse. Military leaders in foreign countries. Hired hit men. Cult leaders who spent every minute of every day getting ready for the Armageddon they were trying to usher in. Camden and Derrick were no danger at all compared to that.

And yet, she was more terrified of them than she'd ever been of anyone. Because they had Beatrice.

She sat in Karen's car, snow falling outside the windows, the night still and quiet around her. She could see the shadows of the police cruisers parked in front of her. They were empty. Just like Dallas's vehicle. The team had headed out thirty minutes ago, and she'd been sitting ever since in the idling car.

Waiting.

Worrying.

Put it in God's hands, and it'll never get dropped, she could almost hear Henry's voice whispering through the darkness.

"Easier said than done," she said out loud, and she knew that if Henry had been around, he'd have laughed.

He'd put everything in God's hands, and he'd never been sorry about it. He'd raised his only son to do the same. Like Henry, Stella's father had been a pastor. She could remember sitting in the wood pew at the front of the church, coloring pictures while he preached.

She'd gotten out of the practice of attending church in recent years. She'd let herself slide away from the old habits that she'd formed as a child. Since she'd returned to Boonsboro, Sunday morning had been for worship again, and she'd found something comforting in that. Seasons changed. People changed. Circumstances and feelings and dreams changed.

But God?

He stayed the same.

Put it in God's hands.

Maybe it wasn't just a pretty little saying designed to make confused and hurting people feel better. Maybe it was something to be done daily: setting all the problems and worries and heartaches in the palms of the one who'd carried every burden, felt every tear.

She really needed to do that.

Now.

Tomorrow.

The day after that.

It's in Your hands, she prayed, closing her eyes, listening to the soft silence that answered.

She used Karen's cell phone and sent Camden a text saying that she'd gotten tired of sitting around the hospital, and she was on the way.

A few minutes later, the phone buzzed a response. She glanced at it.

See you in a minute, kid.

Good. He was waiting, and she was coming.

It was time to do what she'd been trained for.

She checked her hat and hair in the visor mirror. No stray strands hanging out, announcing her true identity. From a distance, at least, she could pass for just about anyone of a similar height and weight. She grabbed the scarf, wrapped it around her nose and mouth. She was as covered up as she could get, as disguised as possible.

She waited another few minutes, letting the time tick away because she didn't want to arrive too soon. Let Camden and Derrick assume they were home free. Let them get complacent and lazy and careless because all of those things would make it easier to free Beatrice.

If she was in a position to be freed.

The *if* was the part that had been haunting her, the word flitting through her mind over and over again as she waited.

What if…

Beatrice was hurt?

Beatrice was sick?

Beatrice was…worse?

She glanced at the dashboard clock, then texted

Chance. Moving in. She put the car in gear and turned onto the gravel driveway that led to the lodge.

She crept along the three-mile stretch, trees brushing the sides of the SUV. The road opened into a clearing, a long building standing in the center of it. The headlights glinted off windows and reflected on the snow that lay on the ground. Karen's cell phone buzzed again and she glanced at it. Bring beer.

Nice thing to ask your daughter to bring to a kidnapping event.

She tucked the phone away. Not bothering to respond.

Karen had mentioned a fork in the road when she'd given directions to the cabin. Stella looked for it, scanning the road, the trees, the tiny little paths that seemed to wind through the forest. When she finally found the forked road, she rolled forward, easing the SUV onto an even narrower stretch of gravel.

Seconds later, she saw a light flashing through the trees. Her pulse jumped, her muscles tense with anticipation. This was it. Everything came down to this one moment.

She thought she saw movement to her left as she climbed out of the car, a shadow shifting at the periphery of her vision. Chance or one of the men moving closer, ready to walk through the door that she was going to leave open.

She stepped onto the porch stairs, and the front door flew open, the man standing in the doorway was the guy from the hospital. She recognized the narrow, wiry build. The height.

Derrick.

She would have said his name, greeted him like an

old friend would, but she didn't want her voice to tip him off.

"Didn't you get your dad's text?" Derrick demanded. "We need some more beer here. That old lady is driving us batty. Go on back to town and get some. Buy some food, too, and don't come back until you do."

He slammed the door, and she thought she heard a bolt slide home.

She tried the knob anyway. Locked.

She could see in the front windows, the living room light making every detail of the room visible. Wide-planked flooring, rough with age and neglect. Easy chair. Saggy couch and beat-up coffee table.

Derrick must have seen her looking. He knocked on the window, motioned for her to go.

"Hurry up. We've got plans for later tonight. Maybe when you come back, you can convince the old lady to cooperate."

He stalked to an easy chair, dropped into it, scowling as he stared Stella down. He didn't seem to know she was an imposter, and she wanted to keep it that way, so she turned her back to the window, hurried down the porch stairs.

No way was she going to give up.

Derrick had mentioned Beatrice. Obviously she was alive and okay.

Stella was going to make sure she stayed that way.

She rounded the small cabin, checking two windows on the side of the small building. Both were locked. She moved around to the back. There was a small deck there, light from a single window illuminating the weathered wood.

She approached it cautiously, easing up the deck

steps and peering into a tiny kitchen. Not much in it but a stove and a miniature fridge. A table stood against one wall. A chair. Beatrice was sitting in another chair, her frilly nightgown splattered with dirt, and what looked like a laptop was sitting on the table in front of her.

Were they trying to get her bank account password?

Stella reached for the window, her hand falling away as Camden Woods stepped into view. He walked to the table, jabbed at the computer screen and yelled something that Stella couldn't hear through the glass.

Beatrice seemed unfazed, her shrug only adding to Camden's fury. He stomped away, came back a second later with a pencil and paper. He thrust both into Beatrice's hands and left.

Out to the living room maybe.

Stella didn't waste time. She tried the window. Locked just like the other ones. There was the back door, though, and she fished in her pocket for the utility tool she'd brought.

Chance wasn't the only one who knew how to pick a lock.

She worked quietly, the snow still falling, the night eerily silent. No animals moving through the trees. No night creatures calling out to each other.

The peace of the forest had been disturbed by humans. She could feel their presence, the weight of the eyes that were watching as she fiddled with the lock.

Was everyone in place? Were they ready to move in?

The lock clicked, and she took a deep breath, pressing her ear against the wood, listening. No more yelling. No voices.

She turned the knob, pulling the stun gun from her pocket. Not her weapon of choice but better than using a gun when Beatrice was in the line of fire. She pushed against the door and it creaked open, the sound breaking the silence, breaking the calm.

A man yelled something from the front of the cabin, and footsteps pounded on the floor.

She knew who was coming, and she was prepared, jabbing the stun gun into Derrick's side as he raced toward her. He dropped like lead, falling to the ground with a loud thud.

Camden hadn't appeared, and Stella darted forward, grabbing Beatrice's hand and pulling her to her feet.

"Come on, Nana. We've got to hurry."

The door was still open, and they were so close to escaping. She thought she heard footsteps pounding up the deck stairs, thought she saw a shadow darting toward the door. Chance?

Someone ran through the room in front of her, slamming the door shut before she and Beatrice could reach it. Camden was there, an old-fashioned derringer in hand.

"You just keep getting in my way, don't you?" he shouted, lifting the derringer.

She knew. Saw it in his eyes.

He was going to pull the trigger. She shoved Beatrice away, diving toward him, her hand on his wrist as he fired.

The report rocked them both, the bullet slicing a path through Stella's upper arm. She fell sideways, her hand still on Camden's wrist. Her shoulder hit the wall. Her head followed. She saw stars, but she didn't release her grip.

Beatrice screamed, the sound mixing with the ringing in Stella's ears, the wild pounding of her heart.

Something else was pounding. She didn't know what. Couldn't concentrate on anything but gaining control of the gun.

She yanked Camden's arm sideways, twisting his forearm until he dropped the gun. She reached for it, would have had it in her hands, but Derrick was up, groggy but moving. He kicked the gun away, snatched Stella up by the front of her shirt.

"I don't like being messed with," he spat.

"Neither do I." She drove her fist into his throat, heard him gag as he fell back.

She swayed, saw the blood dripping from her left arm, pooling on the wood floor. She needed to stop Camden now. Ten minutes from now, she might not be able to. She took her gun from its holster, raised it.

"Don't," Camden said, his voice deadly calm, and she realized he had the derringer in his hand, the barrel pressed against Beatrice's temple. "You even breathe funny, and I'll kill her."

"If you kill me, you'll never get my bank account information," Beatrice said, her voice shaking.

"It's a little late for that, Granny," Derrick snapped, moving past Stella, his gaze never leaving her face. "Your granddaughter has just cost you everything."

He was afraid.

She could see it in his eyes.

"You cost yourself everything. Greed does that to people. It makes them stupid," she said.

"Shut up. Both of you!" Camden barked, the derringer wavering, his attention jumping to the small window. Had he seen something there?

Stella didn't look, but she felt it—the energy humming in the air, the feeling that something big was about to happen.

"Put your gun on the ground," Camden demanded, easing through a narrow doorway that must have led to the living area. "Any sudden movements and Beatrice dies," he warned.

She could have taken the shot, but she was bleeding heavily and dizzy from it.

She didn't want to miss. Didn't want to hit Beatrice. She set her Glock on the floor.

"That's better." Camden nodded, the derringer dropping a little more, the barrel no longer against Beatrice's head. "We're going out the front door. You follow, she dies. You call the police, she dies. You cooperate, and you might get a few more years with her."

"Right. So don't try anything funny," Derrick said.

As he reached for the Glock, all the energy Stella had been feeling suddenly exploded.

The window shattered, and Derrick fell back, blood staining his shoulder and chest.

Stella was already moving, pulling Chance's gun from the ankle holster, aiming for Camden. He had the derringer up again, pressed against Beatrice's cheek, his arm around her waist.

"Nobody move," he said, and the world seemed to stop. The back door was open, and Dallas and Simon were there, guns drawn, expressions grim.

"I just want to leave here," Camden continued conversationally. "I don't want trouble. I don't want to hurt anyone."

"Then let the lady go," Simon suggested. "And walk right on outside."

"Into whatever trap is waiting for me? I don't think

so." He backed up, the gun held against the side of Beatrice's face. She didn't flinch, but Stella could see the whiteness of her skin where the barrel pressed into flesh.

"You're only digging yourself deeper into a hole," Stella said, and she was surprised to hear the thickness of her words. She felt light-headed and woozy, blood still dripping down her fingers. "If you let her go now, you won't face as many charges."

"In for a penny. In for a pound. That's one of the only things my mother ever taught me." Camden's harsh laughter echoed through the room. "Put your weapons down. All of you. If you don't, I will kill Beatrice. I promise you that."

"You really think you're going to make it out of this cabin alive?" Dallas said, taking a step forward, setting his gun on the kitchen table.

Camden still had the derringer, he still had Beatrice and, for the moment, he was still the one in control.

He wouldn't be for long.

Stella knew that.

She trusted that.

Chance was somewhere, and when he showed up, the odds would flip in their favor.

"I said put the weapons down," Camden growled, and Simon finally complied, setting his Glock on the counter as Stella put her weapon on the floor.

"Good. Now where'd your other buddy go?" Camden asked, backing away, his gaze darting from one person to another, trying to track everyone's movements as he eased into the living room.

Stella followed him.

Cold air swept in from the open front door, the frigid breeze hitting her square in the face.

Camden must have felt the cold, too.

He whirled toward the open door, his grip on Beatrice loosening. That was all Stella needed. She tackled him from behind, rolled with him as they landed on the ground. And then he was over her, the gun under her chin, his eyes blazing.

"You should have stayed away," he panted. "You should never have tried to take what belonged to me!"

She expected to feel the bullet ripping through her flesh, feel her life slipping away.

Instead, she felt the weight of Camden's body as he fell on top of her, heard the clatter of the derringer as it dropped to the floor. Felt warm blood sliding down her neck.

Camden's?

Hers?

She tried to shove him away, but her arms were weak, her muscles unresponsive. She felt groggy and a little confused. Not quite sure what had happened. Camden's body had forced the air from her lungs, and she couldn't catch her breath. Couldn't move him.

And then he was gone.

Pulled away by someone.

By Chance.

He was leaning over her, his brow creased with concern, his hand shaking as he brushed hair from her forehead. "It's okay," he said.

"Then why do you look like it's not?" she managed to say.

"Because you're bleeding like a stuck pig, that's

why." He slid out of his jacket, pressed it against the wound in her upper arm.

"Where's Beatrice?"

"Simon brought her outside."

"Is she okay?"

"I didn't see any injuries."

"She needs a coat." She shoved at his hand, trying to push him away so that she could stand. "I've got to find one for her."

"I told Simon to bring her back to the hospital."

"I thought you said she wasn't injured."

"She's still sick, remember," he said gently, and she could see the fear in his eyes. Fear for her.

"I need to see her." She sat up and then realized what a mistake that was. Her head spun, darkness edging in until everything was gone, and it was just her, lying against a warm chest, someone whispering in her ear.

"If you die on me, I'm going to kill you, Stella."

She would have laughed if she could have, would have opened her eyes and told Chance exactly what she thought of him—that he was the best thing that had happened to her in a very long time and that she wasn't sure why it had taken her so long to realize it.

That she loved him, with everything she had. That she was his.

Only her eyes wouldn't open. The words wouldn't come, and she felt herself drifting as voices filled the cabin and the darkness swept her away.

Chapter Fifteen

One man dead.

Another man wounded.

Stella wounded.

It wasn't the outcome that Chance had been hoping for, but it was better than the alternative: Beatrice dead, Stella dead, more hearts broken, more families lost.

His family lost.

That's what it would have felt like because Stella was a part of him. He'd known that for years, but he'd finally accepted what it meant. Not just teamwork. Not just trust or respect or affection. A deep-seated connection that nothing could ever break.

He pressed his jacket against Stella's arm, his grip tight. He didn't like her pallor, the amount of blood that she'd lost, the fact that she'd slipped into unconsciousness.

His phone buzzed, and he knew it was Trinity asking for an update. Simon would fill her in. He was on the way back to the hospital with Beatrice, and he'd said he would contact Trinity and tell her to meet him there. Dallas was a few feet away, being interviewed by a couple of deputies. He'd fired the shot that had taken Derrick down, and that had provided the distraction that had gotten Chance in the front door.

That had been the plan, and it had gone off almost flawlessly.

Almost.

He scowled, eyeing the blood that splattered the floor beneath Stella's arm.

"You'd better get through this," he muttered.

She didn't respond. Just lay still and pale and silent.

That worried him.

A lot.

Because Stella was always moving, always ready, always fighting.

He kept his jacket pressed to her arm as rescue personnel swarmed the cabin, checking pulses, triaging wounds. Two EMTs were crouching beside Camden, calling information into their radios.

He could have told them not to bother.

The bullet he'd fired had gone straight through Camden's head. Not something Chance was proud of. Taking a life was never the right thing, it was never the easy thing, but sometimes it was the *only* thing.

If he hadn't acted, Stella would be dead.

There'd been no doubt about that. Camden's finger had been on the trigger, and he'd been ready to fire.

A split second to act.

That was all that Chance had, and he'd taken the shot, firing the way he'd been trained—accurately, without hesitation.

"What do we have here?" A young EMT knelt beside him, gauze pads in his hand, gloves on. "Mind if I take a look?"

Chance released the pressure, peeled back his jacket so the guy could poke at the wounds. It looked like the bullet had gone right through Stella's upper arm.

"She'll need to get this cleaned and dressed. Have an X-ray to see if the bullet hit the bone." The guy pressed gauze pads to the entrance and exit wounds, wrapped them tightly.

"Let's start an IV," he called, and another EMT rushed over.

Chance waited impatiently while the IV was started, watching as blood seeped through the gauze. He wanted to nudge the EMTs away, take care of things himself. He'd run IVs before. Stella was the one who'd taught him how. She probably wouldn't be happy if he practiced on her, though. She'd told him he was the worst student she'd ever had. The memory would have made him smile if the situation hadn't been so serious, if she hadn't been just as still and silent as when he was holding the jacket to her wound.

"How bad is it?" Cooper appeared at his side, his gaze shifting from the bloody gauze to the blood on the floor and then to Chance's face.

"Not as bad as it could be. Not as good as I'd like."

"Camden didn't fair so well," Cooper responded, gesturing to the sheet-covered body lying a few feet away.

"It was Stella or him, and it wasn't going to be Stella."

"I know. I saw the whole thing. We'll fill out the paperwork, but I can tell you for sure that no charges will be filed."

"You want my gun until that's official?"

"Yeah. Protocol. You'll have it back once you're cleared."

Chance handed him the Glock.

"Thanks." Cooper frowned. "It's amazing what greed will do to a person. All Camden had to do was accept what Larry was willing to give and none of this would have happened."

"None of this would have happened if Larry had been honest with his wife from the beginning."

"Fear and greed, and now a mess to clean up and a man who could have been anything lying dead on the ground. It's a shame and a tragedy. Makes me wonder why I do the job I do."

"To keep this from happening more often?" Chance offered, knowing how much it hurt to see the worst of life, to always view the world through lenses tainted from seeing atrocities, the most heinous of crimes. He fought that every day, worked hard to find the good in the midst of the tragedies. It was tough, though, and obviously Cooper was feeling that.

"I guess you're right about that." He sighed, rubbed the back of his neck. "I'll have to drive out and tell Karen that her father is gone."

"That's hard news to give."

"Hard news to hear, too. She was a pawn in a game she didn't know was being played."

She also committed several crimes for her father.

Maybe she'd learned her lesson. Maybe she hadn't. That wasn't up to Chance to decide.

Camden's army buddy, on the other hand, needed to go away for a long, *long* time.

"How's Smith doing?" he asked. "From what I saw he survived the bullet."

"Looked worse than it was. It glanced off his collarbone. Lots of blood, but he's still alive. Cursing up a storm and threatening all kinds of consequences."

"Like?"

"Guess he thinks he can sue your organization and the Boonsboro Sheriff's Department. He'll be thinking differently once we book him and read him the list of charges."

"Does he know Camden is dead?"

"I told him. That's why he's making threats. Like I said, he'll shut up once he realizes how much trouble he's in. I'm going to ride in the ambulance with him. He's got a lot of questions to answer and a lot of crimes to answer for. I'm bringing the state police in, asking them to process and collect evidence. I don't want the guy to get off on a technicality."

"That's a good call."

"For the record, your team did good. You planning to stick around here? Or are you going to the hospital? I'm going to need to take your statement later. I can do it there or at the station."

"I'll be at the hospital," he responded.

"I'll call you when I'm finished with Smith. We can figure out a place to talk then. When Stella comes to, tell her I'm sorry things went down this way. I was hoping we'd get through this without any casualties."

"I'm not out," Stella murmured. "So I won't be coming to."

She opened her eyes, glanced at the IV the EMT was adjusting. She was pale as paper—her cheeks and lips devoid of color.

"And things happen, right?" she continued. "We can't know every variable, and we can't plan for them all. So what's to apologize for?"

"The fact that you were shot, maybe?" Cooper said.

"I've had way worse than this."

Chance smiled. *This* was the Stella he knew.

"Okay. No apology then, but how about the next time Beatrice needs to be saved it's from somewhere like a flower garden or a grassy meadow. No snow, no guys with guns, no chance for anyone to be hurt."

Stella chuckled, then groaned. "Save the jokes for when my arm isn't about to fall off. I'll be able to appreciate them better."

"You got it, kid." Cooper unloaded Chance's Glock, dropped the gun and the cartridge into an evidence bag. "The ambulance is getting ready to transport Smith. I'm heading out. You need anything before our meeting, let me know."

He walked away, and Stella reached for Chance's hand, her palm cold and dry against his. "You weren't lying to me, were you?"

"About what?"

"Beatrice. She's okay, right?"

"She seemed to be," he answered carefully.

"What aren't you telling me?" she demanded, and he couldn't lie to her.

"She was upset. Her breathing was a little rough. Simon is on the way to the hospital with her. Trinity is going to meet them there."

"Rough how?"

"I was a little distracted by the amount of blood you were losing to qualify the sound," he said dryly.

If she noticed his tone, she didn't let on.

"I need to find out if the X-rays were done."

"They were. The nurse had just wheeled Beatrice

out of X-ray and handed her over to the orderly when she was taken."

"The orderly was Derrick or Camden?" she asked.

"Probably. Cooper is looking into it."

"I'm glad the X-ray was done. I need to see if they're going to put her on antibiotics. If she has pneumonia, she's going to need a stronger treatment protocol." She tried to sit up, and he pressed his hand to her shoulder, looked her straight in the eye.

"Don't."

"Don't what?"

"Try to stand."

"I don't see why I shouldn't."

"Because you're in no shape to, ma'am," the EMT answered. He motioned for two of his coworkers who were standing by with a gurney. "You've lost too much blood. You try to stand up, and you're going to fall over."

Stella frowned. "You don't really think I'm going to let you roll me out on that gurney, do you? Because there's no way—"

Chance scooped her up before she could protest, set her on the gurney and leaned down so that they were eye to eye. He could see the golden tips of her red lashes, the tiny flecks of gold in her blue eyes. He could see the fine lines that fanned out from the corners of them, and the little scar at the edge of her brow.

He could see *her*, every bit of who she was—stubborn and strong and determined to be there for the people she loved.

"You want to check on Beatrice, right?" he asked.

"Yes, but—"

"This is the quickest way to get there."

She frowned, but there was a glint of humor in her eyes. "You're clever, Chance. I'll give you that."

"I'm also worried. Do me a favor and don't make that worse by refusing to cooperate with treatment protocol."

She touched his cheek, shook her head. "You don't have to worry about me, Chance. I'm going to be fine. What choice do I have? Beatrice needs me."

"I need you, too, Stella," he admitted. "So how about we make sure you're as okay as you say you are?"

"You don't need me, Chance. You're the most independent, confident, accomplished person I know. The only thing you need is to loosen up a little, maybe wear those flannel shirts more often. Ditch the tie. Have a little—"

He kissed her softly. Gently. Felt all the words die on her lips and the tension ease from her muscles, and he knew that everything they could be together was right there in that moment—supportive, connected, loved.

"What was that for?" she asked, and he brushed the bangs from her forehead, kissing the silky skin beneath it.

"Just practicing."

"For?"

"Mistletoe moments," he responded, and she smiled.

"You're assuming there will be mistletoe."

"I'm not assuming. I'm planning."

She laughed at that, taking his hand and holding on tight as the EMT wheeled her out into the falling snow.

Epilogue

Christmas had exploded all over the house.

Every nook and cranny was filled with it. Little trees. Big ones. Stockings and tinsel and lights. There were garlands on the banister and wrapped around the porch pillars. Pretty little pinecones, hand-painted with glitter, sat in a basket on the fireplace mantel right next to the photo of Henry and Beatrice that had been found with a cache of antiques in the trunk of Camden's car. Someone had put a red bow on the corner of the frame and sat a porcelain angel next to it.

Yep. Christmas. Everywhere.

The old Stella would have hated it, would have wanted to avoid it like the plague.

The new Stella?

She was enthralled, amazed by the stunning beauty of it all.

She stood in the parlor, looking at the tree she and Chance had helped Beatrice choose and thinking about how lovely it was. A blue spruce, its silvery needles the perfect backdrop for all the ornaments Beatrice and Trinity had hung on it.

Karen had helped, too, but she'd been more somber than the other two, her sadness at losing her father, her disappointment in the choices he'd made, only partially hidden. She'd been given community service and three years probation. She'd also had to return every item she'd taken from Beatrice.

She was facing it all with aplomb.

She knew she'd been wrong.

She knew her situation could be worse.

But she sure wasn't trying to be cheerful about things.

A real downer was what Trinity had whispered in Stella's ear.

It was true, but Karen was family. She had no money and nowhere to go, and Stella hadn't had the heart to send her away. She'd offered a room on the condition that she complete the community service work and go to weekly counseling appointments.

Karen had agreed to the terms. She spent two hours at the community center every week, working with at-risk youth. She worked hard, and was keeping up with her schoolwork and her volunteer work at the hospital. Stella had high hopes that she'd get through the tragedy and become someone better because of it.

Larry and Patty were discussing taking her in and allowing her to stay until her graduation, but the two needed some time to work through Larry's betrayal and his lies.

To her credit, Aunt Patty had been gracious.

She hadn't kicked him out of the house, hadn't demanded a divorce and hadn't told him that what he'd done was unforgivable. She was angry, though, and she'd been more than happy to tell Stella just how heartbroken she felt.

Stella had watched her aunt cry. She'd hugged her. She'd promised that she'd stand beside her. No matter what she decided. In the end, Patty had decided that her marriage was worth fighting for.

One mistake in forty-five years. A big one, but I still love him, and I can't throw away all the good because of something that happened decades ago. That's what she'd said to Stella when she'd asked for help finding a good marriage counselor.

Stella had put out feelers, had gotten her aunt and uncle set up with twice-weekly counseling sessions.

Tonight, Larry and Patty would be at church with their entire family. It was Christmas Eve, and they planned to celebrate that together.

Stella was celebrating, too.

The season. The joy of renewal and hope.

Love.

She smiled, running her hand down the pretty dress Trinity had helped her pick out. Her arm was still in a cast, the cracked bone knitting itself back together, but she'd still managed to shimmy into the outfit, make her hair look presentable and put on a little makeup.

Trinity had approved.

Trinity had come to stay for a while. Supposedly to help Stella while she healed, but Stella thought it had more to do with Beatrice. The two had bonded over *Little Women* and Christmas decorations. Tomorrow, Trinity would make the drive to DC to spend Christmas with her family.

Tonight?

She was in Boonsboro, helping Beatrice get ready for Christmas Eve service.

The doorbell rang, the sound of it making a dozen butterflies take flight in Stella's stomach.

Chance.

He'd had work in DC for the past couple of days, but he'd promised to attend Christmas Eve service with her.

He never broke a promise. She'd always known that about him.

Now she knew even more.

She knew all the little things that made him special.

That he loved to walk through the snowy woods.

That he preferred marshmallows in his hot chocolate.

That he loved her and he always would.

She rushed to the door and opened it, and then she was in his arms, the warmth of his embrace filling her heart with joy.

"You made it," she murmured against his lips.

"I wouldn't have missed it for the world," he responded.

"The world is full of wonderful things," she said, her good arm wrapped around his waist.

"Not as wonderful as Christmas with you," he responded, and she laughed.

"Is your family upset that you and Trinity aren't spending Christmas Eve with them?"

"Actually," he said, "they aren't because I invited them here."

She pulled back, looked into his eyes. "Are you kidding?"

"Do I look like I am?"

"Chance…" She didn't even know what to say because she'd been thinking about his family, about how hard it would be for them to have two members gone on a holiday that they always tried to spend together.

She'd felt guilty for that, but Beatrice had fought two bouts of pneumonia, and she couldn't travel. Stella had tried to convince Chance not to come, but he'd wanted to be there, and she'd wanted him to be, and all of her protests had been weak and a little ambivalent.

So, yes, she'd been thinking about his family, worrying about them. But she hadn't expected them to show up on her doorstep.

She was ready to commit to Chance.

She was ready to move forward with him.

She wasn't sure she was ready to meet his folks.

She smoothed her hand down her dress, eyed the closed door.

"Are they outside?" she asked, wondering if a dozen Millers were pressed against the wood, waiting to enter.

"Yes. We drove here together. I ran it by Beatrice and she approved. Didn't you notice Trinity and Karen cleaning the guest rooms?"

"I thought they'd gone on a Christmas decorating frenzy. I had no idea they were getting ready for company. Are your parents here, too? Or just your siblings and their kids?"

"They're here," he confirmed, and she suddenly felt a little sick and a little excited and a whole lot unsure.

"You should have told me—" she began, but he shook his head and smiled.

"Beatrice and I decided that it would be best to keep you in the dark. She didn't want you to be nervous."

"Nervous? I'm… I don't know if I'm ready."

"For making new memories?" he asked, tucking a strand of hair behind her ear, kissing her again, that one sweet touch of his lips chasing away her anxiety. "Because that's all this is, Stella. A chance to fill all the darkness with light. To see all the beautiful things that have come out of the difficulties."

"It's also an opportunity for me to look like a total idiot. I should have bought more food—"

"Taken care of."

"Gotten gifts for everyone."

"Done."

"Chance," she said, laughing at the joy of having him there, "you make it really difficult to come up with reasons to panic."

"No need to panic, Stella. It's not your style. Now how about we open the door and let the crew in? It's cold out there tonight."

"Was that the doorbell?" Trinity called from the top of the stairs, Beatrice beside her, her face beaming with happiness.

She looked beautiful and content and at peace, and Stella's heart filled with thankfulness that she'd survived, that they'd get to have Christmas together.

"Are they here?" Trinity continued. Chance opened the door, and a dozen people piled in. Men. Women. Kids. All of them smiling and laughing and chatting.

Stella was laughing, too, holding Chance's hand as he tugged her to the doorway that led into the parlor.

"What are you doing?" she asked. "You haven't introduced me to everyone."

"They know who you are," he responded, smiling as he pulled something from his pocket.

A box.

Pretty blue velvet.

Old.

He opened it, and the house went quiet.

Or maybe the sounds just faded away, because there

was a ring inside. A pearl surrounded by emeralds and rubies. Dainty and delicate. Beautiful.

"Chance—" she said, her heart welling up, filling with all the things she'd thought she'd never have— love and family and forever. All the fear of losing, of hurting, of saying goodbye lost in the joy of having this moment with him.

"Christmas colors. For our first Christmas together," he said.

"It's beautiful."

"You're beautiful," he murmured, kissing her softly, the ring still in his hand. "I love you enough for forever, Stella. I can't imagine spending the rest of my life with anyone but you. Will you marry me?"

"She will!" Beatrice called, and Stella laughed through the tears that were filling her eyes.

Tears of happiness for this perfect moment.

This wonderful man.

Her life that had been filled with heartache, and was now filled just as full with love.

"I love you, too, Chance. And Beatrice is right," she said, levering up on her toes, kissing him deeply. "I will."

"Put the ring on her finger and let's get the show on the road," Trinity said, moving in next to them, grinning from ear to ear. "Christmas Eve service waits for no man."

Chance smiled, taking the ring from the box and sliding it onto Stella's finger. Sealing a deal that had been in the making from the moment they'd met.

"I'm thinking a winter wedding," he murmured, his hands on her waist.

"It is winter," she responded.

"I know." He grinned, taking her hand and leading her into the throng of people that were their family.

* * * * *

HIDDEN IN SHADOWS

Hope White

This book is dedicated to my friends
at Sassy Teahouse in Redmond, Washington.

Though a mighty army surrounds me,
my heart will not be afraid. Even if I am attacked,
I will remain confident.
—*Psalm* 27:3

Chapter One

Okay, so Krista didn't expect a welcoming party when she returned home from her mission trip, but she didn't expect the house to be trashed either.

As she stepped inside the front hallway of her bungalow, a shaft of moonlight illuminated the mess in her living room. Sofa cushions were strewn across the shag rug, the end table was tipped over and mail littered the floor.

Anastasia was not happy. Who would have thought a ten-pound cat could actually do so much damage? That she could tip over furniture?

Krista dropped her purse, went to the oak bureau and pulled the chain on the vintage lamp.

Nothing.

"Anastasia," Krista scolded. The cat had probably chewed through the cord again. You'd think one shocking experience would be enough for kitty to keep her fangs off the electrical wire.

"Come on, Natalie took care of you." Krista edged her way through the living room, hoping to find a lamp with an unchewed cord, and hoping she got some light before her attack cat decided to pounce.

She tried a second lamp, with no luck. Being stalked by a crazy cat in broad daylight is one thing, but in pitch black it could be its own kind of shocking experience.

"Kitty, kitty, kitty," she cooed.

Krista was so not in the mood for surprises. Exhaustion filled every cell of her body after spending fourteen hours traveling from Mexico to Michigan. It was bad enough she'd missed her connection, but then they'd lost her luggage. She waited an hour and gave up, asking them to send it home when they found it.

At least she had the important stuff: her Bible, book of inspirational quotes and digital card with the hundreds of pictures she'd taken on the mission trip. She couldn't wait to upload the shots to her Faithgirl blog.

"Ana-sta-sia," she called out. The cat was sure to be in attack mode. After all, Krista had abandoned her for nearly two weeks. How dare she!

"Kitty, kitty, kitty," Krista said, feeling her way down the hall to the kitchen.

It wasn't like Krista had completely abandoned her. Her best friend, Natalie Brown, stopped by to check on the feline.

The wall phone rang, making Krista yelp.

She snatched the receiver. "Hello?"

"Welcome home!" Natalie said.

"Thanks, I'm glad to be home. Just wish I had some light." She ran her hand across the wall in search of the switch.

"What do you mean?"

"The cat ate through my lamp cords." She flicked the

switch but the ceiling light didn't come on. "Did I forget to pay my bill? No, I set it up on bill pay before I left."

"They wouldn't turn off your lights if you missed one payment, silly girl."

"I'm a tired girl and I can't see what I'm doing and any second now Anastasia is going to strike."

"But it was a good trip, right?" Natalie asked.

"It was amazing." Her heart filled with pride at the memory of helping the children in the small Mexican village. "Anything happen while I was gone?"

"Fred Skripps won the fishing contest, the new condo complex on Fourth got approved and they're bringing in a busload of tourists Friday. Be ready, tea mistress."

"Ready is my middle name."

"Bad, Krista, really bad."

"Sorry. Long flight, they lost my luggage and I'm hungry."

"Check your refrigerator."

Krista made her way to the fridge and pulled it open. Unfortunately the fridge light wasn't working either, but moonlight lit the kitchen enough for Krista to see her friend had left her some goodies.

"You're wonderful," Krista said.

"Says the woman who just spent ten days on a mission trip. You're welcome. There's chicken casserole, fresh fruit and takeout from Pekadill's."

"My mouth is watering. But if my power's out I can't heat it in the micro."

"Did you check the fuse box in the garage?" Nat offered.

"That's next. If I don't fall asleep on my way out there."

"Anastasia would have a field day with that."

"Did you see her at all?" Krista fumbled in the kitchen junk drawer.

"Once, the first time I stopped by. She thought I was you."

"How'd that go?" Krista pulled out a red mini flash-light.

"She ran, hid and never came out again."

"Except to trash my living room," Krista said.

"You want me to send Timothy over?"

"No, thanks. I'll be fine."

"He wouldn't mind."

"I'm good, really." Krista liked being able to take care of herself. Natalie had done plenty, and Krista didn't like taking advantage of Natalie's boyfriend's good nature. "I'll give you a call tomorrow."

"I'll stop by the tea shop."

"Sounds good."

She hung up and pointed the flashlight into the living room. "Kitty, kitty." She aimed in all the corners, above the bookshelf, then got down on her knees and held her breath as she flashed the light beneath the sofas.

"This is ridiculous." She stood. "I'm not going to let you punk me, kitty."

Pointing the flashlight ahead of her, she marched into the kitchen and flung open the back door. The smell of winter floated through the yard, wrapping around her shoulders like a soft blanket.

Home. There was nothing like it.

She marched outside to the detached garage. Shoving the flashlight into her sweater pocket, she heaved open the garage door and reached for her flashlight. A crashing sound made her jump back.

"Anastasia, how did you get in here?" Krista aimed the flashlight into the garage—

And screamed at the sight of a large man rummaging through her toolbox.

Instinct demanded she run, but for a second she couldn't move. Then the intruder turned to reveal a skeleton-masked face. He was holding a weapon in his hand.

Panic shot her out of the garage, her heart pounding against her chest. She raced for the house, focusing on the open door...

The man shoved her from behind and she went down against the cobblestone walk, the breath knocked from her lungs. It couldn't end like this. Who would run the tea shop?

Oh, of all the things to be worried about.

Eyes pinched shut, she braced herself.

But nothing happened.

She heard crunching of footsteps through the dormant garden as the man raced off. Could he be some homeless guy trying to stay warm?

"Hey!" a male voice called out behind her.

Followed by a pop. Then another.

She swallowed back the panic that threatened to make her sick.

Special Agent Luke McIntyre hit the ground when he saw the weapon aimed in his direction. Taking cover behind the house, he slipped his Glock from his belt and waited. He didn't want a shoot-out in this small town, but he had to defend himself.

And the woman.

Luke counted to three and poked his head out. The guy was out of sight.

A car's engine sputtered and cracked. Luke raced around the house in time to spot a dark green minivan peeling away from the curb. On the ground lay a nail gun.

Neighbors' lights popped on with interest and he quickly holstered his gun.

There was no doubt Krista Yates was in trouble.

Luke busted tail to get to Wentworth after the tip came in about Victor Garcia. The drug lord was sending men to the quiet Michigan town to finish some business with the Peace Church mission group. Garcia was a bold one to be using a church group to move drugs, but it didn't surprise Luke.

Garcia had been on the DEA's watch list for months and just when they thought they had enough to bring him in, the drug lord fled, probably to Mexico. Luke's office thought they'd lost him for good.

But Luke hadn't given up. Not on this one. There was too much history, too much at stake.

Luke slipped into town and touched base with the police chief, asking that Luke's position as DEA agent be confidential so as not to alert Garcia's men and chase them off. Luke knew that gossip in a small town traveled like wildfire.

Luke wanted to catch Garcia's men in the act of retrieving the drugs so he could hurt Victor Garcia where he'd feel it most: in his business.

No, Luke didn't just want to hurt Garcia. He wanted to destroy him.

The chief explained that Krista Yates coordinated

the mission trip, and had somehow missed her connection, so she was arriving later than the rest of the group.

The question was, what was Garcia's connection to Krista Yates?

Luke started around back, the sound of sirens blaring in the distance. He pulled out his shield and clipped it to his jacket pocket. Didn't want Barney Fife thinking he was the perp.

He turned the corner.

The woman was gone.

"Miss Yates?" he called out.

"Who are you and what did you do with my cat?"

He turned toward the house. She was aiming a fire extinguisher at him.

He raised his hands and bit back a smile at her aggressive stance. "I'm a federal agent, ma'am." He nodded toward his shield.

"Oh." She put down the extinguisher. "Wait, how did you get here so fast? Did you say federal agent?"

He took a step toward her and stopped. She looked shaken, petrified. He couldn't blame her.

"Yes, ma'am. I'm with the DEA."

Her green eyes were innocent, yet weary, and a bruise was starting to form on her cheek.

"You'd better ice your cheek or you're gonna look like Rocky Balboa after ten rounds in the ring." Lowering his hands, he started for the house.

She reached for the fire extinguisher.

"I'm on your side, remember?" he said.

"Then fix my lights."

"Excuse me?"

"There's no light in my house. I went to the garage

to check the fuse box and that guy jumped me, I mean jumped over me." She shook her head in confusion.

"Go on inside and I'll check the fuse box."

"It's dark inside."

"Okay, then wait on the porch. The cops should be pulling up any second now."

She hugged her midsection with one hand and clutched a charm at the base of her neck with the other. Although she acted strong, she looked broken and terrified.

And way too fragile.

Luke went into the garage, pulled out his pen flashlight and inspected the fuse box. As he expected, all switches were in the Off position. Luke snapped them on and light beamed from the house onto the back porch.

"Want me to close the garage door?" he called.

No answer.

Luke peered out from the garage. The woman was gone. What the heck? Did the guy come back? Send an accomplice? He started for the house.

"Police! Freeze!" a female shouted from behind him.

Luke raised his hands. "I'm a federal officer."

"Yeah and I'm Judge Judy. Get down on the ground."

"If you'd let me turn around—"

"Do it!" The woman sounded too young and green to be holding a firearm.

The guys in Luke's division would have a field day if the pipsqueak cop shot him in the back due to lack of experience.

"I'm going, I'm going." Luke dropped to his knees, interlacing his hands behind his head.

"All the way down!"

He hesitated, bitter memories tearing through his chest. Being forced down...

Held there while his partner, Karl, fought for his life.

"I said get down!" she ordered.

"Deanna, what are you doing?" the Yates woman said, coming out of the house.

"Stay in the house, Krista," the cop ordered.

"No, he's a good guy."

Good? Hardly.

Krista walked up to Luke, removed his shield and flashed it at the cop.

He doubted the rookie could see past her adrenaline rush.

Luke heard another car pull up.

"How do you know that's real?" the female cop said.

"It's real," a man offered.

Luke recognized Chief Cunningham's voice. Luke had spent a good hour with him earlier tonight going over the case.

"Lower your weapon, Officer West," the chief said.

From the concerned look on Krista's face, Luke sensed the female cop didn't follow the order. This was probably the most action she'd seen in her entire year on the force. If she'd even been on the force a year.

"West!" the chief threatened.

Krista sighed with relief and touched Luke's shoulder. "You need help getting up?"

Right, he still hadn't moved, paralyzed by the dark memories that he couldn't bury deep enough. Guilt had a way of rising to the surface to mess with your head at the worst possible moments.

Krista gripped his arm to help him stand. As if he needed help from this fragile thing.

Fragile. Innocent. Dangerous.

"I'm fine." Luke stood and turned to the cop. She looked barely twenty.

"Sorry about that," the chief offered.

"No problem," Luke said.

"Yes problem," Krista countered.

They all looked at her.

"Anastasia is missing." With a shake of her head, she went into the house.

Luke glanced at the chief. "Who's Anastasia?"

"Her cat," Officer West said.

Luke glanced at the house. Krista had nearly been taken out by a member of Garcia's gang and all she could think about was a silly cat?

"Officer West, continue your patrol and don't tell anyone about Agent McIntyre's presence in town," Chief Cunningham said. "I'll handle things here."

"The guy who jumped Miss Yates was driving a dark green minivan," Luke said.

"Okay, thanks." Officer West walked to her cruiser.

"These are not teenage pranksters, West. Radio in if you spot the van. That's an order," the chief said.

"Yes, sir."

The chief turned to Luke. "Ready?"

"For what?"

The chief started for the house. "I have a feeling Krista isn't going to be in a talking mood until we find her cat."

"You're kidding."

"Welcome to Wentworth, son." Chief Cunningham climbed the steps and disappeared into the house.

"Fantastic," Luke muttered.

He was allergic to cats, and even more allergic to

small towns. He grew up in one and hightailed it out of there before he hit his seventeenth birthday. There was too much gossip in a small town, too much imagined drama.

He climbed the steps and glanced across the yard. Imagined? Most of the time. In Krista Yates's case he was pretty sure she'd brought it home with her from Mexico, probably in her luggage, or in something she saw or said.

He shook his head. She was a talker, for sure, but he couldn't imagine the sweet-faced blonde saying anything offensive or rude. This wasn't about manners, it was about one of Mexico's biggest drug cartels moving product into the country via innocents.

The Yates woman defined innocent.

Luke stepped into the house and found the chief and Krista in the living room. "So the house was like this when you got home?" the chief said, eyeing the mess.

"I thought it was the cat."

"You thought the cat tipped over your end table?" Luke asked.

"She's a really big cat and she's rather upset with me right now."

"The sooner we can get a description of the man you saw in the garage, the more accurate it will be," the chief said.

"You don't think he killed her, do you?" Krista asked, her eyes rounding with fear. Wide, green, helpless eyes.

"Now, why would he kill your cat, Krista?" the chief said.

Krista narrowed her eyes. "You, of all people, should not be asking me that. Gladys still has scars from the quilting open house."

"Point taken."

"Anastasia? Here, kitty, kitty." She glanced at Luke. "Get the Whiskas. On top of the microwave." She disappeared upstairs.

Luke glanced at the chief.

"The sooner we find the cat…" the chief said with a shrug.

Luke found the bag of cat treats in the kitchen. As he grabbed them, his gaze caught on a photograph on the windowsill of a teenage Krista, and he guessed her mom, and perhaps grandmother. They looked like a team, arms around each other, ready to take on the world.

They were a loving family. He'd always wondered what that looked like.

It's not like he hung out with the guys at work and their families. He'd had a few invitations, but he knew he didn't belong and would make everyone feel awkward.

He never seemed to belong.

And that was fine by him.

"I got the cat treats!" he called out, more than a bit irritated with this diversion from their course of finding her attacker.

The chief was on the phone, and Luke started up the stairs. Krista met him halfway.

"No shouting," she whispered.

"I was shouting?"

"You shake and I'll grab."

"Excuse me?"

"The cat. You go ahead of me and shake the bag and I'll grab her when she comes out."

"Ma'am, we really need to talk about—"

"Shake and grab."

If the guys found out about this, he'd be more of a laughing stock than if he'd been shot by Rookie West.

She motioned for him to slip around her. The staircase was narrow and he couldn't help but brush up against her as he passed. She smelled fresh, like flowers, even after a twelve-plus-hour flight. How was that possible?

Shaking the bag, he started down the hallway, glancing into a bedroom. Neat and tidy, the four-poster bed was covered with a down comforter and the curtains looked handmade.

"Kitty, kitty. I love you, kitty," she crooned.

He kept shaking, ignoring the generous use of a word he'd rarely heard growing up. What the heck was wrong with him tonight?

Lack of sleep. He'd gone too long on five hours a night. It was bound to catch up to him.

"Wait." She touched his arm.

Warmth seeped through his leather jacket as he eyed her petite fingers.

She pointed to the next bedroom and released him, tiptoeing ahead. He glanced at his arm, struggling to remember the last time he'd felt any gentle, nonthreatening human contact.

Yeah, man, you do need sleep.

After he nailed Garcia and his production line. After the murderer was in jail. After...

What? There'd always be another Garcia.

Luke's job would never be over and he'd never be satisfied.

Krista crooked her finger and he followed her into the bedroom. This one had to be hers. A canopy bed centered the room, draped in light purple and pink material. A Bible lay on her nightstand and a tray of antique perfume bottles lined her dresser.

Luke glanced away.

Krista pressed her fingers to her lips and kneeled down pointing beneath the bed. He motioned to the bag of treats and she nodded for him to shake. He shook. They waited. No cat.

"Oh, boy. She's gotta be under here." Krista shimmied beneath the bed.

He felt something brush against his pants and glanced down to see a black-and-white cat doing a figure eight around his legs.

"Miss Yates?" he said.

"Yeah?" her muffled voice answered.

"Is this the cat you're looking for?"

She wiggled back out and sat cross-legged on the floor. "Anastasia?" With a confused frown she glanced up at Luke. "She hates people."

"I'm not people. I'm a federal officer, remember?" He smiled, hoping she'd be able to shift gears quickly and give them the intruder's description before too many other things clouded her memory.

"Wow." She looked up at him with awe. Respect.

He didn't deserve it.

"Not a big deal." He passed her the treat bag and she opened it.

The cat pounced on Krista. "Okay, okay," she laughed, a sweet, carefree sound.

"About your statement…" he said.

The cat purred and rubbed against Krista's knee as she put a treat on the hardwood floor.

"Ready?" he said.

"Sure." She stood and Luke automatically reached out to steady her. He withdrew his hand, afraid his touch might damage her somehow.

He turned to leave the room.

"Wait a second, can you hold this?" She handed him the treat bag.

She put her hands together and stood at her dresser. "Thank you, Lord, for allowing me to help such wonderful children in Mexico, for seeing me home safely, for my friends, for Anastasia and for Agent Luke for being my hero tonight. Amen."

He wanted to correct her, tell her he was no one's hero, not by any stretch of the imagination.

"Okay, let's get this over with," she said. "I'm exhausted."

She took a step toward the door, wearing that pleasant smile.

The crack of a gunshot echoed through the window.

Luke grabbed her and hit the floor.

Chapter Two

Here she was, knocked on the ground again. Not exactly how she pictured her first night home. She'd hoped to get into a bubble bath to wash the plane scum from her skin, sip a cup of chamomile tea and crawl beneath her down comforter.

Instead, someone was shooting at her.

"Stay here." Agent McIntyre stood and pressed his back against the wall.

"But the cat—"

He pressed two fingers to his lips to shush her. His expression was fierce, intense. She was glad she wasn't on his bad side. She started to get up.

"Right there," he ordered, slipping a gun from inside his jacket.

Her breath caught at the memory of little Armando Morales. Images of the little boy covered in blood, moaning in pain, made her freeze in place. Armando had been an innocent bystander caught in a territorial shoot-out among drug dealers.

Yet he was just a child.

The whole experience reminded her how lucky she

was. She may not have had a father or siblings, but she lived a safe, healthy life in Wentworth.

At least she had…until tonight.

The stairs creaked as Agent McIntyre went to investigate. She scooted to the door and leaned into the doorjamb, wishing that this was some kind of crazy dream brought on by exhaustion. Sure, she'd returned home, downed a few scoops of casserole and had crawled into bed. The peas in the casserole didn't agree with her, sparking nightmares that began with her being chased down by her garage stalker.

Another popping sound shattered that wishful thinking. It sounded farther away than the first, definitely from outside. Her windows hadn't been shattered by the shots.

"Anastasia?" she whispered, needing a hug, even from a crazy cat.

Hugs were something she sorely missed since Gran passed away and Mom moved to Florida with Lenny. Krista missed a lot of things and had hoped to fill that emptiness with her missionary work with kids, and maybe, in the not too distant future, a loving husband and children of her own.

Only, she was a disaster in the relationship department and had decided to stop looking so hard. She prayed about her life, asked God to help her find inner peace.

Kind of hard to find peace when people are shooting at you.

"Miss Yates?" Agent McIntyre called from the bottom of the stairs.

"Yes?"

"It's safe. You can come down."

She headed downstairs where the intense, yet handsome, agent was waiting for her. Her eyes caught on the gun in his hand and she froze.

He glanced at his weapon. "Sorry." He shoved it into its holster and pulled his jacket over it to conceal the weapon.

"The gunshot?" she asked.

"A neighbor was trying to scare off a raccoon. The chief's out there talking to him now."

"Probably the Bender kid. Someone should tell his dad to lock up the rifle."

"I'll be sure to do that. Come on, let's take your statement about the man in the garage before you fall asleep on us."

She ambled through the living room. "With all this adrenaline rushing through my body I doubt I'll ever sleep again."

Anastasia raced past her into the kitchen.

"How about some tea?" she offered over her shoulder.

"I'm good, thanks."

Was he ever. Agent McIntyre was good at being there to protect Krista, acting confident and unshakable. He was pretty nice to look at, too.

Warning! Sleep alert!

She was not one to ogle a stranger, but she was tired, hungry and confused. A man had broken into her house and garage. Looking for what? And wait a second, why was a federal agent at her house?

She turned to him. "Hey, you never told me why you're here."

"First things first. Let's get ice for your cheek."

She touched her face. "It looks bad?"

"Not yet, but it will if you don't ice it." He took a kitchen towel from the rack, opened the freezer and dropped a handful of cubes in it. He reached out to place it on the bruise and she took it from him.

"Thanks," she said, holding it in place and leaning against the counter. "You're an expert at first aid?"

"I've been knocked down a few times."

Yeah, she could see that. He was tough, the kind of man who stayed focused and didn't back down from a fight.

"Ready to give a statement?" he said.

"Sure."

Chief Cunningham stepped into the kitchen from the back door. "I gave the Bender kid a lecture about firearms. Took away the rifle for the time being, until his dad gets back from his business trip."

"I was about to question Miss Yates," Agent McIntyre said.

"Please call me Krista. Miss Yates makes me feel like an old maid."

"Okay, Krista." Agent McIntyre sat at the kitchen table and opened a small notebook.

Good, he looked less intimidating sitting instead of towering over her. The man had to be over six feet tall, dwarfing her five-foot-three-inch frame. His good looks and hard-edged demeanor made her uncomfortable. He was different than the few men she'd dated in Wentworth.

Not just different. He was a cynical man who'd chosen a violent career.

She sighed and found a bag of chamomile tea. She'd lost her dad to violence and saw what violence did to innocent children on her mission trips. Krista believed in discussing problems, praying about them. She wondered if a man like Luke McIntyre ever prayed. She doubted it.

"Can you describe the man in your garage?"

"No, I'm sorry. He was wearing a skeleton mask."

The agent hesitated in his note taking. Why?

"Did anything unusual happen at the airport in Mexico before you boarded?" he continued, focusing his blue-green eyes on his notepad. She'd noticed their brilliant color when he'd helped her trap Anastasia.

"Nothing unusual other than missing my first flight, which meant missing my connection in Chicago, and then losing my luggage."

"Did anyone talk to you at the airport?"

"Not really."

"Anyone at all. The slightest, seemingly insignificant conversation could help us."

"I chatted with a young mother. She had the cutest little newborn."

"Any men?"

"I don't like talking to men."

The agent snapped his eyes to meet hers. "You don't talk to men?"

"Strangers. I don't trust them."

"Smart girl."

Irked, she turned her back to him and poured hot water into the cup. "Thank you, Agent McIntyre, but I stopped being a girl ten years ago."

Silence filled the room. She'd overreacted. She couldn't help it. Being called a "girl" hit a nerve.

It reminded her of when she was a little girl, innocent and trusting. When she made the mistake of talking to a stranger.

"Anyway, no talking with strangers," she said, turning to Agent McIntyre.

Chief Cunningham stood quietly in the corner, arms crossed over his chest. He knew the story, the loss and devastation to the Yates family. The chief was the only one who knew the truth, knew that Mom and Krista had fled to Wentworth from California because the little girl had been so close to a killer, looked him in the eye, even shook his hand.

Krista had been only five when she'd told the stranger that Father was still at work in the Lincoln building. No one could have anticipated how that bit of information would change everyone's lives. It led the disheartened investor to Dad's office where an argument turned violent and Dad was killed.

After Dad's death, Mom fretted that the killer would come back for Krista since she'd seen him, so Mom packed up their belongings and moved to Gran's house in Michigan. A year later they got word that Dad's killer had been caught and sentenced to life in prison.

Krista was safe, but Mom and Gran couldn't drop the overprotective parenting style. Mom probably would have objected to Krista going on the mission trip if she'd still been living in Wentworth.

"And when you landed in Grand Rapids?" the agent asked, interrupting her thoughts.

"I got paged."

"For what?"

"Someone found my license, but I had my license so it was a mix-up. By the time I got to baggage claim, I discovered they'd lost my luggage."

"Did you get there as luggage was coming out on the conveyor belt?"

"No."

"So someone could have taken your luggage?"

"I guess, by accident, sure."

The agent and police chief exchanged glances.

"I don't have anything worth stealing, if that's where you're going with this."

"You might have had something you didn't know you had," Agent McIntyre said.

Then again his job was to see conspiracy around every corner.

"Why are you here again?" she asked and sipped her tea with one hand, while holding the ice to her cheek with the other.

"I'm investigating drug trafficking from Mexico into the Midwest."

"You think they used my suitcase to smuggle drugs?" she said, her voice pitched with disbelief.

"It's not that simple," Agent McIntyre said.

"What, then?"

"We got a tip that the leader of the drug cartel sent men to Michigan to tie up some loose ends with a church group. The tip came shortly after your group left Mexicali."

"So, you think someone in the mission group was smuggling drugs?"

"It's a possibility, yes," McIntyre said.

"No. It's not. I know you're used to dealing with criminals, Agent McIntyre, but people like us don't break the law."

"Luke."

"Excuse me?"

"My name is Luke. You don't have to call me Agent McIntyre."

"Oh, okay." But it wasn't okay. She didn't want to call him by his first name, didn't like the fact he was accusing someone in her church of smuggling and she didn't like that he was still here at nearly one in the morning.

"Is that all?" she said.

"You didn't recognize anything about the assailant?"

"The man in the garage? No. He could have been some teenager fooling around for all I know."

"Krista, I want you to stay with me and Jane tonight," Chief Cunningham said.

"Thank you, chief, but I'm fine here."

"You're really not," Luke interjected.

"You don't know that for sure."

"Why risk it?" he said.

"What about staying with your friend, Natalie, or the Sass family?" the chief suggested.

"Look, I haven't had a good night's sleep in nearly two weeks. I need to sleep in my own bed!" she shouted, then slapped her hand to her mouth. She didn't mean to lose it like that. "Sorry, I get cranky when I'm tired."

"I'll stay with her," Luke said to the chief.

"No, really, that's okay." She wasn't sure what scared her more: the stranger jumping out of her garage or the handsome agent offering to sleep under the same roof.

"Krista, you either stay at our house or with the Sasses, or let Agent McIntyre bunk on your couch. You pick."

No one had spent the night since Mom came back for Gran's funeral two years ago. Mom had moved to Florida with Lenny, and since Gran's death Krista had been in the family house alone.

And tonight they were asking her to share it with a stranger.

"I won't let a strange man stay in my house," she said.

"I'm a federal agent and I'm here to protect you. What's the problem?"

"It doesn't look right," she said.

Agent McIntyre glanced at the chief.

"Small town, people talk," the chief explained. He glanced at Krista. "We'll tell them Agent McIntyre is my nephew from upstate New York."

"I don't like lying," Krista said.

"Undercover work isn't the same as lying," Luke said. "It'll help me figure out who's behind all this."

"I understand, but—"

"How about I stay in the loft above your garage? I noticed a room up there."

"Great idea," Chief Cunningham offered. "It's well insulated and heated since the previous owner ran his mechanics business out of the garage."

"It's pretty gross up there," Krista said, feeling bad that she couldn't offer better accommodations.

"I'm sure I've slept in worse."

She wondered what could be worse than a cold, damp garage.

"It's a good compromise," the chief offered. "He can keep an eye on the house from the garage."

True, he could see her bedroom window from the garage. A thought that was both comforting and unsettling.

"It's either your garage or my car," Luke said. "And I don't want your neighbors to think I'm stalking you from the street."

"Okay, fine. There's a cot up there, although we haven't used it in years."

"I wasn't planning on sleeping much anyway."

Of course not. He'd be watching the house. Watching her.

"I'll have patrol swing by every hour." The chief shook Agent McIntyre's hand. "You'll check in tomorrow?"

"Yes, sir."

"Good night, Krista."

"Good night. Thanks, chief."

The chief walked out to his cruiser and Luke hesitated at the back door.

"You should have better security. Anyone could pop one of these windows and—"

"This is not New York City," she argued.

"You're right about that." He turned to her, scribbling something in his notebook.

Probably that she was a smarty-pants, disagreeable, cat-obsessed, crazy woman.

"You ever consider getting a dog?" he said.

"Not really, why?"

"They make great alarm systems."

"You're a dog person?"

"That surprises you?" He looked at her.

It did actually. Dog people were loving and kind. This man seemed guarded and cynical.

"Kind of, I mean, Anastasia adores you and she usually hates dog people."

"Told you that, did she?"

Was he joking with her? No, she was just exhausted and imagining it.

He glanced out the window and back at Krista. "Good night, then."

"Wait, I'll get you some blankets and a pillow." She went upstairs to the hall closet and pulled out pink linens. She guessed not his usual color, but pale pinks and purples were her favorite and she'd decorated the house accordingly.

She wasn't used to having company and wondered what else he needed.

He's not company. He's a cop after a criminal.

What did the man look like? What color was his hair? His eyes? What did he say?

Childhood memories assaulted her. She'd tried to describe the man who came looking for her dad, but she was too upset that Daddy wasn't coming home. Ever.

She hugged the linens and made for the stairs. She thought she'd put it behind her, buried the memories and the fear so deep that they wouldn't rise to scare the wits out of her.

But danger was back, in the form of the DEA agent bunking in her garage.

How on earth did she get embroiled in this mystery? She refused to believe someone on the mission trip had a connection to a drug organization. She just wouldn't accept it.

"Here," she said, stepping into the kitchen.

Agent McIntyre was eyeing photos lined up on the window ledge.

"Your mom and…?" he asked.

"Grandmother. We moved here when—" She stopped short. She couldn't even talk about it. "We moved here when I was five."

He turned and eyed her with speculation. She shoved the linens at him. "This should keep you warm. Sorry about the color."

He took the blankets and pillow. "Hopefully I won't break out in hives."

He was teasing again? She wasn't sure, couldn't be sure of anything right now.

"Yes, well." She opened the back door. "I'm up and out by eight to prep the tea shop for customers."

He stepped onto the back porch and turned to her. "I'm right outside if you need me."

He shot her a half smile, his blue eyes sparkling with color. Oh, heavens, she was tired all right.

"Thanks, good night," she said.

"Lock up behind me."

She shut the door and clicked the lock. He nodded his approval through the window and headed out to the garage.

He's just doing his job, Krista.

Sure, intellectually she knew that, but emotionally? Emotionally she heard Gran's and Mom's worried voices, felt the iron hand of control clamp down on her shoulders. They'd meant it out of love, but sometimes she just couldn't breathe.

Where are you going, Krista? What did you do today? Who did you talk to?

It wasn't until she was in her late teens did they explain that the protective habit was born out of love. They loved her so much they didn't want to see her hurt by a stranger. They'd developed the habit because years ago they'd feared for her safety after her father was killed.

Agent McIntyre wasn't motivated by love, but rather by duty. He'd stay over Krista's garage and unravel this threat before anyone got hurt. She sensed he was a warrior type, a controlling force.

Krista turned off the kitchen light and headed upstairs. She didn't want a controlling force in her life. She'd fought long and hard for her independence. She'd practically begged Mom to relocate to Florida with Lenny. Krista didn't want Mom missing out on wonderful years of retirement with her new husband because she had some irrational fear about Krista being hurt.

The past was the past, long gone, buried with the news that Dad's killer had died in prison.

It had been years since the nightmare resurfaced to haunt Krista. Yet tonight, thanks to a stranger breaking into her house and the DEA agent sleeping in her garage, the violence was back in her life.

Along with the memories.

Chapter Three

The Yates woman might have been exhausted last night, but she woke up with more energy than a kid on a gummy bear high.

By eight she was out the door, headed to the family tea shop. Luke followed close behind, both to protect her and to look for insight into this woman, her friends and the townspeople. Insight that would give him a clue as to who might be Victor Garcia's drug mule. The criminal wouldn't be stupid enough to actually smuggle drugs through Krista's luggage, would he? No, Luke sensed something else was going on. He just didn't know what.

He'd tried talking Krista out of opening the shop today, suggesting she needed a day to recover from her trip. But she was having none of it. She told him this time of year, right before the holidays, people needed the respite from their busy lives to enjoy a cup a tea. She'd said, "It's not about the tea. It's about friendship and connections."

Two things completely foreign to Luke.

Sitting in the back of Grace's Tea Shop, he read the paper to get a handle on the local flavor. He glanced around the shop, painted in pale purple with frilly lace framing the windows. Dainty chairs bordered small, round tables and a lit fireplace took the chill out of the morning air.

Luke did not belong here. This was a woman's place, a peaceful place.

"Coffee?" Krista offered, walking up to him with a pot. She looked enchanting this morning with her long, blond hair pulled back and her cheeks rosy from cooking scones and muffins.

"I thought you specialized in tea?" he said.

"I figured you were a coffee kind of guy."

"You figured right."

He wondered what else she'd figured out about him.

She poured him a cup and said, "Black, right?"

He nodded. "I think we should come up with a story about why I'm here at the tea shop."

"You're a customer, simple enough."

"I have a feeling I'm not your usual demographic."

"I've had men in here before."

He raised an eyebrow. "Really?"

"Okay, well, not every day, but occasionally."

"To ease suspicion, we'll go with the story that I'm Chief Cunningham's nephew and you hired me as your temporary handyman."

She rested the coffeepot on the table. "I told you, I'm not into lying, especially to my friends."

"Then I'll be the chief's friend, and you can give me a list of things you need fixed. I'll be your handyman for real."

She narrowed her eyes.

"What? I'm pretty good with a hammer." Working on his own house had been cathartic after Karl's death.

She placed the coffeepot on the warmer and pulled vegetables from the refrigerator. "I'll think about it."

He could tell the thought of Luke shadowing her, being close, made her uncomfortable. He wasn't sure if it was because he was a constant reminder of the threat hiding in the shadows, or if it was something else.

Maybe she sensed the darkness that haunted him and knew instinctively to keep her distance. From him.

He sipped his coffee and remarked how good it tasted. "What's in this?"

"A secret ingredient." She winked.

He snapped his attention back to the paper. She was too nice, too gentle and it made him uncomfortable.

A tall brunette breezed into the back, oblivious to Luke's presence. The woman was dressed in a tailored suit and high heels. Her perfume filled the kitchen, the smell a sharp contrast to Krista's subtle floral scent.

"She's back!" The brunette rushed to Krista and gave her a hug. "How'd you sleep?"

"Pretty good." Krista motioned to Luke. "This is Luke. Luke, this is Natalie."

The woman turned to Luke, her eyes flaring with interest.

Luke stood and extended his hand. "I'm a friend of Chief Cunningham."

"Well, hello."

They shook hands.

"How long are you staying in Wentworth?" Natalie asked.

"Not sure. A few weeks, I guess."

"Wonderful." She winked at Krista.

Krista blushed. "Knock it off."

Could Krista really be that shy and innocent? One

more reason Luke should stay close. She'd be an easy target for one of Garcia's men. Because she coordinated the mission trip, Luke had to assume Garcia's men would come looking for her first when they got to town. That is, if they weren't already here.

Yet if last night's intruder was with the Garcia operation, he would have done more to Krista than hurdle her and flee the scene.

A short guy, late thirties, marched into the back of the shop. Busy place, and they weren't even open for business yet.

"Krista!" the man said, wrapping his arms around her for a hug. He was either oblivious to Luke or was purposely ignoring him.

Krista made a face at her girlfriend over the man's shoulder and broke the hug. "Good to see you, Alan. I've got to check the soups." She went to stir a pot on the stove.

"I heard the Bender kid shot out your windows last night," Alan said.

"No, they didn't shoot out her windows," Natalie offered. "A stranger was caught rifling through her garage."

"Right on both counts," Krista said.

"Alan, meet the chief's friend," Natalie said, introducing them.

The man turned and his jaw hardened. Alan was in his mid-thirties, clean-shaven with perfectly combed hair and suspicious eyes. He was about four inches shorter than Luke's six-foot-one-inch frame.

Luke shook hands with Alan, who squeezed extra tight. He was making his mark, letting Luke know Krista was off-limits. Whatever. Luke wasn't here for romance and he surely wouldn't get involved with a fragile creature like Krista Yates.

"Nice to meet you, Alan," Luke said.

Alan nodded and turned back to Krista. "So, what really happened last night?"

"Someone broke into the house and the garage," she said.

"What?" Natalie said. "I was there at six to check on Anastasia. Oh, my goodness, is she okay?"

"She's fine. I'm fine. Everything's fine." Krista waved them off and went back to stirring the soup.

"Krista, are you really okay?" Alan placed his hand on her shoulder.

Krista stopped stirring for a second, then continued. Luke didn't miss the hesitation. Alan ignored it.

"I was a little rattled, but I'm okay," Krista said. "The cops got there right away."

"You shouldn't be living in that house alone," Alan said.

"Thanks, but I'm a big girl, Alan."

"She's not alone. I'm staying over the garage," Luke offered.

Alan and Natalie looked at Luke as if he'd just announced Martians had landed in the town square.

"My friend, the chief, was worried about the perpetrator coming back so he asked me to stay close," he explained.

"The perpetrator?" Alan said. "Are you a cop, too?"

"I've had some experience in law enforcement, yes."

"What kind of experience?" Alan pushed.

"You want my résumé?" Luke pushed back.

"Take the discussion outside, guys," Krista said.

"I've got to get moving if I'm going to open by eleven."
She corralled everyone out the back.

Alan hesitated and turned to her. "Dinner tonight?"

"No, but thank you. I'm still jet-lagged."

Alan touched her arm. "You shouldn't have opened
today, Krista."

"It's the busy season, you know that. The Christmas
teas cover half my expenses for the year. I can't lose
that revenue."

"But—"

"Look," she interrupted Alan. "I appreciate your concern, I really do. But the Sass twins won't clock in for
another hour and I need to get back to work."

Natalie and Krista hugged. Krista stepped back into
the shop before Alan could get another hug. She shut
the door, leaving the three of them standing by the herb
garden.

Luke's cell vibrated and he checked the caller ID. It
was his supervisor, Agent Marks.

"Excuse me," he said to Alan and Natalie.

With a nod, Luke walked to his car and answered
his cell.

"McIntyre," he said.

"Any progress?" Agent Marks questioned.

"Not yet, sir."

"Did Miss Yates recognize last night's assailant?"

"He was wearing a mask."

"Do you want to bring her in for protection?"

"She'd fight me on it." Luke saw in her eyes how devoted she was to her business and it sounded like this
was the prime season for revenues.

"It's your call. I've put an alert out on her luggage."

"Thanks."

"Be careful," Marks warned. "And call for backup if you need it."

"Yes, sir."

He pocketed his phone and eyed the tea shop, an old brick house converted into a small restaurant in the heart of town.

"Nice meeting you," Natalie called out to Luke as she breezed to her older-model Volvo in the parking lot.

"You, too," he said.

With a curt nod, Alan walked to a newer SUV and took off. Luke noted Alan's license plate and would call it in later. There was something about that guy…

Luke couldn't be jealous, not over a complete stranger like Krista. More like, his protective instincts were kicking in. He'd seen how Krista needed space, didn't like Alan touching her. Whatever that guy thought of their relationship, Krista had a completely different take on things.

Luke should head back to Krista's house, get tools and start his handyman cover. Instinct told him not to leave her alone, not even for a few minutes. He called the chief's private line.

"Cunningham," the chief answered.

"It's Luke McIntyre."

"Everything okay?"

"Yes, sir. I was wondering if you could do me a favor and swing by the tea shop with some tools. I'd rather not leave Krista alone."

"Put you to work, did she?"

"Not officially, but I'm trying to convince her it's a good cover."

He chuckled. "I'll bring by my toolbox. We think we got something on the perp's car. A dark green minivan with an Ohio plate was dumped on the other side of Silver Lake. Fits the description."

"So the guy's still close."

"Looks that way."

A scream echoed from the tea shop and Luke bolted for the house.

Chapter Four

He should have checked the entire building, every corner, beneath every table, inside every teapot before leaving her alone in there.

He whipped the back door open. "Krista!"

Nothing.

"No, no," he ground out between clenched teeth. He raced to the stairs leading to the second-floor office. Taking the stairs two at a time, he pulled out his firearm, got to the top and spun around, pointing the gun into the room.

Directly at Krista.

With round, terrified green eyes, she dropped the teapot in her hands and it crashed to the floor into pieces. He swung the gun around the room.

They were alone.

"What happened?" He holstered his gun. He took a step toward her and she backed up.

She was scared out of her mind. Because of Luke.

He put out his hands in a calming gesture. "I'm sorry about the gun. Okay? Just breathe."

Luke took a deep breath and she mimicked him.

"Are you okay?" he asked.

She nodded affirmative.

"You screamed. Why?" He didn't move, didn't step closer. But he wanted to. He wanted to put his arm around her and calm her down, stop her trembling.

His touch would probably make her shake more considering he'd just pulled a gun on her.

"What happened?" he asked.

She pointed to the broken teapot on the floor. Lying beside it was a dead mouse.

"That's why you screamed?"

She nodded again. "It was…in the teapot. So, so I was checking other ones and you…" her voice hitched.

He threatened her with a gun.

"I'm sorry. I thought…never mind. I tend to go to the worst-case-scenario places. But you're okay, that's all that matters. Everything's fine."

But it wasn't fine. There was no way a mouse could open the lid of a teapot and climb inside.

"Has this happened before?" he asked.

"We have mice problems. All restaurants do," she said, defensively.

Good, she was coming out of her fright.

"The teapot was on my desk when I came upstairs. Strange, because I don't remember leaving it here."

She touched the calendar desk pad. Somewhere, deep down, she sensed the danger as well. But for now, Luke would shelve the possibility of this being a threat against her and help her get her bearings back.

"Krista!" a girl called from downstairs.

Krista didn't answer at first. She just stared at Luke. He stepped aside, giving her ample room to pass. The last thing he wanted was to make her feel threatened.

She needed to trust him if he had any chance of protecting her.

"I'll clean up," he said. "Broom?"

She pointed to the far end of the long attic office. He stepped around her and she rushed downstairs.

The high pitch of excited female voices drifted up from the restaurant. He grabbed the broom and hesitated, trying to calm the adrenaline rush. Couldn't help reacting the way he did. He'd been a few seconds too late and his partner died because of it. Luke wouldn't make that mistake again, especially not with a complete innocent like Krista.

With a deep breath, Luke got the broom and began sweeping up the mess. Shards of china, loose tea and a few candy wrappers.

He eyed the dead mouse. A few inches away he spotted a white scrap of paper folded a few times. He grabbed a pair of latex gloves used by the kitchen staff and opened the note.

Welcome Home, Pretty Lady.

"Great," Luke muttered. He had to assume this was a threat, right? A dead mouse in a teapot. So Garcia's man had been here in the shop?

"That's too close." It's not like the quaint tea shop would have video surveillance. He'd have to do it the old-fashioned way and check the locks for signs of tampering.

He took his time cleaning up, giving Krista space. She needed to recover from the sight of the dead mouse, and a man pointing a gun at her. But he wasn't going far. When the chief stopped by Luke would hand off the note and have him send it in for prints.

It seemed tame for a drug lord's henchman. Subtlety

wasn't their style. They were more direct, more in-your-face vicious.

Now you get to watch him die.

Garcia's words slashed through Luke's chest like a knife. His best friend, the only guy in the world who both understood and accepted Luke for who he was, broken parts and all, died right in front of Luke. And he was unable to do a thing about it.

Luke shoved back the memory and the pain. Stuffing the note into a plastic baggie and then into his pocket, he headed downstairs to call in this development.

If only he knew what it meant.

Thank goodness Krista was feeling more like herself halfway through the lunch rush. She thought her nerves would never stop skittering.

First a break-in, then a dead mouse, then Luke aiming a gun directly at her chest.

She reminded herself that that was normal behavior for a man like Luke, but still, the image was not easy to shake. Pulling a gun because she'd found a dead mouse was definitely overkill. Then again, he didn't know what had made her scream.

"Table four needs more cream and jam," Tori Sass said, breezing into the kitchen with a handful of plates.

"Right up." Krista squirted sweetened whipped cream onto a plate and spooned a dollop of jam beside it. Some liked their scones extra sweet. She wondered how Agent McIntyre liked his.

No, he'd probably never tried a scone. He seemed more the doughnut type of guy.

Why was she thinking about him again? She was

tired, that's all. Tired and frightened out of her right mind between the mouse and firearm.

She'd never forget the look on his face when he'd swung around and pointed it at her. He looked powerful and determined.

And maybe a little frightened. Was that possible?

Sure, even in his line of work a person felt fear, she reminded herself.

"How's the order for table seven?" Tatum Sass asked.

"Almost there." Krista refocused on the tea sandwiches in front of her and arranged red rose petals in between them.

Make them feel special, Mom had taught her. It was Krista's role to give local women a place to gather, share dreams, hopes and fears, in a safe environment.

Yet Krista wasn't feeling safe right now. Between the jet lag, lack of sleep and this morning's excitement, she was exhausted and more than a little off kilter.

"You look tired," Tatum said, waiting for her order.

"Thanks, now I feel so much better," Krista joked.

"Why don't you take a break? This is the last food order."

Krista nodded. "I'll be out back."

She untied her apron and flung it over the hook. She could use a few minutes of fresh air. Luckily, it was unseasonably warm for a November day in Michigan, so she grabbed a sweater and stepped outside.

And spotted Luke trimming back the rose bushes. She'd meant to do that before her trip, before the fall hit. But she'd run out of time, what with the Sass girls starting up community college and having limited availability.

As Luke tended to the rose bush, she remarked how

normal he looked, like a regular guy. Not like a violent man who packed a gun against his ribcage.

With seemingly gentle fingers, Luke snipped the rose stem with some kind of knife. A pocket knife.

"Hey, I've got pruning shears," she said.

He turned to her and she could have sworn she read regret in his eyes, probably because he'd scared the wits out of her earlier.

"Hang on," she said. She went back inside, dug into the white china cabinet and found the shears. As she opened the door to go back out, she nearly ran into him.

She didn't expect him to be so close. Nor did she expect her heart to skip a few beats. And not out of fear.

She handed him the shears. "Thanks."

"It's the least I can do considering I scared the—" he paused "—you know."

"Have you been out there all afternoon?"

"Pretty much."

"Did you get lunch?"

"Not yet."

"I'll make you a sandwich." She motioned him into the shop, but he hesitated.

"Come on, it's safe," she joked.

He followed her inside and washed his hands.

"Turkey okay?" she asked, putting on gloves.

"You even guessed my favorite sandwich? How do you do that?" He settled at a table in the back.

"Everyone likes turkey." She pulled out bread, lettuce and tomatoes.

Tori came into the back with a tray of plates. She slid them by the sink and turned to Krista. "Who's the guy?"

"A friend of Chief Cunningham," Luke said.

Krista kept working on the sandwich. She couldn't

blame Luke for acting the way he did this morning. It was his job to suspect danger around every corner.

And that suspicion might keep her safe.

Tatum joined her sister in the kitchen.

"Chief Cunningham's friend," Tori explained to her sister.

Tatum walked over to the Luke and shook his hand. "I'm Tatum and this is Tori."

"Tori, can you start on the dishes?" Krista asked. "I'm not sure I've got the energy."

"Sure."

Krista finished making Luke's sandwich, garnished the plate with a pickle and a few olives and put a mini scoop of fruit salad in a dish. She placed it in front of him.

"How much?" he said.

"On the house."

He glanced into her eyes. "I can't do that."

"Why not?" Krista asked.

"It's freeloading. Let me at least do the dishes after I eat."

"Great idea!" Tori said, drying her hands and rushing off into the dining room.

"No, really I couldn't—"

"Sure she could," Tatum said, putting her arm around Krista's shoulder. "In case you haven't noticed, she has a hard time accepting help from people."

"Wise guy," Krista said.

"It's true." Tatum smiled and breezed out of the kitchen.

"Nice kids," Luke said.

"They consider me their auntie."

"Well, Auntie, I'd really like to do your dishes in exchange for lunch. And anything else I can do to help, just say the word. Okay?"

"Sure."

Krista went to clean up the stainless steel prep counter. Her insides warmed at the thought of how nice it was to have a man care about her.

Then she reminded herself he was here for work, and part of his job required him to stick close and catch whoever was working in tandem with the drug cartel.

She rinsed off the prep table with bleach water and started on the dishes.

"Hey, hey, that's my job," Luke said.

"I'll leave some for you, no worries."

The back door opened and Alan stepped into the kitchen. He glared at Luke. "You're still here?"

"I work here."

"Yeah, right." He turned his back to Luke and went to Krista. "Hey, I wanted to make sure you were doing okay."

He touched her arm and she tried not to recoil. Alan wasn't a bad guy, just not a guy she wanted touching her. She knew he wanted more than she had to give him, and she didn't want to encourage the affection.

"I'm fine, thanks."

"Really? Because I was worried this morning."

"Thanks, just tired." She stepped away from him and rearranged the tea jars. Maybe if she kept her distance he'd get the message.

She didn't want to be rude, but she wasn't sure how to handle this situation. She'd been clear with him months ago that she wasn't interested, that she wasn't ready to get serious. With anybody.

Which wasn't exactly true. If she found the right

man, a Christian man as devoted to God as he was to Krista, well, she'd definitely consider. Only there weren't a lot of single guys of her generation left in Wentworth. Most of her classmates had gone off to college, landed important jobs in the city and didn't return home.

"Business run smoothly this morning?" Alan asked, eyeing the tables out front.

"Sure, why?" she asked.

"It's your first day back and you've got to be exhausted. I mean with your long travel day and early morning…"

God give me patience.

If he kept reminding her how tired she was, she was going to pass out right here on the hardwood floor.

She turned to him. "I'm fine, Alan, really. And I appreciate your concern. Now, if you don't mind, I'm going to finish up these dishes, so I can close early this afternoon."

She smiled brightly and hoped she'd been nice about her obvious attempt to kick him out of her space.

"I'll check on you tonight." He reached out to touch her shoulder.

"Great, thanks."

The phone rang, saving her from having to rudely pull away.

She sidestepped Alan to answer the phone. "Grace's Tea Shop."

"Yes, this is Thunder Travel Tour. We're bringing a bus through Wentworth and would like to book your restaurant for a high tea."

"Great, what's the date?"

As she took the order, she spied Alan hovering over

Luke as he ate his sandwich. What was Alan's problem? One, she and Alan weren't dating, and two, Luke wasn't interested in Krista that way.

As if he heard her, Luke glanced at Krista.

She snapped her attention to her reservation book. "That date looks good. How many?"

"Twenty-six."

"We offer a set menu for that number. Would you like me to e-mail it to you?"

"That would be great."

Krista spied Alan hovering by the doorway as if he wasn't leaving without saying a proper goodbye. As she finished the call with the travel agency, she wondered if she needed to be more direct with Alan so he could move on and find another woman to date.

"I look forward to working with you," Krista said and hung up.

Alan took a step toward her just as Tatum rushed into the kitchen. "A group of eight just walked in for high tea."

"Now?" Krista checked her watch. "We didn't have a reservation." It was nearing three, which meant Krista wouldn't be closing up anytime soon.

"No reservation, but they hoped we'd have an opening."

Krista nibbled at her lower lip. She was exhausted.

"Tell them you're booked," Alan offered.

Krista looked at Tatum. "Tell them we'll have a table ready in fifteen minutes."

Tatum nodded and went into the dining room.

"Krista, you're obviously exhausted," Alan said.

"It's all part of running my own business." She opened the refrigerator and pulled out spreads to get working on the tea sandwiches. "Thanks for stopping by, Alan."

He must have heard the dismissal in her tone. She'd been pleasant enough, and hoped he'd take his cue to leave.

"I'll call you later," he said.

With a nod, she focused on the sandwiches. A minute later she heard the door close and she breathed a sigh of relief.

Luke walked behind her to the sink. "Eight is a big order. Sure you're up to it?"

She eyed him. "What is with everybody today? I'm a big girl and I know my limitations," she said a little more firmly than she'd intended.

Luke put up his hands. "Didn't mean to offend."

"You've got a sink full of dishes."

"So I do." He turned and got to work.

Krista was exhausted by the end of the day and looking forward to a nice, quiet evening.

Instead, she came home to a crowded house full of friends who'd orchestrated an official welcome-home party.

As she stood in her living room surrounded by friends she felt so full, so at peace. Yet a part of her had hoped for quiet time to upload more photos to her blog, and maybe even sneak in that long bath she'd been fantasizing about.

She should have known something was up when the Sass girls offered to close the shop. They always had friends to catch up with after work, and church activities to attend, yet today they practically forced Krista out the back door so they could clean up.

They'd all been in on the plan: the Sass twins, Natalie and friends from church. Their goal was to show her how much she'd been missed.

"Krista?" Luke said.

She turned to him. He seemed completely out of place and more than a little uncomfortable surrounded by these down-to-earth folks.

"Looks like you're okay here so I'm going to meet up with the chief for an hour," he said.

"Oh, okay, sure."

"Hang in there." He smiled.

She realized he was the only person in the room who saw through her smile and knew how tired she really was.

"Thanks. And thanks for being my busboy today."

"Maybe you'll promote me to handyman?"

"We'll see."

"Enjoy yourself." He made his way through the crowded living room and practically ran out the front door. She wondered what made him so uneasy about the group. Was it simply that the suspect could be among them? No, she wouldn't accept that possibility.

Natalie weaved her way through the crowd. "Did we surprise you?"

"Totally."

Natalie put her arm around Krista and gave her a squeeze. "I know you're tired, but they insisted."

Krista glanced around the room and spotted Tori and Tatum's mom, Julie Sass, chatting with the youth minister.

"I should have known something was up when the Sass girls offered to close."

"Yeah, why's that?" Natalie asked.

"They've always been nervous about locking up and setting the alarm."

Natalie scanned the room. "Where's Alan?"

"He doesn't like to share me."

Natalie snapped her attention to Krista.

"Sorry, that was mean," Krista said.

"No, it was accurate. I didn't think you noticed."

"I notice a lot. I just keep it to myself."

Like she noticed how Luke bolted from the party as soon as possible. He acted as if being around friendships and laughter physically pained him. Maybe even terrified him.

Her cell vibrated on her hip. It was a text message alerting her that something tripped the alarm at the tea shop.

"Drat. The girls must be having trouble setting the alarm. I've gotta buzz over there for a minute."

"You can't go," Natalie said. "It's your party."

"It will take five minutes."

"Then I'll go with you. You look too tired to drive, anyway."

"Gosh, thanks." With a smile, Krista led Natalie out the front door. Within minutes they were at the shop.

"Stay here," Krista said, grabbed her keys from her purse and went to reset the alarm. The back door was open.

Why would they set the alarm before they locked up?

Panic gripped her stomach. "Tori? Tatum?" Krista called as she stepped into the shop.

No one answered. "Girls!"

She started for the stairs to the office and spotted broken glass and loose-leaf teas sprinkled on the hardwood floor. Backing up, she grabbed her cell phone from her belt and called 9-1-1.

"9-1-1 emergency."

"This is Krista—"

Someone grabbed her from behind, yanking the phone out of her hand and tossing it across the room. He had his arm around her neck and waist.

"Where is it?" he growled into her ear.

"What do you want?"

"Your purse, your money."

"Let me go!" She struggled against him, but he was too strong and about five inches taller than Krista.

Sirens wailed in the distance.

Her attacker shoved her aside and Krista lost her balance, banging her head on the counter as she fell to the floor.

She opened her eyes and spots cluttered her vision. Stunned and confused, she struggled to sit up and lost the battle. Collapsing against the floor, she focused on taking deep, slow breaths.

"Krista!" Natalie cried.

And the world faded to black.

Chapter Five

This couldn't be happening. He'd left her for ten minutes.

Adrenaline rushing through his body, Luke gripped the door handle ready to jump from the chief's cruiser.

Come on, come on. They couldn't get to the shop fast enough.

The chief finally pulled into the parking lot and Luke flung open his door.

"Wait for backup," the chief ordered.

Backup? Small-town law enforcement was no match for the likes of Victor Garcia.

"I got it." Luke jumped out of the chief's cruiser and bolted for the restaurant.

He reached inside his jacket and slipped out his Glock. He turned the corner to the back door and froze at the sight of Natalie kneeling over Krista.

No, he wouldn't accept it. He couldn't handle the possibility that Krista had been hurt…maybe even killed. His shoulder muscles tensed.

The chief rushed into the doorway, along with another cop.

"Natalie, what happened?" Luke demanded, rushing to Krista's side.

"Out front, some guy ran out front!" Natalie shouted.

"We'll check it out," the chief said.

"Someone call an ambulance," Natalie pleaded.

"It's on the way." Luke shoved his gun inside his jacket. Didn't want Krista opening her eyes to see Luke hovering over her brandishing a gun.

He kneeled on the other side of Krista and gently gripped her wrist to take her pulse. Her skin was cool to the touch, but her pulse was strong and steady.

Thatta girl.

He noticed a red bump on her forehead.

"What happened?" He glanced at Natalie. She was pale, looked like she was going to pass out herself.

"Natalie, breathe," Luke ordered. "Krista's going to be okay."

She had to be okay.

"Talk to me," he prompted Natalie.

She sniffled. "Something tripped the alarm and Krista thought the girls were having problems setting it, but we got here and the door was open and the... girls! Where are they?"

Krista moaned. "Why all the shouting?"

The chief kneeled beside them. "How is she?"

"She's coming around." Relief settled low in Luke's gut. He glanced at the chief. "Natalie's worried about the girls who were working here earlier."

"I'll check upstairs and call their mom."

Krista moaned and blinked her eyes open. Luke had never seen anything more beautiful in his life.

Confusion creased her forehead. "I'm on the floor."

"That you are." He placed her hand on her stomach. He'd been holding it while taking her pulse and hadn't let go.

"What happened?" She touched her forehead where an ugly bruise was already forming.

"You don't remember?" Luke asked.

"I was at the party and then, no, it's foggy."

She automatically reached for her silver charm at her neck. He guessed it was her touchstone.

"Where are the paramedics?" Luke whispered, glancing out the back. He couldn't stand seeing her hurt like this, lying on the floor and probably suffering from a concussion.

The chief came downstairs. "The Sass girls are home, safe and sound."

"Thank God," Natalie said.

"Something tripped the alarm," Krista said. "I remember now."

Luke snapped his attention to her. "What else do you remember?"

"The floor, tea and glass everywhere."

Luke glanced over his shoulder at the tea racks. Sure enough the floor was covered with broken glass jars of tea.

"A man was here," Krista whispered.

Luke glanced at her. "Did you recognize him?"

"He grabbed me from behind and…" She closed her eyes.

Luke fought the urge to reach out and hold her hand, tell her everything was going to be okay.

Natalie took Krista's hand and squeezed it. "It's okay, Krista."

Krista opened her eyes and stared directly at Luke. She wanted something. He didn't know what.

"Is it...safe?"

"Yes. He's gone."

But they both knew what she was really asking was if this was connected to Garcia's drug business.

"Did he say anything?" Luke asked.

"He wanted my purse."

"Do you think it was the same guy who was hiding in your garage?"

"I don't know."

Two paramedics rushed into the kitchen and lay a backboard on the floor.

"I'm really okay," Krista protested.

Luke and Natalie stepped aside, letting the EMTs tend to Krista.

"Natalie, where's her purse, do you know?" Luke said.

"In my car."

With a nod, Luke went outside.

And spotted a man digging around in the front seat of the car. Gutsy. The place was swarming with emergency response personnel and he was trying to snatch the car? So much for this being a quiet tourist town.

Luke came up behind the guy, grabbed his arm and twisted it behind his back.

"Find what you're looking for?"

"Hey, what's the problem?" The guy struggled, but Luke pinned him against the car.

"The problem is you breaking into a stranger's car."

"This is my fiancée's car."

Natalie stepped out of the tea shop. "Timothy? What are you doing here?"

"You know this guy?" Luke said.

"He's my fiancé, Timothy Gaines."

Luke released Timothy.

"Who are you?" Timothy demanded as he rubbed his shoulder.

"A friend of the police chief."

With a disgruntled nod, Timothy turned to Natalie. "You okay, honey?" He gave her a brief hug, then stepped back and looked into her eyes. "I was driving by and saw your car in the lot. You left the keys in the ignition."

"I'm okay. Krista was attacked."

Luke studied the dynamic between the couple. Although they were engaged there was something awkward about their interaction. Then again, Luke would have no idea what a loving couple looked like. Dad had abandoned them when Luke was five, and Mom didn't want to complicate her life by getting involved with another man.

Out of the corner of his eye, Luke spotted the EMTs carrying Krista out of the shop.

"The chief will want to talk to both of you," Luke said, and marched to the ambulance. "Where are you taking her?"

"Westfield Clinic. If they think it's more serious they'll transfer her."

"I want to go with her," Natalie said.

"I need you to stay here and give your statement to Officer Sherman," the chief said.

"I'll follow her to the clinic," Luke said.

"Good." The chief and Luke shared a knowing look.

Krista's situation seemed to be getting more dangerous by the hour. Another reason Luke needed to stay close.

Closer than close.

The ambulance pulled away and Luke followed in his car. He'd left Krista in a house full of people, thinking she'd be safe, that no harm could possibly come to her in that environment.

His mistake. One he wouldn't make again.

But he'd been anxious to get out of there, away from the friends and church folk who surrounded her, welcomed her.

Loved her.

Something Luke hadn't experienced much in his life. Mom tried, but Luke always sensed he'd been more of a burden than a bright spot in her life.

Sure he was. He'd been a troublemaker in school, always acting out, getting sent to the principal's office. Looking back, he realized it was anger at his life that drove him to lighting fires and stealing bikes. First abandoned by his father, then ten years later losing his mom to cancer.

Anger didn't begin to describe the war brewing inside Luke's chest as a teenager. After three years of being shuffled around in the foster care system, Luke channeled his anger into a different kind of war. The war in Iraq. At least it made him feel like he was doing something productive with all his rage.

Rage he'd buried, deep. Yet here he was, thinking about the past. A waste of energy.

He needed to focus on keeping Krista Yates safe. The image of her limp body lying on the floor reminded him of…

Karl, a good friend, who'd been just as motionless after Garcia shot him and left him to die.

In front of Luke.

Helpless. Gutted. There was no other way to describe the burn rushing to every nerve ending in Luke's body as he struggled to free himself from the duct tape to save his friend.

He'd felt almost as helpless when he'd heard dispatch radio the call from Krista's tea shop.

She was Luke's lead to the Garcia gang. Luke's only lead.

Yet something other than nailing Garcia made him rush out of the chief's car and into the tea shop.

Luke was worried, truly, genuinely worried.

About Krista.

"Not good," he whispered as he parked in the clinic's lot.

He had to shelve the compassionate feelings he was developing for Krista. It was ludicrous to even go there, to consider the thought of Luke and Krista being friends, much less anything more. She needed a nice, Christian man devoted to God and family.

Luke had given up on God a long time ago. About the time God took his mother and left Luke floundering in a foster care system that had no place for a teenager.

He'd seen enough violence and death in Iraq to further destroy any belief in a loving God.

He shook his head, snapping out of his analysis of his life and how Christ had failed him. Being around Krista brought it all to the surface. She glowed with the love she felt for God, her devotion to doing good deeds and caring for others.

That kind of energy was foreign to Luke and made him uneasy. That very uneasiness would be his constant reminder not to let this case get too personal, not to let Krista Yates get too close. Or was it that he didn't want her seeing all of his imperfections, especially the biggest one of all: that he couldn't protect the people he loved most?

He'd stay physically close but emotionally distant. Easy for a guy like him, at least he thought so until he saw them wheeling her into the hospital.

Something knotted in his gut and he stormed ahead.

* * *

"You can't come in here, sir," Nurse Ruth Rankin said on the other side of the curtain. Ruth and her sister often visited the tea shop and it was nice to see a friendly face at the clinic. But Ruth didn't sound friendly, alarming Krista.

"I have to see her."

Luke's voice. Krista smiled, oddly relieved to hear the deep timbre through the curtain.

"Are you her boyfriend?" Nurse Rankin said.

"No, absolutely not," he said, panic edging his voice. "She's a friend. I need to make sure she's okay."

"Why don't you wait outside? The doctor will know more after the CT scan."

"Wait," Krista said. "Ruth?"

Ruth pushed aside the curtain. Luke eyed Krista, concern etching his forehead.

"Can he stay with me?" Krista said.

Ruth sighed. "Okay, but just until we take you up for the scan. I'll be right back."

Ruth disappeared and Luke stood there, waiting. For what, permission to step closer?

Krista wanted to reach for his hand, but felt it was inappropriate. Still, she wished she had someone's hand to hold on to. Mom. Gran. Someone.

A wave of loneliness washed over her. She touched the silver charm at her neck and found solace.

"How are you feeling?" Luke stepped closer, within inches of her bed.

She sensed his uneasiness. Why, because he didn't like hospitals? Or was it something else?

"My head hurts, but otherwise I'm okay," she said.

"Can you tell me exactly what happened at the tea shop?" He pulled out a small notebook.

Back to business.

"A guy grabbed me, demanded my purse, then threw me to the ground. I hit my head on the counter as I fell."

He scribbled something, then pinned her with intense blue eyes. "Why did you leave the party? What were you thinking?"

She was put off by his anger and critical tone.

"The alarm tripped and I figured the girls were having trouble setting it, so Natalie and I went to reset it. What did you expect me to do?"

"Be smarter than that."

"Excuse me?" She'd never seen this rude side of him.

He stepped closer. "You need to accept that this situation is dangerous, Krista. You have to…" His voice trailed off. He snapped his notebook shut. "Never mind."

He shoved his notebook into his jacket pocket and turned to leave.

She was physically bruised and emotionally exhausted. She needed comforting words, not a lecture. Yet she suspected Luke's reaction had more to do with something in his past than Krista's experience today. She sensed he felt…guilty.

"Wait," she said.

He hesitated beside the curtain. A few seconds later he turned to her, his eyes guarded.

"I'm a small-town girl, Luke. I run a tea shop and attend church every Sunday and, well, stuff like this is foreign to me. I get that you deal with it every day, so you're smarter—"

"Don't. I shouldn't have said the thing about being smarter, that was…"

"Mean?"

He glanced at the floor. "Yeah, mean."

"But you said it because—" she hesitated "—you feel guilty?"

Clenching his jaw, he snapped his attention to her eyes. He leaned away from her, as if she'd exposed him.

"It's not your fault," she said. "It's not my fault either. How could I know someone really tripped the alarm? We've had problems with it for months. The girls don't set it often, so it would make sense they'd have difficulties."

"If I would have been at the house, I would have gone with you."

"We can't be together twenty-four/seven."

"We can and we will be. No arguments."

The determination in his voice surprised her.

"It's the only way I'm going to nail Garcia," he added.

Right. The case. This had nothing to do with Luke wanting to keep her safe because he cared about her. This was all about nailing the bad guy.

She studied his clenched jaw and piercing eyes. "Why is this case so important to you?"

"It's my job."

"I sense there's more to it."

He glanced down, as if he didn't want her looking too long into his eyes for fear she'd see something he desperately wanted to keep hidden.

"Luke?"

"Garcia killed my partner. In front of me."

A chill skittered down her arms.

"I'm so sorry." She reached out and touched his jacket sleeve, a natural, compassionate act. Luke glanced at her hand. She thought he might pull away.

"I've gotta call in." He stepped back, breaking the connection. "Don't go anywhere without me." With a nod, he walked out.

More like ran. From her.

Krista sensed he hadn't told many people about his partner, and she suspected Luke blamed himself for his death. But why?

She'd probably never find out. Truly, what mattered most was that he caught Garcia and closed down his business so he couldn't make money off hooking children on drugs.

Krista still couldn't believe the ugliness had permeated the small town of Wentworth. The tourist town of not quite three thousand was known for its vacation activities, access to both White Lake and Lake Michigan and an annual summer festival. She couldn't fathom how crime had edged its way into the safe community.

But after today's break-in, she could no longer hope that her garage attacker was some teenager out for a thrill.

Now Grace's Tea Shop had been broken into, as if someone was looking for something very specific.

"The shop," she whispered, searching the chair next to her for her purse. She should call the Sass girls and ask if they'd clean up, restock the teas for tomorrow's business.

Nurse Rankin came around the corner with a clipboard in her hand. "Where's the boyfriend?" She winked.

"He's not my boyfriend."

"He sure acts like it."

"He's…" She didn't like keeping the truth from people in town, but knew that for Luke to solve the case he had to keep his identity a secret. "He's the protective type."

"Men only protect women they're interested in, honey. He's cute."

"I hadn't noticed."

"Uh-huh." Ruth placed the clipboard on the bed and pulled the gurney away from the wall.

Ruth wheeled Krista out of the emergency room to the elevator.

"I need to make a call," Krista said.

"After the scan." Ruth glanced over her shoulder. "Don't look now, but we're being stalked."

"What? Who?" Krista leaned up on her elbow and glanced over her shoulder.

Luke walked a couple of feet behind them. He shot her a comforting smile.

"That protective boyfriend of yours isn't letting you out of his sight, is he?" Ruth pushed.

"It's been a wacky twenty-four hours."

"I heard about the lavender garden sniffer and the Bender kid shooting out your windows.

"He didn't shoot out the windows. Just fired off some rounds, I guess. And tonight someone broke into the shop."

"What for? Your hazelnut scone recipe?"

"I have no idea."

"McIntyre," Luke said.

Ruth glanced over her shoulder. "Sir, you can't use a cell phone—"

"When? How many? Hang on." Luke rushed past Krista and pointed at the nurse. "Don't let her out of your sight."

Chapter Six

Two of Garcia's suspected henchmen were spotted boarding a plane for the States.

Then who the hell broke into the tea shop and attacked Krista?

"Destination?" Luke asked his boss.

"Chicago, so maybe it's not related to your case."

"Chicago, Detroit, they're equidistant from Wentworth. But I'm afraid someone's already here."

"Why?"

"In addition to the attack last night, someone broke into the tea shop just now." Luke glanced across the town square where city workers were putting up Christmas decorations. Krista was attacked, nearly killed, and yet life went on as if nothing had happened.

"You think one of Garcia's men broke into the shop?"

"Can't be sure," Luke said. "If not, and it's someone from a rival drug organization, it could mean a drug war is brewing."

"Two rival groups after the same thing. But what?"

"I think her luggage is the key."

"Still missing?"

"Yes, sir."

"I'll put agents in Chicago on alert to find and tail Garcia's men once they land. Is the woman all right?"

"Says she's fine, but they're doing a CT scan to be sure."

"Ready for backup?" Agent Marks said.

"Not yet. More strangers in town will stir suspicion. I don't want to scare off the local contact. He's our best link."

"Have you gone through the list of people who went on the mission trip?"

"Was about to when the tea shop was hit." He'd been going over the list of names with the chief, flagging a few and forwarding them to the office for background checks. Then they got the call that the tea shop had been hit.

"Stick close to the girl. She's our best lead."

"Yes, sir."

He pocketed the cell phone and glanced up at the gray sky. It smelled like snow.

He hesitated before going back into the hospital, needing a minute to ground himself. Seeing Krista hurt, lying on the ground, had ripped open the old wounds. She shouldn't have gone to the tea shop, especially without him. What was she thinking?

She thought the girls were having problems setting the alarm and they needed her help.

Krista was always thinking about others, helping others. Knowing this was her M.O., it was Luke's job to put her first, make sure she was safe and protected.

He'd take her home and set the ground rules: He was going to be her handyman whether she liked it or not.

He would always be close, within arm's reach when she went into work, to make sure she was safe.

Not an easy assignment for Luke. She was bright and cheerful, even in the face of danger. He suspected she got that energy from God, something Luke had turned his back on years ago. She was lucky to have that kind of faith.

He wasn't sure he knew how to comfort a traumatized Krista, but her faith kept her strong.

"Comfort her? What are you thinking about?" he muttered.

This wasn't about Krista, the woman. It was about Krista, his lead to busting a major drug dealer. Losing his perspective could get them both hurt, or worse. Garcia showed no mercy when dealing with his enemies. He killed as easily as he ate lunch.

With that thought, he marched back into the clinic to find Krista. He wasn't sure why this woman got to him and he didn't care. He'd fight it, shove the edginess deep down so it wouldn't cloud his goal: nailing Garcia.

And getting out of Wentworth.

"I'm really fine," Krista said, as Luke walked her to his car.

He eyed her with suspicion.

"Okay, so I have a headache." She pinched her fore-finger and thumb together. "A teensy one."

"You're lucky you only have a minor concussion."

"I'm lucky you showed up when you did. That's twice now."

"You're welcome. Just so we're clear, I'm officially taking the job as your handyman and personal body-guard. No discussion."

"I'm too tired to argue."

"Good." He opened the car door.

"Krista? Krista!" Alan called, rushing across the parking lot.

"Hi, Alan."

The man ignored Luke and hugged Krista. With a sigh she pressed her cheek against his chest. Luke clenched his jaw.

"I'm fine." Krista broke the embrace. "I'm really fine."

"You need to close the shop," Alan said. "At least until this guy's caught."

"Absolutely not. If I close for a few days this time of year I might as well close up for good."

"Is it worth your life?"

"Hey," Luke warned. "No one's out to kill her."

Alan turned to Luke. "You don't know that."

"Who on earth would want to hurt this sweet woman?" Luke let slip.

"I have no idea, but twice in twenty-four hours—"

"Enough. I need to get her home to rest."

Krista was looking a little pale.

"I'll take her," Alan said, puffing out his chest.

"I've got it, thanks."

Alan blocked Luke from Krista. Luke didn't want trouble, although he was tempted to put this guy in a headlock and leave him gasping in the parking lot.

"Look, man," Luke started. "The chief will have my head if I don't do exactly what he asked. He asked me to see Krista safely home."

Luke stepped around the guy and opened the car door for Krista.

"Thanks," Krista said to Alan, then slid into the front seat. Luke shut the door and turned to Alan.

"If you know anything about someone wanting to hurt her, you'd better tell the chief."

The man's face hardened. "I don't know anything."

Luke studied the guy, his receding hairline, cold, judgmental eyes and thin lips. He fit way too many criminal profiles for Luke's taste.

"Good night." With a curt nod, Luke got behind the wheel and pulled out.

Just as he'd suspected, Alan was trying to make Krista nervous with his comment about her choosing between the tea shop and her life. What a ridiculous statement, at least for a local who knew nothing about the possible drug connection to Peace Church. It seemed to Luke that Alan's goal was to frighten Krista into giving up her business, giving up her independence, so she'd be dependent on others. On Alan, perhaps?

Now there's a manipulative way to get the girl of your dreams. Didn't take Luke long to figure out Alan had a major crush on Krista, but it was also obvious that Krista wasn't interested. At least it was obvious to Luke.

"I really appreciate this," she said.

"What, driving you home?"

"And offering to be my undercover bodyguard."

"It's nothing."

"Yeah, you haven't seen my handyman list of chores yet."

He appreciated her sense of humor when he knew she must still be rattled by tonight's assault.

"As long as you don't ask me to rewire the place. Not so good with electrical."

"How about hanging Christmas lights? The Christmas tea events start before Thanksgiving. Have to satisfy the tourists who come out here to shop for Christmas."

"Smart businesswoman."

"I try."

"That's why you won't close, even for a few days? We could wrap this thing up and you'd be—"

"I said no to Alan and I've known him for ten years. What makes you think I'm going to change my answer for you?"

"I carry a badge?"

"Not impressed, sorry." She smiled.

He snapped his gaze from her and stared hard at the tree-lined street ahead. He had to. That adorable smile threatened to make him forget why he was in Wentworth.

"So, what's the deal with Alan?" he said.

"He's a nice guy."

"But?" Luke pushed.

"But what?"

"It's obvious he likes you, a lot."

"I know." She slumped back against the seat.

"But you don't return the feelings. So, what's the problem?" Luke mentally scolded himself. He had no right asking her such a personal question. Yet a part of him wanted to know what qualities a woman like Krista looked for in a man.

"The problem is, I'm an independent woman. I know Alan's type. He'd suffocate me."

"Ah, the possessive type?"

"Possessive, protective, controlling."

"Sounds like there's a story there."

"I don't like to gossip."

Just as well, Luke didn't want her sharing personal feelings about another man. He shouldn't care.

But he did.

They pulled onto her street and a handful of cars were lined up in front of her house.

"The party's still going?" she said, with a desperate quiver to her voice.

"I doubt it. They're probably hanging around to make sure you're okay."

He pulled into the driveway and eyed the house. Light spilled out from the windows, giving it a warm and inviting glow. If only the houseful of friends would stay 24/7. The power in numbers would surely keep Krista safe.

But then these locals didn't know about the real danger threatening Krista.

Natalie rushed to the passenger side of the car and yanked open the door. "You're okay, thank God."

Krista got out of the car and Natalie gave her a hug.

"I'm fine, just a headache," Krista said.

Just a headache? He bet her head throbbed like a jackhammer pounding cement. Luke got out of the car and followed the women to the house.

Krista slowed as they approached the back porch. "Who's inside?"

"Timothy, Julie Sass and the girls and Pastor White. They're helping clean up and they wanted to make sure you were okay. Don't worry, they're not staying."

Krista sighed. "Thanks."

Natalie led Krista toward the house and Luke hesitated. "Krista?"

She turned to Luke.

"Don't forget, I'm close." He pointed to the garage.

"You could always come inside and help us clean up," Natalie said.

But he couldn't, couldn't handle being surrounded by so much love, so much compassion.

"It's okay," Krista said, touching his coat sleeve. "You've done plenty. Thanks."

Natalie looped her arm through Krista's and led her up the porch steps. As they opened the back door, cheers echoed from the house.

The door slammed on the welcoming sound, shutting Luke out. Yet he stood there for a few seconds. He wasn't sure why.

"You got work to do." He went back to the car and got the files. He'd take them up to his room in the garage and get started on identifying connections between mission volunteers and the drug ring.

Working would keep his mind focused and his thoughts off of the beautiful Krista Yates.

Krista wasn't sure where she got the energy to open the next day, so she thanked the Lord for the much-needed strength.

She made a pot of coffee at home, threw in a couple of pieces of toast and was ready when Luke knocked at eight. She handed him a mug of coffee and piece of toast with peanut butter.

He was dressed more casually today. He'd traded his dress slacks, collared shirt and tie for jeans, a Chicago Bears sweatshirt over a black T-shirt and gym shoes. He leaned against the counter as he ate, Anastasia weaving between his legs. Luckily Luke wasn't much of a morning person either. Either that or he wasn't sleeping well in her drafty garage.

Guilt snagged her conscience.

"You warm enough up in the attic?" she asked, and took a bite of her toast.

"I'm fine."

"You sure?"

"I can take care of myself, no worries." He sipped his coffee.

"You're sleeping okay?"

"Not really."

"Because it's cold?"

"Because I'm worried about you." He dipped his toast in his coffee. "I've decided to get you a dog."

"What?"

"A watch dog will alert me if someone's outside."

"I can't have a dog. Anastasia—"

"I'll keep the dog outside with me."

"And when you leave?"

"We'll deal with that when the time comes."

"I don't need a dog."

"Everybody needs a dog."

That comment shocked her. Dogs were lovable and loyal and wonderfully innocent. She would have a dog except it would interfere with her travels and long work hours. It just wasn't fair to the pet.

Anastasia, on the other hand, was independent and low maintenance.

"You ready?" he asked, rinsing his plate and mug.

"Yeah." She grabbed her purse from the counter.

When she turned, he was standing a bit close, looking deeply into her eyes.

"You sure you're up to this?"

He acted like she was about to take the stage in front of a thousand people. He sounded like he really cared about her. She studied his bright blue eyes and caught herself. *Silly girl. He's a cop out to nail a criminal.*

"The question is, are you sure you're up to my handyman list?" she shot back.

"Already put tools in the car."

"All right, then."

He led her out of the kitchen, triple-checked the lock on the back door, and they took off. When they pulled into the tea shop parking lot she noticed her little Ford Focus parked in the corner. She'd forgotten she'd left it behind last night.

She'd tried to completely forget what happened last night, the shock of the intruder, his hard grip and verbal demand for her purse. But why? She didn't carry more than twenty dollars in there.

It wasn't a random purse snatching and you know it.

"Hey, you okay?" Luke asked, pulling up next to her car.

Great, now the guy could tell when she was sliding into the dark, scary places of her mind?

"Busy day ahead," she said and got out of the car. She didn't want to talk about any of it anymore: Garcia, the house intruder the other night, the break-in at the shop.

She wanted life to get back to normal. She approached the back door, deactivated the alarm and stuck her key in the door.

"Hang on, let me do the honors." Luke smiled and acted as if this was a polite gesture, not a protective one.

He swung the door open and stepped inside. Krista followed, her heartbeat thumping against her throat with the panic of what she'd find.

Oh, good grief, you can't be afraid of going to work.

She glanced in the direction of the tea racks. They'd

been restocked with new glass jars filled with the twenty-three varieties of teas she kept on hand for customers. Someone had been busy last night. They'd cleaned up the tea and glass on the floor, found new jars upstairs and restocked everything.

She must have beamed because Luke winked at her.

"The tea fairies were here, huh?"

"It's good to have friends."

His smile faded. Reading pain in his eyes, she regretted saying the words and didn't know how to make him feel better.

"I'll pull the chairs down off tables while you work on my handyman list." Luke went into the dining area and got to work.

Krista checked the reservation book. They only had one, a table for four, which was good considering the decorating Krista wanted to get done for Christmas. Sure, some folks thought decorating a week before Thanksgiving was a little premature, but Krista couldn't get enough of Christmas and all it represented.

She put on a pot of coffee and started warming soups. There were enough frozen scones to hold her through the first rush, but she should probably bake more.

Krista checked the restaurant voice mail. There was only one message from the nearby Michigan Shores Resort, asking to reserve a table of six for their guests. They would be filling up for the holidays. The resort, run by Don and Marilyn Baker, put on fantastic events around the holidays.

Tourism kept the economy alive around here, but money wasn't the only reason Krista wanted the family tea shop to thrive. She loved offering people a place to gather and relax, share stories and laugh.

Of course, a man like Luke McIntyre would never understand that motivation. He was all business. She wondered when was the last time he laughed and what it sounded like.

"So, you got my list?" Luke said, coming up behind her.

"We'll start with decorating."

"For Christmas."

"Yep. Upstairs in the corner of the office are four boxes marked 'Christmas.'" She rubbed her hands together. "This is going to be fun."

"Bah humbug." He turned and disappeared up the stairs.

She wished she could brighten his attitude, make God and Christmas and community seem less threatening, but she guessed that would take a miracle.

"The Christmas season is upon us," she whispered with hope in her heart.

Christmas was a time for celebrating the birth of our Lord, a time to rejoice and be thankful. And Krista was thankful, for so many things.

She pulled the laptop out from the cabinet below the counter and powered up. She hadn't checked e-mail since she'd been home, not that she expected anything exciting. After all, everyone she knew lived in this small town and knew of her return, and the disastrous twenty-four hours that followed.

"Positive thoughts," she whispered.

Because it was a quiet day and Luke was here to put up the decorations, she'd sneak in a moment to upload a few more photos to her blog. She pulled the thumb drive off her keychain and inserted it into the laptop.

Luke pounded down the stairs into the kitchen with box number one. "You going to help me?"

"Yeah, in a sec. I haven't checked e-mail since I've been back and want to update my blog."

"You've got a blog?" He put the box down on the counter.

"Yep."

"You blog about your cat, right?" he teased.

"Sometimes. But mostly I try to inspire people, which is why I'm posting photos from my mission trip." She typed in "proverbsbabe3.com" and clicked Go.

"What's the three for?"

"My lucky number. It symbolizes the Trinity and there are three people in my family."

She waited for the blog to open. And waited. "I need a faster computer."

It finally popped open, but her page was blank. Then, suddenly, the image of a coffin floated across the screen.

Chapter Seven

"What the...?" Krista said.

Luke nudged her out of the way. "Someone broke into your account."

"How can they do that? Why would they do that?"

"Could be kids messing around." But Luke knew that possibility was slim. "Let's not assume anything until I check it out. Get me your Internet provider information and pass codes and I'll have my people look into it."

"Okay, thanks." She went upstairs to her office.

Luke knew it was safe up there because he'd checked it out when he got the box of Christmas decorations. He eyed the screen with the floating coffin. What had this woman stepped into? Now they were coming after her online?

Holiday music drifted through the shop from the corner speakers. She must have turned it on upstairs. Although it brightened most people's lives, Christmas songs were just another reminder of the things Luke never had: thoughtful gifts of love, family gatherings, turkey with cranberry sauce and stuffing.

His dad had died in a freak car accident when Luke

was only five, leaving Mom to raise him by herself. Mom could barely pay the light bill much less buy unnecessary presents for her kid. She did the best she could on her secretary's salary. For the first few years after Dad's death, their local church had provided them with holiday meals and presents from strangers.

Luke felt ashamed about needing handouts. At ten he told his mom he didn't want anything from the church people. He'd rather go without than suffer the embarrassment of kids at school knowing what he got for Christmas because, well, their families footed the bill.

He wondered if that's what drove Krista to being so independent. He'd read her background, knew about her father's murder and her mother moving to Wentworth when Krista was young.

It seemed he and Krista had more in common than Luke wanted to admit, only, Luke never found comfort in a God who took both of his parents away.

"Hey, is Natalie here?"

Luke turned to the back door. Timothy, Natalie's fiancé, stepped into the kitchen.

"I haven't seen her."

"Huh. I thought she said to meet her here at nine."

"We don't open until eleven," Luke said.

"We?" the man chuckled.

Luke didn't answer. He didn't have to explain himself to this guy.

"So you're the chief's friend from New York?" Timothy strolled into the kitchen and leaned against the counter to face Luke.

"I don't remember saying I was from New York, but yes, I'm friends with the chief."

"What's your interest in Krista?"

Luke narrowed his eyes at the guy. "Who wants to know?"

"My fiancée, actually. She can't figure out why you're always hanging around."

"The chief is worried about Krista and asked me to keep an eye on her."

"Yeah, well, there are lots of guys who would kill for that job. Why you?"

"Maybe because I'm former military and the chief trusts me to follow orders?"

Timothy nodded and glanced at the laptop. "Whoa, what happened there?"

"Either the site is down or someone broke in. Not sure yet."

"Kinda strange, all this stuff that's been happening. Someone breaks into Krista's house, the shop and now her computer?"

"A lot of action for a small town."

Timothy crossed his arms over his chest. "Yeah, ever since you showed up."

The guy was a few inches shorter than Luke but built like a wrestler. Still, Luke didn't want to get into a shoving match in the shop.

"You accusing me of something?" Luke said.

"I just don't like coincidences. And since my fiancée is best friends with Krista, I feel protective of both of them."

"It's not me you have to worry about."

"Yeah, then who?"

"How would I know?" Luke said.

Good thing Luke left his shoulder firearm in the glove box. He'd be too tempted to threaten idiot Tim with it. Luke had left it in the car out of respect for

Krista; plus, it wasn't easy hiding a firearm when you were only wearing a T-shirt and jeans.

"I think you know a lot more than you're saying." Timothy leaned closer.

Great. He really wanted a fistfight here, in the shop?

"Hey, Timothy," Krista said, breezing up to them with a file folder. "You looking for Nat?"

Timothy kept his gaze focused on Luke. "She was supposed to meet me at nine for scones."

"Huh, she didn't tell me. I usually wouldn't be here this early, but we've got to get the Christmas decorations up."

"Yeah, well, she probably had problems with that old clunker of hers."

"Wouldn't surprise me," Krista said, setting down the file.

A few seconds of silence passed. Timothy didn't move to leave. Luke didn't budge from his spot in front of the laptop. Krista glanced from Timothy to Luke and back to Timothy.

"What'd I miss?"

"Not a thing," Luke said.

"Great, then here's the information you asked about." She handed Luke the file and smiled at Timothy. "You want to help decorate?"

"Maybe another time. Natalie and I would love to help out."

"Oh, okay."

Luke heard the question in her voice.

"Take care, Krista." Timothy kissed her on the cheek and left.

Krista stood in the doorway for a minute and watched him leave. "What on earth was that about?"

"He thinks I brought trouble to town."

She snapped around, blond strands of hair breaking free from her clip and trailing down the side of her face. "That's ridiculous."

"He doesn't know me, Krista. And everything started happening when I showed up. It's logical."

"But untrue and unfair to accuse you."

"He's being protective. Nothing wrong with that."

"I wish you could tell everyone who you really are."

"Bad idea. I have a better chance of finding the drug contact in Wentworth by being as nonthreatening as possible. I'm just a guy, passing through town to visit his friend."

She planted her hands on her hips as if gearing up for an argument. She looked adorable.

He tapped the file folder to his palm. "I'm going to the car to call this in. I'll be right back."

"Good, because we have holly to hang."

"Can hardly wait."

It was bad enough that Timothy stopped by and gave Luke a hard time, but an hour later Alan made his daily appearance.

"Just checking in on my favorite girl," he said, coming in for a kiss. Krista turned her cheek.

This had to stop.

"I'm fine, Alan, truly." And she was getting really tired of people checking on her.

She'd received a phone call earlier from Mom and Lenny asking if she wanted them to fly to Michigan because they'd heard someone had broken into the house. Then Timothy stopped by, Natalie made an appearance and now Alan was thrusting himself into her life. They needed to stop suffocating her.

And she needed to focus on getting the shop ready to open for the lunch rush, which meant she had to get rid of Alan so she could finish decorating with Luke.

"I called early this morning. Didn't you get my message?" Alan asked.

"I was tired. Look, Alan, I have a lot of work to do this morning. Can we talk later?"

"How about dinner?"

Alan was a decent man and she didn't feel right dumping him abruptly, although in her mind they were never together. Out of respect for his feelings, she'd agree to have dinner.

"How about a sandwich at Ruby's Pub?" she offered.

"I was thinking we could drive into Grand Rapids for a more romantic setting."

Just then, Luke came downstairs with another box of decorations and nodded as he passed them on his way into the dining room.

"What's he doing here?" Alan scowled.

"Ruby's Pub," Krista confirmed. "I'll meet you there at seven."

"I could always stay and help decorate." He spied around the corner at Luke.

"We're almost done. Thanks anyway." She led Alan to the back door. "Go on. I'll see you later."

He turned to hug her goodbye, and the shop's phone rang, praise the Lord. "Gotta go."

She shut the door behind him and went to answer the phone. Luke came around the corner and grabbed it.

"Hello?" he said, then eyed the phone and hung up. "Wrong number."

"More like you scared them off."

"How do ya figure?"

"They call Grace's Tea Shop and a deep male voice answers 'hello'," she imitated.

"I don't really sound like that, do I?" He smiled.

In the flash of a second she realized she shared a comfortable connection with Luke that she'd never felt with other men, especially not Alan.

"What?" he said, studying her.

"Nothing, just an aha moment."

"Want to share?"

"Nope. Like to keep you guessing." She strolled into the dining room. The tree filled the corner of the shop, the holly garland was strung from the windows and photographs in holiday frames lined the mantel over the fireplace. "Looking good, handyman."

"One more box and we're done with inside work. The other two boxes are outside lights." He turned to her. "You ready for customers?"

"Yep, food prep is done. We've only got two reservations, which is good because Tatum can't get here until one."

"So you're on your own," he said.

"Unless you want to strap on an apron and help me out up front."

"Uh, I'd probably break your dainty cups."

"They're stronger than they look."

"I'll bet they are."

His blue eyes captivated her, and for a second she forgot why this man had come to Wentworth. More like, she wished it wasn't because he was a federal officer out to get a drug-dealing killer. She wished...

With a forced smile, she turned her back to him and

dug into the box of decorations. She pulled out the first thing she touched: a ball of mistletoe.

Oh, boy.

"What is it?" he said.

"You've never seen mistletoe?"

"Not like that I haven't." He fingered it like a kid fascinated by a new toy. Then his eyes caught hers. "What do you want me to do with it?"

She couldn't help but glance at his lips. Talk about awkward.

"Hang it in the doorway." She shoved it at him and turned back to the contents of the box. *Focus,* she coached herself.

Why couldn't she feel this kind of attraction to a solid, safe man like Alan? Why did a guarded man in a violent career be the one who drew her in?

Shaking off her thoughts, she pulled out a box of ornaments and opened the top. She smiled as her eyes caught on the nativity scene ornament she'd made in the fifth grade. This was possibly her favorite: the birth of baby Jesus with the star sparkling above.

"What else did you find there?" Luke said, walking up to her.

"Ornaments for the tree." She placed the nativity scene ornament on the tree front and center.

"You make that?"

"Yep. I made most of these. They're dated on the back." She pulled out another ornament, this one of a cross with the word *Faith* running vertically down the center. "Dive in."

She and Luke hung ornaments for the next few minutes as soft holiday music filled the shop.

Krista hung the Kitten in a Box ornament. "I love this time of year."

Luke kept pulling out ornaments, putting some down and looking at others.

"There's nothing here dated before 1988. Guess you weren't much of an artist before then?"

"Actually, we had to leave those ornaments behind."

"Behind? Oh, right." He placed a lighthouse ornament on the tree.

"You know, don't you?" She eyed him.

"About?"

"Me and my mom fleeing California after my dad was killed."

"I read your background file." He placed his hands on his hips. "I'm sorry I brought it up."

She shrugged. "It was a long time ago."

But they both knew it still haunted her, especially considering recent events.

"I guess you were lucky to find a home here in Wentworth," he said.

"Yep, in a safe, quiet town. At least it was until this week."

Luke stepped closer and placed his hands on her shoulders. "Things will be safe again, I promise."

"I don't even know you, yet I totally believe you. How do you do that?"

He smiled. "Charisma?"

"I guess. Okay, you know all about me. When do I get to read your background file?"

He dropped his hands to his sides. "It would put you to sleep."

"I doubt that." She bent down for another ornament. "Come on, tell me about your family."

She grabbed a foam ornament covered with sequins

and started to place it on the tree. She paused at the odd expression on Luke's face.

"It's not a hard question," she prompted. "Where did you grow up? Do you have brothers and sisters? What made you become an federal agent?"

"What, you writing an article for the local paper?" He pulled an ornament from the box and casually placed it on the tree.

Krista sensed the tension in his body. She could see it in the way he held his shoulders.

"Hey, if you're going to be my shadow until this is over I'd like to know something about you," Krista said.

Luke hung the ornament and stared her down. "All you need to know is I'm going to keep you alive."

He turned and left the dining room.

Did she hit a nerve or what? Was it possible that Luke had an even darker history than Krista?

Fine, she wouldn't push him. She felt sure that given enough time he'd open up to her. *Why is it so important to you?*

"It shouldn't be," she muttered.

But it was. Probably because of the angst she read in his eyes when he wasn't covering with bravado or humor.

Krista finished with the last of the ornaments and carried the box into the back. Luke was nowhere to be seen. Yeah, he was probably hiding in his car. Whatever. She had to respect his need to keep his life private.

He came downstairs carrying another box. "I'm goin' outside to do the lights."

She grabbed her coat and followed him out the back door.

"Don't you have scones or something to bake?" he said, as if he didn't want her around.

Whenever his curt side popped out, she couldn't decide if she should turn and walk away, point her finger in his face and give him a lecture or shower him with compassion.

She chose compassion, because that was the most Christian thing to do. She grabbed the ladder and followed him to the front of the shop.

"I'm very particular about my lights," she said.

"I'll bet you are," he joked.

So he was covering with humor again. Interesting. She leaned the ladder up against the house and shook it to make sure it was secure.

He started up the ladder with the box in his hands.

"Careful," she warned.

"You're making me nervous."

"Sorry." She gripped the ladder so it wouldn't budge.

Luke slid the box onto the asphalt shingles and climbed onto the roof. "Okay, boss, where do I start?" he asked with a smile.

"String the bigger lights along the roof line. The clips should be there from last year."

Luke kneeled down and fingered the edge of the roof. "Okay. You want them to go all around the roof or just in the front?"

"All around, please."

"Yes, ma'am."

A car pulled into the lot with three ladies inside.

"Looks like you've got customers. I can handle this." She hesitated.

"Go on. I won't mess up, too badly." He disappeared to the other side of the roof and she headed inside to prepare for the first customers of the day.

Shucking her coat, she tossed it on the stairs going

up to the office and grabbed a few menus. She took a deep breath and greeted the three middle-aged women.

"Good morning, ladies," she said. "You have your choice of tables."

The short blonde woman with a round face pointed to the corner table by the tree and her friends followed.

"Have you ever been to Grace's Tea Shop before?" Krista asked.

"I came last year with my mom while staying at the Lakeside Resort. I'm back for a girls' weekend." She smiled at her friends.

"Sounds great. We specialize in high tea, offering three different versions."

The ladies sat down and Krista handed them menus. "We also have salads, soups and sandwiches. I'll give you a few minutes to—"

A loud bang echoed from outside, followed by pounding from the ceiling. Krista instinctively ducked and glanced out the window...

...just as Luke dropped off the roof.

Chapter Eight

Stunned, Luke struggled to breathe as he stared up at the gray November sky. What on earth just happened? He heard a loud crack, like a gunshot, lost his footing and tumbled off the roof.

Which meant someone was shooting at him? He had to get up, protect Krista.

He pinched his eyes shut against the frustrating paralysis of his lungs. That was the only thing he could feel right now, not the pain of a possible broken limb or concussion. He couldn't even tell where he'd been hurt. He just knew he had to have done some kind of damage in the fall.

"Luke?"

He looked up into Krista's warm green eyes. And for a second he felt a kind of peace he'd never experienced before.

Then panic set in.

"Got to..." He struggled for air to form the rest of his sentence. He had to get up, get her inside where it was safe.

"Don't move. An ambulance is on the way."

"No," he gasped. "Can't leave you."

"Don't argue with me or…or I'll fire you." She shot him a stern look and placed her hand to his chest.

Her touch made him relax, helped him focus. Should he tell her he'd been shot at? And that they could be aiming for her next?

No, it made no sense to kill Krista. Abduct her, maybe, but not kill her. She had something Garcia's men wanted. She'd be no good to them dead.

He got it together, took a deep breath. "You need to get inside."

The squeal of a siren echoed across the parking lot. "Help is here. Everything's going to be fine."

He didn't believe it, wouldn't believe it until he nailed Garcia and got this woman out of danger.

"Over here!" she called out.

A second later Officer West came into view.

"I was a block away when I heard your call. What happened?" Officer West asked.

"I heard a bang—"

"It sounded like a gunshot," Luke interrupted Krista.

With a nod, Officer West took a few steps away and spoke low into her radio.

Luke tried to push himself up, but Krista wasn't having any of it.

"Don't you dare move," she ordered. "The cops are here, the ambulance is coming. You just stay put."

"I'm fine." In truth he had no idea how fine he was until he stood up. "Get inside. You've got customers."

"They'll wait. You think that bang was a gunshot?"

"It sounded like it. I ducked, but lost my footing."

She glanced nervously over her shoulder. "Where is that ambulance?"

"Krista?"

She glanced at him. "I never should have asked you to put up my lights."

"Stop, this is not your fault." He placed his hand over hers. But he could tell she didn't believe him. "Help me up."

"I will not."

"Fine, then I'll get up by myself."

With a fortifying breath, he pushed off the ground and stood, wavering slightly against pain in his left ankle. Krista grabbed his arm for support.

"Hey, wait for the ambulance," Officer West said as the ambulance pulled into the parking lot.

"I don't need paramedics."

"Stop being a jerk and let them take a look at you," Krista argued.

"Is than an order, boss?"

"Yes, it is." She waved the EMTs over.

Luke didn't know any other way to deal with this situation than to try and lighten the mood. Deep down he was worried that if someone was bold enough to shoot at him in public, who knows what they'd do next.

To Krista.

Two EMTs rolled a stretcher over to the sidewalk.

"I don't need that." Luke started for the ambulance and Krista wouldn't leave his side. He wished she'd go into the shop, although he felt they were pretty safe out here with the cops and emergency crews swarming the lot. The perp would be a fool to take another shot at him.

If someone was shooting at him, that meant he'd blown his cover.

Clenching his jaw against the pain, he hobbled to the

ambulance. It wouldn't hurt to let them get a look at his ankle, maybe wrap it for support.

He sat on the edge of the ambulance. "I'm not going to the hospital."

The younger EMT glanced at Krista. She shook her head. "He's a grown man. We can't force him."

"Sir, where are you hurt?" an older guy, with jet-black hair asked.

"My ankle." He stretched it out and winced.

"Okay, sir. We're going to check your vitals and your eyes for signs of a concussion."

Krista stayed close, nibbled at her fingernail. She looked worried, truly concerned about Luke's well-being. Sure she was. He was her only protection against Garcia.

"Krista!" Alan called from behind her.

She didn't budge from her spot next to Luke.

"Krista, what happened?" Alan nudged his way beside Krista.

"I fell off the roof," Luke said. He made eye contact with Krista and a silent understanding passed between them. He didn't want to discuss the shooting with just anybody. At this point Luke wanted to keep it between the chief, Officer West, Luke and Krista.

"Thank goodness you're okay," Alan said to Krista and pulled her aside.

Luke wanted her to stay close where he could keep an eye on her. Yeah, like he'd be able to protect her in his condition?

The older EMT checked his blood pressure, flashed a light in his eyes and then got a look at his ankle.

"Will I live?" Luke said.

"The ankle is definitely sprained, but I can't tell you

if it's broken until you get an X-ray." The guy straightened. "You probably have a concussion. You were lucky you landed on the pile of broken-down boxes."

Luke glanced across the parking lot. He was lucky it was recycling day and the shop's delivery boxes were stacked and laying just right to break Luke's fall.

"You sure we can't convince you to take a ride?" the EMT encouraged.

"No, thanks anyway."

"We'll wrap the ankle. Get crutches and stay off it for a couple of days," the younger EMT said.

"Will do."

Luke watched Krista and Alan across the parking lot as the younger EMT wrapped his ankle. He hated weakness of any kind, especially physical weakness. He had no intention of using crutches. It would make him look weak, vulnerable.

Luke stepped away from the ambulance, clenching his jaw against the pain. Officer West stepped up to him. "Need a hand?"

"I'm good, thanks."

Officer West glanced across the parking lot at Alan who was in a heated discussion with Krista. "That guy creeps me out."

"What do you know about him?"

"He moved here a few years ago to get away from the city. I guess he's some kind of techno geek. He's dense, that's for sure. I mean she obviously isn't interested."

Chief Cunningham pulled up and got out of his cruiser. "What in the name of sweet peaches happened here?"

Luke motioned him closer. "I heard what sounded like a gunshot and lost my footing. Fell off the roof."

The ambulance pulled out.

"Shouldn't you be going with them?" the chief asked.

"He's stubborn," Officer West said.

"Do I have to pull rank?" the chief threatened.

"Thanks for the concern, sir, but I'm really okay," Luke said. "Just a sprained ankle."

"Lucky you," the chief said. "Officer West, canvass the area and determine if anyone else heard anything resembling a gunshot."

"You don't believe me?" Luke said.

"I believe you, son. But let's rule out other possibilities first. There's construction on the north end of town, and the local mechanic could be working on a stubborn car. We'll do a canvass just to be sure."

"I'll radio in, sir." Officer West got in her patrol car and took off.

"Anything else you can tell me?" the chief said.

"No, sir."

"Okay, then get inside and ice that ankle before it blows up like a hot air balloon." He glanced across the parking lot. "Krista!"

She sidestepped Alan and rushed over to Luke and the chief. "Thanks, chief," she whispered.

The chief eyed Alan, who hovered in the parking lot for a minute before getting into his car.

"Take Luke inside and make him ice that ankle. I'll bring some crutches by later."

"I don't need crutches," Luke said.

"Yes, you do," Krista said, leading him to the back of the shop. She frowned and Luke eyed her.

"The chief thinks the sound could have been a car backfiring," Luke offered, hoping it would ease her concern. But he wasn't letting his guard down.

"It's not that." She got him set up at the employee break table in the back.

"What, boyfriend trouble?" He shifted into the chair with a groan.

"He's not my boyfriend." She scooped cubes into a dish towel. "I'd planned to clear things up with Alan tonight at dinner, but I can't leave you in this condition."

"It's a sprained ankle, Krista. I'll live. But I don't want you going anywhere without me."

"Three's a crowd, or haven't you heard?" She pulled out a second chair and she placed his foot on it.

She gently adjusted the ice pack to his ankle and he clenched his jaw against the cold.

"Don't worry about it," she said. "I need to make sure you take it easy."

He started to argue with her, then realized if a guilt trip kept her from running off to meet Alan, then Luke would go along.

He'd use whatever means necessary to keep her close and out of danger.

"Stop fretting." He motioned her to back off. "You've got customers."

"But you'll—"

"Stop babying me or I'll climb back on the roof and finish the lights."

"You wouldn't dare."

"Try me." He smiled.

"Okay, message received." With a shake of her head, she grabbed an order pad and disappeared into the dining room.

He pulled out his cell. If someone had been shooting at him that meant the threat was already here.

Only, why couldn't they see it? Especially the locals?

The chief seemed pretty sharp and on top of his game. He'd have to know about strangers in town.

Unless Garcia had enlisted the help of a local, someone that no one would suspect, someone they all trusted as one of their own. Luke needed the folder of names and background information he'd left in the car.

His foot was pounding and his head still buzzed from the fall, but he couldn't just sit here doing nothing. He grabbed the ice pack and placed it on the table. Pushing the chair back, he lowered his foot and started to get up.

"Don't even think about it," Krista said, walking into the kitchen. "You're staying put if I have to duct tape you to the chair."

The man was impossible. It was bad enough Krista had to run the shop single-handedly, but she also had to play babysitter to a stubborn federal agent who was cranky as anything.

But he was alive.

She sighed at the thought as she spread dilled cream cheese on a slice of bread. If he'd fallen differently off the roof…

No, she wouldn't go there. Things happened for a reason. Luke's job wasn't finished here in Wentworth. He was meant to survive the fall and close his case.

And make her life miserable in the process.

"I hate to bother you, but—"

"Give me two minutes," Krista interrupted him, wanting to put the finishing touches on the tea sandwich.

"I'm leaking," Luke said.

She turned to see a puddle forming on the hardwood floor.

"Shoot." She dropped the knife and rushed to him. She kneeled beside the chair and gently removed the ice pack. "I'm sorry."

"It's not your fault."

Just then, Tatum Sass waltzed into the back of the shop. "Whoa, did I interrupt something?"

"Just the first lunch rush," Krista said, racing across the kitchen to dump the towel in the sink.

"What happened to him?" Tatum asked.

"Fell off the roof," Luke said.

"What were you doing on the roof?"

"Hanging lights," Krista answered. "Which means I'm going to have to finish hanging them tonight after work."

"Oh, no, you're not," Luke argued.

"Boy, you guys sound like Tori and her old boyfriend. Argued all the time." Tatum hung up her jacket and grabbed an apron. "Status out front?"

Krista put on a new pair of gloves and went back to working on tea sandwiches. "You need to take a food order for table five, table three is waiting on the Duchess's Tea and table two is ready for a check."

"Check," Tatum joked.

"Go on, get out there. This order will be ready in five." Krista nodded at the three-tiered tower that was waiting for sandwiches, fruit and scones.

"Oh, and he needs more ice for his ankle," Krista said. "Can you do that first?"

"No," Luke protested. "It's better. Go on and take care of customers."

Tatum shrugged and went out into the dining room.

"It only would have taken her a minute," Krista said over her shoulder.

"Don't make me feel guilty about you neglecting your customers on my account."

"Why not? I already feel guilty about your injury."

"Stop, or I'm going to get my own ice."

She turned to him. "Don't you dare."

"Then stop worrying about me." He smiled and went back to studying the contents of his folder. A folder he wouldn't let Krista get from his car because he wouldn't let her out of his sight.

So he'd called the chief who'd sent Deanna West back to get Luke's keys and retrieve the folder. He'd been engrossed in the contents, jotting down notes and flipping pages for the past three hours.

When Krista slid a cup of soup and a sandwich in front of him, he'd barely noticed but managed to grunt out a "thanks." He was absorbed all right. She wished she knew what was so fascinating, but simply didn't have time to ask.

The second rush hit just about the time Tatum showed up. Thanks goodness for the teenager's arrival, and her efficiency.

Someone tapped on the back door. Good grief, if it was Alan again she was going to lose it. He'd called her every hour to make sure she was okay.

Instead, Chief Cunningham stepped into the kitchen. He nodded at Krista.

"Hey, chief," Krista said. "Need some lunch?"

"No, no, just stopped by to bring some crutches for gimp here." The chief offered the crutches to Luke.

"Thanks." Luke pushed the chair aside and stood on one foot, adjusting the crutches under each arm.

"Should fit about right. My son broke his leg a few

years ago. He's about your height." He motioned to the door. "You mind giving those a spin outside?"

Krista didn't miss the chief's subtle nod. She suspected he had news about the case and didn't want anyone overhearing. Still, Krista should be kept in the loop, shouldn't she?

Luke glanced at Krista. "I'll be right back."

Another group of four wandered into the shop, keeping Krista distracted from the goings-on outside. A good thing. Although she wanted to know what was happening with the case, and if someone had really taken a shot at Luke, she had to stay on top of her game if she was to serve customers.

Making delicious food presented in a beautiful manner, served in a charming setting was her ministry in life. Just like catching criminals was Luke's.

She wondered how many drug dealers or murderers he'd put away in his career as a federal agent. Well, she thanked God for people like Luke, men who were dedicated to justice and protecting innocent people.

She also thanked God for bringing Luke into her life at this tumultuous time. She realized that after knowing him only briefly, she'd miss him when this was over: his surly nature, teasing tone and protective attitude. But that was the way of things. It's not like she could ever have a relationship with a man who thrived on the rush of violence. She'd had enough violence in her life, thank you very much.

And once this drug-smuggling case was closed, she hoped to go back to her old, normal life. She sighed as relief washed over her. Or was it melancholy?

As she and Tatum cleaned up at the end of the day, Krista puzzled over Luke's mood. The chief had told him that the gunshot sound was actually a car's backfire. Dispatch received four calls about the same time Luke fell off the roof.

Luke didn't seem convinced.

"Dining room's done, sinks and coffeemaker are rinsed," Tatum said, planting her hands on her hips, waiting for orders.

"Then we're good." Krista untied her apron. "Not bad for just two of us."

"Cool." Tatum pulled out her cell phone. "And it's only four. Awesome. I've got plenty of time before my date."

"Gabe again?"

Tatum smiled. "Yup. Pizza and a movie in Muskegon."

"A movie." Krista leaned against the counter. "I haven't seen one of those in ages."

"I'll let you know if it's any good." Tatum grabbed her jacket and stepped into the doorway. "It's a romantic comedy called Sugar and Spies."

"The kid must really like you to sit through a chick flick," Luke interjected, closing his folder and leaning against the table to stand.

Krista rushed over to assist, but he put out his hand to stop her. She tried not to feel offended. Why wouldn't he accept her help?

"Bye, guys." Tatum breezed out the back.

"So, you hungry?" Krista said.

"Got a stop to make first."

"Where?"

"Surprise. You want to drive?"

He must be in more pain than he was letting on.

"Sure. Your car or mine?"

"Mine, if that's okay." Using the crutches, he managed his way to the door and scanned the surrounding buildings.

Krista set the alarm and locked up. "Where are we going?"

"The pound."

"But I can't have—"

"Look," Luke interrupted. "I've made up my mind on this. We could use the added security at your house."

It did no good to argue with him. The man was determined to get her a watch dog.

Wentworth didn't have a pound, so they ended up at an animal shelter one county over where, of course, she wanted to rescue all of the twenty-plus dogs barking and shivering and begging to go home with someone.

That is why she avoided these places. She couldn't stand the pain of seeing abandoned animals. She hugged her midsection and glanced down the center aisle at the poor creatures, God's creatures.

Luke touched her arm. "This upsets you. I'm sorry."

She shrugged. Luke placed his forefinger and thumb to her chin and lifted her gaze to meet his. "Look at it this way, we're saving one of these dogs tonight, right?"

She nodded. "But how do you choose?"

Luke scanned the row of barking dogs and a slow smile curved his lips. "That's him." He pointed his crutch at a barrel-chested, big white dog with a small, black-and-white head.

"Why him?"

"He's stubborn, he's a survivor. I can tell."

Krista wondered if Luke was describing the dog or himself. She wondered what else Luke had survived and how he'd managed to make it without the comforting hand of Jesus.

"What's his name?" she said.

They ambled toward the black-and-white dog.

Luke tilted his head to read the chart. "Roscoe." Luke leaned his crutches against the cage and kneeled down. "You wanna come home with me, buddy?"

Roscoe crouched low and barked, wagging his tail.

They checked out quickly thanks to Luke's federal ID. Krista suspected there would usually be a lot more paperwork and screening involved to make sure the people adopting the pet were qualified.

An hour later they pulled up at Krista's house. Luke and Roscoe headed for the garage. "Wanna check out your new home, buddy?"

Suddenly it dawned on Krista that Luke would have to manage the loft stairs on crutches. He must have read regret on her face.

"What?" he said. "I told you I'd keep him in the garage with me."

"The stairs."

"What about them?"

"Your crutches."

"Enough already. You need to stop worrying about me. Now, come on, help us get set up in the garage."

Krista couldn't stop worrying. She moved boxes around to make room for the dog kennel, and stacked more wood for the stove in case it turned bitter cold. Sure, the garage was heated, but it never seemed to get as warm as the house because of the peaked roof.

She was on her way back in with a pile of wood when something dropped from the loft. She shrieked and jumped back. Luke had tossed the mattress over the railing.

"You're going to freeze down here," Krista said.

"First you don't want me doing the stairs, now you don't want me sleeping down here."

He was right, everything coming out of her mouth sounded like an argument. She couldn't help it. She was worried about Luke, and more than she should be for a man just doing his job.

As she built a hearty fire, he came up behind her and touched her shoulder.

"Hey, relax for a second." He led her toward the stairs with a hand to the small of her back.

His hand felt warm and solid against her body, not itchy like whenever Alan touched her.

Alan. Drat.

"What time is it?" She pulled out her cell phone. It was only six.

"You late?"

"I told you, I had a dinner date, but I'm not going," she said, cutting off his protest. "Still, I need to call Alan."

Luke adjusted himself on the stairs and patted his leg. "Come here, buddy." Roscoe trotted over to him.

Krista walked to the doorway and made her call. Alan's voice mail picked up and she breathed a sigh of relief. It wasn't going to be easy letting him down.

"Hey, Alan, it's Krista. I'm sorry but we're going to have to reschedule dinner. I ran into a problem tonight." She glanced at Luke, who studied her with intense blue eyes. "But everything's okay, no worries." She turned away from Luke. "Call me and we'll figure out another time. Thanks. And I really am sorry."

She slipped her phone into her pocket.

"So, I'm a conflict?" Luke raised a brow.

"Well, it is a problem that you're hurt and need someone to look after you and since there's no one else in town—"

"I don't need looking after, but I don't want you going out with that guy alone, either."

"Come on, Alan's harmless."

"That's debatable." He narrowed his eyes at her. "Even so, you and I are joined at the hip, remember? At least until this case is closed."

"And then you're gone, off to save some other damsel in distress." She smiled at him.

Luke wasn't smiling. He clenched his jaw and his blue eyes darkened. Her heart raced at his intense expression.

With a tennis ball in his mouth, Roscoe nudged Luke's knee to play.

Luke broke eye contact and she had to remind herself to breathe. What had just happened?

"Where'd you get that, buddy?" Luke said.

"We've got all kinds of treasures in here," Krista recovered. "Boxes and boxes of family stuff."

Luke glanced at the shelves stuffed with boxes marked by year. Mom and Gran kept nearly every art project, every handmade Christmas ornament, Mother's Day projects and birthday presents Krista made them.

"I'm envious." Luke patted Roscoe's furry mane. "I mean, to have this kind of history of your life, to have family and friends."

"Surely you have friends."

"Had one."

She suspected his one friend was the partner who

was killed by Victor Garcia. She said a silent prayer
to the Lord to help open Luke's heart to people again.

To risk loving again.

"Brothers and sisters?" she tentatively asked.

"Nope, just me."

"What about your parents?"

Luke snapped his attention to her and her breath
caught at the pain in his eyes. She wanted to reach out,
touch his cheek and tell him everything was going to
be okay.

How crazy was that?

She glanced at his lips, just for a second, and found
herself wanting to kiss him to warm the chill from his
eyes.

"Krista," he whispered.

Did he sense her thoughts? Would he…kiss her?
She'd kissed a few other men, sure, but never a man
like this, a broken warrior bent on exacting justice.

Suddenly a low, menacing growl rumbled in Roscoe's throat.

Chapter Nine

Luke grabbed Roscoe's collar so he wouldn't bolt, and leaned close to Krista. "Take Roscoe and hide under the stairs until I tell you to come out," he whispered. He inhaled her floral scent, so incongruous to the danger hovering outside the garage.

"But—"

He placed his forefinger to her lips. Not a good idea.

"Go on," he ordered.

She nodded and led the dog beneath the stairs. Once they were out of sight, Luke slipped his off-duty revolver from his ankle and started for the door.

He didn't like waving a gun around in Krista's presence. It upset her and the look in her eye made him feel like a monster.

Luke hobbled out of the garage into the night, barely noticing the pain of a sprained ankle thanks to the adrenaline rush. The chill cleared his focus and he made his way along the side of the house to the front.

The sound of pounding made him hesitate. Someone was trying to break into her house in the front.

Luke turned the corner and aimed his firearm at a tall, skinny guy, mid-twenties with spiked red hair.

"Freeze!" Luke ordered.

"Don't shoot!" The guy stumbled backward.

Luke flashed his badge. "I'm a cop. Who are you?"

"Flower delivery for…for…" He looked at the gift card. "For Krista Yates."

"Bring it down here."

With a nervous nod, the guy walked down the stairs toward Luke.

"ID," Luke said.

The guy blinked, staring at Luke's gun.

"Put the flowers down and show me some ID."

With trembling hands, the guy put the flowers on the ground and pulled out his wallet. His license read Brent Baker of Wentworth.

"Hands against the porch, Brent," Luke said. He wasn't taking any chances.

Brent turned around and grabbed the porch railing. Luke shoved the gun into the waistband of his jeans and patted down Brent. He didn't find a firearm, but found a multifunctional pocketknife clipped to his belt.

Luke snapped it off and waved it in the guy's face.

"Come on, man, everyone's got one of those," Brent protested.

"Luke?"

Luke snapped his attention to Krista who was peeking around the house.

"I told you to stay in the garage," Luke snapped.

Brent took a few steps away from Luke.

"Where are you going, kid?" Luke said.

The guy put his hands out. "I don't need a tip, it's fine, really, it's okay."

The guy stared at Luke's gun, tucked in his waist-band, then glanced up at Luke, terrified.

Luke was losing it, suspecting everyone and their sisters of being involved in the Garcia conspiracy. Brent was an innocent kid who'd crossed paths with a crabby agent thanks to a sprained ankle and lack of sleep.

"Sorry." Luke pulled a five-dollar bill from his wallet and handed it to the guy. Brent took another step back.

"Go on, take it," Luke said as pleasantly as he could.

Brent dodged forward, snatched it and ran. He jumped in his van and peeled out.

"Your knife!" Luke called after him. But he was halfway down the block. Luke slipped the knife into his jeans pocket.

"What's this?" Krista approached Luke, Roscoe following close behind. She kneeled beside the flowers and pulled the card from the outside of the package.

"Hang on, let me check it out first," Luke said.

She looked up and smiled. "You're kidding, right?"

"No, ma'am."

"It's just flowers." Her expression was a cross between disbelief and anger.

"We can't be too careful—"

"Okay, fine. Take it." She shoved the card at his chest and went around back.

He couldn't blame her for being upset. Her life had been turned upside down and crooked, all because she'd gone on the mission trip, done something selfless and good, without expecting anything in return.

She certainly didn't expect danger to follow her back to Wentworth.

Luke picked up the flowers and hobbled around to

the back porch. The mutt pranced beside him. "Good boy, Roscoe."

The dog had done his job, alerting them to potential danger.

Luke sat on the back porch and put his weapon back in his ankle holster. He carefully unwrapped the flowers to reveal a colorful bouquet in a glass jar with a red ribbon. He fingered the card feeling a bit like a jerk, but he had to be suspicious of everything and everyone.

Except Krista. Her innocence and compassion was the only truth he knew for sure. That, and he wouldn't let anyone hurt her.

He ripped open the card. It read: Looking forward to tonight. Love, Alan.

Love? Did the guy really think she loved him when it was painfully obvious she didn't have strong feelings for the guy?

He shoved the note into the envelope and blew out a slow, deep breath. Alan definitely knew what he wanted and wasn't giving up.

Well, that made two of them. Luke wasn't going to let Garcia's men get to Krista. So Alan and Luke had something in common: They both cared about Krista.

Cared about her? *Only in relation to the case, buddy. Don't lose your head.*

Luke stood, picked up the flowers and started for the back door. The adrenaline rush from their unexpected visitor had worn off, and the ankle pain was back, irritating him, making him feel weak and dependent. He tapped on the glass window of the back door with his knuckles.

Krista took her time answering. When she finally opened the door she wouldn't look at him.

"I'm sorry," he said. He hadn't a clue how those words slipped out. "The flowers are fine. I wish I could say they're from me." He joked, holding them out to her.

She took them and went into the kitchen. "Who are they from?" She turned to him. "You read the card, right?"

"Alan," he said.

She shook her head. "Oh, boy."

With a burst of excitement, Roscoe bolted past Luke into the kitchen.

"Roscoe, no!" Luke lunged for the dog and tripped on the threshold, grabbing for a chair, table, anything as he went down. Instead, he completely lost his balance and hit the kitchen floor with a thud.

Lying flat on his back, humiliation flooded his chest. Then the dog rushed him and started licking his face.

"Enough!" Luke said, grabbing him by the collar.

Luke scrambled to get control of the situation, pushing the dog away with one hand, while trying to sit up against the wall. It was more of a struggle than it should have been, and he was breathing heavily by the time he got control of things.

"Sit!" he ordered. Roscoe obeyed, his tongue hanging out, ready for more action.

Krista closed the back door and put her hand to her lips, covering up a smile that made her green eyes sparkle.

"What's so funny?" he said, with more edge than necessary. But he didn't like being out of control, looking like a fool.

"Sorry, you just, for a second you seemed like—"

"What, stupid?"

"No, human."

Which meant she thought him nonhuman before?

"Wait, that's not the right word," she corrected, kneeling beside him. She pinned him with her green eyes and he couldn't look away. "I guess the word is relaxed, laid-back, you know, not so uptight." She smiled, and he found himself wanting to brush his thumb across her lips to absorb her warmth. The thought created an ache in his chest for something he thought cold and dead.

"How about dinner?" She stood, breaking the spell.

"I should take Roscoe outside."

"No, I can gate off the kitchen so he won't terrorize Anastasia."

"Are you sure it won't be the other way around?"

"Very funny." She pulled an expandable gate from the pantry and set it up between the living room and kitchen.

"That should work." She pulled out a pot and filled it with water.

"Hang on, you've been cooking all day," Luke protested.

"I still have to cook for myself. Besides, I don't think it's a great idea for you to be standing at the stove, do you?"

"Guess not."

"What time did you take your last pain reliever?"

"Why, do I look that bad?"

"You do that a lot." She turned on the gas burner.

"What?"

"Avoid the question with a question."

"I'm used to asking questions, not answering them."

"No kidding."

He didn't miss the sarcasm in her voice.

"One-thirty," he answered.

"Five hours ago. You're due. I'll get the ice first."

She filled a dish towel with ice and put it in a plastic bag.

"Try not to leak this time." She winked and shifted the ice bag in place, studying his expression, probably to determine if she was hurting him.

He snapped his attention from her brilliant green eyes to his ankle, where she carefully adjusted the ice pack. He couldn't stand much more of this, her tending to him, icing his injury, making him dinner. It made him…edgy.

"What else can I get you?" she said, sounding like she really cared, like her goal in life was to take care of Luke.

He wanted her out of his space. Out of his head.

"You've done enough." He stared at the ice pack.

"Okay." She went to the stove and got out another pot. "Spaghetti sound good?"

"Anything's fine." He really needed to get out of here and away from the illusion of a woman cooking for him, nurturing him.

Loving him.

It wasn't real. It was all part of the job.

Her cell phone rang from her coat pocket and she glared at it.

"Not answering it?" Luke asked.

"It's probably Alan. This is going to be messy."

She filled a glass with water and brought him a few pain reliever tablets.

"You don't have to wait on me," he said.

She stared him down. "Okay, what's with you? You

obviously don't want me helping you. With anything. Why? What's the big deal?"

"I'm supposed to be protecting you."

"And you are."

He swallowed back the pills and stared at the dog.

"Look," she said. "People have been taking care of me my whole life. Now it's my turn. That's why I do the mission work, volunteer at church and run the tea shop. It's my way of returning the favor. I like doing it. I'd like to take care of you."

"No. Thank you."

"Why not?"

He snapped his gaze to meet hers. "I'm just not comfortable with it, okay?"

"Tough marshmallows." She went to the stove.

She wasn't going to give up and he wasn't sure how much fight he had left. He couldn't remember anyone ever taking care of him. Well, maybe Mom, before she got sick and their lives fell apart. But somewhere, deep down, he knew he didn't deserve someone's compassion, someone's love, and that was what caring for someone was about, right?

Krista's wall phone rang. "This can't go on all night or I'll go bonkers." She picked up the receiver.

"Hello...yes?"

She turned her back to Luke and he suspected it was Alan.

"I know...okay. I can't tonight. No, it's really not necessary. I understand but... Okay. Bye."

She sighed and hung up the phone.

"Bad news?"

She turned to him. "Alan. He wants to check in on me. I tried talking him out of it."

"No problem, I'll go back in the garage." Luke started to get up.

"You will do no such thing." She adjusted his arm around her shoulder to help him stand. "But you should probably sit in a chair instead of on my floor."

"I was getting used to your floor."

"Ha, ha." She pulled out a second chair and lifted his ankle, putting the ice pack on it. "Good, stay."

"Arf."

"See, how do you do that?"

"What?"

"One minute you're incorrigible and mean, and the next, you're joking around."

"I'm..." he paused. "Mean?"

"Sometimes, yeah." She planted her hands to her hips.

He glanced at his ice pack. She'd been good to him even though he'd ripped through her life like a lightning storm, blasting everything apart. "Sorry."

That was the second time he'd said that word tonight. Not like him. Not one bit.

Her wall phone rang again. "Oh, drat." She grabbed it. "Hello," she snapped. "Oh, hey, Nat. I thought you were...oh, no, I'm sorry. Hang on." Krista put her hand over the mouthpiece. "Can you give me a ride to and from work tomorrow?"

"Sure."

She turned back to her friend. "No problem, but it's at the shop, so you'll have to... I'm at home. No, I had to cancel, but I have a feeling he's coming over anyway.... Because I have to make sure Luke is okay."

"Luke can take care of himself," he called out.

She flashed her hand like a stop sign to silence him.

It was a small, cute hand, one he realized he'd probably crush if he tried to hold it.

Still, he'd like to try.

He rolled his neck. Man, he needed a good workout, something to get his balance back. Being around this woman made him go to strange places in his head, places he most certainly didn't belong.

"Sure, come over," she said to her friend. "Very funny. I'll see you later." She hung up and went back to the stove.

"More company?" Luke asked.

"Nat's Volvo died and she's supposed to meet Timothy in Muskegon for a romantic dinner, so she asked to borrow my car."

"And of course, you said yes."

"That's what friends are for." She opened a box of pasta and dropped it into the boiling water.

Friends. A foreign concept.

The slamming of a car door echoed from outside.

"Speaking of friends, that must be your boyfriend," Luke said.

"Could you watch the pasta?"

"Aren't you going to invite him in for dinner?"

"Probably not a good idea."

"Ah, he's the jealous type, I forgot."

She slipped errant strands of blond hair behind her ears, put on her jacket and hesitated. "If he does come in, you'll behave, right?"

Luke placed an open palm to his chest. "Like a true gentleman."

She shot him a half smile and went to greet Alan.

Luke got up to stir the pasta. He wasn't in the mood to verbally spar with Alan. Luke couldn't trust his edgy mood not to get him into trouble and pick a fight with the guy, who was most definitely not good enough for Krista Yates.

And Luke was?

He ripped his cell phone off his belt and called in, needing to remind himself why he was here in Krista's home.

"Agent Marks."

"It's Luke. Any word on the guys in Chicago or the blog site access?"

"The tech guy is still working on the source, but he says it looks like the hacker pretty much wiped everything clean."

"From a religious blog? That makes no sense."

"Unless she posted something she didn't realize was threatening. Oh, we traced her luggage. They put it on a truck this morning."

"And it's not here yet."

"They had other stops."

"That's too simple."

"At least you don't have to worry about Garcia's men. They're still in Chicago. Any flags in the community file you want us to follow up on?" Marks said.

"Actually," Luke paused. "I need a background check on Alan Jameson, loan officer at National Bank and Trust in Wentworth."

"Got it."

"Also, Phillip Barton and Lucy and Ralph Grimes."

"I'll get back to you."

"Thanks." The water boiled over, making a hissing sound as it hit the burner. Luke turned down the heat. "I'll check in tomorrow."

Luke pocketed his phone and stirred the pasta with

a fork, feeling better about helping out with dinner as opposed to her waiting on him. He glanced out the window, but Krista and Alan were nowhere in sight. He put down the fork and looked out the side window. They weren't there either.

Hobbling to the back door, he whipped it open.

No Krista. No Alan.

"Krista!"

Chapter Ten

Luke grabbed the crutches and went outside, his heart pounding against his rib cage. What kind of idiot would assume their visitor was the boyfriend? Luke, that's who, because he'd been so distracted by Krista's charming smile and gentle nature.

Practically falling off her porch, he stumbled out to the garage. Also empty. He stepped into the yard.

Calmed his breathing.

Scanned the property.

Listened for sounds of distress.

The haunting quiet of a snowy night rang in his ears. He ignored the chill in his bones and started up the driveway to the front of the house. He was greeted by blinding headlights.

Natalie got out of a taxi and looked at him in question. "What's wrong?"

"Krista," he panted, having crutch-sprinted up the driveway. "She's gone."

"Gone, where?"

"I have no idea."

Natalie casually adjusted her purse over her shoulder. "She's a big girl. I'm sure she'll be back soon."

He glared at Natalie and headed back to the house. Needed to call the chief. Find her.

Save her.

"Hey, don't you think you're overreacting?" Natalie said, following him.

He ignored her, couldn't get past the fact he'd failed again, let down an innocent.

Let down Krista.

"Luke, calm down," she said.

He spun on her. "You have no idea what's going on here."

"I'm her best friend, so you'd better tell me what on earth is going on."

He waved his hand in dismissal and pulled out his cell to call the chief.

"Who are you calling?"

"Chief Cunningham."

"Stop. Did you try calling her first?"

"No."

"That seems like an obvious thing to do, doesn't it?"

He clenched his jaw, unable to answer her. He wasn't thinking straight, couldn't even see clearly past the panic burning its way up his chest.

"Maybe there's a simple explanation." She dug out her cell phone from her purse and pressed Krista's speed dial. "Krista, thank goodness you answered." Natalie raised a brow at Luke.

Relief calmed his racing heartbeat. Then anger took hold. Krista left him, knowing it would make him insane with worry? Where could she have possibly gone and with whom?

"I'm at the house, where are you?... Uh-huh. Okay, yeah, well Luke is a little crazed, so as the saying goes, you should have called." Natalie chuckled. "Okay, I'll tell him."

Natalie dropped her phone in her purse. "She's with Alan. They're taking a walk around the block."

"It's too dangerous," Luke ground out.

"Hang on, what is so dangerous about a walk around the block?"

He went back inside, still reeling from panic. Natalie followed and dropped her coat on a kitchen chair. Roscoe ran up to greet her.

"A dog? What is going on?"

Luke ignored her and called the chief.

"Cunningham," the chief answered.

"It's Luke. Sorry to bother you, but Krista went out for a walk and I'm not sure it's safe."

"Alone? What's she thinking?"

"She's with Alan."

"Was probably his idea. I'll send a patrol to her neighborhood."

"Thanks."

"You bet."

Luke went back to stirring the pasta.

"Okay, enough of this cloak-and-dagger stuff," Natalie said. "What's really going on?"

Luke considered how much he should tell her, if anything.

"Look, buster." She grabbed the fork from his hand. "Since you've come to town all kinds of freaky stuff's been happening—the guy in her garage, the tea shop break-in. We're starting to think you're trouble. Yet the chief's on your speed dial. So what gives?"

"I'm here to protect Krista."

He thought maybe if Natalie knew how dangerous this situation was she'd help keep an eye on Krista, maybe she could work with him instead of against him. Still, he wouldn't share everything, especially not the fact they suspected a local of being a drug contact.

"I'm a federal agent," he said. "We think Krista has been targeted by a drug cartel."

"What?" She stepped back. "Our sweet Krista? Why?"

"Not sure." He stared her down. "Natalie, it's imperative that you not tell anyone about this. We need to keep it quiet in order to investigate properly. Can you do that?"

She nodded.

"Say yes," he said.

"Yes, of course."

"Even your fiancé," he pressed.

"Okay, sure. I'm just…stunned."

"So you can see why I'm worried about her."

"Why didn't she tell me?" she said.

"We asked her not to."

"But she'd never have anything to do with drugs."

"We think it's related to her mission trip. We're not sure how. But you're right, since her return from Mexico strange things have been happening and there's a possibility it's related to drug smuggling."

"I… I don't know what to say."

They shared a worried silence. If this woman truly cared about her friend, she'd do the right thing and be more protective. And not tell anyone about the threat.

"That's why you're here, isn't it?" she asked.

"Yes."

"And why you're sticking so close to her?"

"Yes."

Too bad it wasn't for other, nonprofessional reasons. *Yeah, buddy, that kind of thinking could get her killed.*

"But obviously I didn't stick close enough since she slipped out so easily. If it were up to me she'd stay in her house under armed guard."

"Don't even joke about it. She recoils from the thought of overprotective men, women or dogs, for that matter." With a smile, she stroked Roscoe's neck.

The thump of footsteps pounded up the back porch. The door swung open and Krista walked in, followed by Officer West, but no Alan. Good.

"Krista," Natalie said, rushing to her friend and hugging her. "Are you okay?"

"Hey, what's this all about?" Krista asked her friend.

"I was so worried," Natalie said.

"I'm fine, although a little peeved that you called the cops on me," she shot at Luke.

"You disappeared without an explanation." It was everything he could do not to lose his temper in front of these three women.

"Alan wanted some privacy. We needed to talk."

"You know it's not safe," Luke warned.

Krista glanced at her friend. "Another overprotective guy, just my luck."

"He told me what's going on," Natalie said.

Officer West shut the door. "And the chief fully briefed me as well."

"I'm fine," Krista huffed, taking off her coat. "Everyone's overreacting."

"I disagree," Luke said.

"I'd have to agree with Luke," Officer West said.

Krista squared off at Luke. "I needed to have a private talk with Alan, not within earshot of the kitchen."

"Did you get everything resolved?" Luke asked.

Krista shook her head and sat at the kitchen table.

"Krista?" Natalie said. "How did he take it?"

"I don't want to talk about it, especially not with an audience."

"Come on." With an arm around Krista, Natalie led her into the living room.

"Don't leave the house," Luke called after them. He couldn't stop himself.

A few minutes passed, Luke struggling with the raw panic that had probably shaved a few years off his life.

"That was a little over the top, telling her not to leave the house," Officer West said, leaning against the counter.

"I don't know what else to do. I'm with her and she disappears. The woman has no sense."

"She was trying to be sensitive to Alan's feelings. You can't fault her for that."

"I do if it puts her in danger."

"She's not like us. She's trusting and optimistic."

"And we are...?"

"Suspicious and cynical." She smiled. "Look, if it would make you feel better I could offer to spend the night on her couch until you find the perp."

"She'll probably fight us."

"It's worth a try. What's your next step with the case?"

"Investigating the locals."

"You really think someone in Wentworth is involved?"

"Absolutely. That's why I don't trust anyone, not even harmless Alan."

"Yeah, well that guy creeps me out so you're not alone there."

"You got any ideas how I can control this woman?" He nodded toward the living room.

"First, don't think in terms of controlling her. And second, let her know you trust her."

An impossible request.

The next morning Krista woke up feeling bad, both about making Natalie late for her dinner with Timothy, and the disastrous conversation with Alan. She'd nearly had him convinced to move on, explaining that she wasn't ready for a long-term relationship.

Then Officer West pulled up, police lights flashing. Horrified, Alan had left in a huff, feeling humiliated, which is what Krista had been trying to avoid.

"I can't believe Luke called the cops on me," she said to Anastasia. The cat peered down from the top of Krista's oak bureau. She'd meowed at Krista on and off all night, letting her owner know how displeased she was with their canine visitor.

Krista finished dressing and read a Bible passage about patience. She'd need an extra dose of it to deal with Luke McIntyre. He didn't want her help and demanded she tell him every detail of her plans, yet she knew he didn't tell her everything. She suspected he'd been given information from his superiors about the case, but wouldn't share it with her.

She went downstairs to make coffee and toast. The couch, where Officer West had insisted she sleep, was empty and the blankets folded neatly.

Krista wanted to feel appreciation for her houseguest, not resentment, but she couldn't help feeling smothered.

"Shake it off," she said to herself.

She stepped into the kitchen to find Luke sitting at the table drinking coffee, Roscoe by his side.

"Shake what off?" he said, glancing up from a smattering of open files. Some days she couldn't even describe the color of his eyes other than brilliant.

"My crabby mood," she recovered. Had she been staring into his eyes too long?

"Didn't sleep well?" he asked.

"Anastasia kept me up complaining about Roscoe."

"She didn't even see him."

"But she knew he was here. Want toast?"

"Sure. I boiled water, too. For your tea."

"Thanks." When he did stuff like that it made it hard for her to be cross with him.

"We've gotta move fast this morning," she said.

"Why's that?"

"The girls are opening for me, so I can cater a ladies' tea at the resort. We'll stop by the shop to pick up supplies, then head to Michigan Shores."

"A ladies' tea," he muttered.

"You can always stay back and work."

He closed a file folder and shot her a look like she'd just suggested he dress as Santa and greet little kids in the town square.

Twenty minutes later they swung by the shop. Luke was a big help, loading the boxes of scones, china cups and silverware into the trunk of his car. He wasn't using his crutches today, so his ankle must have felt better. Either that or he was covering his pain well.

Krista drove because she knew how to get there, and

she suspected Luke wasn't fond of taking direction. She caught herself. Why did she think she knew so much about him, a virtual stranger?

As they headed to Michigan Shores Luke got a call and his congenial mood faded.

"I understand," he said. "Yes, I will." He pocketed his phone.

"Bad news?" she said.

He glanced in the side-view mirror and frowned. "Your luggage was supposed to be delivered yesterday. The truck driver claims he delivered it late last night."

"But we were home all night."

We were home all night. It sounded like they were a couple enjoying a night at home by the fire, watching a Hallmark movie.

"I guess we have to assume it's gone for good," he said.

"That's going to cost me. I'll have to buy a new wardrobe."

"Maybe the airline will reimburse you."

"Perhaps."

What really bothered Krista was the thought of someone, a stranger, going through her things, taking her comfortable jeans and her favorite wool sweater Mom had given her for Christmas before she'd moved to Florida.

"Don't think about it," he said.

He must have read her mind.

"Does that work for you? Not thinking about it?" Krista asked.

He glanced across the car and smiled. "Most of the time."

"Well, I'm a little old to use the 'ignore it and it will go away' tack."

"Yeah, you're ancient," he teased, glancing at the side-view mirror again.

"See anything interesting?"

"Not really."

They turned onto the long drive of the resort. Small cabins lined the property, and at the end of the driveway was the mansion-like lodge that housed guests and offered dining and entertainment. She pulled up to the front door and he put his hand on her shoulder.

"Give me a few seconds to scan the property, okay?"

His blue eyes caught her in a way that made her fidget in her seat. She looked away. "Sure."

He got out and glanced across the property, its leafless trees and tennis court, and pool that was packed with tourists during the summer season. Today a layer of snow blanketed the plastic covering.

Luke poked his head into the car. "Okay, let's go."

Krista went inside and got a few of the staff members to help bring in the boxes. The tea party was being held in a small room off the dining room with a picturesque view of Lake Michigan. Each table featured a vibrant centerpiece of alstroemerias, roses and carnations. It reminded her of the flowers she'd received from Alan last night.

Drat. In all the excitement she didn't get a chance to appreciate them. Or Alan. Was she making the wrong decision by cooling off their relationship? Maybe she wasn't seeing something in him, appreciating all his fine qualities.

Yet Mom always said Krista would know when she

met the man who'd be her partner in Christ's love. She'd feel it in her heart.

She felt nothing for Alan but regret. Regret at leading him on, regret she couldn't care more about him, and regret that he couldn't accept her decision.

"What's wrong?" Luke asked, as he placed a saucer and teacup on a table.

"What do you mean?" she glanced at him.

"Something's bothering you."

"Just tired." Which she was. Besides there was no reason to bare her heart to him. This was a professional partnership, not a personal one.

"Maybe you should call in reinforcements to help out today," he suggested.

"Now you're telling me my business?" she said.

"Boy, you are crabby."

"Sorry." That wasn't like her, but she hadn't been able to get grounded since she returned home from the mission trip.

Luke shot her a tender smile. "Hey, we'll get these guys and put them away, and your life will get back to normal. This won't last forever."

For a split second, she wondered what forever would look like with Luke McIntyre. His smile faded, his blue eyes darkening.

"I should brew the tea," she whispered.

"What do you want me to do?"

Kiss me.

As if he'd read her thoughts, he leaned forward and did just that. He placed a sweet, warm kiss on her lips that took the chill out of her chest and cast aside the worry from her mind.

It was the first time she'd experienced a kiss like this, a kiss that reached far deeper than her lips.

He broke the kiss and grabbed on to the back of a chair for support. Did the kiss affect him as much as it did Krista?

"Ankle's weaker than I thought," he said, glancing down at the floor.

"Goodness, sit down." She pulled out a chair and held on to his arm as he sat. This time he didn't pull away. He also wouldn't look at her.

"Luke?" she whispered, searching his face.

Someone cleared his throat from the doorway and Krista looked up. Chief Cunningham started toward them.

"Chief?" she said. "Did my luggage turn up?"

"It's not about your luggage." He glanced at Luke, then back to Krista. "There was an accident last night. Your friend Natalie is in the hospital."

Chapter Eleven

As they went into the hospital, Luke realized he'd never felt this helpless.

There seemed to be no words to comfort Krista. And he'd tried, talked more to her in the thirty-minute car ride to the hospital than he had all week. Talking, questioning, trying to get her to open up, share some of her worry so she wouldn't let it bottle up inside and eat away at her.

He didn't stop his attempts until they reached the hospital. With an arm around her shoulder, he escorted Krista down the corridor to Natalie's room. Yet she didn't seem comforted by his touch.

She seemed stunned, defeated.

Of course she was. They'd been on guard for a threat from Garcia's men, but no one could see this coming, a random car accident.

In Krista's car.

What if it wasn't a random accident? It was Krista's car that had been forced off the road. Krista should have been behind the wheel.

He'd focus on that later, when he wasn't reassuring Krista, holding Krista.

They approached room 314 and Krista hesitated. She looked up at him with such fear in her eyes, fear of her friend's condition.

"Do you want me to go in with you?" he offered, yet he wasn't sure how he'd do it. It wasn't the injured friend that scared him, but Krista's reaction.

A nurse came out of the room.

"How's she doing?" Krista asked.

"Stable," the nurse offered. "She's got some lacerations, a broken wrist, but otherwise, she's a very lucky lady."

"Can I see her, just for a minute? It might brighten her spirits," Krista said.

"Only one of you."

Luke nodded. "I'll be right here."

With a sigh, Krista went into the room and closed the door behind her.

He automatically put his hand to the door, wishing he could be there for her to ease some of the burden. Instead, he was an outsider again, looking on as someone he cared about was gutted by emotional pain.

He cared about her. He couldn't deny it any longer.

He paced the hallway outside Natalie's room and let himself have it for allowing that kiss to happen at the resort. What was he thinking? He wasn't. He was acting on instinct, naturally leaning forward, making the connection that was sure to haunt him for the rest of his life.

"Get away from her room!" Natalie's fiancé, Timothy, shouted coming down the hall.

A nurse chased after Timothy. "Sir, please keep your voice down."

"Get out of here before I beat you senseless!" Timothy threatened.

"Call security!" the nurse ordered.

Timothy charged. Luke grabbed the guy's arm, swung it around his back and slammed him against the wall.

"Calm down," Luke said.

"It's your fault! You brought this here!" Timothy squirmed against Luke's hold.

"Take it easy. You don't want them to kick you out of the hospital."

"Don't tell me what I want."

"You want to see her, don't you?"

"Stupid question."

"Then behave like a sane human being."

Timothy stopped struggling and Luke released him. The guy turned around and rubbed his shoulder. "I know it's your fault. I know you're not what you pretend to be. I heard you threatened Brent with a gun."

A security guard sprinted up to them and Luke waved him off.

"They should be kicking you out of the hospital and locking you up," Timothy said.

Chief Cunningham approached the three of them. "Timothy, take it easy."

"I don't care if he is your friend, Chief. This guy shows up in town and all kinds of violent stuff starts happening." He narrowed his eyes at Luke. "It followed him here."

"Back off, son. You're upset," the chief said.

"You bet I'm upset. Natalie is…she's…" His voice caught in his throat.

"She's going to be okay." The chief put a firm hand on Timothy's shoulder. "Why don't you go see her?"

Timothy turned and went into the hospital room. The chief glanced at the security officer. "Thanks. I've got this."

With a nod, the guard left.

Luke took a calming breath, easing the tension in his shoulders from being in the defensive position. He didn't want to hurt Timothy. Luke understood why the guy was so upset, but he didn't want Timothy drawing unwanted attention to Luke, either.

"It's an emotional time when a loved one is hurt," Chief Cunningham said.

Luke pushed back the memory of Karl dying in front of him. "Yep. Tell me about the car accident."

"Sounds like a pickup was passing Natalie and clipped her, sending the car into a ditch. Maybe a DUI—"

"Or not." Luke eyed the chief. "It was Krista's car. Maybe someone thought Krista was behind the wheel."

"Let's not jump to conclusions until we talk to Natalie. She's been in and out of it all night."

"All night? And her fiancé just got here?"

"They had a hard time with identification. Natalie was unconscious when they got to her, and her purse was missing from the scene."

"You mean someone hit her, then stopped to swipe her purse?"

That could have been Krista, unconscious and vulnerable behind the wheel of the car, waiting for someone to help and instead being stalked and having her purse stolen.

Luke fisted his hand. "Then this was not a random hit and run."

Resting his hand on his firearm, the chief didn't argue. "Maybe Krista should take a vacation, leave town."

A pit grew in Luke's stomach at the thought of sending her away. But he knew better than anyone you could run from trouble, but that didn't mean you'd escape its reach.

"If they want her badly enough, they'll find her."

"What, then?"

"They stole Natalie's purse thinking it was Krista's. That's taking a big chance in public like that. We need to figure out what Krista's got that they want so badly."

"The luggage is still missing."

"Which means they got it, but didn't find what they were looking for. They thought she had it on her and sent someone to get it." Luke leaned against the wall and crossed his arms over his chest.

"She doesn't even know what they want," the chief said.

"Yeah, but by putting her in the hospital they gain access to her house."

"We should do a full search."

"I agree. And it wouldn't be a bad idea to have Officer West move in with Krista until this thing is over."

"I'll speak with her."

The door to Natalie's hospital room opened and Krista wandered out. She turned to Luke wearing a pale, distant expression.

"How is she?" the chief asked.

"Bruised. Tired. I offered to bring her some things

from home but…" Her voice trailed off and she glanced over her shoulder at Natalie's room.

"But what?" Luke pushed.

"Timothy said he'd handle it."

"What else did Timothy say?" Luke asked.

She shook her head. "It's not important."

Maybe not, but it had upset her. Luke guessed the jerk must have been trash-talking him.

"I don't know if I should go or stay," she said, fiddling with her silver charm.

"We can hang around if you'd like," Luke said.

She shrugged. "Timothy made it pretty clear that he's got this covered. I guess we should head back."

The devastation in her voice caused an ache in Luke's chest. She felt so utterly helpless. He knew that feeling.

And he wanted to fix it, but hadn't a clue how.

"Krista, I'd like to search your house, if that's okay," the chief said.

"Sure. Whatever. I'm going to hit the ladies' room first." Krista nodded and walked down the hall.

"I'll get started on the search," the chief said. "You have any idea what we're looking for?"

"Wish I did."

"You'll be at the tea shop?"

"I'll be wherever she is."

Krista said silent prayers all the way back to Wentworth, prayers for Natalie's recovery and thanks to God that she wasn't injured more severely.

Krista simply couldn't imagine visiting her friend in worse condition than she'd seen her today. Bruises were forming around Natalie's eyes, her arms were scratched and her eyes bloodshot. She looked like she'd been beaten up.

Closing her eyes, Krista took a deep breath. *Please God, give me strength to help my friend, to know what to say to comfort her.*

Timothy had certainly said enough. He'd scolded Krista for bringing Luke with her to the hospital. Luke was the stranger who Timothy had decided was the cause of all the trouble in Wentworth over the past few days.

If only Timothy knew the truth. But he couldn't. No one could.

"She'll be okay," Luke offered, pulling into the parking lot of a family restaurant outside of Wentworth.

Again, it was like he'd read her thoughts.

"What are we doing here?" she asked.

"Lunch," he said.

"But—"

"Look." He parked and turned to her. "It's been a rough morning. Let's relax for a few minutes, have a cup of soup and regain some strength."

For once, Krista didn't mind being handled and told what to do. She didn't want to make any decisions or think for a little while. She just wanted to be.

They went inside Earl's Pancake House and took a booth in the corner. Luke ordered coffee and handed her a menu. She stared at the words, the block print swimming across the laminated beige page.

"Krista?" he said.

She glanced up and struggled to smile. "Sorry. I can't get the image of Natalie's bruised face out of my mind."

"I know." He reached over and placed his hand over hers. "She was actually very lucky."

"To think someone would bump into your car and drive off like that, without stopping to help or calling the paramedics." She sighed and welcomed the warmth coming from Luke's palm. "To think that could have been me."

He glanced down at their hands.

Reality struck her smack in the face. "Wait a second, do you think the accident was intentional? That someone ran the car off the road thinking I was inside?"

Luke slipped his hand from hers and searched the restaurant. "Where's our waitress?"

She knew by his reaction that her suspicions were true. The collision was meant for Krista. It should be Krista lying in the hospital bed with bruises and bumps.

It should have been Krista who was almost killed, but instead it was Natalie.

And it was Krista's fault.

The buried pain of a five-year-old clawed its way up her chest, as flashes of memory assaulted her.

A tall man towering over her at the front door.

Krista telling him Dad was still at work.

Policemen standing on her front porch.

Mom collapsing when they told her...

Krista bolted from the booth and sprinted for the door. She needed fresh, cold air to shock her back to the present and snap the images from her mind.

"Krista!" Luke called after her.

She barely heard him. All she heard were her mother's cries and the policeman's questions. She remembered the look on her mother's face, a horrified look that haunted Krista to this day.

Krista thought it was the look of blame, because it was Krista's fault the bad man found her dad. In reality it was Mom's fear that the killer would come back to hurt Krista because she could identify him.

And then Krista and Mom ran. Just like Krista was doing right now.

Luke grabbed her arm. "Where are you going?"

Glancing around, she realized she'd made it into the parking lot, her instinct driving her to run, to escape.

Coward.

She'd never quite forgiven herself for uprooting Mom from friends and her church community in California to hide out in Michigan with Gran.

"Krista, talk to me," Luke demanded.

She shook off the chill of a cold November day and looked into his blue eyes. "It's my fault. I should have been in the car instead of Natalie. Someone was after me, right?"

"We don't know that."

She pulled away from him. "It's true. Just like before."

"Before?"

"I can't go through that again, Luke. I won't let the people I love get hurt because of me."

"Listen, sweetheart." He cupped her shoulders with firm, gentle hands.

She wondered if he even knew he'd used the endearment.

"This is not your fault," he said.

It wasn't your fault, pumpkin. Mom's words. Krista never quite believed her. Just like she didn't believe Luke right now.

"Krista, do not blame yourself for this. You didn't put Natalie in the hospital."

"Sure I did. I loaned her my car."

"Because you're a good friend. Don't beat yourself up for that."

"You don't understand."

"Then come inside and explain it to me."

Krista glanced at the cars passing by. Her friend was nearly killed, but life went on as usual, just like it did when her father was killed. She never understood how life could go on as normal when her world had been blown apart.

With his forefinger to her chin, Luke guided her eyes to meet his. "Please, come inside."

When she looked into his concerned eyes, she felt grounded again. Her heart still raced, only not with anger at whoever rammed into Natalie. Her heart raced for a completely different reason.

With a comforting smile, he took her hand and led her into the restaurant. They went to their booth and hot coffee was waiting for them.

For once, she welcomed the bitter brew. She sipped the coffee and glanced out the window.

"I thought I'd left all that behind," she whispered.

"Your father?"

She nodded.

"Maybe you should take a break, a vacation."

She snapped her attention to him. "I won't run again."

"It's not running. It's…evading."

"I have a better idea. I'm going to help you catch them."

Luke leaned back in the booth. "Not a good idea."

"This whole time I've been taking things as they come, letting you and the chief figure out why these guys are in Wentworth. Well, no more. They've hurt my friend and I want to put an end to it."

"You're doing enough just by staying safe."

"I disagree. I could be doing more."

"I don't like the sound of this." He eyed his coffee.

"I'll find out whatever you need to know from the community. No one will suspect what I'm doing."

"I don't want you putting yourself at risk."

"I'm already at risk. You know that, Luke."

He crossed his arms over his chest. Worry lines creased his forehead and his lips pinched into a thin, contemplative line.

She thought he was worried about her, but then she noticed his gaze drift to the front of the restaurant.

He shifted out of the booth and planted his hand on her shoulder. "Stay here."

She turned around and watched him leave the restaurant, disappearing around the corner. Just then her cell phone rang. Hoping it was Natalie, she answered without looking at the caller ID.

"Hello, Nat?"

Nothing.

"Hello?"

"It should have been you in the car."

Chapter Twelve

The black pickup cruising the parking lot fit the description of the one that rammed Natalie last night. It parked and someone opened the tinted window and blew cigarette smoke out the crack. Instinct drove Luke outside to investigate. Maybe he was being paranoid.

As Luke got closer, he slipped his hand inside his coat and gripped his firearm.

Suddenly the truck's engine roared and the driver spun out of the lot.

"Hey!" Luke called after him.

He was right. The driver of the car was keeping an eye on Krista. Had he been hovering close by when Krista fled into the parking lot a few minutes ago? The thought of the truck barreling toward her and finishing the job shot panic through Luke's veins.

One thing for sure: Garcia's men knew Krista wasn't lying helpless in a hospital bed. And she was still a target.

If only Luke knew what they wanted from her.

"Luke!" Krista called.

Luke spun around to see Krista racing toward him.

He scanned the trees surrounding the parking lot wondering if the driver of the pickup left someone behind to finish what they'd started last night.

She had to stop putting herself in danger like this.

"Someone called and—"

"I told you to stay inside." He grabbed her arm and pulled her back to the restaurant.

"What's wrong?" she asked, her eyes wide.

"Nothing."

She jerked her arm free. "Look, I can't help you or protect myself if you keep things from me."

But he wanted to; he wanted to distance her from the ugliness of the Garcia family. *Too late, buddy. You know that.*

"I think I just saw the truck that ran into Natalie," he said.

"Here? Why?"

When he hesitated, she said, "Oh, he was here for me. I guess he's the one who just called me, too."

"What did he say?"

"That it should have been me in the car."

Luke put his arm around her and led her inside. "I'm sorry."

With a shake of her head, she went back into the restaurant and sat down. The waitress approached them, order pad in hand. "You love birds staying this time?" she smiled.

Love birds. Right. Like that could ever happen between Krista and Luke.

"I'll have the soup and sandwich special, make it a burger," Luke said.

"And you, miss?" the waitress asked Krista.

"I'm not sure," she said, distracted as she eyed the menu.

"How about a grilled cheese sandwich and soup?" Luke offered.

Krista put down the menu. "Yes, I'll do that."

With a smile, the waitress took their menus and went into the kitchen.

"Krista," Luke said.

She glanced at him, but he sensed he didn't have her complete attention. Of course not, she was worried about what was coming next.

"I'm not going to let anything happen to you," he said.

"Thanks," she sighed and glanced out the window.

Now, if he could only keep that promise.

After stopping by Michigan Shores to pick up supplies, Krista insisted on going straight to the tea shop. A good thing in Luke's opinion because if she was at work, she couldn't go snooping around, looking for clues and getting herself hurt.

He appreciated her determination to help solve this case, but he didn't want her putting herself at risk. Yet he knew Krista. Once she set her mind on something, there was no changing it.

"It was lucky they had staff available to serve the ladies tea," she said.

He sensed guilt in her voice, guilt about having to abandon the tea party.

A few minutes later they pulled up to the tea shop and Krista opened her car door.

"Wait." He touched her arm.

"No, listen, they aren't going to kill me. If they do, they'll never find whatever it is they're looking for. I can't live in fear, Luke. I just won't do it." She whipped open her car door and headed for the shop.

Luke eyed her through the windshield, figuring this wasn't solely about the current threat, but that her past was adding fuel to her emotional fire. He couldn't imagine losing a father to murder and blaming yourself. Then again it was kind of like Luke blaming himself for his partner's death.

No, that was different. If Luke had been smarter, taken things slower, he would have sensed the danger instead of jumping in and putting himself and Karl at risk.

This case was messing with both his and Krista's heads in a big way. His priorities had shifted from finding the perp to protecting Krista. Yet they were one and the same, right?

Rationalize it any way you want. You're getting too involved with this case. With Krista.

He paced the cobblestone sidewalk next to the tea shop and called the chief.

"Cunningham."

"It's Luke. The truck that hit Natalie was stalking us, and Krista got a threatening phone call."

"Did you get a plate number on the truck?"

Luke gave him the number and leaned against the brick building. "Find anything at her house?"

"Not yet."

"Oh, and she's decided to launch her own investigation to expose the perp because they hurt her friend."

"Sounds like Krista."

Alan pulled up in his sedan and rushed into the shop. Didn't that guy get the message? Krista wasn't interested. End of story.

"They found Natalie's purse at a truck stop off Highway 31, money and credit cards still in the wallet."

"That's not what they were looking for."

"I'd give my bass fishing trophy to know what they wanted so badly."

"They broke into the shop looking for something. I'm going to do a little investigating around here, maybe find some answers."

"Good plan. We'll talk later."

"Thanks."

Luke pocketed his phone and headed for the back door, not looking forward to an Alan encounter.

When he entered the back, the place was up for grabs. Tori was frantically making sandwiches, while Krista had four teapots lined up, and was scooping loose tea into the strainers. The water in the sink was running, a timer was beeping and the phone was ringing.

And Alan hovered over Krista's shoulder. Luke wanted to grab the guy and toss him out the back door.

"When I heard about Natalie's accident in your car—"

"You're a great friend, Alan, but right now I need to focus on the lunch rush," Krista said. "I'm going to have to ask you to leave."

Even Luke was surprised by her short, businesslike tone.

Alan's expression changed from concern to anger. Krista couldn't see it. Her back was to him.

Luke took a step toward him. "Anything I can do, Krista?"

Alan snapped his head around to glare at Luke. The guy's squinty eyes radiated fire, and for a second Luke thought he could be more dangerous than he seemed.

"Finish filling the sanitizing sink, wipe down the counter and get Tori some clean dishes," she ordered.

"Excuse me," Luke said, shouldering his way past Alan into the tight quarters.

Although Luke ignored Alan and got to work, he sensed the guy hovering, waiting for something.

"As long as you're okay," Alan said to Krista.

"I'm fine, Alan. Thanks for stopping by."

A minute later the back door clicked shut. With a shake of her head, she set five timers to brew tea and shifted beside Luke to wash dishes. "I was rude, wasn't I?"

"Not rude. A little short maybe."

"I just couldn't help it. What with everything that's happened in the past twenty-four hours, I just couldn't deal with him."

"Understandable. Listen, the chief and Officer West are searching your house."

"For what?"

"Clues as to what you have that Garcia wants. Someone grabbed Natalie's purse after the crash, but when they found it the perp hadn't taken money or credit cards. You have any idea what they're after? Did you buy any trinkets or gifts that you brought back from Mexico?"

"Just a diary."

"Where is it?"

"In my suitcase."

"Krista, table four is complaining about their refill and table two says the soup is cold," Tatum said, hovering in the doorway holding a half-empty bowl of soup. "Oh, and I've gotta be at a thing in twenty minutes."

"What thing?" her sister questioned from the prep table.

"None of you business."

"Does Mom know about your thing?" Tori glared.

"Focus, girls," Krista said. "We're a team, remember?"

The girls stopped arguing and Luke admired her ability to shut them down.

"Luke, ladle a new bowl of soup, heat it in the micro for a minute and I'll take it out. Tatum, finish up the dishes. I'll take over the dining room. Tori?" Krista stepped into her line of vision. "Good job on the food prep. You comfortable here or do you want the dining room?"

"I'm good."

"Great, then let's move it."

After a few hours of serving customers the guilt and fear started to ease. Guilt about Natalie's accident and fear of being stalked and attacked. Krista was just too exhausted to worry.

She wasn't too tired to chat with customers, ask pleasant but pertinent questions and gather information for Luke's investigation. She listened for mention of anything odd or out of line with the normal happenings of Wentworth.

It was typical for her to talk up customers. She liked the interaction and liked hearing what they had to say about their families, current events and plans for vacations. Some customers even asked about Natalie.

That connection was the real joy of owning a shop like this, a connection she suspected Luke found useless, maybe even terrifying.

They locked up at five and headed home. She steeled herself against what her house would look like. Did the chief and Officer West rip the place apart? She hoped not but would accept it if it meant getting that much closer to ending this nightmare.

"You're quiet," Luke said, pulling into her driveway.

"Pensive."

"I saw you grilling your customers. You shouldn't do that."

She squared off at him. "I wasn't grilling anyone. I was being friendly."

"Still, someone could figure out you're playing investigator."

"Oh, yeah, because I got great clues today," she said with sarcasm in her voice. "Ruth and Gerry are going on a cruise in March, Nancy Patterson sold her vintage sewing machine, and the Cooper boys were suspended for two days for squirting hair gel on their biology teacher's keyboard."

"What would give a kid the idea to do that?"

"They're bored. I suspect smart, too."

"That's all you got?" he joked.

"Annette Winters said they were looking forward to my cranberry scones at the church potluck tonight." She glanced at Luke. "I totally forgot about that one."

"Don't go. Tell them you've had a rough week, you're still jet-lagged and—"

"I can't renege on cranberry scones, no matter how tired I am." *Or what criminals are after me.*

Luke gripped the steering wheel tighter. He seemed genuinely worried about her, which meant he cared about her more than an agent would normally care about a witness, right? Or was he worried about being around church folk? Because wherever she went, he'd surely be inches behind her.

They parked on her driveway and could hear Roscoe barking from the garage. He was a good watchdog, for sure.

With files tucked under one arm, Luke escorted her to the back door with a gentle hand at her elbow.

She realized she liked having him close, enjoyed the supportive hand of a strong man. Then she remembered that all too soon he'd be gone. She quickened her pace and pulled away from him.

She was starting to fall for the grumpy federal agent, against her will and all good sense in her head.

Once inside, she dropped her purse on the table and tentatively eyed the living room. It wasn't too bad. Sure, things were out of place, but it wasn't messy.

She was strung tight, like a tennis racket, and needed to decompress with a little baking, maybe blogging.

"I'm going to check on Roscoe, let him out," Luke said, coming up behind her. "You stay here, got it?"

"Where else would I go?"

"Off to do more snooping around? I don't know."

"I'm too exhausted to do anything but collapse."

"Good. I'll be back in a few minutes." He left and she shut and locked the back door.

Alone. Finally. She welcomed the solace without her shadow looking over her shoulder. Sure, she appreciated his help today at the shop, and of course she was thankful that he was here in Wentworth to protect her.

But she desperately needed time alone to breathe, think and fully come down from the adrenaline rush that started this morning when she visited Natalie.

Speaking of which, she hadn't spoken to Nat since

she'd seen her at the hospital. Krista had called, but Timothy intercepted the call and said Nat was too tired to talk.

She pulled out ingredients for cranberry scones and got busy, while dialing the hospital to check on her friend.

"Mercy General."

"Room 314, bed A please."

"One moment."

While Krista waited she assembled the dry ingredients. The line rang repeatedly, six, seven, eight times, but no one answered. She cut the butter into the dry mixture, added the cranberries and sugar in a separate bowl and beat together the cream and egg. A good thing she could make these in her sleep.

"Answer, already," she whispered.

"Mercy General."

"Oh, hi. I was trying to reach my friend, Natalie Brown?"

"Hold please."

Krista blended the dry mixture with the cream mixture and dumped the dough on the counter. Kneading the dough seemed to ease her nerves a bit.

The operator came back on the line. "Miss Brown was discharged late this afternoon."

"Really? She didn't look in any condition to leave the hospital."

"I'm sorry, ma'am, I can't give out information about a patient's condition. I can only tell you if she's here or not."

"Okay, thank you."

She spread and cut the dough into triangles, placed them on the cookie sheets and popped them into the oven.

Natalie, out of the hospital? Curious.

She set the timer for twenty minutes, washed her hands and called Nat's house. The call went to voice mail.

"Hey, Nat, it's Krista. Could you give me a call and let me know what I can do to help? Thanks."

Krista thought it odd that Nat was released and wasn't answering her home phone. Then again, Timothy was probably micromanaging her, protecting her from too much activity or stress.

Although Krista's feelings had been hurt by Timothy's harsh words earlier today, she knew they were born of love for his fiancée. The thought of her being seriously injured was tearing him apart.

Krista hoped someone would someday love her as much as Timothy loved Nat. Well, Alan had claimed he loved her.

"Move on," she whispered to herself.

But she couldn't really move on until this case was solved, she got her life back to normal and Luke disappeared, back to his work chasing criminals.

Criminals like the ones hounding her. They broke into her shop, her home and her blog. Well, they might be threatening her from the shadows, but they couldn't stop her from blogging. The blog was her way of taking control of her situation. She'd re-create it and bring joy to others' lives, regardless of the criminals threatening her.

She grabbed her purse and sat at the computer nook. Blogging about her mission trip always brightened her spirits. So someone breached her Faithgirl blog. She'd just start a new one using a different name.

She grabbed her key chain from her purse and pulled

off the thumb drive. She stuck it into her computer and created a new blog on blogworld.com.

Scanning through her pictures helped her instantly relax as she remembered how it felt to help the children in the small village outside of Mexicali. Krista felt like she was part of something bigger than herself, something Christ had called her to do. All the petty stresses of life dissolved and the tightening in her chest over her current situation eased a bit.

Luke tapped on the back door. She got up and let him in. "What, isn't Roscoe coming?"

"I thought I'd better ask first."

"Sure, you can bring him in."

While Luke went back to the garage, Krista put up the baby gate between the kitchen and living room. "Sorry, Anastasia," she called into the house. The princess cat had been in hiding ever since Roscoe's appearance.

Just as Luke and Roscoe came up the back steps, someone rang the front doorbell.

"I'll answer it," Luke said. "You have your cell?"

She nodded and grabbed it out of her purse.

"Be ready to call for help. Stay out of sight, got it?"

"Sure."

A few seconds passed, her heart pounding, Roscoe dancing by the baby gate, wanting to get to Luke.

She heard him open the front door. Then nothing. It was eerily quiet. A few seconds later the door shut, and she heard footsteps headed her way.

Were the footsteps even Luke's? Should she call the police? She whipped her head around and spotted a can of starch. She grabbed it and pointed at whoever was coming into the kitchen.

Luke stepped over the baby gate carrying her suitcase.

"They finally delivered it. Fantastic." She reached for the black suitcase, but Luke cautioned her.

"This is evidence."

"Luke, I really miss my sweater. Please?"

He placed the suitcase on the kitchen table, grabbed a paper napkin and unzipped it, slowly.

"Come on, come on," she joked.

"Look, we don't know who dropped this off. No one asked me to sign, it was just there on your porch."

"You're right. Sorry."

He finished unzipping it and flipped it open.

She spotted her sweater, all right, shredded to pieces, along with the rest of her clothes.

Chapter Thirteen

"Don't touch anything," Luke said, studying the suit-case. "I'll call the chief to come get this for forensic testing."

Luke closed the suitcase, wanting to shut out the violence that had destroyed Krista's things. He wanted to wipe that look off her face. Was it fear or sadness? Either way, it tore him apart.

"Was that really necessary?" she said. "The whole shredding my clothes thing?"

"I'm guessing they meant to frighten you." He eyed her. "Are you frightened?"

She leveled him with brilliant green eyes. "I'm angry."

"Good, then they failed." He glanced at the bag.

"I don't suppose the airline will reimburse me for my clothes?"

"It's possible. Why don't you call them and give it a try?"

"After I finish uploading pictures to my blog." She sat down at the computer.

"I thought—"

"I created another one." She shot him a victorious grin.

"Nice."

She went back to work on the blog. It amazed him how she was able to snap out of her anger and launch into a new project. But then in her mind, blogging about her mission trip was probably her way of taking control of the chaos.

He admired her for that. As he pulled out his phone to call the chief, he realized he admired a lot of things about Krista. Topping the list was the fact she did not let Garcia's men rattle her to the point of locking herself up in her house. On some level he wished she would. It would make his job a lot easier.

"Cunningham."

"Chief, it's Luke McIntyre. Krista's suitcase was anonymously delivered to the house. Everything inside was destroyed."

"Sorry to hear that. Want me to get it to the forensics lab in Grand Rapids?"

"That would be great." Luke moved the suitcase off the table and next to the door.

"I'll send an officer over."

"Thanks."

"You coming to the potluck tonight?" the chief asked.

"How'd you know?"

"Word travels fast in Wentworth. Like a sled goin' ninety down a luge track."

"I should have figured."

"How's Krista doing?"

"She's—" he paused and glanced at Krista, focused on the computer screen. "Determined."

"Good. I'll see you later, then."

"Yep." Luke turned to Krista and eyed the new blog

over her shoulder. She dropped in a photograph of her kneeling and talking to a little girl.

"Nice shot."

"Thanks. That's Maria. Her brother, Armando, was injured by a drug dealer's bullet."

"Wait, so your mission work was that close to Garcia's compound?"

"I don't know. I guess it's possible."

Luke scooted a chair next to Krista and she turned to him. "What?"

"Maybe you saw something you weren't supposed to, or heard something or—"

"Like what?"

"I don't know." Luke glanced at the floor and back up at Krista. "Names, do you remember hearing any names, or places or anything about Michigan?"

She shook her head. "No, sorry. I would have remembered that."

The timer went off and she jumped up to pull out the scones. The kitchen smelled of home, not like a home Luke had ever known, but he imagined this is what a happy one smelled like.

"We'll head over to church in about an hour, after I whip up another two dozen," Krista said.

"They smell great."

She measured some flour and dumped it into a bowl. "Didn't your mom ever bake for you?"

"No." A one-syllable answer. He couldn't risk anything more.

"Huh. I thought all moms baked." She put cream and sugar into another bowl and blended it.

She glanced at him, expectant.

"My mother had—" he paused "—health problems."

Krista hesitated as she mixed the dry ingredients in with the creamy mixture. "I'm sorry."

"It's fine."

His way of shutting down. If he didn't, he might end up in that place where he blamed himself for her drinking, and the health complications that followed. It must have been difficult raising a kid like Luke all by herself.

"What?" Krista prodded.

Luke glanced up.

"You got a strange look on your face. Were you thinking about her?"

"No, I was trying to figure out how to keep from eating all your scones before we get to church."

"Very funny. Like I believe that."

"Believe it. They smell delicious."

Krista smiled and glanced over her shoulder at him. Her gaze caught on the suitcase by the door and her smile faded. He wanted to do something, brush his thumb across her cheek and make her smile again.

"What kinds of things do you need to know about people?" She snapped her attention back to kneading the dough.

"I'd rather you not—"

"I'm going to, so tell me what you're looking for."

"A large influx of money, someone bragging about buying expensive jewelry or a new car, when you know they probably couldn't afford it. Anyone who's taken a trip recently, people who vacation in Mexico."

"Anything else?"

"That's a good start."

With a spatula she transferred the scones to a cooling rack, put scone dough on the baking sheet and slid it into the oven.

"One more batch and we're ready to go. Wanna taste?"

"Sure."

She dropped two scones on a plate and put the kettle on.

"Must have tea with your scone," she said.

Her wall phone rang and she grabbed it. "Hello. Hello. I'm sorry, I can't hear you."

Luke stepped up beside her and leaned in to listen. Wasn't easy to stay focused with the heat of her skin warming his cheek.

"Who is this?"

Heavy breathing echoed across the line.

Luke took the phone from her. "There's a trace on this call."

More breathing. Luke hung up and sat down at the kitchen table. "Is the tea ready?"

"Almost." She sat down and studied him. "Do you think that was…?"

"Doesn't matter. They can't touch you as long as I'm here, but it wouldn't hurt to put a trace on your phone. I'll mention it to my supervisor when I call in."

"Thanks," she said.

"Don't expect much. If they're smart, they'll hang up before we can get a location."

"Well, thanks anyway." She continued to study him.

Luke patted his leg for Roscoe's attention. He didn't like it when Krista looked too deeply into his eyes. He feared she'd see things no one else could see, things Luke tried to hide even from himself.

"Might as well go through some files while we wait," he said, opening a folder. Work would distract him and keep him focused on what he was here to do, because he surely was not here to fall for a sweet, Christian woman with a generous spirit.

She deserved better.

"Can I help?" she said.

"Nah, thanks."

Resting her chin on an upturned palm, she didn't take her eyes off him.

"See anything interesting?" he said.

"Yeah, actually, I do."

He ignored her comment and the kettle whistled, saving him from another uncomfortable moment. Why? It's not like she was judging him or criticizing him. That wasn't Krista's way. No, it seemed more like she was trying to figure him out, maybe even appreciate him.

Not possible.

She put a flowered teapot on the table, and a flowered plate with a scone in front of him. "They taste best when they're warm."

He closed his file and took a bite of the scone. It tasted like nothing he'd ever tried before, the tart cranberries complemented the sweetness of the flaky biscuit.

"You like?" She smiled.

"This is great."

"Good." She poured tea into two teacups and leaned back in her chair.

They slipped into a comfortable silence, enjoying tea, scones and each other's company. He shouldn't be this comfortable or this relaxed. Luke should be on guard, waiting for the next assault. He glanced at Roscoe, who was happily lying beside Luke's chair.

He scanned the kitchen and his gaze caught on the

photograph of Krista, her mom and grandmother. Somehow he felt the closeness and intimacy of a loving family.

Roscoe growled low in his throat, snapping Luke out of the moment.

"What is it, boy?" Luke rubbed his neck.

Roscoe whined, then barked and rushed the kitchen window. Luke flipped off the light to get a better view. He stepped closer to the window and spotted a squad car pulling into the driveway.

"Luke?" Krista said with worry in her voice.

"It's the officer for the suitcase. I'll take it out to him."

"Great, I'll go get ready."

Luke grabbed the suitcase, opened the door and met the cop on the back porch.

"How about some I.D.?" Luke asked.

The kid flashed his badge. It read John Fritz, Community Service Officer. Luke handed him the suitcase. "You don't carry a firearm?"

"Not as a community service officer."

"Okay, well, be careful with this."

"Yes, sir."

Luke watched the CSO put the suitcase into the back of his squad car and take off.

Luke went into the kitchen and paused. He realized Roscoe could have been barking at one of Garcia's men stalking the house instead of the service officer pulling into the drive. And Luke had been so comfortable, so relaxed, that he hadn't even realized he'd drifted off into fantasyland.

"Don't let it happen again," he warned himself.

He couldn't breathe.

Luke grabbed at his shirt collar, but realized he'd

already unbuttoned it. The community room at Peace Church was packed. Packed with conversation, love and laughter.

And he couldn't take much more.

"Here," Krista said, shoving a plate full of food at him. "You look pale."

"That obvious?"

"Only to me." She glanced across the room. "I love these events."

"That makes one of us." He couldn't stand how all these people got into each other's business and offered advice, butted into someone's life without being asked.

"What freaks you out so much?" she asked.

"I'm not good with people."

She smiled up at him. "You're good with me."

He opened his mouth to quip back, but couldn't come up with the right words.

She was right. He didn't have to work at being comfortable with Krista, even though she scared him, especially her ability to see through his angry exterior into the heart of a little boy.

A wounded little boy.

"I don't like that look," she said. "Have a cookie."

She grabbed a sugar cookie off his plate and held it to his mouth.

"Well, ain't that sweet?" Chief Cunningham said walking up to them.

Krista placed the cookie back on the plate and brushed off her fingertips. "Just trying to cheer up our friend with some sugar. You two talk while I make the rounds."

"Haven't you already made the rounds?" Luke said, desperate to get out of here.

"Can't hurt to make them again." With a smile she breezed into the crowd, touching a young woman's elbow to join in on a conversation.

"How you holding up, son?" the chief asked.

"Do I look that bad?"

"No, not bad at all. Just uncomfortable."

"I'm not used to these kinds of things."

"Guessed as much." The chief glanced across the room. "Anyone from the files look like a person of interest?"

"Phillip Barton has relatives in Mexico. Is he here?"

"Over by the punch bowl. Probably spiking it, if I know Phillip."

Phillip was mid-fifties with short, black hair and a square jaw.

"Tell me about his business," Luke asked.

"Said he owns a seat on the board of trade and doesn't need to work. Moved to Wentworth five years ago and opened a boat cruise business for tourists. Takes them out on Silver Lake and Lake Michigan. Does pretty good, I think."

"He fits the profile."

Luke spotted Alan hovering behind Krista.

"Alan the banker is a possible," Luke said.

"You think he's smart enough to be connected to a drug cartel?"

"We're not looking for smart. We're looking for someone who can take orders," Luke said.

"Did you finish going over the mission group list?"

"I did. All twelve seem clean to me. I'm starting to think Garcia's men might have smuggled something into the country through someone's luggage without their knowledge."

"And it was to be collected by their man in town?"

"Makes the most sense."

"Which doesn't explain why they're after Krista."

"No, it doesn't."

Which is what kept Luke from getting a good night's sleep. He not only had to figure out how Garcia's men got drugs into the country and where the drugs ended up, but also why they were after Krista. Until he knew why, she wouldn't be safe.

An elderly woman with silver hair and a warm smile wandered up to the chief and Luke with a pan in one hand and spatula in the other. "Boys, did you try my blueberry streusel?"

"Not yet, ma'am." Luke nodded to his plate. "I'd better finish my dinner first."

"Nonsense." She cut a small wedge and placed it on top of Luke's other desserts. "So, how are things at the tea shop?"

"Ma'am?" Luke questioned.

"You're the handyman, correct? How're the projects coming along?"

"Good, very good."

"I'm so glad. I don't know what we'd do without Grace's Tea Shop. It's magical, you know." She smiled.

"Yes, ma'am."

A younger woman in her thirties approached Luke. "Hi, I'm Julie Sass. My daughters work for Krista."

Luke shook her hand. "Luke McIntyre."

"The girls say you've been doing wonders at the shop." She leaned closer. "And with Krista." She winked.

Luke shot a panicked look at the chief, who shrugged.

"Ah, well, I'm pretty good with drains, but nearly

killed myself hanging Christmas lights," Luke said, avoiding the comment about Krista.

"I heard. How's the ankle?"

"It's good, thanks."

"Mr. McIntyre?" An elderly woman stepped in front of the streusel lady. "I'm Delores Frupp, Doe for short. If you have any pain from the ankle, I use arnica, an herbal cream that reduces the swelling."

"Thanks, I'll remember that, but I'm really—"

"Or aloe vera. That's always helped me," streusel lady offered.

"R.I.C.E.," Julie Sass said. They all looked at her.

"Rest, ice, compression and elevation. That's what the coach told Tori to do when she sprained her ankle in soccer."

The three women discussed the benefits of the various forms of first aid for sprained ankles. Luke glanced at his plate of food, wondering why it bothered him that they seemed to care so much about him.

It reminded him of something, someone…

The many someone's from his childhood church. They'd visit once a month after services bringing food and clothes, sometimes toys for Luke.

He'd hear the doorbell ring and he'd hide in his room as Mom welcomed the group into the living room, offering them a beverage…

While she threw back her fourth glass of scotch.

At one in the afternoon.

Buried memories shot to the surface, blinding him, suffocating him.

The women's voices, the cacophony of the crowd rose to an unbearable pitch. His heart pounded against his chest.

"I gotta go." He handed the chief his plate and made for the door.

He needed fresh air, needed to get out of here and shake the memories from his mind. Get his head back in the game.

Mom was an alcoholic.

He'd never admitted it before.

Shame coursed through him.

He stormed out the back of the church toward the garden.

That's why she died: because she drank herself to death. Everyone in town, all the church people knew it.

They knew his shame.

Which was why, after two years in foster care, he'd lied about his age and joined the army.

He ran, just like he was now. Had to get away from the crowd of people inside who reminded him of his childhood church community, the people who knew the truth—Luke was so bad that he drove his mother to kill herself with booze.

He went outside to the back garden that was covered in snow, the plants dormant until spring.

Dormant, like his memories.

Until now.

"Mom," he whispered as frustration ripped through his chest.

A crunching sound drew his attention and he turned.

Just as something hit him in the back of the head. He dropped to the ground, face-first into the snow. His cheek chilled as he struggled to focus, to figure out...

He gasped and passed out.

Chapter Fourteen

When Krista saw Luke bolt out of the community room, she wondered if he'd received word about the case. Then she caught the look in his eye and she instantly wanted to follow him, find out what caused the desperation she read there.

It wasn't about the case. It ran deeper than that and she wanted to help him.

Unfortunately she was surrounded by church friends who wanted to hear more details about the mission trip. She directed them to her new blog site, and politely excused herself, saying she had to visit the ladies' room.

She made a beeline for the back door, whipped it open and froze at the sight of a tall, hooded figure standing over a motionless body in the snow.

Even from here she recognized the fallen man's black boots. Luke's boots.

"Luke!" she cried.

The hooded man sprinted away, disappearing through nearby bushes.

She opened the door to the community room and grabbed Tori Sass, who happened to be standing there with her boyfriend. "Tori, go get the chief and send him out back, now."

Krista turned and rushed down the back steps, instinct driving her across the property. Luke's normally strong, large body looked dwarfed in the snow.

Panic flooded her chest at the thought of him being—

"Krista?" the chief called from the back door.

"It's Luke, someone hurt him!" She skidded to a stop and kneeled beside him, brushing her hand against his cheek. He was so cold, so still.

The chief rushed up behind her.

"Did you see—"

"The bushes." She pointed, but could hardly say more in her distraught state.

The chief called across the property, but she could hardly hear him past the pounding of her heart.

"Luke, open your eyes," she whispered, placing her palm to his cheek to warm him.

Please God, don't take him yet. Not like this.

"What happened?" Dr. Langston said, rushing up to her. A small group was forming.

She glanced up at the tall, elderly doctor. "I'm not sure. He's unconscious."

"Krista?" Luke moaned.

She turned to him. "Luke, you're okay, it's going to be okay." She glanced at the doctor, looking for confirmation.

He motioned for her to move aside and she did, but she didn't break the contact with Luke's cheek.

"Do you remember what happened to you, son?" Dr. Langston asked.

"No, sir."

"I need to call an ambulance," Krista said.

"No." Luke grunted and pushed up with his hands. Krista helped him stand.

He wavered a bit and she put her arm around his waist to steady him. Dr. Langston came around the other side for support.

"Let's get him into the pastor's office," the doctor said.

Krista nodded and the three of them shuffled past the growing crowd into the back of the church.

"Give us space," the doctor ordered the group, then nodded at Julie Sass. "Can you get my car keys out of my parka inside and get my bag out of the car?"

"Absolutely." She ran ahead, while Krista and the doctor helped Luke up the back steps and down the hallway toward Pastor White's office.

The concerned mumblings of church friends echoed down the hall behind them. There was no way around it, everyone was going to find out who Luke was and why he was here.

And how much danger Krista had somehow brought back with her to Wentworth.

"What happened?" Tatum asked someone behind them.

"Looks like he slipped on the ice. Happens to the best of us," the chief offered. "Everyone, back to the potluck."

Krista understood his motivation to keep the real danger a secret. His job was to protect the people of Wentworth, and find the Garcia threat as quickly and quietly as possible.

Krista and the doctor led Luke around the corner to a chair in the pastor's office. She kneeled beside him.

She didn't like the way he looked. His skin was pale and his eyes creased with confusion.

"Do you feel faint?" the doctor asked.

"No, but I've got a massive headache."

Julie rushed into the room. "Your bag."

Dr. Langston opened it and pulled out a penlight to examine Luke's eyes.

"Let's start with a few questions," the doctor said, shining the light in one eye, then the other. "What day of the week is it?"

"Friday."

"What's your name?"

"Luke McIntyre."

"Where are you?"

Luke glanced around the room. Krista mouthed "church" and Doc Langston raised a brow.

"Sorry, sorry," Krista said. She couldn't help herself. She wanted him to be okay.

Julie touched Krista's arm. "Come here," Julie motioned.

Krista glanced at Luke and he shot her a hint of a smile, indicating he'd be okay without her hovering over him.

She wandered to the other side of the room with Julie. "What happened?" Julie asked.

"I have no idea. I went looking for Luke, and spotted some guy standing over him in the snow."

"What happened to the guy?"

"When I called out for Luke, he took off."

Julie's gaze drifted to the doctor's examination of Luke. "So some guy attacked Luke?"

"Let's not assume that. But he sure didn't do anything to get help."

The chief came into the pastor's office. "Well, that's more excitement than we've had at a potluck in ten years. They need you out there, Julie. Something about the kids spiking the punch?"

"Oh, no." Julie rushed out of the office and the chief closed the door.

"How is he?" the chief asked.

"Fine," Luke said.

"His eyes look fine, motor skills good," Doc Langston said. "He's got a nasty contusion on the back of his head. You get that from falling on the ice, son?"

"I…" He paused. "Don't remember, sorry."

"Nothing to be sorry about." The doctor stood and glanced at Krista. "Wouldn't hurt to put ice on his head, get fluids into him and ask him questions every hour or so until he goes to bed. If he seems disoriented or starts vomiting, get him to the clinic."

"Should I take him to the clinic now?" Krista said.

"No," Luke argued. "Just get me some aspirin and I'll be fine."

The doctor glanced at Luke, then Krista. "I don't think it's serious. Still, wish you could remember what happened, son."

Luke rubbed the back of his head. "Me, too."

"Well, I'm headed back inside." Dr. Langston packed up his bag.

"Thanks." The chief opened the door, and closed it behind him.

Luke glanced up at Krista. "Stop looking at me like that."

"Like what?"

"Like I'm dying or something."

"I was worried."

"Don't be. I've been through worse."

The comment stung, especially because it drove home the violence he'd survived as a federal agent, violence that disturbed her way too much to be a part of her life.

"What happened out there?" the chief asked.

"I told you, I don't remember," Luke snapped.

"Luke," Krista hushed.

"I'm frustrated, okay? One minute I'm in the community room staring at a plate of food, and the next thing I know I'm facedown in the snow."

"Do you remember handing me your plate and saying you had to get outside?" the chief said.

Luke's eyebrows furrowed and dawning colored his blue eyes, then he glanced away. "No."

Either he didn't remember or he didn't want to share. Krista guessed it was door number two.

Krista wondered if his disorientation was freaking him out. She touched his shoulder. "It's okay. You're safe."

He stood and paced to the window, breaking their connection.

She wasn't sure how much more of this she could take. Although his reaction was probably born of frustration and helplessness, it cut deep into her heart.

"I need to talk to the chief." Luke turned to her. "Alone."

"I thought we agreed you'd keep me in the loop from now on?"

"Just…" He bit back what he was about to say. "Can you get me some aspirin?"

"Sure." Krista left before doing something stupid,

like getting in his face and demanding he stop shutting her out.

She headed down the hall, calming her breathing, fighting back the wave of frustration that made her tear up.

Why did he get to her like this?

Because you care about him more than you're supposed to. Her heart plummeted when she saw his body lying there in the snow. If he had died…

No, she couldn't think about that now.

Thank you, Lord, for protecting Luke. Please help me with my feelings for him, and please help me show him the grace of God.

He was angry and embarrassed, and the pain reliever did little to ease the pounding in his head. And all he wanted to do was go back to his temporary home and chill out with Roscoe.

But Krista was determined to check in on Natalie and bring her food from the potluck. Krista was concerned because she hadn't spoken to her friend since she'd been released from the hospital.

"Head still hurt?" she asked.

"Yep."

"Want me to drop you at home?"

"Nope."

"I'm sure I'd be safe at Natalie's."

"Just as I was sure I'd be safe at church." The minute he said it he regretted the words. They weren't necessary. He didn't have to bite her head off.

"Sorry," he said.

"I know."

He suspected she really did know, and that terrified

him. He could face off some of the deadliest criminals, but what scared him more was this woman's ability to see into his heart.

"I'll only be a few minutes," she said, turning down a side street.

"I'm going in with you."

"I'm not sure Timothy will like that."

"He'll get used to me." He eyed her. "You have."

She smiled, then redirected her attention to the street. A good thing.

"That's odd," she said.

"What?"

"Her house is completely dark."

"Maybe she's asleep."

"No, she always leaves the porch light on, and the light in the living room is on a timer. It stays on all night for her cat."

"Cat's afraid of the dark, is it?"

"Natalie thinks so."

"Drive past the house a block and park."

"But—"

"Please, just do it."

With a disgruntled sigh, Krista passed Natalie's house and pulled up behind a blue sedan.

"Call her," Luke ordered.

Krista dug in her pocket for her cell and made the call.

"Voice mail," she said.

"Try again."

She called her friend, tapping her fingers on the steering wheel. "It's no use, she's not—" Krista sat up straight. "Natalie?... Where are you?... But... I know, but..."

While Krista caught up with her friend Luke scanned the neighborhood. He was seeing shadows everywhere now, behind trees, beside cars, even in living room windows.

He'd let his guard down earlier, allowed ghosts of the past to mess with his head and throw him off course for only a few minutes. That's all it took for someone to whack him but good.

But why? If they'd wanted him dead they would have finished him off in the church garden.

Then again, it seemed like Krista had interrupted the attack. He fisted his hand. She could have been kidnapped, or worse, and he would have been lying there, unconscious. Helpless. Unable to protect her.

"I don't understand," Krista said. Luke figured she was still talking to her friend. "Luke?"

He turned to her perplexed expression. "Excuse me?"

"She's at Timothy's. I guess he doesn't want her at home by herself."

"That's decent of him."

"He's really not the nurturing type and has little patience."

"He must love her."

The words hung in the air between them. Love, a confusing and complicated emotion at best.

"She's lucky," Krista whispered, and started the car.

"So we're going to Timothy's?" Luke asked.

"No. She doesn't want to upset him and he, well, doesn't want me around right now."

"What's that about?"

"He blames me for the car accident."

"That's ridiculous."

"He feels the way he feels."

Yep, just like Luke felt something for Krista, even though he knew it was inappropriate and wrong on so many levels.

"May I ask you something?" she said.

"Sure."

"Do you really not remember what drove you outside at church?"

"It's a little foggy, why?"

"Because the look in your eye just before you ran out of church was, I don't know, well it spooked me."

That's the look of raw anguish, sweetheart.

"What did I look like?" he said.

She glanced at him, then back at the road. "Like you just found out your mom died."

His gaze drifted out the side window. She'd read it in his eyes, read the heartbreak and agony that followed. Amazing.

"If you want to talk…" She hesitated. "I'm a really good listener."

"I'll bet you are," he whispered. But talking to her, sharing his buried shame would only weaken his ability to protect her.

"It might make you feel better," she prompted.

"I doubt that."

"Try it."

"I remembered something about my mom." Although his mind told him to shut his mouth, his heart couldn't stop the words.

"Is she…?"

"Dead. Passed away when I was fifteen."

"Oh, Luke, I'm so sorry."

"It happens."

A few minutes of silence passed as they drove

through the heart of town to get to Krista's house. He thought he was off the hook.

"Do the holidays make you sad because you think of your mom?"

"Has nothing to do with the holidays."

"Then what—"

"I remembered she was a drunk, okay? And all the church people knew about it and pitied me and gave me handouts. I hated it."

"They were trying to help."

"I don't need anybody's help, not now, and I certainly didn't need it then."

"Everyone needs help once in a while, Luke."

"Not me. Don't need it, don't want it."

"Ever?"

"Never."

"But why—"

"Because when I let someone help I get them killed."

Chapter Fifteen

Krista gripped the steering wheel, shocked by his confession. She knew how she wanted to respond. She wanted to ask him pointed questions about what happened and why he blamed himself for needing someone's help. She suspected it had to do with his partner.

She glanced his way, but his eyes were closed and he was rubbing his temples. He'd shut down. He was in pain, and she should give him space. For now.

They pulled into her driveway and she noticed the kitchen light on. "I don't remember leaving the light on."

He snapped his attention to the house and squinted. Opening his door, he said, "I'll check it out."

"I'm going with you."

He shot her that look she figured was meant to intimidate her into staying in the car, but she ignored it. There was no way she was letting him walk into a potentially dangerous situation after just being knocked out. She grabbed the plate of food meant for Natalie and followed him.

"Let's get Roscoe to help us out." He went to the garage and opened the side door. He'd left a lamp on for the dog, only...

...the dog wasn't there.

"Roscoe," she hushed.

"Stay here, got it? No back talk on this one."

She nodded, remorse gripping her chest at the thought that someone had taken or hurt the dog. He closed the garage door and she clicked off the light to watch him approach the house. He crept toward the back door and reached inside his jacket for his gun. She swallowed back her panic, slowed her breathing so she wouldn't pass out.

She wanted this whole thing over, wanted to get back to her uneventful, normal life. She'd collected some good information for Luke tonight at the potluck, and was looking forward to sharing it, yet they hadn't had a chance to talk about it since they'd left church.

Pulling out her phone, she got ready to call 9-1-1.

Roscoe's bark echoed from the house.

"What the...?" she whispered to herself. How did he get inside? The back door opened and Luke holstered his gun. Officer Deanna West stood in the doorway. Luke motioned for Krista to join him.

Krista went to the back door. "Hey, Deanna."

"Hi, Krista. Food for me? Thanks." Her brown eyes widened with anticipation.

"I'd brought it for Natalie, but she's not up for visitors." Krista slid the plate onto the counter.

"More like the ball and chain isn't up for visitors," Deanna added.

"You don't like Timothy?" Luke asked, settling into a kitchen chair.

"He's a wee bit possessive for my taste. Hey, as long as you're here with Krista, I need to run a few errands."

"No problem," Luke said.

"I'll be back in an hour. I've got a key, obviously."

"Where did you—"

"Under the purple pot outside," Deanna interrupted Krista. "Anyone who knows you could figure that out."

"I'm so transparent," Krista said.

"You can say that again," Luke added while petting Roscoe.

"You say it like it's a bad thing," Krista retorted.

"Well, I'll leave you kids to fight." Deanna winked and breezed out the back door.

Krista leaned against the counter. It was nearly nine and she was beat, but she needed to share information with Luke in hopes of helping him solve this case.

"Wanna know what I found out tonight?" she said.

Luke glanced up.

"I heard a few interesting things that may or may not mean anything." She sat down next to him and propped her chin on her upturned palm. "First, someone broke into Luanne Sparks's car two days ago."

"And this is important because…?"

"She went to Mexico with us and hadn't unloaded her souvenirs from the car yet. Her daughter got sick and couldn't watch the twins, so Grandma Luanne had to jump in and while the car was parked outside someone got into the trunk and emptied it out. And I'm sure this is nothing, but Alan bought a hunting rifle a few days ago. He told Ned at the hardware store that he was concerned about the sudden crime wave in Wentworth and needed it to scare off any potential intruders."

"That guy with any kind of gun…" He shook his head.

"Timothy's sheet metal business is going well. He just got a big contract from All Star Roofing, which accounts for his buying property up north. Lucy and Ralph Grimes bought an old farmhouse outside of Muskegon to rehab, and there was one other thing." She paused and tapped her forefinger to her chin. "Oh, Phillip Barton bought a new car."

"That's big news," he said, half kidding.

"It is if the guy runs a boat business. He can't make that much money."

"The chief told me he owns a seat on the board of trade."

"Yeah, but a Mercedes SL?" She shook her head. "Has to cost—"

"They start at around a hundred thousand."

"Who can afford that? And who needs it?"

"Have you ever driven one?"

"Have you?"

"No, but I can imagine it's a pretty nice ride."

She made a face.

"I was going to look into Phillip a little more anyway."

"I'd better warn you, some of the ladies are asking for your number so when you're done at the tea shop you could to do some 'honey do' chores for them."

"You'd better add to my list."

He seemed less intense for the moment, so she dived in. "I'm taking a guess, but did you ask your partner for help and that's when he was killed?"

Luke leaned back in his chair. "Boy, woman, you switch gears faster than a driver at Indy."

She studied him, wondering if he'd answer. It was a nosy question, sure, but she really felt like she could help him, ease some of the angst twisting him in knots, if she knew more about his situation.

Through the grace of God anything was possible.

"I should have handled it on my own," Luke whispered.

"Handled what?"

"I got a tip, thought I could use backup, so I called Karl. I should have alerted my supervisor. He would have sent a team, but I thought I had it under control." He pinned her with cool, blue eyes. "I didn't."

"And Karl was killed."

Luke slowly tapped his finger on the kitchen table as if calming himself. "He left behind a wife and two-year-old. I have no family. I should have been the one to die."

"But you didn't and you've gone on to catch plenty of criminals."

"Doesn't justify his death."

"Nothing justifies an untimely death of a loved one." She could barely hear her own voice, and realized she was sinking into her own dark memories.

"I'm sorry," he said, leaning forward and placing his hand over hers. "We've both experienced some pretty ugly things."

"And some beautiful ones as well, don't forget."

"Yeah, like what?"

"The support of the community when Mom and I moved here. Wentworth adopted us, even though frightening rumors preceded us to town. The people here didn't care, and the folks at Peace Church were amazing."

"You were lucky."

"It's not about luck. It's about love. The love of God."

Luke slipped his hand away.

"God forgives and loves you, Luke."

He snapped his gaze to hers and she nearly scooted back at the intensity she read there.

"He couldn't possibly forgive me," Luke said.

"For what happened to your partner?"

"For what I did to my mother."

Krista steeled herself with a prayer. *Jesus, help me listen with an open heart, and offer forgiveness where You surely would.*

"What did you do to your mom?"

"I made her life miserable." He glanced at the floor.

She waited, sensing there was more.

"Always in trouble, getting arrested when I was thirteen. She said I drove her so crazy she had to drink to stay sane."

"And you believed her?"

Luke glanced up. "She was my mom."

Right, and we all believe our parents, especially at that age.

"What happened to your dad?" she asked.

"Left when I was little." Luke's cell vibrated and he snatched it from his belt. He paced into the living room. "McIntyre."

As the low timbre of his voice drifted into the kitchen, she sighed and touched her silver charm. It all made sense—Luke's self-loathing because he thought he drove away his father and felt responsible for his mother's drinking. That was so cruel to do to a child. Yet he'd survived his upbringing and grew up to be an honorable man who sacrificed his own safety to protect others.

He was a fine human being. He should be proud of himself instead of hearing his mother's words haunt him from the past.

How could she convince him of that?

* * *

"You wanted to know if anyone strange came to town and this is pretty strange," Chief Cunningham said.

Three men had checked into the Crocker Hotel on the outskirts of town. They were sharing a room, and specifically asked for a view of the parking lot.

As if they were waiting for someone. Were they Garcia's men?

"Did the clerk give you a description?" Luke asked.

"Thirties, scruffy-lookin', polite. Two of them were wearing cowboy hats. Said they were here for a party."

Garcia owned a number of ranches staffed by cowboys to get the work done.

"I need to go with you," Luke said.

"You sure you're up to it?"

"I'm fine. Send Officer West back to watch over Krista. Better yet, have her take Krista somewhere else for the night, just until we figure this out."

"Good thinking. I'll swing by to pick you up."

"Thanks." Luke ended the call and glanced at the kitchen. The sound of Krista humming drifted into the living room.

For once Luke welcomed bad news. It meant he'd be out investigating instead of sitting in Krista's kitchen letting her do emotional open-heart surgery on him. He still couldn't believe he'd exposed himself like that, that he'd told her about Dad…about Mom.

He figured he was still off kilter from the knock to the head. He straightened. Could his attacker have been one of Garcia's men who'd registered at Crocker Hotel? Waiting for Krista to come out of church so he could take a shot at her?

He went into the kitchen and found Krista repackaging the leftovers from the potluck.

"Who was that?" she asked, casually, as if the call hadn't just interrupted a raw moment for him.

"The chief. He's picking me up and sending Officer West back to take you someplace for the night."

She froze in mid scoop of stuffing. "Why?"

"Three suspicious-looking men rented a room at the Crocker Hotel. The chief wants to check it out."

"So why do you have to go?"

"They could be Garcia's men. I won't let him go into this alone."

"But you were unconscious a few hours ago."

"I'm fine."

"You're limping."

"My ankle's a little sore. No big deal."

She took a step toward him. "It is if you need to run away from the bad guys."

"Krista—"

"You can't go. I won't let you."

"You won't let me?" He smiled, trying to make light of her comment.

"I don't think this is funny."

"It's my job."

"Don't remind me." She turned her back to him and went back to scooping food into a plastic container.

He'd upset her. He didn't mean to. But this job, going out in the late hours and investigating suspects, was part of the deal. It's what drove him, kept him running at high speed.

Then she turned to him, her green eyes misting, and he wasn't sure about anything anymore.

"I will pray for your safety."

"Thanks."

She closed in on him and the room got incredibly small. Unhooking her necklace, she said, "I want you to take this, for luck."

He eyed the silver charm. "I'll be fine. You hold on to it for luck."

Gripping his biceps, she stood on her tiptoes and kissed his cheek.

Goose bumps shot down his arms and he struggled to catch his breath. This was inappropriate for so many reasons, yet he loved the way her lips felt against his cheek.

The back door clicked open. "The chief is—whoa, sorry," Officer West said.

Krista released Luke and rushed past him into the living room. "Good luck!" she called and raced up the stairs.

"Sorry," Officer West said.

Luke went to the door but didn't make eye contact with the cop. "Get her out of here, somewhere safe, I don't care where."

"I will."

He snapped around and pointed his finger, as if to punctuate his order, as if he had something important to add but nothing came out.

"It's okay," Deanna assured. "I'll take care of her."

With a nod, he marched down the back steps to the chief's car.

Ten minutes later Luke and the chief were at the hotel asking questions.

"Did you see them leave?" the chief asked the teen-age clerk.

"Nah, but I've been texting my boyfriend on and off for the past hour."

"Describe the guests," Luke asked.

"Tall, dark and one was actually handsome," she joked.

"Did they speak with an accent?" Luke pushed.

She glanced up, as if thinking. "Yeah, actually the one dude had an accent."

Luke and the chief shared a look.

She shrugged and handed Luke a key.

"Don't text your boyfriend about this, or tell anyone else until we figure out what's going on, got it?" Chief Cunningham said to the girl.

She nibbled her lower lip and glanced away.

"Who did you tell?" the chief said.

"That's what Ryan and I've been texting about. Trying to figure out who these guys are."

"Don't tell him we're here or what we're doing. We wouldn't want any innocent bystanders getting hurt because they showed up to check it out."

"Okay, sure. But I hate lying to Ryan."

Luke snatched her cell phone and turned it off. "Now you're not lying."

She nodded, a little taken aback by Luke's behavior. Didn't surprise him, but he didn't know what else to do.

With a nod, the chief led them outside to room 7.

A part of Luke hoped this was it, that these were the guys that would put an end to this case and the constant adrenaline flowing through his body because he was afraid Krista would be hurt.

Yet another part of him dreaded the day he'd have to say goodbye to her.

Focus, McIntyre!

They approached the room and Luke motioned for the chief to stand on the other side of the door. Luke calmed his breathing and readied for an assault.

The sound of male laughter filtered through the window. The chief raised an eyebrow and Luke shrugged. Maybe they were killing time before they carried out their assignment.

Luke tapped on the door with the barrel of his gun, but the guys didn't hear him. He banged louder.

The room went silent. A few seconds passed.

"Who is it?" a deep male voice called out.

"Hotel manager."

"What? We're not being that loud."

"Open the door, sir."

Luke readied himself to kick in the door once they cracked it open.

The seconds seemed to drag on for hours.

Ready.

Set.

The door opened.

Luke kicked the door open in the guy's face and charged into the room, gun drawn.

At three guys playing poker and smoking cigars.

"What on earth, man?" said the guy who answered the door. He stumbled back onto the bed, holding his nose.

Two of the men dropped their cards and raised their hands. The third, a big guy in a checked flannel shirt, glared at Luke.

"Edie sent you, didn't she?" flannel shirt said.

"I'm a federal agent. This is the Wentworth police chief. We need to see some I.D."

The three guys sitting at the table pulled out their

wallets. They passed them to the chief who glanced at them, then back at the men.

"Looks legit," the chief said.

Luke holstered his gun. "So what's the deal here?"

"Texas hold 'em," a guy said.

"No, I mean why rent the room to play cards?"

"You kidding? You think our wives would let us have a card game at any of our houses? They hate the smoke, the jokes, the whole thing," one of the guys said.

"So we said we were going hunting for the weekend and we rented a room."

"Just one?"

"I rented one, too," the guy with the bloody nose said, raising his hand.

"The three of us checked in together and Dave came later."

"Suzy wouldn't let me go before I bathed the kids," Dave explained.

Unbelievable. Luke just gave a guy a bloody nose and ruined these guys' night of male bonding.

"Why rent a room in Wentworth?" the chief asked.

"It's far enough away from Stillwater that no one would recognize us and report to our wives," Dave said.

"Although now we'll probably be in the paper," the skinny dude added. "Are we going to be arrested?"

Flannel shirt looked at his friend. "For what? Playing cards?"

"You're not going to be arrested. Our mistake," the chief apologized.

"Sorry, guys," Luke said. "We're investigating a case and three guys checking into one hotel room sounded suspicious."

"Well, we'll leave you to your game." The chief nodded to Luke and they left the room.

Luke was embarrassed, sure, and more than a little frustrated. But he'd do whatever was necessary to protect Krista and put an end to Garcia's reign.

Interesting how he was thinking of her first.

"Well, that's a relief," the chief said.

"Not really."

They got into the squad car and the chief glanced at Luke. "Why not?"

"Someone's still after Krista and won't stop until they get what they want."

Chapter Sixteen

Krista paced Julie Sass's living room, glancing out the window every few minutes hoping for the chief's car to pull up.

"You'd think *you* were the mother of nineteen-year-old twins," Julie said, sipping her tea in an easy chair.

"We should have heard something by now." Krista glanced at Deanna, who doodled in a sketchbook. "Shouldn't we have heard something?"

"I'm sure they'll notify us the minute they know anything."

Krista glanced back outside. A few minutes later she felt Julie's hand on her shoulder and glanced at her friend.

"Oh, sweetheart, you got it bad," Julie said.

Deanna winked at her.

"Stop, both of you." Krista paced to the sofa, sat down and fingered her charm. She wished Luke would have taken it with him.

Julie sat next to her. "Come on, spill it."

"I'm a little anxious."

"And in love?" Julie offered.

Krista squared off at her. "This can't be love, I mean, it's not supposed to feel this way."

"What way?" Deanna prodded.

"Like, like I'm antsy, nervous, something, I don't know."

Deanna smiled and focused on her sketchpad.

"What's so funny?" Krista said.

"You've never been in love before, so it might feel a little uncomfortable," Julie offered.

"I thought it's supposed to feel wonderful and peaceful and...and—"

"It's nerve-wracking," Deanna said.

"And sometimes frustrating," Julie added.

"And chaotic."

"And thrilling."

"And sometimes, confusing," Julie explained. "But I've seen you two together. I recognize that look. On both your faces."

Krista held her friend's gaze. "It's a disaster."

"I'm an expert on disaster," Deanna offered.

"I should have fallen for Alan," Krista said.

Deanna glanced up from her sketchbook. "That would have been a major disaster."

"Look." Julie took Krista's hand. "If it's meant to be, it will work out."

"How do I know this isn't just happening because he's here to protect me?"

"That's true, there's that thing called transference," Deanna said.

"I know you, Krista, probably as well as your mom knows you. This is the real deal."

"Then it's the ultimate disaster because he lives in New York and I live here, and I run a tea shop and he hunts criminals and—"

"Criminals?" Julie questioned.

"And now I've blown his cover."

Deanna stopped drawing and joined the ladies in the living room. "Julie, it's important that you not say anything to anyone about Luke's real reason for being here."

"Which is what?"

"He's working on a case. He's with the DEA."

"Drugs? Here in Wentworth?"

"We're not sure," Deanna said.

"It's my fault." Krista paced back to the window. "It has something to do with my trip to Mexico. They think someone smuggled something into to my things and a drug lord wants to retrieve it." She glanced at Julie. "That's our theory, anyway."

"Oh, Krista, I'm sorry." Julie went to Krista and gave her a hug. "You must be so scared."

"Not really. I've got Luke as my personal protector."

"Handyman at the tea shop, staying in your garage. It all makes sense now."

"Except for the fact I'm falling for him."

"Speaking of which…" Julie nodded at the window. The chief's cruiser pulled into the driveway.

"Please don't tell anyone about what's really going on," Deanna said, opening the door. "It could put your family in danger."

"I won't," Julie said.

Deanna went to greet the chief and Luke.

Julie turned back to Krista. "What are you going to do about Luke?"

"There's nothing to do. There's no future there."

"Your faith is your strength, Krista. Don't give up on it now."

Krista smiled and hugged her friend. "Thanks."

"What's wrong?" Luke said, approaching Krista.

"I was just getting advice from my big sister," Krista said.

Julie shot Krista a knowing smile.

"You okay?" Luke touched her arm and looked deep into her eyes.

"Yeah, just tired," her voice caught. He cared about her. A lot. She cleared her throat. "What happened at the hotel?"

"I'll tell you on the way home," Luke said.

Home. Her chest tightened. If only that were true, if only she and Luke shared a home.

"Did you three have a nice visit?" the chief said, eyeing them suspiciously. The chief had been married for thirty years. He recognized girl talk when he saw it.

"Very nice," Julie said.

The twins pounded up the steps and raced through the front door. "Why are the cops here?" Tatum asked.

"I'm here to bust you girls on curfew," Chief Cunningham said.

"Hey, I'm nineteen," Tatum said.

"Me, too," Tori said.

"He's teasing, sweetheart," Julie said. "My girls are home. I can go to sleep."

"Thanks for everything," Krista said, envious of Julie's beautiful family.

"Good night, all," the chief said.

Deanna drove Luke and Krista back to the house and made herself comfortable in the guest bedroom upstairs. Luke went through the house and rechecked all the locks, windows, doors, everything.

It seemed like he was stalling.

"Keep Roscoe inside with you tonight. A barking dog can deter someone from breaking in."

"You didn't tell me what happened at the Crocker." She sat at the kitchen table and stretched out her legs.

"We busted up a card game."

"You're kidding."

"Nope. Four guys needing some cave time."

"Cave time?"

"Guys need to retreat into their caves once in a while to get a break from their women."

"You make us sound like shrews."

Luke shrugged. "It's normal, at least that's what my partner used to say."

"You miss him."

"He was a good man."

"So are you."

"Thanks, but…"

"What?"

"Never mind. What's on the agenda for tomorrow?" he asked.

She realized he was keeping her at a distance.

"I have to set up for a reception at the Silver Lake Lighthouse. They're doing a dessert fundraiser."

"Man, this little town is a busy place."

Luke started for the back door, but she jumped up and caught his arm. He stiffened, his eyes growing dark.

"Tonight, when you went to the hotel… I was so worried," she said. "I paced and I fretted and—"

"It's part of the job. It's what I do." He glanced at the floor, breaking eye contact.

"I know that. But what I realized was—"

He pressed his forefinger to her lips. "Don't say it."

She tenderly kissed his finger. He slid his hand down to rest on her shoulder.

"Why not?" she whispered.

"It's impossible."

"Not if you have faith."

He rolled his eyes, and with a hand on his cheek, she made him focus on her. "I have enough for both of us. Trust me, Luke. Trust God."

She leaned forward and kissed him. The subtle vibration of his moan tickled her lips. It was just as she'd remembered, soft and sweet, with a hint of desperation.

She'd never felt so safe, so at peace, as she did in Luke's arms.

Suddenly he broke the kiss and stepped back. She searched his eyes, but he wouldn't look at her.

"We can't." He reached for the back door, but she blocked him.

"Look at me."

He planted his hands to his hips and looked over her shoulder.

"Luke?"

Clenching his jaw, his eyes drifted to meet hers.

"It's okay," she said. "I wanted you to kiss me."

"But I shouldn't have."

"Sure you—"

"Do you want to die, Krista? Because getting close to me will get you killed."

She touched his cheek. He closed his eyes and sighed. A few seconds later, he reached around her to open the door.

"See you tomorrow," he said and walked out to the garage.

* * *

She fretted, paced and worried about him.

Three more reasons to add to the list of why Luke shouldn't let this thing with Krista go any farther. Forget the top two reasons, the fact he lived in a big city miles away from here and his violent career was his priority.

Krista had experienced her share of violence. He wouldn't bring more into her life.

He spent part of the day doing legitimate chores upstairs, building bookshelves and organizing supplies. The rest of the time he spent on reviewing suspects and making calls.

Yet he felt no closer to exposing the local contact. He looked over his list: Phillip Barton, Ralph Grimes, Alan and perhaps, yes, he had to accept it, Krista's friend, Natalie. Luke wondered if Natalie was the target of the car accident all along.

The fact was Natalie's financials were a mess. She was in debt up to her eyeballs, in part because of the floundering real estate market and having loaned her fiancé money to keep his business solvent.

Folks on the verge of financial disaster were the easiest targets for people like Garcia.

"Luke?" Krista called upstairs. "We're taking off in twenty minutes."

"Thanks."

He e-mailed his supervisor a request for a more extensive background check on Phillip, Ralph, Alan and Natalie. A deeper look into their backgrounds could turn up more clues, maybe even a direct connection to Garcia.

He packed up his folders, glanced at the newly organized office and a sense of pride washed over him. He liked doing things for Krista.

You've completely lost it, buddy. Shaking his head, he went downstairs. It was time to load up his car with food and supplies for the lighthouse event.

"Krista?" he said, walking into the dining room. The chairs were flipped onto tables, and the mop lay on the floor as if someone had been interrupted.

He marched into the back and found Timothy, Natalie's fiancé, blocking the back door. "Looking for someone?" the guy said.

"Krista."

"She's outside with Natalie."

Luke started for the door.

"Don't even think about it," Timothy said. "Natalie's doing an intervention."

"Excuse me?"

"To get you out of Krista's life."

"I think that's up to Krista."

"Yeah, well, she's a sweet girl," Timothy said. "Her mom and grandmother protected her most of her life, so she's lacking the skills needed in this situation."

"And what skills are those?"

"To be able to discern friend from enemy."

"I'm not her enemy."

"You're using her as bait for your criminal case."

"How did you—"

"Natalie told me and I confirmed it with the chief."

"The fewer people who know about this, the better chance I have to find the perp."

"Yeah, well, I won't tell anyone." He paused, looked up and shot Luke a sinister smile. "As long as you leave Krista alone."

"It's kind of hard to keep my distance when I'm here to protect her."

"Correction, you're here to solve your case. She just happens to be collateral damage."

"You could be arrested for interfering with a federal investigation."

Timothy took a step toward him. "Well, you should be arrested for messing with that girl's head and making her fall in love with you."

Silence stretched between them. Love? Had Krista said that?

"Natalie is the love of my life and Krista is her best friend," Timothy said. "She's like my sister, so leave her alone."

"I have a job to do."

"You're a selfish jerk out for yourself no matter who gets hurt."

Krista breezed into the back. "Hey, what's going on?" Neither man spoke.

"Guys?" She glanced from Timothy to Luke.

"Timothy, Nat's really tired. You'd better get going." She gave Timothy a hug and Luke wanted to rip them apart.

Not because Timothy thought of her in a romantic way, but because Luke wanted her depending on Luke, leaning on him, not on this jerk.

She stepped back and patted Timothy's shoulder. "Thanks for bringing Nat over."

"Sure thing." Timothy glanced at Krista. "You take care of yourself."

"I will."

Timothy shot one warning glare at Luke and walked away.

She turned to Luke. "Whoa, what was that about?"

"Not important."

Yet it was very important. Krista's friends were worried about her. Luke actually agreed with Timothy. Krista falling in love with Luke was a disaster with a capital *D*.

"You sure you're okay?" Krista grabbed a box of dishes.

"Yep." Or he would be as soon as he figured out how to stop her from falling in love with him.

Yeah, and how are you going to do that, McIntyre? Especially because he was feeling the pull himself, the pull toward something he'd never felt before.

Love.

Not good. He would have to distance himself from her in every way possible. He'd let things slip, things about Karl, his parents, things that made her feel sorry for him and caused her to have feelings she confused with love. No more. He'd put up the wall and do his job.

Regardless of how he was feeling about the adorable Krista Yates.

"It's going to be perfect," Krista said in a singsong voice.

Luke finished unpacking the last of the teacups and glanced at Krista. The woman was being hunted by drug thugs, yet she still enjoyed the moment and took pleasure in her work. How was that possible?

She eyed him and tipped her head slightly. "You're awfully quiet."

"Got nothing to say."

"Uh, right. Try again. Timothy upset you. What happened?"

"You first. What did you and Natalie talk about?"

"The potluck, her latest real estate sale, the wedding. They've rented Michigan Shores for July of next year."

"She didn't—" he paused "—say anything about me?"

She shrugged.

"She told Timothy I was a federal agent," Luke said.

"Yeah, I heard that." She sprinkled rose petals across the buffet table. "He was freaking out, saying I should stay away from you because you're not good for me. Natalie explained what was going on and why we're—" she hesitated "—together all the time."

"Maybe he's right."

Krista focused on her rose petal display. "What do you mean?"

"About me not being good for you."

She waved him off. "Timothy doesn't even know you."

"Neither do you, Krista."

She straightened. "I disagree."

"I'm here to protect you. Naturally you're going to be drawn to me. It happens all the time."

"Not to me it doesn't."

"Whatever you think is happening—"

"I don't think, I know."

"Krista—"

"I left something in the car," she interrupted, and walked to the spiral staircase leading downstairs.

"Stop. I'll get it." He didn't want her going out there alone.

She handed him her car keys, but didn't make eye contact. "The lighter should be in the front seat. I need it for the candles." She put on latex gloves and placed tea sandwiches on a china plate.

He didn't want to hurt her, but the sooner she stopped this fantasy about she and Luke, the better she'd be. He went outside, scanning the property for danger.

He'd been here for days, yet still wasn't any closer to knowing who hunted Krista and what he wanted. Luke felt like a fool, and wondered if his feelings for Krista were messing with his ability to close this case.

Maybe it was time to bring in someone else to lead the investigation, or at least act as Krista's bodyguard while Luke flushed out the perp. Another agent would have the distance needed to focus on keeping her safe.

His cell vibrated and he noticed he was low on battery. He'd been so distracted by potlucks and random kisses that he forgot to do the most basic things.

"McIntyre," he answered.

"It's Marks. Got prints on the note. You know someone named Alan Jameson?"

Luke's straightened. Alan was always close to Krista, checking on her, touching her.

"I'll question him as soon as I can," Luke said.

"Anything else you need from us?"

"Don't suppose the suitcase was any help?"

"Haven't got the labs back. I'll call as soon as I do."

"Thanks."

Luke grabbed the lighter from the car and walked back to the lighthouse, waiting for Alan to pop out of the shadows. Luke had a hard time believing he was involved in an international drug ring.

He made his way up the spiral staircase and handed Krista the lighter.

"Thanks."

She smiled, as if they hadn't just argued about their

relationship, as if he hadn't just hurt her feelings. But he knew he had. He'd seen it in her green eyes.

"My boss called with a lead," he said.

He hesitated. "And?"

"How well do you really know Alan?"

She pinned him with disbelief in her eyes. "You're kidding me."

"Afraid not."

"Alan is always so nice and solicitous. I guess the whole time he was playing me because he wanted to smuggle drugs?"

"I doubt it's that simple."

She shrugged. He knew she didn't like Alan romantically, but still, she'd developed a certain amount of trust for the man.

Trust now broken.

"I'll call the chief and ask him to bring Alan in for questioning. What's left to do here?"

"I can teach you how to fold napkins," she offered as she lit a candle on the buffet table.

Luke groaned, then pulled out his cell and called the chief with the news about Alan.

Suddenly the lights went out, plunging them into darkness.

Chapter Seventeen

Luke grabbed Krista's hand and shifted her behind him. He slipped his other hand inside his jacket and pulled out the Glock, careful not to flash it to Krista.

"Someone forget to pay his light bill?" he joked.

"The wiring is pretty outdated."

They shared a knowing look in the candlelight. This wasn't about old wiring or light bills.

He should check it out, but for all he knew this could be a diversion to get him to leave her alone, unprotected and vulnerable.

"Has this ever happened before?" he asked.

"Once."

"What did you do?"

"Called Luther, the maintenance guy."

"Call him."

"My purse is under the table."

Pointing his gun at the stairs, he led her to the buffet table and she got her cell phone from her purse.

"It's going to voice mail," she said.

"Leave a message. Then call the chief."

She made the calls. "What now?"

"We wait." He didn't have much choice. Once people started arriving, they'd be relatively safe. A crowd would chase off the stalker, if he's what caused this blackout. It could just be a power surge, after all, she had hot pots and soup warmers plugged in.

He scanned the room and spotted an ice chest in the corner. "Let's get behind the ice chest."

Their position behind the wooden icebox shielded them from a frontal assault. Although if there were more than one guy coming up those stairs and they packed more than a typical handgun, Luke was toast.

"It's Garcia's men, isn't it?" Krista asked.

"Maybe, maybe not."

She put trembling hands together in prayer and whispered under her breath. Her prayers seeped into his chest and he found himself wanting to whisper along with her.

But God didn't answer prayers for people like Luke McIntyre.

"…Lord, all-forgiving…" she whispered.

Luke blocked out her voice and focused on the stairs, on the attacker.

But no one came. The lighthouse drifted into an eerie silence.

Krista stopped praying. Seconds slowly ticked by, adrenaline flowing through his body, making his heart race triple time.

"Luke?" she whispered.

"Yeah?" He didn't look at her.

"If we die—"

He glanced at her. "I won't let that happen. Not to you."

"I want you to know I've never felt this strongly about a man, I mean, the way I feel for you."

He redirected his attention to the stairs. "It's transference, Krista. It happens in cases like these."

"Then why do you feel it, too?"

A door slammed downstairs. "Krista?" a male voice called.

"Timothy?" she said, scooting out from behind Luke.

He holstered his gun and accompanied her to the top of the stairs. "Don't go down there."

"It's just Timothy," she said.

"What happened to the lights?" Timothy said, coming up the stairs with a flashlight.

He flashed it in Luke's face, probably to irritate him. "What's going on here?"

"We were setting up and the lights went out," Krista explained. "What are you doing here?"

"Natalie asked me to drop off some brochures for the new property in Millstown. Who were the two guys outside?"

"What guys?" Luke said.

"Two guys hovering by the garage. They saw me and took off."

"Did either of them look familiar, like Alan Jameson?"

"No, they were bigger than Alan."

"Which direction?"

"Toward Alpine Lodge next door."

"Stay with her," Luke said and rushed past Timothy.

"Luke, don't," Krista called after him.

Nothing was going to stop him from pursuing the guys who'd been stalking Krista. He flew down the stairs and out the back door.

He kept flush to the garage, took a deep breath, and eyed Alpine Lodge. Besides the news about Alan, this was the best lead they'd had and he wasn't letting it slip through his fingers.

Keeping low, he sprinted across the property to the lobby and peeked inside. There was a woman behind a desk reading a magazine, but no customers in sight. Luke slipped his gun into his holster and stepped into the lobby.

The middle-aged woman glanced up and smiled. "Hi. What kind of room would you like?"

"Actually, I don't need a room." Luke flashed his I.D. "I'm looking for two guys, husky-looking?"

"Don't have anyone like that staying here."

"Did you see anything strange or unusual outside tonight?"

"It's so dark out, I can hardly see anything but my own reflection in the window. Sorry."

"Who are your guests?"

"You mean all four of them?" she chuckled. "Let's see, Mr. Pete Ingram, in town on business. Wanda and Monroe Casperson, in town visiting their grown kids. And Lyle Alder." She glanced up. "Traveling salesman on his way to Traverse City."

"You always know so much about your customers?"

"I like them to feel at home." She smiled.

"Okay, well, if you think of anything…" He handed her a card. "Have a good night."

"You, too."

He stepped back outside into the frigid night. Chasing his tail again, yep, that's what he was doing. Round and round, and never catching it.

As he headed back to the lighthouse, a small pickup

pulled into the driveway. An older gentleman got out and grabbed a toolbox.

"You Luther?" Luke said.

"Yep. Lost power again, did she?"

"She?"

"Madeline, the house." He pointed.

"Yeah." Okay, so some people named cars, and this guy named houses.

"I'll start with the fuse box," Luther said.

"Mind if I look on?"

"Doesn't bother me."

Flashing lights sparked across the property as the chief pulled up behind the pickup. He swung open the door. "What's going on?"

"Lights went out," Luke said. "Krista's upstairs. Could you check on her?"

With a nod, the chief went into the lighthouse and Luke followed Luther into the basement. Luther flipped the switch for the basement light. It didn't come on.

Luther pointed the flashlight at the fuse box and hummed.

"Easy fix," Luther said. He flipped the fuse switch and lights popped on. "Wish they were all this easy."

Luther headed upstairs. "You comin'?"

"In a minute."

The guy nodded and went upstairs.

Luke glanced at the dirt floor and spotted an orange, foil candy wrapper. He squatted and picked it up, thinking it looked familiar, but he couldn't place where he'd seen it.

So it wasn't a random blown fuse. Someone had purposely shut off the power…to what? Scare Krista? Attack her?

The guy had to assume Luke would be close and because word had gotten out that Luke carried a firearm,
the perp would know she'd be protected.

Something was off. A smart perp would go after
Krista when she was alone, or at least not with Luke.

He went upstairs where the chief was grilling Krista.

"The lights went out, that's all," she said, glancing
at Luke.

That wasn't all. A few minutes ago he'd stopped her
from professing her love for him. He knew that's what
she was about to say, and he couldn't let her, wouldn't
let her say it out loud. Then it would be real, and he'd
have to deal with his own feelings.

She was right. This wasn't simple transference.

Timothy placed his hand on Krista's shoulder. "You
sure you're okay?"

"I'm fine. And I have to get ready for the reception."

"You call if you need anything," Timothy offered.

"Of course. Love to Natalie."

He kissed her cheek. With a curt nod to Luke, Timothy left.

Krista got busy putting baked goods on a plate.

"Can I talk to you downstairs?" Luke said to the
chief.

Krista glanced over her shoulder, but didn't say anything. No, they'd both said enough.

Once downstairs, Luke turned to the chief.

"So it wasn't a random outage?" the chief asked.

"No, sir."

"What are you thinking?"

"That someone knocked the lights out figuring I'd come
after them, leaving her alone and giving them access."

"They're like a hound dog sniffing out a trail."

"Timothy saw two guys running toward Alpine Lodge. I spoke to the woman at the desk. She didn't see anyone or anything suspicious."

The chief shook his head. "This is getting stranger and stranger."

"I'm thinking of requesting backup."

"Probably a good idea, for everyone." The chief pursed his lips.

"What do you mean?"

The chief nodded toward the lighthouse. "She's taken to you. It's obvious. And she's gonna get hurt."

"Not intentionally."

"I know that, son, but all the same…"

"I'll have the other agent stick close to her while I finish the investigation."

"Good plan. What's on the schedule for tomorrow?"

"I'm hoping a day off."

"That's right, it's Sunday. Okay, we'll see you at church, then."

Church? He had to be kidding.

As he watched the chief drive off, Luke realized he might not have a choice. If Krista went to church Luke would have to follow her, sit with her…

…pray with her.

Surprisingly, he wasn't turned off by the thought after everything he and Krista had been through these last few days. They'd been lucky so far, Krista hadn't been hurt and somehow he'd been able to protect her.

He had a little help with that. Divine help.

That's when it hit him—he should go to church with Krista if for no other reason than to thank God for allowing him to protect her.

Protect her…and fall in love with her.

* * *

It was Sunday, church day. He still couldn't believe he was here, sitting next to Krista in church.

Halfway through the service, the knot in Luke's chest seemed to melt away. He let the music drift over him and released the tension he'd been holding on to for the past few days.

Krista was right. He did feel safe here, accepted in a way he'd never felt before.

Walking into the place hadn't been easy. He'd hesitated at the door.

"There are no enemies here," Krista had whispered and led him inside. She assumed he was scanning the place for suspects, when in fact he was in awe of the atmosphere of Peace Church.

Then again, it had been years since he'd stepped into a church. It had been…

His mother's funeral. The day he'd been completely abandoned. Dad had been gone for years; Grandma Annie and Grandpa Joe had passed away when Luke was young. Luke had been left all alone.

You're never alone, an inner voice whispered.

He glanced up at the colorful stained-glass windows. Oddly, here, in this place, he didn't feel so alone.

Yet deep down he didn't feel that he deserved forgiveness.

Krista squeezed his hand. He glanced into her eyes and was immediately transported into a fantasy of living in Wentworth with her, helping her run the shop, taking Roscoe on walks around Silver Lake.

"Amen," the congregation said.

People gathered their things, the hum of conversation floating in the air.

"See, that wasn't so bad, was it?" she said with a smile.

"No, it wasn't."

"Hey, Krista, Luke," Julie Sass greeted them. "You guys coming to the warming house for caroling after the tree lighting tonight?"

"It's not even Thanksgiving yet," Luke said.

"It's a tourist town. We start the celebration before Thanksgiving to give retailers a bump just before Turkey Day," Julie explained. "So what do you think? Stop by for hot chocolate later? Or did you guys have something else planned?" Julie smiled.

Krista actually blushed and Luke found himself drifting, toying with the possibilities.

"We'll see," Krista said.

"Hey, Krista, they're having problems with the coffeepot again," an older woman said from the back of church.

"Duty calls." She squeezed Luke's hand and headed down the aisle toward the back of the church.

"I can help," he called after her.

She turned. "Stay. I'll be right back."

He was about to follow her, but was flanked by Lucy and Ralph Grimes. He'd scratched them off the suspect list after the background check.

"When can you stop by the farm to do some handiwork?" Lucy asked.

"I didn't know—"

"I can do it," Ralph argued with her.

"You cannot. You should see what this boy has done with Krista's tea shop."

"I asked him first," the streusel lady from the potluck said.

"Wow, now you've got them fighting over you," Julie joked.

"Let's go, Lucy." Ralph glanced at Luke. "Nice to see you at church, son."

"You, too."

Son. The chief called him son and Mr. Grimes called him son. And for some reason, Luke didn't mind.

He realized standing here amongst the congregation that he felt a part of something bigger than himself, bigger than the DEA and catching bad guys.

He liked the feeling.

"We'll see you tonight, then?" Julie said.

"Most likely."

"By the way, thanks," she offered.

"For what?"

"Being good to Krista. I've never seen her smile this much."

With a nod, Julie walked away.

Leaving Luke with a whole slew of guilt to process. He was here to protect Krista, but he was also using her for his case, sticking close to get a lead on what Garcia's men were after.

No, that was his original motivation for coming here. Find the bad guy and shut him down.

Things had changed.

As people filed out of church Luke sat back down, taking a second to evaluate the turn of events.

He wasn't just here to close the Garcia case. He was here to protect Krista.

Because he was falling in love with her.

Help me, God, he prayed silently. *I want to do right by her.*

For the first time in forever he wondered, was forgiveness possible? Could he have another chance to live a normal, productive life with a generous and kind woman like Krista?

"Hey," Krista said, sitting next to him.

He glanced at her. "Everything okay with the coffeepot?"

"It's old and stubborn. Sometimes you need to get rid of the old stuff to make way for the new."

"Very true."

She took his hand and held it for a few minutes. He could tell she reveled in the peaceful atmosphere of her church.

"Did you enjoy the service?" she said.

"It wasn't as bad as I thought."

"It was wonderful." She looped her arm through his and glanced out the top windows.

He'd always remember her this way, tipping her face to the light, a slight smile curving her lips. She was sweet and gentle. And perfect.

"Okay, love birds, time to fly out of here," Pastor White said from the back.

"Sorry, Pastor," Krista said, standing.

"Don't be sorry. I'd let you stay longer, but I need to visit Dorothy Greko at the hospital."

Luke and Krista shifted out of the pew and walked up the aisle, still holding hands.

The pastor smiled at them. "See you at the tree lighting?"

"We'll be there." She glanced at Luke and smiled.

"So, what's on the agenda for the rest of your day?" he said.

"Relax, update my blog, pet the cat, if she's still talking to me."

"Cats talk?" he teased, walking her to the car.

"Do they ever."

"I'd like to see that."

"You mean hear it."

"That, too."

He opened the passenger door for her and his cell vibrated. "McIntyre," he answered.

"They lost Garcia's men in Chicago. It's a pretty good bet they're coming your way."

Chapter Eighteen

Krista wasn't sure what the phone call was about, but it completely changed Luke's mood from warm and friendly to cool and distant.

He was back in agent mode, continually scanning their surroundings, giving one syllable answers, not engaging in conversation.

She knew what she'd seen in church. Luke had made a connection to God. She read it in his blue eyes as they walked out together, holding hands.

But now, as she sat in her kitchen working on her blog, she could feel his tension from across the room as he stared out the side window, waiting for something or someone.

She wanted the warm and caring Luke back.

"Wanna see the rest my pictures?" she said.

He glanced over his shoulder. "Of what?"

"My mission trip."

He glanced out the window, then back at Krista. "Sure."

She clicked on the slide show of children in class, attending church service, and the trip to the countryside.

"Was the countryside pretty flat?" he asked.

"Some of it. But there were mountains as well."

A picture flashed on the screen of Krista kneeling beside a group of children.

"You look like a natural with kids," Luke said.

"Thanks."

"What's that?" He pointed to a bright red building in the background.

"I don't know. Some kind of manufacturing plant, I guess."

She clicked through the photos and landed on a little boy with his arm around a little girl's shoulder.

"Cute," he said.

She sighed and leaned back in her chair. "I would have taken more, but two guys were swearing at me in Spanish, telling me to get away from the kids."

"Why? Because you were taking pictures?" Luke squinted to see two guys in the background, one bald, the other with thick, black curly hair.

"I guess. They don't trust us."

Someone tapped on the back door.

"I wasn't expecting anyone," Krista said.

"I am."

He opened the door and the chief stepped into the kitchen. "Krista," he greeted, then eyed Luke. "Want to talk outside?"

"No." Krista stood and planted her hands on her hips. "You have to stop keeping things from me. It's my life that's in danger."

"I'm trying to protect you," Luke said.

"By keeping me in the dark?"

Luke sighed and glanced at the chief. "Go ahead."

"He wasn't home and no one's seen him."

"Who?" Krista pushed.

"Alan," Luke said.

"Why are you looking for Alan?"

"We found his fingerprints on something at the tea shop," Luke said.

"He's my friend, he's been there a lot. What's the big deal?"

"It was a threatening note. I found it in your office and sent it in."

She shook her head in disbelief. "But why would he...you think he's the local contact for the drug cartel? No, that's not possible."

"His house was locked up tight, lights were off, car was in the garage," the chief said.

"So he hasn't left town."

None of this made sense. Alan was a nice, polite man, always protective of Krista.

"He was our best lead," Luke said.

"What should we do next?" the chief said.

"Tell your officers to be on the lookout for two strangers, guys who work for Garcia."

He thought for a minute, then pinned her with his dark blue eyes. "Do you trust me?"

"Of course."

"Good. We're going to put an end to this. Tonight."

Excitement buzzed in the air as flurries drifted down to coat the branches of the city's official Christmas tree.

Krista clung to Luke's arm, pretending, just for a second, that this moment was real, and not some strategy to expose the bad guys who'd been hounding her since her return from Mexico.

The moment passed when someone bumped into her

and she practically launched into Luke's arms for protection.

"You really came!" Julie Sass said, hugging Krista.

"I really did," Krista said.

"Not you." She pointed to Luke. "Him."

Luke smiled, but continued to scan the crowd for danger.

"I don't go anywhere without him," Krista covered for him.

"No, you don't, do you?" With a sad smile, she said, "Well, I'm doing cider, so I'd better scoot. Hey," she said to Luke.

Krista nudged him to pay attention.

"What? Sorry."

"Take care of my friend," Julie said.

"Yes, ma'am, I plan to."

Julie drifted off into the crowd. There must have been a few hundred folks in the town square. It was the biggest thing to happen in Wentworth County besides the summer boat races.

Luke led Krista toward the Christmas tree. "Any advice on the best vantage point?"

"It really doesn't matter. Once the tree's lit, you can see it from anywhere."

They edged their way into the crowd just as the carolers burst into a chorus of "Winter Wonderland." Krista glanced across the square at the shops, lit up and offering cocoa and cookies in hopes of jump-starting the retail season.

As her gaze drifted back to the tree, she spotted a familiar face in the crowd. Timothy.

She waved and smiled.

Timothy glared at Luke and disappeared into the

crowd. He was being way too protective of Krista, especially now that he knew Luke was here to protect her, not hurt her.

At least he wouldn't mean to hurt her. But the truth was, he'd leave and she'd be heartbroken.

It was her own fault for falling in love with him.

"What happens next?" she asked.

"What do you mean?"

"We wait for someone to attack me?"

He glanced into her eyes. "No, I'd never put you in that kind of danger. He won't risk doing anything in such a public setting. But once he spots you, he'll follow us to the decoy location at which point he'll be arrested." He tipped her chin up with his bent forefinger. "I'm not going to let anything happen to you, got it?"

"Yep." It's all she could get out. She wanted to keep looking into those blue eyes of his, wanted to make him smile, make him laugh so she could see his eyes sparkle.

He turned back to the crowd, his jaw clenched and his body tight.

This was his job. To protect her, put Garcia's men behind bars and move on to the next assignment.

But tonight she could honestly say there was more to Luke than scouting suspects and nailing the bad guy. Something had changed since that first night she'd met him outside her house.

He had changed since then, gone from emotionally guarded federal agent to considerate man. Maybe he'd changed enough to consider a life with Krista?

"What's wrong?" Luke said, his eyes focused on the crowd.

"Why do you think anything's wrong?"

"You're staring at me."

She snapped her gaze from studying his profile. "I was thinking about…" she hesitated. Did she dare? "If you and I had met under different circumstances."

"Yeah, I know what you mean."

"You do?" She didn't risk looking at him.

"Let's talk about this later, when you're safe."

"Sure, okay." They were going to talk about it? She wanted to do the happy dance right here in the middle of the town square. He was admitting to feeling something for her, right? Admitting that there was *something* to talk about.

"So about my honey-do list," Lucy Grimes said, brushing up against Luke.

"Mrs. Grimes, you are relentless." Luke smiled. "I haven't forgotten about you."

Three more church friends greeted them, Luke plastering a fake smile on his face. He looked like he was in physical pain.

Once they were alone again, she asked, "Is it that hard to be friendly?"

"It is when I'm supposed to be focused on protecting you."

"Oh, right, sorry."

He squeezed her hand and she looked into his eyes. "You never have to be sorry. For anything."

She thought he might kiss her, but he turned his head to continue his search of the crowd.

"Something's off," he muttered.

"What?"

"I'm not sure. Come here, get in front of me."

He shifted her in front of him and wrapped his arms around her waist, interlocking his fingers in front. She closed her eyes and leaned back into his chest. They swayed slightly to the music.

This was heaven on earth, leaning against the man she loved, listening to Christmas songs, and being surrounded by friends in the first of the town's celebration of the birth of Jesus.

She could stay here all night in Luke's arms, rocking, humming, wishing.

She wasn't afraid. She knew in her heart that the Lord wouldn't have finally brought love into her life only to take Luke away from her.

He needs me, Lord.

She wasn't sure how much time had passed cradled in his arms, but the music stopped and people started moving around.

"Where did you go?" he teased.

"I was dreaming."

"About hot chocolate?" he asked.

About you.

"No, I dreamed about going home and having a cup of lavender-white tea."

"Well, let's make that dream come true, shall we?"

With his arm protectively around her, they walked to the car. Luke glanced over her head into the crowd.

"Anything?" she said.

"No, but that doesn't surprise me. He's probably going to follow us. That's the plan anyway."

They got in the car and pulled away from the festivities. She glanced in the rearview mirror, but didn't see any headlights.

"Nothin'," Luke muttered.

She could tell he really wanted to finish this off tonight because he'd made a promise to Krista.

He'd keep his promise.

Then leave her.

No, she had more faith than that.

"Chief Cunningham, come in, over," the dispatch operator's voice called through a radio the chief had given Luke.

"This is Cunningham, over."

"We've got shots fired at 112 Cherry Street."

Krista sat straight. "That's my house."

Chapter Nineteen

Luke didn't want to take her to the scene of a shooting, but he couldn't let her out of his sight.

"Why would someone shoot up my house?" Krista asked, gripping her down jacket.

"Let's not overreact. It could be the Bender kid shooting off a pellet gun again."

She nodded, but didn't look convinced.

"Is there anyplace I can drop you where you'd feel safe?" he asked.

"I only feel safe with you." She glanced out the window.

"How about—"

"No. I have to stay with you."

He took a deep breath and kept under the 35 speed limit. He didn't want to be the first to respond to the scene of a shooting with Krista in the car. Yet he was anxious to know what had happened.

Krista wasn't home. Why would someone shoot at her house? Or did the perp get inside?

"We'll cruise by your house, but you stay in the car," he ordered.

"Okay."

She didn't fight him this time. She'd surrendered completely to his decisions and it scared him. He liked it better when she fought him, argued and stood her ground. He felt completely responsible for her in a way he hadn't before.

A few minutes later they turned the corner to her house and flashing blue lights lit the street. Two squad cars and an ambulance were parked out front.

Luke pulled up behind a squad car. "Stay here."

He got out and walked around the front of the car. He glanced at Krista and changed his mind about leaving her. He opened her door and offered his hand. "On second thought, I'd better keep you close."

With a nod, she got out of the car and they started up the driveway. The sound of an excited Roscoe barking from the garage echoed through the yard. Two EMTs were treating a man in the back of the ambulance. Luke recognized Alan Jameson as the victim.

A police officer stood guard.

"What happened here?" Luke flashed his badge at the cop.

"Chief said to bring this guy in once they treated his flesh wound."

"Alan?" Krista said, stepping toward him.

Luke put out his arm to block her.

"Why's he being questioned?" Luke asked.

"He took a couple of shots at Officer West."

"What? Alan?" Krista said, shocked.

Alan stared at the ground, ashamed, maybe even dazed.

"Come on." Luke led Krista to the back of the house and they went inside. Officer West and the chief sat at the kitchen table. West's hair was messed up and her hands were shaking.

"I thought it was one of them. How could I know?" she said, staring at her firearm on the table. "I mean, why was he shooting at me?"

"Because he thought you were Krista," Luke offered.

Krista pulled away from him. "Why would Alan shoot me? He—" she paused "—likes me."

"It has nothing to do with like or dislike, Krista. If he's the local contact, his job was to get whatever you brought back from Mexico to the right people in the States."

"Alan can't be a drug dealer. I won't believe it."

"Believe it, Krista." Officer West glanced up from her gun. "He shot out the windows. He thought I was you."

Silence blanketed the room.

A third officer came into the kitchen with a rifle. "It's a pellet gun, sir." He handed it to the chief.

"He was going to kill her with a pellet gun?" Chief Cunningham said in disbelief.

"I need to question him," Luke said. He turned and took Krista's hand. "First, we need to get you someplace safe, a place no one knows about."

"But Alan's in custody."

"And Garcia still has men out there. Chief, any ideas?"

"Everyone knows everyone in this town. If Alan has been working with the two guys, they'd probably know where to look for her."

"Natalie," Krista whispered.

"What about her?" Luke questioned.

"She manages all kinds of property. Maybe she has an empty unit?"

"Give her a call," Luke said.

With a nod, she pulled out her cell phone and went into the living room.

Chief Cunningham tapped his fingers on the kitchen table to get Officer West's attention. She glanced up.

"You okay, West?" he asked.

"Yes, sir."

"I'm going to hold on to this for a few days until we wrap this thing up." He took her gun and she closed her eyes.

Surrendering your firearm was procedure after you shot someone. She had to know that, but still it stung.

Krista wandered back into the room. "Natalie said she's got an open condo unit five miles north of Wentworth."

"Good." Luke glanced at the chief. "Can one of your officers take her to the condo?"

"Officer Sherman can do it. I'll take Alan to the station and you can meet us there."

Luke placed his hand on Krista's shoulder. "It's almost over, sweetheart."

Without warning, she wrapped her arms around him and pressed her cheek against his chest. He didn't return the hug at first, embarrassed to do so in front of the chief and Officer West.

"West, why don't you get your coat and I'll drop you off on the way to the station," the chief said.

With a nod, she grabbed her jacket.

"I'll meet you at the station," the chief said to Luke. He and Officer West left and shut the door.

Luke slipped his arms around Krista's lower back

and gently squeezed. "It's okay, honey. Everything's going to be fine."

She looked up at him. "How can it be fine when you'll be gone?"

Luke paced the chief's office as they discussed the best way to interrogate Alan. They had to find out how Alan was involved and, more importantly, what Garcia wanted from Krista.

Unfortunately nothing tied Alan to Garcia's business. Luke had requested a trace history on Alan's phone logs and e-mail account. Nothing popped. There seemed to be no connection between them.

"You've got more experience with this kind of thing," the chief said. "I'll follow your lead."

Luke knew he had to choose his words carefully with Alan, question him in such a way that he'd want to come clean. It had to be to his advantage to turn on his drug boss.

"Let's go," Luke said.

They went into the conference room where Alan was sitting at a table. Luke sat down across from him. Alan stared at his handcuffed hands in his lap.

"Alan, want to tell us why you were shooting at Officer West?" Luke said.

Alan didn't answer.

Luke pounded his fist on the table. Alan jerked and glanced up.

"Why would you try to kill a police officer?" Luke pressed.

"I wasn't. I didn't know—"

"Did Garcia give the order? You were trying to kill Krista, right?"

His eyes widened in horror. "I'd never hurt Krista."

"Why, because you love her? Makes sense, right, Chief? You love someone so you try to kill them? How does that work, Alan?"

"I wasn't trying to kill her."

"Sure you were. Garcia told you to take her out so you could get your hands on whatever it is she brought back with her from Mexico."

"I don't know anyone named Garcia."

"Stop lying and tell us why you tried to kill Krista!"

Alan jumped to his feet. "I wasn't trying to kill her, just scare her!" The chief put his hand on Alan's shoulder and encouraged him to sit down. Alan collapsed in the chair and rested his cuffed hands on the table.

"Scare her?" Luke said. "Why?"

"Because then she'd need me."

"Come again?" Luke leaned back in his chair.

"I couldn't get her to commit to our relationship, so I thought if she saw the value in having me around to protect her…"

"So you broke into her house and tea shop and sent the threatening note?"

"I didn't break into her house. I did some other stuff."

"What other stuff?"

Alan shrugged.

"You've gotta tell us or we're going to assume you were behind everything including running Natalie off the road thinking it was Krista."

Alan glared at Luke. "I left the note with the dead mouse, took a shot at the tea shop and shredded her clothes. That's all. I would never hurt Krista. Not like you." He leaned forward across the table. "I know your type. You'll get what you want from her and leave."

"We're not talking about me. We're talking about you terrorizing Miss Yates."

"She needs me. She needs to be taken care of, but she's so independent she can't accept the love of a nice man. No, she'd rather fall in love with a stranger who's going to break her heart."

Luke glared at Alan. There was truth to his words. Luke shoved that thought way back.

Luke's phone vibrated and he glanced at the caller. It was a text from his boss to call in immediately.

"Excuse me," Luke said. He went into the hall and called in. "Yes, sir?"

"Garcia's men were spotted on a toll exchange in Indiana two hours ago. I'm faxing you their picture so you'll know who you're looking for. What's the fax number there?"

Luke went to the fax in the chief's office and read him the number.

"Backup is on the way," Marks said.

"Thank you, sir."

Luke hung up and the fax came through. He picked up the sheet and remarked that the two men looked familiar: one bald, one with thick, black curly hair.

The men from Krista's photographs.

Photographs she'd been putting up on her blog. Her first blog site had been destroyed. Which meant… Had she somehow taken pictures of Garcia's operation in Mexico? Is that what they wanted from her? Could it be that simple?

The authorities had no idea where the base of operations was, although they knew it was within a hundred-mile radius of Mexicali.

Could it be this whole time they were after her photographs, needing to destroy them? Luke knew she always carried her thumb drive on her keychain, which meant they'd never find it, unless they got their hands on her.

If Alan was telling the truth and he wasn't tied to Garcia, and if this was all about her taking the wrong pictures on her trip...

They were still coming for the thumb drive.

And Krista.

Planning his next move, he glanced at the chief's desk and spotted an orange, foil candy wrapper.

Just like the one he'd found at the lighthouse...at the tea shop when he'd found the dead mouse.

"Everything okay in here, son?" the chief said, standing in the doorway.

Luke eyed the chief. "I don't know, is it?"

The chief couldn't be involved in this. Luke's instincts would have alerted him that the guy was dirty. Then again, Luke had been distracted by a sweet and wonderful woman these past few days.

"I don't think Alan's involved with the drug case." The chief glanced at the fax in Luke's hand. "Those Garcia's men?"

"Yes." Luke shifted back a step and held out the candy wrapper. "Is this yours?"

"Timothy recommended them, said they're the best thing for a sore throat in the winter."

"Timothy, as in Natalie's fiancé?"

"Yeah, why?"

"We've got to get to Krista."

Chapter Twenty

Krista gazed at the snowfall from the living room window of the condo. Snow always reminded her of Christmas, her favorite holiday.

It's almost over.

Luke's words filled her with a kind of dread she'd never felt before. It was the first time in her adult life she'd experienced love, the kind that kept her awake at night thinking about the possibilities. Thinking about Luke.

Yet for Luke this was about getting the bad guy and earning redemption for his partner's death.

"How about tea?" Natalie said from the sofa. She started to get up.

"Hey, hey, you're still recovering." Krista rushed over and sat on the coffee table across from her. "You shouldn't have come with me. You should have stayed home and taken care of yourself."

"Timothy thought it was a good idea. With friends around, you won't feel so scared."

"I'm not scared. Luke said the case is almost over."

"And then...?" Natalie shot her a sympathetic look.

"I get back to my normal life. Yay," she said, half-heartedly.

"I'm sorry."

"You're sorry? For what? It's my fault you were run off the road."

"Don't say that. It wasn't your fault. It was the drug guy's fault, whoever has been after you for the past week."

Frustrated, Krista stood. "But why? They got my luggage, they've broken into my house and business and—"

"How about some tea, ladies?" Timothy said, carrying in a tray with cups and saucers.

"If only I had a boyfriend like you," Krista joked.

"Fiancé," Natalie corrected.

"You have a brother or cousin that you haven't told us about, I hope?" Krista joked.

"Sorry, can't help you out there. But I make a mean cup of chamomile tea." He put the tray down and Natalie reached for a cup.

"Hang on, sweetheart," Timothy said. "That one's Krista's."

"What's the difference?" Natalie eyed them.

They looked the same to Krista.

Timothy kissed Natalie on the forehead. "Yours has an herbal supplement I got at the health food store to help you heal."

Natalie and Krista exchanged smiles.

"He's a keeper," Krista said. She took her tea and sat down. Timothy went back into the kitchen.

Krista sipped her tea. It tasted bitter and she figured he'd steeped it too long.

"So, seriously," Natalie started. "Have you told Luke how you feel?"

"Yes, but he can't think about stuff like that right now."

"Stuff? You're in love with him, Krista. That's important."

"And unfortunate."

"Don't say that. Love is a gift." Natalie shifted back into the cushions and sipped her tea.

"I know. But I have to be a realist. Luke lives in another part of the country and works in a violent career. I couldn't go through my life waiting for that day when a police officer came knocking on my door to tell me someone I loved had been killed."

"Right, I forgot about your dad, sorry. Maybe Luke would quit his job."

"That would never happen. You haven't seen the determined look in his eyes."

"To protect you." Natalie yawned. "I'm sorry. My brain needs oxygen," she joked.

"Go ahead and rest. I'm fine."

"Just for a second." Natalie closed her eyes. Krista took the empty teacup from her hand and placed it on the tray.

Krista closed her eyes as well and drifted into a fantasy about Luke being on the police force, attending community events with her, praying with her in church.

If only they'd met under different circumstances, if he weren't a cop and she didn't have such strong ties to Wentworth.

But all the "if onlys" in the world wouldn't change the fact she'd admitted her feelings for him and he kept pushing her away.

It wasn't meant to be.

A door crashed open and Krista sat up.

"Where is she?" a man shouted.

"Why are you here?" Timothy shouted back.

Krista jumped to her feet as Timothy was dragged into the living room...

By two men she recognized. They were the same guys who yelled at her for taking pictures of the children in Mexico.

They shoved Timothy to the floor.

"¡Estupido!" the curly-haired guy shouted.

The bald guy pulled a gun, pointed it at Timothy and glared at Krista. "Where is it?"

Krista put up her hands. "What, what do you want?" Adrenaline racing through her body, all she could think about was Luke. How much she loved him. How her death would destroy him.

"Tell us or I shoot him!" the bald guy threatened.

"Krista, please!" Timothy croaked.

"You have to tell me what it is you're looking for."

The bald guy re-aimed his gun at Natalie's sleeping form.

"Krista!" Timothy shouted.

Krista rushed over to shield Natalie's body. "What do you want?"

"Pictures," the curly-haired guy said. "Where you keep pictures?"

"What pictures?"

"From your Internet site. You took pictures in Mexico. We want them."

Heart racing, Krista grabbed her purse and dug for her keys. "They're on my keychain."

"You lie to us!"

"No! They're—" she grabbed them "—here." She tossed her key chain at the curly-haired guy.

"Show us." He motioned for Krista to join him in the kitchen. The guy had a laptop set up. Krista put the thumb drive in place and scanned the pictures.

"Good." He grabbed the thumb drive, then dragged her back into the living room.

This was it. She was going to die.

She kneeled beside Natalie and placed a hand on her back.

"Stand up," the curly-haired guy ordered Timothy.

Timothy stood and squared off at him.

"Garcia es furioso," he said to Timothy. "You finish. We wait outside."

He handed Timothy the gun.

The floor shifted under Krista's knees with the realization that Timothy was working *with* these men. The two men walked out, leaving Krista, Timothy and Natalie alone. Krista wondered if Timothy had drugged Natalie's tea because he didn't want her to know about his involvement with the drug cartel.

"Timothy?" Krista stood. "What's going on?"

"I'm sorry, Krista. They weren't supposed to come." He shot her a pleading look. "If only you would have given up the thumb drive."

"Given it up? I didn't know they wanted it. And you…you're involved in this?"

"I needed the money."

"That doesn't justify you breaking the law and…and what, you're going to shoot me?"

"I have to. If I don't, they'll kill Natalie. That's why I took her out of the hospital, because I knew they'd come after her!"

"Timothy, take a deep breath. Listen to how absurd this sounds. You're not a killer. How did you get involved in this?"

"It doesn't matter," he said, clutching the gun.

"It matters to me. My father was killed by a gun and if I'm to die the same way I'd like to know why."

Every bone in her body told her to keep him talking, in hopes of making an ally out of him.

"Why?" she pushed.

"Natalie deserves things, nice things. A big wedding, honeymoon, a second house up north. I took out a loan from a guy and couldn't pay him back. He had ties to Garcia's organization and made me an offer to clear my debt. They paid me to smuggle a drug concentrate into the country through souvenirs."

"That's why they broke into Luanne Sparks's car?"

He didn't answer, just stared at the gun in his hand. "All I had to do was get them and hand them off to Garcia's men in Detroit."

"But I didn't buy any souvenirs," Krista said.

"No, you took pictures." He pinned her with empty, dark eyes. "Pictures that exposed Garcia's base of operations."

"I didn't know that. I took pictures of little kids."

Timothy sighed and glanced at the couch. "Natalie wants kids."

"I know."

He glared at Krista. "But I can't have kids if I'm in prison. I'm sorry, Krista."

Timothy raised the gun. Krista dropped to her knees and put her hands together.

"Dear Lord, forgive Timothy for his actions. He's lost and needs Your guidance."

"Stop talking," Timothy shouted.

"Timothy, put the gun down!" Luke ordered from the doorway.

Surprised, Timothy spun around.

A shot rang out, blasting her eardrums, and Krista hit the floor, body trembling.

"Got him?" Luke said.

"Yeah, I'll call for an ambulance," the chief answered.

Eyes squeezed tight, Krista struggled to breathe, fear clogging her throat.

She could hear Timothy moaning in pain a few feet away from her, but didn't want to open her eyes.

Natalie's loving fiancé had almost killed her.

"Krista," Luke said, placing his hand on her shoulder. "Sweetheart, it's okay. Open your eyes."

She did and saw Luke's bright blue eyes staring back at her. Then she caught sight of his gun and thought she might be sick.

A wave of sadness spread across his face as he shoved his gun out of sight. He helped her up and wrapped his arms around her. "It's over, honey. It's all over."

"Two men…"

"We got 'em."

"From Mexico."

"Garcia sent them to destroy the pictures that Timothy couldn't find."

"Drugs."

"What about them?" He looked into her eyes.

"Drug concentrate smuggled into the country through souvenirs."

"We'll get it. We'll shut them down. Come on." As he led her out of the living room, she glanced at Timothy and a choke-sob caught in her throat. Sadness over-whelmed her for her friend Nat. How could she ever come to terms with her fiancé being a violent criminal?

Through friends, church and plenty of time. Krista knew how it worked. She'd been there herself.

"I'm going to have Officer Sherman take you home," Luke said.

"No." Krista clung to his jacket and looked up into his eyes. "Please, don't go. Luke, I love you."

Chapter Twenty-One

It felt like a machete had ripped through his chest.

She loved him. Poor Krista because Luke wasn't worth loving. He wasn't nearly good enough for her.

But as she stood there, pleading green eyes looking up at him, he wanted to surrender, just for a second, and tell her he loved her, too.

It was the truth.

Also true was the fact his life's work was a violent one, and this fragile creature needed someone grounded and safe.

And worthy.

He led her to the patrol car. "Are you up to giving a statement?"

"Stop a second." She hesitated and looked up at him. "I promised myself if I lived through this that I would tell you how I felt. I just bared my soul to you. Don't you have anything to say?"

He glanced at the patrol car. "Like what?"

"How do you feel about what I said?"

"Sad."

"Why?" she hushed, squeezing his hand.

"Because I can't give you what you need, Krista. You're confused right now because you've been through a traumatic experience and you almost died and it would have been my fault."

She framed his face with her warm hands. "I didn't die. You saved me."

"It's my job. And it's that very job that makes this thing between us impossible."

"Then get a new one."

"Krista," he scolded.

"What? You couldn't join a less dangerous branch of law enforcement?"

"This is what I do." He opened the patrol car door.

"Because you're paying a penance."

"Because I'm good at it."

"I'll bet you're good at a lot of things."

"Look, I have to stay focused on the case right now."

She sighed and looked at him with those amazing green eyes. "Do you love me?"

"Yes, Krista, which is why I have to leave."

Krista shifted in the chair beside the chief's desk and signed her statement. It was nearly impossible to hold it together, especially when she knew what was coming next.

Luke loved her.

And he was going to leave.

It made no sense, and her frustration was quickly turning into anger...

...and grief. Gut-wrenching grief that rivaled the pain she felt at the loss of her father.

There had to be something she could do, something she could say to change his mind.

"Hard to believe Timothy was involved in this," Chief Cunningham said. "He was the one who broke into the tea shop and drove Natalie off the road, thinking it was Krista."

"He was trying to kill me, even then?" Krista asked.

"No, he was trying to get your purse so he could figure out where you kept the thumb drive. When he went to the car and saw Natalie, he called emergency right away." Chief Cunningham stood and closed the file. "I wondered how he got to the scene so fast."

"And the first night in my garage?" Krista asked.

"Timothy. Did a search of your house and came up empty. Figured out you weren't home yet, so he went to the garage to shut off your lights. If Luke hadn't shown up he probably would have…" The chief glanced up. "Well, no reason talking about it. This case is closed."

"It will be closed once we charge Garcia. Lucky thing Timothy didn't have time to pass off the concentrate to Garcia's men."

"So, what's next?" the chief asked.

"Since Garcia is an American citizen, we'll get moving on the provisional arrest warrant so they can extradite him back to the States for the murder of my partner."

"And the manufacturing plant?" the chief pressed.

"We have no jurisdiction in Mexico, but we'll make our request through the Office of International Affairs. Then it's up to the local law enforcement in Mexico to take action."

"Your work here is done, then."

"Yes." He didn't look at Krista. He hadn't made eye contact with her since they arrived at the station. It was like they were strangers, and she was just another witness in a federal drug case.

But she knew better.

"Well, I should let you go, then."

The chief left his office and shut the door.

"When do you leave?" Krista asked.

"Tonight."

"So you're running away."

He snapped his gaze to meet hers. "I'm trying to put criminals behind bars."

"At the expense of your own life?"

"It's my job."

"Stop staying that. Your life is worth more than any job."

"My life is my job which is why anything that happened between us is irrelevant."

"It's relevant to me." She stood and reached out, but he stepped away.

"Don't make this harder than it has to be," he said, glancing down. "I've enjoyed our time together, but it's over."

"It doesn't have to be."

"No? How does that look, Krista? Us getting married, you pacing the floors at night waiting for me to come home? Or worse." He turned his back on her. "Work following me home, some thug figuring out where I live and coming to the house?"

"No, because you'll be in a different line of work."

"Can't happen."

"You're using your job to punish yourself for your partner's death. Let it go, Luke. He wouldn't have wanted you to live this way."

"It's best for everyone."

"Forgive yourself. God forgives you."

He glanced into her eyes and for half a second she saw a flash of understanding, maybe even peace.

His cell vibrated and he snapped it from his belt. "Yes, sir?"

As he spoke to, she guessed, his boss, she knew no words would change his mind. She took off her necklace and clutched it in her palm.

She couldn't make him stay with her, forgive himself or allow himself to love her, but she could send a piece of herself with him.

He turned back to her. "Gotta go."

Don't cry, girl. Don't you dare cry.

"I'm sorry you have to go." She went to him and hugged him tight, slipping the charm into his jacket pocket. "I will pray for your safety." She looked up at him. "And your safe return."

With a sad smile, he kissed her. Soft, sweet and vulnerable. She wanted to hold on, but he gripped her shoulders and broke the kiss.

"Roscoe, I forgot—"

"I've gotten used to him. It's fine."

"You sure, because I can ask the chief—"

"It's fine." Having Roscoe around would remind her how much Luke cared for her.

"Take care of yourself," he said.

"You, too."

He turned and walked to the door.

"God bless you, Luke McIntyre."

He hesitated, opened the door and disappeared out of her life.

Chapter Twenty-Two

As Krista set the tables for the first of many Christmas teas, she realized that Christmas at the tea shop was her saving grace. Preparing for the event gave her purpose and distracted her from the ache in her chest.

Three weeks had passed without any word from Luke. A part of her didn't expect to ever hear from him again.

But that other part, the idealistic part that believed in love, taunted her with hope. She said special prayers for Luke every night before bed, prayers for his safety and self-forgiveness.

That's all she could do. Well, that and mend her own broken heart.

She'd spent many hours consoling Natalie, trying to make sense of how everything had fallen apart in her friend's life. But it would be months, maybe even years before Nat would fully understand and recover. The man Natalie had given her heart to had been seduced by evil and Natalie had no clue what was going on. How did someone recover from that kind of betrayal? Krista wasn't sure, but she'd do her best to help her friend.

"How many do we got tonight?" Tatum Sass said, strolling into the dining room from the back.

"How many do we have," Krista corrected.

"That, too."

Krista smiled. "Twenty-four."

"We're short on sugar cubes."

"Rats, I meant to stop by the grocery store last night."

"I can go," Tatum offered.

"You sure?"

"No prob. I'll be back." Tatum breezed out.

Krista had been a little off, a little distracted since everything happened. Her friends knew it. They were doing a good job of taking care of her, picking up the slack and checking on Krista.

For the first time in a long time Krista didn't mind being taken care of instead of taking care of others. She didn't see it as people trying to control her or tell her what's best. She understood it was about friends rallying to her side because they loved her. Their love was appreciated, but she wanted another kind of love, a kind of love only Luke McIntyre could give her.

"Stop it," she scolded herself. She had to pick herself up and move on. Twenty-four people were coming for dinner, for crying out loud.

Krista clicked into gear and raced around the shop setting tables, lighting candles and brewing tea.

An hour later Krista carefully set the rose petals on a high tea tower and slid it to the side where one of the girls could grab it.

Except for a stubborn whipped creamer and leaky faucet, they'd avoided any major catastrophes tonight. The roomful of customers seemed joyful and content as they nibbled tea sandwiches, sipped tea and enjoyed Christmas music.

Suddenly Tatum slid into the kitchen.

"Tatum, no sliding," Krista reminded.

"We've got a problem."

Tori slid in behind her. "A major one."

"What?"

"There's some guy out there with a badge, I think he's with the health department," Tatum said.

"He needs to talk to you," Tori added. "Right now."

"In the middle of an event?"

"He said now," Tori punctuated.

"Fine. Tell him I'll be right out."

The girls disappeared back into the dining room. Krista grabbed her coat thinking maybe she'd convince him to talk code violations outside. She was strict about following the rules and had no idea what could warrant a visit from the health department.

She stepped around the corner into the quiet dining room. All chatter had stopped as the ladies stared at a man standing by the fireplace. It looked like...

Luke turned around and shot her an apologetic smile.

Krista froze, unable to speak or even think straight.

Luke walked over to her and took her hand. "I've missed you."

"I'm having a Christmas fantasy, right?" she said.

"If you are, it's about to get better." He got down on one knee. "Krista Yates, will you be my wife?"

It felt like they were completely alone, no customers, no staff, even the music faded into the background. He pulled out a black box from his pocket and opened it to reveal a beautiful solitaire diamond ring.

"I don't know what to say," she said.

"There's a first," Tatum joked.

"Shh," a customer scolded.

"What do you think?" Luke pressed.

"It's beautiful."

"I mean about my proposal?"

She looked into his warm blue eyes and her heart filled with love. "Of course I'll marry you."

The group of ladies applauded. Luke stood and put the ring on her finger. A little embarrassed, she led him out to the front porch and closed the door.

"I'm—I'm," she stuttered.

"You're the most amazing thing that's happened to me, Krista."

"But your case—"

"The strangest thing happened." He put his arm around her and looked up at the dark sky dotted with stars. "I was at the airport about to board the plane to Mexico when I reached into my pocket for change and instead pulled out this." He opened his palm to reveal her charm. "And that hole in my heart opened up and was filled with something more powerful than anger or revenge." He grazed his thumb across her cheek. "Your love and your love of God brought me back, Krista. It saved me from myself. I never want to spend another day without you in my life."

They kissed and it felt like a dream. He was here, holding her, loving her.

They broke the kiss and she narrowed her eyes at him. "Why did it take you three weeks to find your way back to me?"

"I had to wrap things up at work, put my condo on the market, find a job."

"You quit the agency?"

"I did. You're looking at the new security supervisor for Andmark properties. They run Michigan Shores and a handful of other resorts in the area."

"You're kidding."

"What, you don't think I'm qualified?" he teased.

"No, I mean, how did you do that so fast?"

"I guess I've got friends in high places."

"You mean the chief."

"Him, too."

Meaning Luke had done his share of praying for guidance and help. And it led him back to Wentworth.

To Krista.

She wrapped her arms around him and glanced up at the sky. "Isn't it beautiful?"

Out of the corner of her eye, she could tell he was still looking at her. "It sure is."

* * * * *

WE HOPE YOU ENJOYED
THIS BOOK FROM

LOVE INSPIRED SUSPENSE
INSPIRATIONAL ROMANCE

Courage. Danger. Faith.

Find strength and determination in stories of faith and love in the face of danger.

6 NEW BOOKS AVAILABLE EVERY MONTH!

LISHALO2021